One

Déjà vu swept over Eve Winchester. *Not again. This* cannot *be happening again.*

The two pink lines mocked her denial.

Eve clutched the pregnancy test, gripping the side of her white pedestal sink with her other hand.

Sheets rustled in the bedroom. Through the crack in the bathroom door, Eve could see Graham Newport lying in her bed.

Now that she knew her predicament, she had no idea what step to take next. For someone who prided herself on plans, on spreadsheets and following through on details in a timely fashion, she was completely lost.

But her unknowns stemmed from the fear of what Graham would do. How would he react? How would their families, whose rivalry was legendary in Chicago, deal with this shocking news? The Newports and the Winchesters had enough drama on their hands lately.

The Newport brothers' paternity had been thrown into question earlier this year. Graham and his brother Brooks were still up in the air after their paternity tests came back negative, but their other brother, Carson, had discovered who his real father was—Sutton Winchester, who happened to be Eve's, too.

Yeah, they were all in a state of upheaval right now and this unexpected pregnancy would just toss a stick of dynamite into the fire.

With shaky hands, Eve quickly put the test back in the box and shoved it beneath some trash in the can under the sink. Finally, risking another glance over her shoulder, she peered through the slight opening in the door and noted that Graham was still asleep. He had one toned leg thrown over white sheets, one arm stretched out to the side. Eve closed her eyes and pulled in a deep breath. After the paternity test had proven Graham wasn't related to her in any way, they'd finally given in to the feelings they'd fought so hard against. They'd been so careful to keep this heated affair a secret. But when their instant attraction had become evident, they'd both gotten backlash from their siblings. Fine, they could sneak around and leave the siblings out of it, right?

Yeah, that had worked for the past six weeks. So much for keeping their families out of their private lives.

Now she was having a baby. A second pregnancy… this one much scarier than the last. This time she knew the ugly horrors that could happen. She'd lived through them, still bore the internal scars, and now she'd have to find a way to push through again. Could fate be that cruel?

Eve slid her hand over her silk chemise. Her flat stomach had once been round, once held another life taken all too soon. As much as she wanted to take her father's company global and focus on being in charge, she refused to let an innocent baby feel anything but loved and secure. And above all, this child would not be a victim in the war between the families.

That is, if she made it to full-term.

Fear coursed through her. The fear of telling Graham weighed heavily on her, but the fear of losing another child was absolutely crippling. Going through such grief again might very well destroy her. Added to that, her father was terminal. How much pain could one woman endure and still keep going?

The sheets rustled again and Eve knew she couldn't hide in the bathroom forever. Graham had come over late last night and they'd quickly tumbled into bed, as was their habit. No sweet-talking, no romantic walks for them. Eve had a passion for Graham and the family feud between the Winchesters and the Newports had no place in their affair.

Unfortunately, their worlds were about to collide in ways they never dreamed.

Stepping back into her bedroom, Eve pulled in a deep breath. Even though her entire world was completely turned upside down, she still had obligations, and Elite Industries needed their new president to be in top form at all times. The man in her bed would have to go because she had a meeting shortly and she needed to prepare. Plus, she needed some time alone to process her situation.

The second Eve crossed the room, Graham's intense aqua eyes were on her. That heavy-lidded gaze did amazing things to her body. Just one stare, one simple touch, and the man had her under his spell. The potency he projected was unlike anything she'd ever known.

With a cockeyed grin, he jerked back the sheet in

a silent invitation for her to join him. He never had to say a word to get her right where he wanted her. There had been an unspoken agreement that this was sex only. Clearly they didn't want more because they were both married to their jobs and the intensity of their passion was off the charts. A committed relationship couldn't be this hot this fast. But they were about to enter a committed relationship of a totally different nature.

Eve shook her head. "As much as I'd love to take you up on your offer, I need to get some work done."

He raised one dark blond brow. "On Sunday morning? I can make you forget all about work."

Graham Newport could charm the crown from a queen…which was why he was one of Chicago's finest lawyers. Despite his young age of thirty-two, Graham had made full law partner at Mayer, Mayer and Newport. And it wasn't just the charm that catapulted him into his prestigious position. That reserved, quiet, yet lethal strength had him soaring to the top.

"Maybe so," she agreed, trying to sound casual, though the hidden pregnancy test mocked her. "But I have an online meeting later with a group from Australia because it will be their Monday morning."

Graham sat up, the sheet pooling around his bare, sculpted waist. Raking a hand through his disheveled hair, he sighed. "I hate when you want to be responsible."

Eve nearly cringed. If he thought she was responsible now, wait until he discovered the pregnancy. But that would have to wait. She needed to cope with this shock first, needed to make sure everything was all right. Granted, everything had appeared to be fine with her last pregnancy…then suddenly it wasn't.

Even though she and Graham had a physical relationship only, he had every right to know. But until she saw a doctor, she was keeping this news to herself. The last thing she'd ever want anyone to feel was the empty void and crushing ache of losing a child.

"You okay?"

Eve blinked, pulling herself back to the moment. Graham's aqua eyes held hers. Pasting on a smile, she nodded. "How could I not be after last night?"

Get it together, Eve.

Graham jerked the sheet aside and stalked across the room to gather his clothes. The man was completely comfortable with his body and she was completely comfortable enjoying the view.

Eve smoothed her silk robe with shaky hands before adjusting the covers and pillows on the bed. She needed to focus on something other than the sexy man in her bedroom, who never failed to satisfy her every desire, and the unborn child they'd made.

Graham would demand to know how this happened. She'd told him she was on birth control, and she was. But she'd switched types right about the time of the children's hospital charity ball…their first night together.

Strong arms circled her waist as she fell back against Graham's hard chest. Her body instantly responded to his touch and when his lips caressed the side of her neck, Eve couldn't stop her head from tilting, her lashes from closing and a moan from seeping out. She had no willpower when it came to Graham and the bedroom. Obviously.

"Maybe I could help you with preparing for this meeting," he muttered against her ear. "I do my best thinking in the shower."

Eve had been prepared for this meeting for weeks. That was her thing. She was always professional, always prompt, and she always had a plan B. Her spreadsheets had spreadsheets, and her period was never a day late.

Which is how she'd known when she needed to buy a pregnancy test.

And, if Graham really knew her, he would've caught her in the lie about needing to get ready for a meeting. He would've known she had her notes and speech down pat in order to win over the prospective new company. Which just went to prove, they didn't know each other very well at all outside the bedroom.

With a quick, effective tug, Graham pulled the knot free on her robe. Eve gripped his hands. "You may think in the shower, but I guarantee I won't be able to."

Graham playfully nipped at her earlobe and released her. "You're always flattering me."

As if his ego needed any more stroking.

Eve finished making the bed as Graham sat in the corner accent chair and slipped his dress shoes on. The man was hot as hell naked, but designer suits did some amazing things for him. And each time he showed up after work, she had a hard time resisting that *GQ* look with a touch of unkempt hair going on. How could one look like one needed a haircut and still have the entire Chicago power-lawyer look going?

It was the side eye. He had the sexiest side eye she'd ever seen. He'd tip his head in that George Clooney kind of way and peer at you from beneath those thick lashes. Yeah, those aqua eyes were the main component of his charm to get you hooked. Once he had you under his spell, he pulled you in tighter, snaring you with the rest of all of his seductive ways.

"I actually have a case I'm working on." He came to his feet and rolled up the sleeves of his black dress shirt.

"Brooks and I are meeting later. Say the word, though, and I'll gladly cancel."

Laughing, Eve shook her head. "We both have meetings. And if our families keep noticing how you and I are both MIA at the same time, they're going to stage an intervention."

Without a word, he closed the space between them, wrapped her in his arms and kissed her. Could something so potent, toe-curling and heart-clenching be summed up in such a simple word as *kiss*? Being kissed by Graham was an event, something she should prepare for, but there was no way she could ever prepare her body for the onslaught of passion and desire that slammed into her each time he touched her.

He ran his hands up and down her back, the silky material gliding against her skin. Nipping at her lips, he murmured, "I'll be back tonight."

With that whispered promise, he released her and walked away. Eve remained still, clutching her robe, staring at the neatly made bed and trying to figure out exactly how this unplanned pregnancy would weave into her perfectly planned life...and how Graham would take the news that he was going to be a father.

"Sutton will not win in the end," Brooks threatened. "If it's the last thing I do, I'll expose that man for the cheating bastard he is."

Pinching the bridge of his nose between his finger and thumb, Graham blew out a breath. Sutton Lazarus Winchester had always been a thorn in their side—his real estate business was Newport Corporation's main competition—but ever since they'd discovered Sutton had had an affair with their mother, Cynthia Newport, things had been much worse.

It had all started when she had first come to Chicago. Her real name was Amy Jo Turner, which she'd used until she fled her abusive father when she'd been pregnant with twins. With a brand-new name and town, Cynthia had gone to work in a coffee shop, saving money to raise two boys. She'd ultimately been taken under the wing of Gerty, a retired waitress. It was at this coffee shop that Cynthia met Sutton and wound up going to work for him. Cue illicit affair and their half brother, Carson.

The entire string of events was a complete mess. But now that the DNA test was official, Graham and Brooks knew for a fact Sutton wasn't their father. Which had made Graham's seduction of Eve possible. The woman kept him tied in knots. He counted down the time to when he could get his hands on her again, have her panting his name and wrapping that curvy body around his.

"Are you even listening?"

Graham dropped his hand to the arm of the leather club chair in his brother's office and sighed. He was half listening, half fantasizing new ways to make Eve lose control.

"I hear you," he confirmed. "And I agree. Carson is entitled to an inheritance when Sutton passes. It's only fair seeing as how Carson is his child, as well. The estate shouldn't just be split among the girls."

Sutton's three daughters were fighting this battle, as well. Nora, Grace and Eve weren't quite ready to welcome another sibling, but too bad, because the tests proved Carson was indeed a Winchester no matter how many people disliked the fact.

And Graham despised that he and his brothers were technically teaming up against Eve and her sisters. But it was only fair that when Sutton finally passed, Carson got his fair share of what was rightfully his. It would be in the Winchesters' best interest not to fight this matter because Graham would fight back…and win.

This entire mess was just another reason Graham and Eve had to keep their affair a secret and 100 percent physical. Nothing too heavy, no commitments and nothing long-term.

And no way in hell could their siblings ever come to know the full truth of just how hot their attraction burned. They'd not been too secretive about their initial attraction, but quickly discovered discretion was the best way to go. Considering what he and Eve did was no one's business, they'd opted to take things to the bedroom and ignore the turmoil surrounding them.

Keeping things simple—no talk of families or wills and Sutton's health—was the only way this affair was working and Graham was in no hurry to end it. A physical relationship with a woman who matched his passion like no other wasn't something he was ready to toss aside.

"So I need you to subpoena Eve."

The cold, harsh words jerked him from his thoughts. Graham sat up in his seat. "Excuse me?"

"I didn't think you were listening," Brooks growled. "We need her and her sisters to testify at the hearing regarding Sutton's estate. I need you to hand deliver those subpoenas."

So much for attempting to keep his relationship with Eve impersonal. Damn it. He wholeheartedly agreed that Carson was due his percentage, but he didn't want to go to battle with Eve. Not that he wouldn't win. Winning had never been an issue because when Graham Newport went into a courtroom, he was there for battle and came out on top. Always. But to get into a war with Eve…

He blew out a breath. That would destroy this chemistry they'd discovered.

Not that he wanted anything long-term or serious with her, but he wasn't ready to put the brakes on this amazing secret affair they had going. And he had to admit, the whole sneaking-around thing did thrill him on a new level he never knew existed. Sex had always come easy for him, but to know Eve matched his passion, his fire, was something he'd never found before. So, for now, he'd really like to keep this subpoena out of his personal life.

"When's the court date?" Graham asked.

Brooks rested his forearms on his neat, mahogany desk. "Two weeks. I'd rather have it moved up because, with Sutton's health declining, I don't want to take any chances."

Sutton wasn't doing well at all. The man was on his last leg and Graham wasn't sorry the old bastard was fading. Sure, that sounded cold and harsh, but it was fitting for the man who was ruthless and conniving. The man had taken advantage of Graham's mother, whether she would've admitted it or not. He'd gotten her pregnant, unbeknownst to him, but he'd still tossed Cynthia aside when he was done with her. Clearly his high-society wife was all he needed at the end of the day, though she'd ultimately ended up leaving him.

Graham's own mother had recently died, too, which is how the paternity issues had come to light in the first place. But the loss was still too fresh, too heart wrenching, so he turned his focus back to Brooks. Letting the void in his heart consume him would be all too easy.

"What did Roman find out?"

The private investigator Brooks had hired to uncover Brooks and Graham's paternity had been working diligently on the case, yet hadn't come up with a name yet. They'd never known who their father was and, for a brief time, they feared Sutton was the one. Now that Roman Slater had found out that Sutton had fathered Carson and abandoned their mother, Brooks and Graham were out for blood. The only way to take Sutton down was to hit him where he'd feel it the most. Considering the man didn't have a heart, Brooks and Graham were going after his finances on Carson's behalf, and ultimately that would trickle down to his daughters. Graham ignored the guilt gnawing away at his chest. Business and sex were two areas where he never got emotionally attached.

"I'm waiting to find out, but he's almost positive he's uncovered more children Sutton fathered from his affairs. If that's the case, I won't hesitate to use it against him."

Graham muttered a curse and stared out the floor-to-ceiling window behind Brooks. The Chicago skyline was one he never took for granted. He loved his city, loved working here and taking charge. The ambiance of such a powerful city gave him ammunition each day to fight his battles.

"If he uncovers too many, they'll all want a share of Sutton's assets."

Graham crossed his ankle over his knee and raked a hand over the back of his neck. Maybe he should get a haircut. No. He liked Eve's fingers running through his hair. He liked the way she toyed with the strands on his neck when…

Damn it. He was here for Brooks. How could he concentrate when Eve kept creeping to the forefront of his mind?

"I thought of that, too," Brooks agreed. "Which is another reason I want this finalized before Sutton passes.

So those subpoenas need to be delivered as soon as you can draw them up."

Graham nodded. He might not want to do this, he might hate mixing this business with his personal life, but there was no other way. And Graham knew Brooks wasn't usually this ruthless. But his twin was angry, hurt. They both were. With Sutton so hush-hush about what he knew, and right on the tail of their mother's passing, there was just so much emotion and nowhere to put it all.

Sutton was a man who deserved to be destroyed, and if Eve and her sisters got in the Newports' way, well... they better just cooperate because Graham would win this fight for Carson. Taking prisoners along the way wasn't ideal, but he'd do so for the sake of his brothers. Family was everything, after all.

Two

Two days had passed since the test. Two hours had passed since her doctor had done an exam and confirmed the pregnancy, assuring her everything looked fine. She'd held it together until she made it back to her car. In the quiet of the parking garage, she'd wept for the innocent life growing inside her and prayed she'd have the strength to make it through.

Just because children weren't something she'd set her sights on for her future didn't mean she didn't want this baby. Years ago she'd been naive and unprepared for what life threw her way. Now Eve was ready to do anything and everything to keep her baby safe and secure. She'd started taking vitamins the day she took the home test. At this point all she could do was relax and attempt some sort of stress-free life…as much as was possible when she was planning global domination.

As president of Elite Industries, she was more than ready to broaden the scope of the company's dealings. Her father had created a good foundation, but she wanted more. She wanted to prove to herself, and to her ailing father, that she could make this company even better. Before he passed, she wanted him to be proud of what she'd done.

Back at the office, Eve closed her eyes and tipped her head back against her leather office chair. Her father's days were numbered, there was no denying the truth that faced them. Sliding a hand over her stomach, Eve wondered at what point she should tell him about this next generation. Would he be excited she was carrying on the name? But if she told him about the baby, she'd have to tell him about the baby's father. Eve wasn't ready to expose her child to this ugly war just yet.

Once she told Graham, then they could decide when to tell everyone else. He needed to know; she just had no idea how to go about telling him. Would he be angry? Would he blame her or would he embrace fatherhood? How on earth would they deal with shared parenting?

Questions whirled around inside her head as her office door burst open and slammed against the wall. Eve jerked upright, shocked to see Graham striding through, her assistant, Rebecca, right on his heels.

"I'm sorry, Ms. Winchester," Rebecca stated nervously. "I tried to stop him."

What was he doing here? Nobody knew about their affair and they'd purposely gone out of their way to avoid being seen together in public. His barging into her office could jeopardize everything.

"It's fine." Eve shot her assistant a smile and nodded in a silent dismissal. Once the door was closed, she glared at Graham. "What the hell are you thinking coming here? The last thing we need is gossip about your being in my office."

Graham crossed to her desk and slammed a piece of paper down, the force sending other paperwork fluttering to the floor. "We need you to testify."

Shocked, Eve came to her feet and braced her palms on the top of her desk, completely ignoring the paper. "What?"

"This is a subpoena regarding your father's assets and Carson's interest in them."

Rage bubbled within her. This is why he'd come? Was this also the same reason he looked so angry? What was he thinking doing this to her, to her family?

"How dare you order me to testify against my father?"

The muscle in Graham's jaw tightened, a tic she'd noticed when he was angry with himself. So, that was the real issue here. Why was he doing this if he didn't want to?

What was going on and why was he doing this to her?

"You have to see what your father is, Eve." Graham's bright eyes held hers. Those same eyes that had devoured her body just yesterday now held so much anger, resentment. "Carson is entitled to his share of the inheritance. Plus, our PI has uncovered some other nasty facts regarding Sutton."

As much as Eve wanted to close her eyes to battle the pain, she couldn't. Her father may not be a popular man, but he was still her father and she wouldn't let anyone stand in her office and throw ugly rumors around. Yes, he'd admitted to affairs while married to her mother, but that was in the past. Couldn't people change? Did he have to pay for his sins forever? He was dying. Couldn't everyone just let him live out his last days in peace?

Enough. She refused to allow this to happen, let alone

in her own office…her father's old office. Reaching for her phone, Eve started to dial her assistant. Instantly Graham's fingers encircled her wrist.

"What are you doing?"

She glared at him. "Having security escort you out."

The pressure around her wrist increased, but not to the point of hurting. "Hang up, Eve. Hear me out for two minutes and I'll go."

Still gripping the phone, Eve stared into his eyes, and her first thought was whether their child would have those mesmerizing baby blues. How could she resist him and tell him no when she couldn't get her own hormones in check?

And, how could she fault his loyalty for standing up for his brother? Wasn't she standing up for her father? They both held family bonds high and she had to admire that, but she still couldn't allow him to shove his weight around. Not here on her turf.

She hung the phone up and pulled away from his touch. Crossing her arms over her chest, Eve tipped her chin. "Two minutes."

A hint of a smile danced around those kissable lips. No. She couldn't think of him in those terms right now. The way he came barging into her office, forcing this subpoena on her had nothing to do with what they did in the bedroom. Right this minute, they were enemies… and soon to be parents. Talk about a conflict of interest.

"Carson is your half brother, too," Graham began in that steady, low tone of his that no doubt always had the judge and jury hanging on his every word. "He deserves part of your father's assets."

"Considering my father is very much alive, that's not my call," she argued. Eve hated discussing the fact that her father's health was failing, but the harsh truth was always at the forefront of her mind. "Is that all you barged in here for?"

"Eve, you have to see this is the right thing to do for Carson. Don't let Sutton's hatred and hardheaded notions trickle down to you. You're too good for that."

For a split second, Eve wanted to melt at his words, but then she recalled who she was dealing with. Chicago's youngest, fastest-rising attorney who marched through court and came out with a victory every time. He had Charm with a capital C. He oozed it and exploited it in order to get what he wanted.

"I have no hatred toward Carson," she stated firmly. Carson was just as much an innocent as she and her sisters were. "I simply don't feel it's my decision to say what happens to my father's things. He has a will, Graham."

"One that was implemented before he knew of Carson's existence." Graham pressed his palms on her desk and leaned forward. "Regardless of what you want to do, you've been served, Eve."

Part of her wanted to applaud him for holding his ground and having his brother's back. The other part of her wanted to slap him, tear this subpoena to shreds and toss it like confetti in his face. But she refused to let her emotions show.

"I believe your two minutes are up."

His eyes held hers for a moment longer, but he finally turned and walked out, his exit much less dramatic than his entrance. Once the doorway was clear, Eve's legs gave out and she sank back to her chair. With shaky hands, she unfolded the document and stared at the date she was due in court. Whatever was going on with the Newport brothers, she sincerely wished they'd leave her out of it. Her father was dying, she was pushing to acquire another real estate company in Australia and now she was expecting the baby of a man who should be her enemy.

What more could life throw at her?

"Ms. Winchester?"

Eve glanced up to see Rebecca standing in the doorway. "Do you want me to have security make sure Mr. Newport is out of the building?"

"No, Rebecca. That won't be necessary. Mr. Newport's business is done here. He won't return."

There. Hopefully that would help quash any rumors about Graham's unexpected visit. Rebecca wasn't one to gossip, though. Eve wouldn't have her as an assistant if she were, but she still wanted the utmost respect from her staff.

"We had a mutual client and he was dropping off some paperwork," Eve added. "Thank you."

With a slight nod, Rebecca stepped back out and closed the door.

So much for telling Graham about the baby soon. Now she had to figure out where they stood because he'd drawn a battle line the moment he'd opted to show up at her office. He could've had anyone on his staff deliver that subpoena.

Again, this proved how his family loyalties and his career were his top priorities. Which only made Eve wonder: Once he knew they'd created a baby, would she and the child be included in that inner circle?

The following morning, Eve's patience had run out. Graham hadn't contacted her since he'd burst into her office yesterday, and now the glaring headline mocked her from the front page of the paper: Chicago Kingpin Sutton Winchester's Infidelity Produces More Heirs.

She began reading the article and literally had to take a seat on a stool at her kitchen island when she hit the line about his "fathering numerous children out of secret affairs." Her stomach churned, and the nausea had nothing to do with the baby.

Tears pricked her eyes as anger rushed through her. There was only one family who wanted to stir the proverbial pot and that was the Newports. Brooks may be the ringleader in this agenda to bring down her father, but Carson and Graham were right there with him. And no doubt Graham had known all about this little media exposé when he was in her office yesterday.

Betrayal was a sickening feeling. But how could she feel betrayed? He'd never pretended to be on her side when it came to their families. They had sex, plenty of sex, but that didn't make them a couple. That didn't mean he had to be loyal to her or defend her to his family.

Eve knew very well who Graham was when she'd gotten together with him, so if blame was to be placed, she needed to point the finger at herself. She just wished she weren't getting so personally wrapped up in a man who was 100 percent wrong for her.

And what the hell was this about her father having "numerous" other children? Carson was the only child she knew of. Perhaps now that his secret son had come to light, others wanted a share of her father's holdings. The man was worth billions. Vultures would be swooping in wanting money, especially with his health failing.

An ache spread through her chest. People were picking away at her father. He was still alive, he was still in control of his will, and all of these people vying for a piece of something that didn't belong to them were seriously making her turn into someone she didn't want to be. If anyone, Graham included, wanted a fight, she'd give them one. She would protect her father, especially now, and she had no doubt her sisters would happily join her in the battle.

Eve finished her orange juice and dry toast so she could take her vitamin and keep it down. She'd learned on day one not to take that pill on an empty stomach and lately she was nauseous anyway. Whether from the pregnancy or from the constant roller coaster with the Newport men, she wasn't sure.

But if Graham expected her to show up in court and do dirty work on behalf of his brothers, she expected something in return.

She shot off a quick text to her assistant to reschedule any morning meetings. Eve already knew there were two, but both were with coworkers and could be adjusted. Nobody would second-guess the president's orders.

Once she finished with Rebecca, Eve sent Graham a text demanding an immediate meeting at her house. If he was going to play hardball, then so was she. Maybe he only knew her well in the bedroom, which was fine, but now the proverbial tables had turned. Hell, they hadn't just turned, they'd been flipped completely over.

Eve quickly showered and threw on her favorite crimson suit. The V of the jacket's lapels was just low enough to be sexy, yet high enough to be professional. She was gearing up for battle and she wanted to look her best.

She'd just applied her lip gloss when her doorbell rang. Eve's master suite was on the first floor of her Chicago mansion. Five bedrooms upstairs were available for any guests, but she rarely went up there. Maybe she'd reconsider once the baby came. She wasn't comfortable being on a separate floor from her child. Of course, at first she'd like the bassinet to be in her room so she could be close to her baby for nightly feedings.

Eve paused and pulled in a breath. That was the exact attitude she needed to keep in regards to this baby. A positive attitude, an outlook that planned for a future with her child. Because nothing would go wrong...fate wasn't so cruel as to take away a second child.

Eve gripped the door handle and gave herself a mental pep talk. The second she opened this door, she had to forget Graham was the father of her child and remember he was the man trying to ruin her father.

Opening the door, Eve stepped back and gestured for Graham to come in. They'd never been formal, and perhaps she should've had this chat on neutral territory, but she wanted to be here, on her turf. This was her day to win the battle.

The moment she closed them inside and turned to face him, her body heated. Damn it. Why did he have to slide that sultry gaze over her? When he started to step toward her, Eve held her hands up.

"This isn't a social call."

Her words didn't deter him as he closed the space between them and slid his hands over her waist, down her hips, and pulled her against him.

"I'm not in the mood to talk anyway," he replied with a slight grin.

When he went for her lips, Eve skirted out from his hold. One kiss and she'd be a goner. There was absolutely no room for hormones right now.

"What was that stunt in the paper all about?" she demanded. Certainly mentioning their family drama would douse any desire he had.

Graham shrugged. "The truth was uncovered."

"The truth," she repeated. "You expect me to believe

my father has Winchester heirs milling about Chicago? Sounds too convenient for this news to come out now."

"Our investigator turned up quite a bit on your father." Graham took one step toward her. "I don't want to argue with you about this. You have to see the truth and accept it."

With a very unladylike growl, Eve turned on her Christian Louboutin heels and made her way into the formal living room. This was one of the few rooms left in her home where they hadn't had sex. She had to focus on the fact that, even though she was expecting, this affair might be coming to an end. How could she continue when he was so adamant about destroying her family?

"I know you're trying to look out for the best interest of Carson," she started before he could say a word. "But you have to see it from my point of view, too. This is my father. I know you all hate him. I know he wasn't the nicest man to you guys."

"He's a bastard."

Crossing her arms over her chest, Eve forged on. "He's dying." Those words hurt to say, but she was fighting for him, so remaining strong was the only option. "This is not the time to drag his name through mud in the press."

"Eve—"

"No. If you want me to come to court, you better get your brother and that investigator to back the hell up." Eve hadn't realized she'd stepped forward until the tips of her shoes were touching Graham's. "I will not negotiate."

A corner of his mouth kicked up into a grin. Eve didn't want to give in to the ridiculous schoolgirl flutter in her belly; she couldn't let her emotions take over.

She was already personally involved with him, already carrying his child. She had to have some sort of hold on this…what? Relationship? Did they actually have a relationship? Was there a label that could be placed on whatever they were doing?

Not likely. They were both a mess. The only time things ever seemed to be going their way was in the bedroom. Sex had a way of making you think your world was perfectly fine. Then the cold slap of reality hit.

"If you start laughing—"

Graham snaked an around her waist and pulled her in tight. "Wouldn't dream of it."

"Don't kiss me." Did that protest sound weak? "This isn't a good idea."

He nipped at her jawline, traveled up to her ear and whispered, "Feels like a great idea." His hands curved over her backside, pulling her hips into his.

Graham's hands and mouth, his body for that matter, always seemed like the answer. He made her forget everything except for how her body seemed to zing to life. But she couldn't zing, not today.

Eve pressed her palms to his chest and eased back. "No. I won't be distracted by sex. I want your brother to back off the media attacks and insults."

The muscle in his jaw clenched. "Fine."

Narrowing her eyes, Eve shifted from his grasp. "It's that easy? You agree and know he'll just back down?"

Graham shrugged. "He's acting out of hurt, not rage. I can reason with him."

Eve wanted to believe Graham, but she didn't know Brooks very well. All she knew was how much of a mess they'd created with this secret affair. She was a fool to think their actions wouldn't trickle into their families' lives.

She turned, needing to put some space between them. Having him so close was difficult. They never just talked and she wasn't immune to his charm...much as she'd like to be.

But just as she spun away, a wave of dizziness overcame her. The room tilted before her eyes, and she reached out for any stationary surface. Everything seemed to be moving in slow motion, but Eve cringed, waiting for the hard hit to the floor.

At the last minute, her hand went to her stomach just as strong arms wrapped around her torso.

Secure against Graham's chest, Eve kept her eyes shut as she pulled in a shaky breath. The dizziness remained. It was the first time she'd experienced this pregnancy symptom.

"Okay?" he whispered in her ear.

Not really.

Eve patted the hand he had around her. "I'm okay." She hoped. "Just lost my balance."

Opening her eyes, she focused on the chair and eased from Graham's hold to have a seat. Crossing her legs, she wasn't a bit surprised when his gaze landed directly on her bare skin.

"I want to know what Brooks says and if he plans on getting your PI to ease up. You're attacking a dying man."

Graham unbuttoned his black jacket and crouched at her knees. "We're not attacking, Eve. We simply want your father to do what is right for our half brother. Surely you can see that he's entitled."

"My opinion is irrelevant."

Why was her stomach threatening to revolt? She'd been hoping to bypass this common symptom of pregnancy. She'd rather skip straight to that miracle glow so many raved about. Actually, she'd rather skip to the end when her baby was safe and healthy in her arms.

Heat washed over her. That clammy, instantly hot type of feeling that swept through you when you had the flu…or morning sickness apparently. Why now? Why did this have to happen with Graham here?

"I need to get to work," she told him, hoping he'd leave so she could be miserable all on her own. "Text me later after you talk to Brooks."

Graham's hand slid over her knee. "You're looking pale. Are you okay?"

Of course she looked pale. One minute she was fine, the next she felt like death. Why wasn't he leaving so she could battle this on her own? Why did Mr. Always-Polished-and-Sexy have to see her like this? She prided herself on being that sultry vixen he seemed to believe she was. If she tossed her toast on his Ferragamo shoes, she'd totally ruin her image.

"Eve?"

He wouldn't leave until she assured him she was fine. "Just tired," she told him, attempting to hold her head high and show as little weakness as possible, considering.

His brows dipped. "Are you coming down with something?"

Just a child.

If he didn't think she was fine, he'd never get out of here. With all the energy she had left, Eve pushed herself out of the chair, forcing Graham to come to his feet, as well. She ignored his worried look and started toward the open foyer. Time to show her guest the door before she made a complete fool of herself and he figured out she was pregnant. She couldn't tell him just yet.

"I'm running late," she lied. "You let me know how we're going to proceed after you talk to your brother."

As she reached for the door handle, his hand covered hers.

"Don't push me out."

"We both have work." Why was he so close? His familiar cologne enveloped her, but to her surprise, it didn't turn her stomach. His warm breath tickled her cheek, and any other time she'd relish the moment. Now was definitely not that time.

"I mean mentally," he corrected. Taking her by the shoulders he turned her around. "Whatever is going on with your dad, the courts and my brothers doesn't have to affect us."

Eve couldn't help the laughter that bubbled up. "You're a fool if you believe that. It has already affected us. Until today, we've never kept our clothes on when you came here."

His aqua eyes darkened. "I'm more than ready to rip that suit off you."

And he would. Graham didn't make veiled threats or empty promises. Right now, though, sex was not the answer.

Eve reached behind her and turned the doorknob. "You talk to your brother—we'll talk about the suit ripping later."

His eyes darted down to the V of her jacket, then back to her mouth.

"When I come back later, I want you to still have this on."

With a quick, promising kiss that was anything but innocent and sweet, Graham walked out. Eve shut the door at her back and rested against the wood. How could she feel so nauseous and yet still be reacting to this man?

One thing was sure: until she knew where he stood with this whole inheritance issue, and until the ultrasound came back okay, she wasn't telling him anything. They'd continue on as they had been…having sex and pretending the world around them didn't exist.

Three

Three

"Tell me this is your idea and you're not being persuaded by a woman you should consider our enemy."

Graham eyed his brother, hating how much this paternity issue was eating away at them. They both just wanted answers...answers Sutton had, but refused to share. The man was dying. Why was he now choosing to be loyal to Cynthia? He hadn't chosen her years ago, so this sudden burst of emotion was completely out of character.

And Brooks's actions were also out of character. "This isn't you," Graham stated, eyeing his twin. "Being vindictive. I know you're reacting out of frustration and hurt, but attacking Sutton in the media isn't the way to deal with it."

Brooks grabbed a tumbler from behind the bar in his study and poured two fingers of bourbon. Gripping the glass, he stared down at the contents as if weighing his actions. Eve wasn't forcing Graham to do anything. What she said made sense, and Graham knew his brother wasn't a hateful man. Brooks was fair, honest and loyal...quite the opposite of Sutton Winchester.

"Are you sleeping with her?"

The quietly spoken question hovered in the air. Brooks didn't even look up, but Graham felt the punch to the gut just the same as if his brother had shouted the question.

"Are you going to ease off with the media?" Graham countered. "If you want Eve to cooperate, or any her sisters, we can't come at them like we're coming in for the kill."

Graham winced at his poor choice of words considering the state of the old man. But still, Nora, Grace and Eve weren't to blame. They didn't choose to be born to a man as evil and self-righteous as Sutton.

Brooks tipped back the contents and slammed his glass down onto the polished mahogany bar. "You can't be loyal to your lover and to your family. Your promiscuous ways are going to bite you in the ass."

Graham paced across the room to the floor-to-ceiling window overlooking the city below. This penthouse suite was perfect for a bachelor with a busy lifestyle. "I've gotten along just fine in my professional and personal life without your input."

"If you think getting into bed with a Winchester isn't going to do damage to our family, you're even more blindsided by lust than I first thought. Didn't we agree you'd stay away from her?"

Graham fisted his hands at his side. This was his brother, his twin. They were so similar, yet different. Brooks was the outgoing type, the go-getter, the grounded brother. Graham was definitely outgoing and a go-getter, but he also enjoyed a good time, a good woman. He'd been told often that his quiet charm won him cases and had women falling at his feet. He was just fine with that assessment.

But Graham wasn't ready to give up what he and Eve were doing. Why should he? He'd never experienced anything like Eve before and he sure as hell wasn't going to let Sutton Winchester's will come between them. He'd find a way to make everything work, play the peacemaker and get the job done. Isn't that what he excelled at?

"We didn't agree on anything," Graham stated. "Eve and I are adults. I know where my loyalties are and I won't let anything stand in the way of getting Carson what is rightfully his and getting Sutton to tell us the name of our father. But attacking him in the press isn't the way to go. We need to go in with a milder approach, for a stronger impact."

Brooks quirked a brow. "And how do you suggest doing that?"

Pulling in a breath, Graham turned from the window. "Stop the press war and put a hold on the legal proceedings."

Brooks opened his mouth, but Graham lifted his hand. "Leave this to me. We want Sutton to suffer, but not necessarily his daughters. They'll be hurt, but we can make it less of a blow to them. Sutton is still alive, so as long as he is, we go straight to him. Play hardball with him. Introduce the evidence Roman has discovered and let Sutton make a choice. Tell him we'll go to the media with all the facts, and the lineup of women claiming to have a child by him, or he can put Carson in his will as a beneficiary and give him his share. I'm demanding he give us the name of our father no matter what he chooses to do about the other issues. I refuse to back down on that."

Brooks raked his thumb back and forth on his glass of bourbon, considering all the options. Graham knew he could make this work. He knew Eve would see his side so long as they quit attacking her father. Damn, but he admired her loyalty. Graham just wished she didn't have to be so faithful to such a bastard.

"We'll try your way." Brooks came around the bar, leaned an elbow on top and shot Graham a look. "But you better remember what team you're fighting for."

Graham nodded. "I never forget who I'm fighting for. Carson and you are my top priorities."

Brooks nodded. "Good. I have another topic I want to discuss."

"Does it require more bourbon?"

With a shrug, Brooks crossed the room and took a seat on the leather sofa. "I want to talk to Sutton. In person."

Inwardly cringing, Graham glanced toward the ceiling and wondered why he was surprised. Brooks was a man on a mission. He was determined.

"You want to leave the girls out of this, fine. For now," Brooks added, aiming a hard look at his twin. "But the three of us—Carson, you, me—we're going to talk to Sutton. He's growing weaker every day and I know it may be cruel to go to him and put the pressure on, but we have to try."

Their mother had passed just months ago, taking the secret of who fathered them to her grave. Graham had no idea why she didn't tell them. At first, he'd thought for sure Sutton was their father and she'd been afraid, ashamed. But the DNA test had come back, proving Sutton had only fathered Carson, leaving Brooks and Graham confused and hurt.

While they yearned to know who their father was,

Graham was elated that old bastard wasn't his. Not to mention the fact that it had left the path wide open to seduce Eve the night of the charity ball for the children's hospital. He'd gotten the results right before the gala. Eve had shown up wearing a body-hugging gold gown. That honey-brown hair she'd piled perfectly on top of her head came tumbling down all around him when he'd finally gotten her to his penthouse. They'd barely survived the cab ride.

"I'll go with you," Graham stated, pulling himself back into the moment. He needed to be strong for his brothers, needed them to know they were a team. "Sutton isn't as strong as he used to be."

Brooks sent a malevolent grin. "That's what I'm counting on."

After a long day, exhaustion finally won. Eve nearly wept as she submerged herself in the soaker tub in her master suite. All the symptoms of her first pregnancy had come back full force: the need to rest at all times, the nausea that slammed into her with no warning, the emotions that were all over the place. Just trying to keep herself in check at work today had been trying. When someone from a newly acquired company in Barcelona offered condolences for Eve's father, she nearly lost it. Thankfully they had only been chatting on the phone and not via video conference because the tears welled up in her eyes and flowed, but Eve managed to clear her throat, offer thanks and keep her tone neutral.

Why were people acting like he was already gone? That was the part that completely gutted her. He was very much alive, though his health was failing.

Her hand slid down through the lavender-scented bubbles to rest on her flat stomach. Babies were a blessing. The innocence they injected into your life couldn't be matched. Eve wanted to tell her father, wanted to be excited about this new life, but first she had to talk to Graham.

Keeping their child from being a victim in this family war was going to be a struggle, but she refused to believe it was impossible. She knew Graham was loyal to his family—that much was obvious. But how would he react to this child? How would he treat her?

She didn't want him to hover, didn't want him to assume she wanted him as a permanent fixture in her life. She had a plan, goals, a career that was taking off better than she'd ever anticipated.

Tears pricked her eyes. She didn't want this career at the expense of her father's health, his life. She'd taken over as president when he could no longer run Elite Industries.

When her cell chimed, Eve jumped. She should've left the thing in her purse, but she'd been carrying it around like a pacifier lately…because one day she'd get the inevitable call about her father.

The cell lay on the edge of the tub surround. Eve glanced at the screen and saw Nora's name. Worried this might have something to do with her dad, Eve dried her hands off on her towel and quickly read the text.

Relief slid through her when she saw it was just a Halloween party invitation. Sounded fun. In terms of costumes, Eve could go as an overworked, worn down, emotional mess. Maybe she could go in her pajamas with bed hair to really play up the part.

Eve shot back a quick reply to tell her sister she'd be there. Asking if Graham could come as her date probably wasn't the smart thing to do.

Wait. Why was she thinking of taking him anywhere as her date? They weren't dating, they were...

Eve dropped her head against her bath pillow and groaned. She didn't know what they were exactly and that's what annoyed her. She had her life all mapped out with color-coded tabs to tell her when and where to do everything. She prided herself on being efficient, planning everything and knowing exactly what was coming her way.

What she hadn't planned on was the onslaught of desire associated with Graham Newport. One look led to another, then to flirting, which was put on hold when they both realized her father had been involved with his mother. The second they knew Sutton wasn't Graham's father, all bets had been off, all warnings from family ignored.

Eve hadn't been able to get Graham alone fast enough that first night after the children's hospital gala, and from the way he practically tore her dress off her, the feeling was mutual.

That had to have been when she got pregnant. She'd only switched her birth control a week before, thinking it was a safe time since she wasn't seeing anyone. They'd been all over each other before condoms were mentioned, but she'd assured him she was on the pill and they'd quickly had the "I'm clean" conversation.

Thinking back now, Eve realized he would blame her for this pregnancy. She'd assured him she was covered, that they were safe. Well, he could blame her all he wanted, so long as this child remained unaffected by any wrath from the Newports.

When her cell chimed again, Eve jerked from her relaxed position. Even though her body was calm and resting, her mind never shut off. She zeroed in on the screen and saw Graham's name this time. Once again, she dried her hands and checked his message, cursing herself for acting like a teenager.

Meet me at my penthouse. 30 min.

Eve gritted her teeth. While some may go for the demanding attitude, she did not. Besides, she was exhausted. If she could sleep in this warm bubble bath and not drown, she would.

Because she didn't want him to think she jumped when he texted, though she did, Eve set her phone back down without replying. There was no reason to pretend that the thought of Graham didn't have her body humming, but now she had to be realistic. She was expecting his child, and she was entering into a battle over her father… Sex couldn't be the main thread that held them together at this point.

Eve closed her eyes for just a moment, needing to push aside all the fears, all the questions, and just relax. Her doctor told her to try to take as much downtime as possible. Even if she could grab five minutes here and there, she would have to for the sake of the baby and her own health.

All too easily she could let her mind drift into the worry of whether she was carrying a healthy baby, but she wanted to focus on the positive. Would she have a boy or a girl? Would her baby have Graham's striking aqua eyes and her honey hair? One thing was for sure— this child would be strong-willed, determined and take charge, all qualities she and Graham possessed.

Eve's mind went to the nursery, and she instantly envisioned Nora and Grace helping her decorate. She could hire a decorator, but this wasn't a kitchen or bathroom job. No, Eve would take a hands-on approach to her baby's room.

The water had cooled, but Eve was still content to just lie there and relax. The quiet of her home was a welcome reprieve. She'd been in meetings all day, had made numerous decisions regarding offices in several different countries. She wasn't one to have idle time, but she had to admit this felt amazing.

She definitely had to listen to her body, and her body was tired and in need of some downtime.

"Eve."

Water sloshed as she jerked and opened her eyes to see Graham standing in the door separating her bedroom from the bath. Her heart beat out of control in her chest. He'd scared the hell out of her.

She blinked, realizing she'd fallen asleep. The water chilled her now and she shivered as she started to get up.

"What are you doing here?" she asked, stepping from the tub to reach for the towel from the heated bar. "How did you get in?"

His eyes raked over her, causing her chills to multiply for a totally different reason. "You were supposed to meet me an hour ago."

Eve wrapped herself in the towel and secured the edge between her breasts. She'd been asleep that long? Maybe she was more tired than she'd thought.

"First, I never agreed to meet you after you demanded it." She crossed her arms, rolling her eyes when his gaze dipped to her cleavage. "Second, you didn't tell me how you got into my house."

One slow step turned into two and suddenly he was in front of her. His fingertips trailed up her bare arms and shivers wracked her body. Without a word, he tipped his head to rake his lips lightly across her jawline. Eve fisted her hands at her sides. She wanted to clutch him and give in to what he was obviously offering, but she had to think with her head, too.

"You smell amazing," he muttered as his mouth continued to explore her skin. "I worried when you didn't show up."

Eve cursed herself when her head tipped back. With this man, she didn't have control over her body. The fact that he worried about her warmed her, but she couldn't think like that. They weren't in a relationship. In fact, last time she'd talked to him, they were more divided than ever.

"Graham." She pushed at his chest. "We can't do this."

Her slight shove did nothing to budge him. Wrapping his arms around her, he met her eyes.

"Brooks and I have an unspoken understanding."

Eve narrowed her gaze, waiting for him to elaborate. "And that's him keeping his investigator out of my family's business?" she asked when it was clear he wasn't going to go into detail.

"He's staying out of this for now. I don't want to talk about my brothers or your father." He nipped at her lips. "Trust me, Eve. I won't hurt you."

Trust him. Oh, how she wished she could. She had a secret she wasn't ready to reveal and *he* wanted *her* trust. And he may not intend to hurt her, but he was hell-bent on destroying her father, which in turn would most definitely hurt her.

With an expert flick, he had her towel open and gliding to the floor before she could stop him. Every intimate encounter before now had been frenzied, frantic, clothes flying and lips exploring. Something about this slow seduction in her bathroom seemed even more…intimate. Were they crossing a line or was she just reading into this?

"Stop thinking," he demanded in a whisper against her ear. "Feel, Eve. Only feel."

As if she had any other choice.

Four

He couldn't touch her, taste her enough. When she hadn't shown, he'd wondered if she was working, but then she hadn't even replied so he'd panicked like some lovestruck fool. Considering he was neither in love, nor a fool, Graham hated how he'd let his imagination run away from him.

But then he'd gotten into her place, using the security code he'd seen her type in one other time, and every worry fled. Seeing her wet in that tub full of disappearing bubbles, he'd had one mission and that was to get his body on hers as soon as possible.

But he wanted to go slow. She looked positively exhausted, not that he'd ever tell her. He wasn't an idiot when it came to women. Something about how vulnerable Eve looked resting in the bath stirred deeper feelings in him that he'd quickly tamped down, but he welcomed the rush of lust and desire.

He wanted her, he needed her and he planned on having her. Now.

Her bathroom was spacious, complete with a vanity island in the middle. Perfect. He scooped her up, sat her on the edge and stepped between her thighs.

Running his hands up her legs, over those rounded hips and over her waist, Graham wasn't surprised when she trembled beneath his touch. Trembling was a nice start, but he planned on having her writhing, panting his name.

Her fingers curled around his shoulders. "We shouldn't do this anymore," she argued, but her words came out on a whisper, betraying her true feelings.

Graham slid one fingertip between her breasts and down to her abdomen. "And why is that?"

Eve sucked in a breath as her lids lowered. Yes. That was the reaction he wanted to see. Complete surrender.

"B-because. We want…"

Graham leaned forward, his mouth trailing along the path his finger had just traveled. "Oh, yes. We want."

Her hands framed his face as she urged him back up to look at her. "We want different things," she stated, her eyes holding on to his.

"Right now I'd say we want the exact same thing."

"It's not in here that I'm worried about."

She had every reason to worry, but he meant it when he said he wouldn't hurt her. Eve was innocent, but she may feel some of the aftershock of her father's wrath. Everything that was coming down on them was a result of Sutton's actions. If anyone was hurting Eve, it was her father. Couldn't she see that?

"I told you to trust me," Graham reminded her. His hand settled between her thighs. "No more talking."

The second he touched her, she moaned. Leaning back on her hands, she offered herself up exactly the way he'd been fantasizing about all day. He'd wanted her in his penthouse with the city lights flooding into his living room, but this was fine, too. If anyone stopped by to visit, they wouldn't see his car because she'd given him a bay in the second garage in the back of the house for such eventualities. This sneaking around only amped up his desire. Graham never backed away from a challenge and he damn well wouldn't start now that Eve was having doubts.

The more his hand moved over her center, the more she let out those sexy little moans. Then she'd bite her lip as if she hadn't meant to show how much she enjoyed what they were doing.

He wanted to bite that lip.

Graham continued stroking her as he leaned forward and took her mouth with his. She instantly opened to him, matching his need with her own. And that's what made Eve so perfect in the bedroom. They had the exact same needs, they knew how to pleasure each other without a single word and neither of them expected anything beyond exactly this.

Eve tore her mouth away and shut her eyes as her entire body tightened. Watching her come undone was the sexiest experience of his entire life. She had no qualms about the noises she made, or the way her damp hair clung to the side of her cheek when she'd thrown her head to the side. This was Eve. His Eve.

No. Not his. She would never be his. This was temporary, no more.

The moment her body relaxed, Graham jerked her to the edge of the counter and unfastened his pants. He couldn't wait another minute. He needed to have her and didn't want her coming off the high she'd just had. She was everything he needed at this exact moment, and he refused to look beyond that. There was no future…not for them.

Her arms wrapped around his neck, her breasts pressed up against his dress shirt and he didn't even care that he was still technically fully clothed. That was the need he had for this woman.

Eve's ankles locked behind him and Graham bent his head to claim that precious mouth once more as he joined their bodies.

Would he ever get enough of her? He kept waiting for this new sensation to wear off, but it had been several weeks now and he was just as achy for her as ever. There was a desire inside him that he hadn't known before her. Part of him wondered if they'd still sneak around if their families weren't the Newports and the Winchesters.

When Eve arched her back, pulling her mouth from his, he took the opportunity to capture one perfect breast with his lips. His actions were rewarded with another soft moan as she gripped his shoulders. Her body quickened the pace, and he was all too eager to join her.

When she cried out his name, it was the green light he needed from her to follow her over the edge. He held her as they trembled together, held her after their bodies had cooled and then carried her into her bed.

And Graham refused to even think about why he was feeling so protective of her right now. This had nothing to do with Sutton, Brooks or Carson. His actions had nothing to do with how worn she'd looked when he'd arrived.

No, this was only sex. Nothing more. It couldn't be.

Eve finished the conference call with one of her father's established clients in Miami. Even though she was taking Elite Industries into global territory, there was still a need to keep the current clients satisfied. Now that Eve was president, she intended to not only continue building on current relationships, but also adding to their Elite family. This business was all she'd known; she was molded to fill this role and she took every bit of it seriously.

Eve popped in another peppermint and willed the flavor to calm her queasy stomach. She'd read from multiple sites—and her doctor had confirmed—that peppermint would alleviate the queasiness.

Two days had passed since Graham had shown up in her bathroom. Two days since she'd had the opportunity to tell him about the baby. But there was that whole family rivalry standing between them, driving the wedge deeper with each passing day. Graham had urged her to trust him, but that word was too easily thrown around. And what had he meant by that? He'd implored her at her weakest moment, and damn if she hadn't given in.

She wanted to trust him in more areas than just her body. She had to believe that he'd taken care of getting Brooks to stay away from the media. Dirty rumors could damage her family's reputation. Something that would start a domino effect and impact Elite Industries.

She refused to allow Graham, Brooks or Carson to destroy the only life she'd ever known. The life she needed to secure for her child.

A light tap on her door had Eve straightening in her seat. Shoving the peppermint into the side of her mouth, she called, "Come in."

The door swung open and Eve's younger sister, Nora, stepped in. Nora in all her beauty and radiance. She'd fallen in love with hotelier Reid Chamberlain and the two were deliriously happy. Reid had also taken to Nora's son and they were absolutely adorable together. Over the past several weeks, the trio had become inseparable. Eve was thrilled to see her sister find her soul mate. Being a single mother had to be so difficult, but Nora had always made life look like a breeze.

The tug on Eve's heart had her cursing herself. She wasn't jealous. Jealousy meant she wanted love, a man in her life. She didn't need, nor did she want those things. Staying focused on Elite, and now this precious baby she carried, was all she had time for. Being a single mom would be difficult, but women did it every single day and, damn it, Eve wouldn't fail. She refused to be intimidated by her fears.

"I hope you're not busy." Nora slid her plaid scarf from around her neck and dropped it, and her designer purse, onto the chair across from Eve's desk. "I was out and wanted to swing by. I haven't seen you in a few days."

Eve pasted a smile on her face. "I've been busy. I got your text about the party."

Nora beamed. "You have to be there, Eve. Grace won't tell me her costume but swears it's going to be awesome. Reid and I are thinking of either going as a Viking couple or as Superman and Lois Lane."

"Sounds fun."

Nora tipped her head to the side. "You're bringing a date, right?"

Everything inside Eve stilled. A date. Probably not, considering that she'd only been with Graham for the past six weeks. Plus, they weren't dating, not by any means. And with the way things were going in the press, there was no way in hell a Newport would be allowed inside a Winchester's home. Well, Eve's home didn't count, but her sisters would never stand for Eve and Graham being an item.

Eve cringed. An item? They'd never been on a date. They snuck around, they'd created a child and now she had to figure out a way to tell him, considering they were definitely *not* an item. So, no. No date for her at the party.

"I've been a little too busy to date." Too busy sneaking in time between the sheets with a Newport. "But I promise I'll be there in costume."

Nora rolled her eyes and dropped onto the other leather chair. "You work too hard, Eve. You need to date. There's not one man you can ask to be your date?"

Well, there was a man, but...

"I don't need a date," Eve stated, propping her elbows on her desk. "I'm happy for you and Reid, but not all of us want that happily-ever-after. I'm building Elite and taking it into the next generation. It's not easy work, so I haven't had much social life."

Okay, two days ago she'd done social life right on the vanity in her bathroom, but that wasn't necessary to point out here.

A solemn look instantly came over Nora's face. "Have you been to see Dad in the past couple days?"

Guilt ate away at Eve. She'd been busy building this company he'd left in her care. She wanted him to see how far she could take it before he...passed. But thinking about the inevitable had tears burning her eyes.

"I know," Nora whispered, swiping at her own eyes. "I'm on my way there, actually. Grace was there last night and said he was having a good day. I hope he's still the same when I get there."

Their father was in his home being nursed by the best caregivers they could find. He was a man of dignity; he didn't want his last days to be in a nursing home or hospital and Eve couldn't blame him. She and her sisters were just fine with granting him any wish he had right now.

"Have you seen Carson?" Nora asked.

Blinking away the tears, Eve shook her head. "I haven't."

Their new half brother. To find out after all this time they had a brother was definitely a blow. Sutton had been known to have affairs, or so the rumor mill had spun it over the past several years, but now there was proof. Eve wasn't quite sure how to handle Carson, but she did know he didn't deserve any of her father's holdings. He knew nothing of her father. They shared DNA only. There was no bond, there were no treasured moments. Not that any of that was Carson's fault, but Eve wasn't ready to embrace him just yet. And she certainly wasn't ready to argue over her father's assets while he was still alive.

"He's requested to see father."

Eve straightened. "What?"

"He wants to talk," Nora clarified. "We can't deny him, Eve. He has every right to see his father."

Before he dies. The unspoken words hovered between them, driving home the point that their father was human. He'd cheated on their mother, now he was dying. He shouldn't have to keep paying for his sins, and he shouldn't have his name tarnished when his days were numbered.

And that brought Eve's thoughts right back to Graham. Was Carson requesting to see their father because he was trying to gain ammunition for their media campaign? Every protective instinct welled up inside her.

"It's a bad idea," Eve told her sister. "He could be plotting with Brooks and Graham."

"I don't think that's what he's doing. Brooks hired a private investigator. If they want to dig up Dad's past, we can't stop them and I highly doubt Dad will give up any skeletons in his closet on his own at this point."

Nora's words sank in, and actually made sense. Still...

Graham had wanted her to trust him. Those words kept bouncing back and forth in her head and she truly wished she knew what the answer was.

"What does Grace think?" Eve asked.

Nora lifted a slender shoulder. "She's fine with letting Carson in. She's not as cynical as you are, though."

"I prefer the term *realistic*," Eve countered. With a heavy sigh, she nodded. "Fine. But one of us needs to be in the room."

Nora nodded. "I agree. I'll let Carson know and we can set up a time."

"Wait." Eve pressed her palms to her desk and eased back in her seat. "Have you asked Dad?"

"He wants to see his son."

Those simple words were what this all boiled down to. Carson was Sutton's son. The final say belonged to their father and he would never turn away family...especially a newly discovered son.

"Let me know when and I'll make sure I'm there," Eve told her sister.

Nora got to her feet and pulled her scarf back around her neck. After adjusting her navy cardigan, she grabbed her handbag and hooked the strap on her forearm.

"Try not to work so hard," Nora said, a soft, caring tone lacing her voice. "You're looking tired and you have assistants who can help."

Eve laughed. "Wow, thanks for the confidence booster."

Circling the desk, Nora embraced her. "I say this because I love you. Don't let work rule your life like Dad did. Take time for yourself. Who knows? You may change your mind about that happily-ever-after but find your Prince Charming has passed you by while you were stuck in your office."

Graham's face instantly came to mind, but he was far from Prince Charming. He was more the evil villain with charm and charisma that made him impossible to resist. Besides, she didn't need anyone to rescue her—prince or peasant.

"I promise to get more rest," Eve assured her as she eased back. "Now, go on and see Dad. Tell him I'll be by later."

Once Nora was gone, Eve fell back into her seat. She was exhausted, and it was showing. She was going to have to take better care of herself. Her life wasn't just about her anymore. She had an innocent child to care for, and she would do anything to keep her child safe.

Reliving the nightmare of losing a baby wasn't an option. But fear had a crippling hold over her. Between the worry of miscarriage and telling Graham, she had some legitimate concerns. Would this be a replay of the last time? Granted, before she'd thought herself in love. She wasn't as naive this time. But she still wanted Graham to be accepting of their child, wanted him to take part in the baby's life.

She had to tell him. Tonight. There was no easy way to drop this bomb and she wasn't a coward. No matter what happened after she told him, she'd be just fine.

Five

She'd avoided him for two days. Two. Damn. Days.

Graham had gone to bat for her, going against his brothers, and Eve had dodged his texts and calls. The fact that he'd thrown away all common sense when Eve had pleaded with him to not ruin her father spoke volumes. That's something someone in a relationship would do. They weren't in a relationship. They had sex. Private, sneaking-around, amazing sex.

Well, they had been. But when he'd been at her place and they'd been intimate, she'd turned down any further advances the morning after. Did she want to call this affair quits? Too bad. He wasn't ready and her body's response to his touch told him otherwise. Not that he would beg. Hell, no. And he didn't want a relationship, but he certainly wasn't ready to end this.

Even if he wanted something more, he was too swamped with being a partner in his law firm to feed any type of relationship. Sex was a stress reliever and Eve was definitely on the same page, though she may have been fighting herself on this matter. She was just as vigilant in her career and wanted nothing more. So, when she ignored his texts, it shouldn't have bothered him…but it did. Eve wasn't one to play games, and if she wanted to put on the brakes, he imagined that she'd just tell him so.

Then, as if she hadn't been silent for two days, she texted him to say she needed to talk.

He didn't like the sound of that. The whole we-need-to-talk thing was such a veiled subject and he didn't like how it eluded to the fact that she may want to call this quits.

Eve possessed every quality he'd ever wanted in a lover. She was career driven—so she wasn't monopolizing his time—she was passionate and damn if she didn't challenge him…in bed and out.

He'd never cared when another woman blew off his calls, though that rarely happened. The few times it had, he'd moved on. No worries. Yet with Eve, he wasn't going to have her call it quits without seducing her one last time. If she wanted to move on, he wouldn't stop her, but he sure as hell would give her a send-off she'd never forget.

Just the thought of getting his hands on her again had Graham hurrying to get to her office. He'd purposely waited until it was good and dark before setting out. With the skies darkening earlier this time of year, he was able to log in more hours with her.

Damn. He shouldn't keep track of the hours he'd spent with her. He should be going with the flow in this casual hookup arrangement. But he was human and

Eve turned him on like no one else ever had. So what if he wasn't ready to put the brakes on just yet?

Graham wasn't oblivious to the fact that he hadn't seen anyone else since that night at the ball when he'd seduced Eve. Had he ever gone this long with the same woman? Other women would think things were getting serious, but not Eve. She knew the boundaries. Besides, even if they wanted to make this something more permanent, no way in hell would their family feud allow that to happen. The last thing he wanted was his brothers or her sisters in their business.

No, it was all about sneaking and seducing. That was the name of the game. He'd been looking for a label and he'd found one. Simple as that.

So what if he had a designated bay in her second garage all to himself. He refused to believe this was serious. Hiding his car when he visited her at her house was merely precautionary, that was all. If one of her sisters or assistants stopped by, he could easily hide in one of the rooms of her sprawling mansion. A car would be a bit harder to explain if it was out in the open.

But now he was at her office, parking in a public garage, so there. Why the hell was he arguing with himself? He'd rather concentrate on Eve and how quickly he could have her on her desk panting his name. Ironically, she was the perfect distraction from the investigation and beating his head against the wall where Sutton was concerned.

Graham took the elevator up to her office. Nobody would be there this time of the evening, and Eve wouldn't have requested he come if her assistant or any other staff members were hanging around. Their offices had quickly become the go-to choice for late-night rendezvous.

As he made his way down the wide, tiled hall, the intense, familiar scent of Eve's jasmine perfume enveloped him. Would he ever tire of smelling it? When she'd wrapped herself around him after her bubble bath the night before last, he'd inhaled that sweet scent. Everything about Eve was a punch to his gut. The desire for her hadn't lessened one bit—if anything, he only craved her more. That was dangerous territory to venture into, but he was in complete control. He had to be.

Her office door was slightly cracked, a sliver of light slashing the dark floor tiles. Without bothering to knock or give a warning, he pushed open the door and found her at her computer. As Graham moved closer, he realized she was staring at her screen, scrolling with her mouse, but she didn't seem to be focusing in on any one thing.

She hadn't said a word, hadn't even turned to acknowledge his presence. As he came behind her chair, he glanced at the screen. Photo after photo of Eve with her sisters and their father in various places and times continued to scroll up the monitor. Sometimes she'd stop, scroll back down, then commence to go up again. Eve was a brilliant photographer. The images around the entire floor of her office proved that. She claimed her photography was a hobby, but he knew full well if she ever opted out of the real estate industry, she could turn pro without fail.

Graham swallowed. Whatever she'd called him here for had to do with that old bastard. Talk about a mood killer.

When she didn't say anything, Graham surveyed her spacious office overlooking the city. The floor-to-ceiling windows showed off a brilliant Chicago skyline dotted with lights. As he turned, he noted the built-in bookshelves on the far wall were full of books, mostly on photography and real estate. When Eve was passionate about something, she put her whole self into it. He could attest to that.

But the fact that he admired and cared about her hobbies was even more dangerous than having his physical desire escalate. Getting too personal meant setting down roots. He wasn't about to set down roots with any woman. Ever. Let alone a woman whose family bitterly rivaled his.

Graham walked back to the desk, setting his hip on the edge beside her chair. The picture she'd homed in on now was of a smiling Sutton surrounded by his daughters. This had to have been taken recently. Eve wore that killer red suit she'd had on a few days ago and Sutton wasn't looking well. But he actually smiled in these pictures. Graham didn't want to see his old rival as a human being capable of such emotions.

"I'm almost done," she told him, without turning. "I have a few more to upload."

Graham didn't want to see Sutton's face on the screen another second, especially not with Eve smiling back from the picture. Guilt twisted the knife in his chest. He had no right to hate the relationship between Eve and her father. He had no right to...what? Be jealous? No way was he jealous. That was absolutely...

Damn it. Maybe he was jealous. How did a man like Sutton deserve love and loyalty from someone so caring and trusting as Eve? Sutton was a bastard and that he'd managed to raise three amazing women was a miracle.

Sutton may have been a conniving jerk, but he'd made the right choice putting Eve in charge of his company. There was no one better to run Elite Industries. She had a vision, something fresh that would drive the company into the next several decades. She was brilliant, independent and charming. She had all the traits that would make Elite expand in the exact ways she wanted it to because she refused to take no for an answer, and she refused to fail.

"I saw my father today." Her soft words cut into the silence. "Grace and Nora happened to be there at the same time. Dad knows I always have my camera on hand, so he wanted family pictures in case…"

Graham didn't like that vulnerable, lost tone in her voice. Selfish as Graham was, and as much as he loathed Sutton, he wasn't going to let Eve grieve alone. The loss of a parent was still too fresh, too painful for him. Nobody should have to face such emptiness on their own.

Squatting down beside her chair, he gripped the arms and turned her to face him. Finally, her bright green gaze landed on his. "It's good you have these pictures. Many family members don't get to say goodbye, let alone capture the final memories."

Moisture gathered in her eyes as she nodded. When one lone tear slipped down her cheek, Graham reached to swipe it away. But his hand lingered on her cheek, his thumb sliding across the darkness beneath her eye.

"You're tired," he said before he could catch himself. "Maybe you should go home and rest."

"I'm fine. It's only seven. I wouldn't sleep now, anyway."

Stubborn. Hardheaded. So much like himself, he felt as if he were looking in a mirror. Still, he wouldn't let her work herself to death and that had nothing to do with their intimacy. He wouldn't want to see anyone this exhausted and worn down.

"What time did you come in today?"

She pursed her lips and looked away. "I think five. Or maybe it was five yesterday and six today. I can't remember right now."

He clenched his teeth and counted backward from ten. She was pushing herself too hard and someone needed to intervene.

"You have spreadsheets scheduling your bathroom breaks at work and you can't recall when you came in or how long you worked today?"

Eve's sharp gaze collided with his. "So?"

"You're working too hard. You're going to break if you don't slow down."

Narrowing her eyes, Eve stood up, but Graham didn't get out of her way. "That's the second time today someone has said that to me. My apologies if I look tired. I'm in negotiations with a company we want to take over, my sister is pressuring me to bring a date to some silly costume party and my father is dying. I'll try to look less exhausted tomorrow and double up on concealer."

Her words sank in and Graham got to his feet and reached up to cup her shoulders. Closing the miniscule gap between them, he brought her body flush against his.

"I'll be your date." Because no way in hell was another man going on her arm.

Eve blinked away her unshed tears. "You can't be my date. Nora and Reid are hosting the party at my dad's. You think they're just going to let a Newport onto the Winchester estate?"

Graham shrugged. "I'll wear a mask and a great costume. Introduce me as whoever you want. But I'm your date."

"No," she said with a shake of her head. "I'll go alone."

So long as no schmuck was escorting her, Graham

was fine. Still, part of him wanted to go with her, but she was right: that was ridiculous thinking. They weren't a couple, so why pretend to be one? He hated how his instant go-to idea was to be with her as her date. They didn't date. Sneaking around after dark, parking their cars where they couldn't be seen and sending texts in code was not dating.

Circling back around to the original topic, Graham asked, "What are you doing to yourself?" Sliding his thumbs beneath her eyes, he let out a sigh.

Eve blinked but remained silent. Something was going on with her. He wasn't sure what, but he wasn't leaving until he knew. Maybe it was the stress from her father's illness and from buying another company, just as she'd said. But could it be something else?

"If you want to end things, just say so."

Her eyes widened as she shifted back slightly. "What?"

Graham dropped his hands. He couldn't touch her and not want her, but he'd be damned if he begged. "If you want to bring this arrangement to a close, that's fine."

The color drained from her face. She started to step back, but hit her chair and lost her balance. Graham reached around to grab her, but she pushed away. Struggling out of his hold, she ended up moving around him and putting a good bit of distance between them.

"That's fine?" she repeated. "If you're that detached from this…whatever this is, then leave."

Careful of his next words, Graham slid his hands into his pockets. Eve was clearly on edge and his blasé words hadn't helped. He hadn't expected her to be so upset. Still, this was useful information to have. Clearly she wasn't calling him here to break things off.

He closed the gap between them, following her when she took two more steps back. Those expressive green eyes remained locked onto his, but her never-ending steely determination had her jaw clenched, her nostrils flaring.

"I'm not leaving," he finally replied. She may try to be fierce, but she looked as if she'd break at any moment. "Tell me why you called me here."

She blinked once, then shook her head. "It can wait."

When she attempted to skirt him once more, Graham reached out to grip her biceps. "Stop running. Tell me, Eve. I haven't heard from you in two days and I haven't felt you beneath me in just as long. What's going on if you're not ending things?"

She continued to stare at him as she bit the inside of her cheek. Whatever she was gearing up to tell him must be something major. Obviously she wasn't going to tell him to take a hike, but what else was there? Did she have news on Sutton she was afraid to share?

Eve pulled in a shaky breath, her body trembling beneath his hands. She was scared. Whatever was going on had her terrified because he'd never seen Eve this run-down, this unsure of her words.

"Just tell me," he stated, sounding harsher than he intended. "My mind is spinning and I have no clue what you want to tell me."

"I've rehearsed this in my head, but now that you're here, I can't find the words."

Worry coursed through him. They may not be a serious item, but Graham wanted to reassure her he wasn't some unfeeling ass. He framed her face and nipped at her lips.

"Whatever you need to tell me, we'll deal with it.

Are you sick? Is it something with your dad you think I won't care about? What, Eve?"

Her dark lashes rested against her cheeks as she let out a sigh. Finally, she lifted her lids, and her eyes locked onto his.

"I'm pregnant."

Six

Graham didn't release her. He couldn't even think, so getting his brain in gear to let go wasn't happening.

Pregnant. How could one word cause such panic and uncertainty? And why did this room seem to be closing in on him?

His hands fell from her arms. Graham raked his fingers through his hair and attempted to pull his scattered thoughts together. Over the past six weeks they'd been intimate so many times. He had no idea when this had happened. All he recalled was that first time when they'd been in such a rush and she'd assured him she was on birth control.

"Say something," she whispered.

"Did you plan this?"

Eve jerked as if she'd been slapped by his words. "I would never do that."

Graham shrugged. "How do I know? Despite the past month and a half, I don't know you that well."

Eve's cheeks pinkened with rage the instant before her hand came up in a flash and struck his face. The crack seemed to echo in the open office. Graham's head jerked, but he didn't reach up to touch the sting.

"You can't blame me for asking," he countered, refusing to feel sympathy despite the hurt in her eyes. "I assume this baby is mine."

Her eyes narrowed. "I haven't been with anyone else since we started seeing each other."

He firmly believed that. Eve was too busy at work for fun and he occupied her evenings, save for the past couple. Still, a paternity test would be required considering he had quite a padded bank account. Someone like Eve wouldn't be after a man's money, though. But he would be smart about this. And being smart, he wouldn't bring up the test right now or his other cheek may feel the same sting.

"I don't expect anything from you," she went on, crossing her arms over her chest. "In fact, maybe we should bring what's between us to a close and focus on what's best for the baby."

Graham didn't know what he wanted right now. His entire world had been flipped and control had never been so out of his reach. But he didn't want to just end things with Eve, especially now.

"That won't change the situation." Graham struggled to keep his distance, but he needed to play his cards right. "I will be here every step of the way, Eve. Whether you want me around or not. This child is a Newport and I never turn my back on my responsibilities."

"Is that what I am now?" she asked. "A responsibility?"

So maybe he hadn't chosen his words as wisely as he'd intended. "You're the mother of my child."

He watched her shoulders relax as relief slid over her. But then Eve blinked and her gaze darted away. Was she worried he'd reject her and the child? Didn't she know him at all?

Of course she didn't. He'd even thrown that fact in her face moments ago. They truly didn't know each other. And now they were going to be parents.

Brooks and Carson were going to…hell, he didn't know what their reaction would be. But for now, he was keeping this information to himself.

What would Sutton say? Once the man found out his responsible daughter was pregnant by his enemy, would he change his mind and give up the secrets he was keeping about Graham and Brooks's paternity? A plan started forming in Graham's mind.

"Have you told your sisters?"

Eve shook her head. "I haven't told anyone. I… I'm not sure they'll take this very well."

Most likely not. And he knew Sutton wouldn't take it well, either. The man probably had higher hopes for his daughter and new president of Elite Industries than having a child by a Newport. But Graham was serious when he said he'd be there through everything. He may not have planned on having a child with anyone, let alone Eve, but he would never turn his back on an innocent child…especially his own.

A possessive streak shot through him as he stared back at Eve. This was why she looked so tired, why she was likely running herself ragged. She was scared of the pregnancy, worried about the backlash when the rest of their world discovered the truth. Again, he would be there. Nobody would hurt his child or the child's mother, no matter what their relationship status was.

"Let's keep this between us until we know how to deliver the news."

Eve nodded. Her arms went around her waist, as if to somehow protect their child. "I don't want our baby to receive backlash from either of our families. No matter what's going on or not going on between you and me, please promise me you'll protect our child."

The urgency in her tone had Graham stepping toward her. "I promise."

The vow came easily because he'd walk through hell to keep his child safe. Odd how he'd only known about this baby for mere minutes and already his priorities had changed. And one thing was certain: his child would have his last name, even if he had to marry Eve.

The idea made him cringe. Not that being married to Eve would be terrible, but he didn't want to be married to anybody. Still, some marriages were made of lesser things. At least he and Eve understood the importance of each other's work and they would both love this child.

"When is your doctor's appointment? I want to go."

Eve shook her head. "That isn't necessary."

"I'm going."

Chewing on her bottom lip, she nodded. "Fine. It's next week. I went the other day for initial blood work. He said everything looked fine and gave me vitamins and my due date."

As Graham listened to her, he was already thinking about the time when the baby would arrive. All work would have to be put on hold. No way in hell was he missing the birth of his child.

His child.

Unable to stop himself, Graham reached out and

eased her arms aside before placing his flat palm against her stomach. To even think there was a life growing inside of her, a life he'd helped create, absolutely humbled him.

Eve stilled beneath him. When he glanced up to her face and caught sight of her wide eyes, he swallowed and stepped back.

"I have no idea how to act," he admitted, shoving his hands in his pockets. "I don't want to upset you, but I want you to be aware how serious I'm going to take this."

"Honestly, I just want to figure out how to make sure our families won't turn against us or this child. That's all I care about. Anything between us doesn't matter anymore."

A point he wholeheartedly disagreed with, but his actions would speak for him over time. He wasn't going anywhere, and keeping Eve close would be simple. No way was another man moving in. Eve and this child were his. Period.

Graham made sure that if there was something he wanted, nothing stood in his way. He may not want a family in the traditional sense, but letting Eve just put up a barrier between them was out of the question. His desire for her hadn't diminished one bit. In fact, knowing she carried his child was the biggest turn-on he'd ever experienced.

"How are you feeling?" He hadn't even asked her. He'd jumped straight into wondering if she'd trapped him, to asking about paternity, to wanting to feel her still-flat stomach.

"Fine."

The clenched half smile betrayed her. Graham tipped

his head. "You can't lie to me, Eve. You're exhausted—you admitted that earlier. But how else are you feeling? Does the doctor think you can keep working all these crazy hours or should you be resting?"

She stared at him, not answering, not even attempting to answer. Her eyes welled up once again and Graham waited. What had he said wrong? He had a million questions, but right now he wanted to know how she was feeling.

"I know this is your child, but..." Eve's words died away as she turned her back to him. Graham reached for her shoulders, but pulled back at the last minute.

The only sound in the room was Eve's shaky breathing. The lights of the Chicago skyline spilled in from the window. They'd shared some intense experiences in this office, but nothing compared to the intensity of this moment.

"Why do you care?" she whispered.

"Because you're carrying a Newport." Damn, that sounded heartless. Why was that his first response? Why did he have to sound so cold?

Because he couldn't let himself feel anything else for Eve. He had to remain detached. Their families made the Montagues and the Capulets look like besties and he couldn't cross the emotional boundary with her. Granted, having a child together was crossing the point of no return, but that didn't mean they had to set up and play house together. Plenty of children had parents who didn't live together. Whatever the arrangement, Graham wouldn't let his child ever want for love, stability or a solid foundation.

Squaring her shoulders, Eve turned and swiped her damp cheeks. "Well, I have some emails to send. I'll text you all the specifics about my doctor's appointment, but if anyone sees us coming and going—"

"You're dismissing me?" Unbelievable.

Her eyes didn't hold the heat or the light he was used to seeing. Now she stared at him as if he were merely a business associate. "I have work. Surely you understand."

"I understand you're trying to keep some ridiculous wall between us." Anger bubbled within him. He didn't know what he wanted her to do or say, but he sure as hell didn't want this unfeeling Eve. "I'll be at the damn appointment if I have to sneak in the back way."

Eve nodded and moved around him to settle back in at her desk. She wiggled her mouse until her screen came back to life. And right there was Sutton's face smiling back, with his hand holding Eve's. Graham had not only been dismissed, he was being mocked by a man who wasn't even in the room.

"We'll talk later," he promised, heading toward the door. "Don't believe for one second this changes what we had going, Eve. I still want you, and if you're honest, you want me, too. That passion isn't something that can be turned off."

Her hands froze as she gave him a sidelong glance.

"I'll give you the space you want," he went on, gripping the door handle. "But you better get ready because I won't be far and I won't wait long."

With that vow, Graham stormed out. *Game on.* Graham wasn't concerned about how their families would react to the baby. He refused to allow anything other than complete and utter love and acceptance. No, what Graham needed to concentrate on was the fact he wasn't

done with Eve, in the personal sense that had nothing
to do with their child.

And if she thought he was going to walk away from
her or their child, well, she was about to find out that a
Newport always got what he wanted.

Seven

"What the hell is wrong with you?" Carson threw his cards down onto the green felt and leaned back in his seat. "You're moping like a woman."

Graham wasn't in the mood for company, let alone playing poker and chatting with his brothers. But when Carson had stopped by earlier, he'd apparently picked up on Graham's doldrums right away and called for reinforcements, texting Brooks to come, as well. Now here they all were.

Graham proudly laid down his royal flush and raked in the chips. Maybe he wasn't in the mood, but he'd been on a winning streak. After sorting the chips by color and putting them away, Graham got to his feet and took his empty tumbler back to the built-in bar.

"I'm done here." Graham refilled his glass with his favorite bourbon. "I'll go put on *The Maltese Falcon*."

They had an ongoing tradition that stretched back

to a time when they lived with their mother and Gerty. Gerty introduced them to the Hollywood classics and insisted they watch them together. To this day, they continued to honor her tradition.

Graham missed her. She was a strong woman, a woman who refused to let life knock her down, and she'd do anything to help others. His mother had been just as strong. A lump formed in his throat as he slid his fingers over the remote to start the movie. Each day seemed to be better than the last, but he knew he'd always feel the void from the loss of Gerty and his mother.

Graham had so many questions now that his mother was gone. She'd been single, pregnant and scared when she'd come to Chicago. Had she even told Graham and Brooks's father that they existed? Had he knowingly turned his back on her or did he have no clue he'd fathered twin boys?

These were questions Graham may never have an answer to. Cynthia took her secrets to her grave. The truth would be something he and Brooks would have to uncover all on their own. At least they had ruled out Sutton as their father, which was a blessing in itself. But the bastard knew the truth and was dodging them. His time was limited, which meant that Graham had to take drastic action if he wanted answers.

The idea of using Eve to obtain the information had his stomach in knots, but she was carrying his child and if Graham had to let that news slip to Sutton in order to get information…well…

Graham heard his brothers behind him as they came into the home theater. But his mind wasn't on the movie or even the idea of his father out in the world somewhere. His mind was on Eve. The parallel between her and his mother's experiences wasn't lost on him, but there was a huge difference. Graham planned on being part of this child's life. Eve wouldn't be alone, she wouldn't have to worry about facing this without support.

"He's still got that look," Brooks muttered. "He won every damn hand and still looks like he's ready to punch the wall."

"Your face would do," Graham replied without glancing over. "I like my walls intact."

"If you're going to fight, at least pause the movie," Carson interjected. "I know we just watched this one a few weeks ago, but it's still my favorite."

Graham shook the ice cubes around in his glass. "I'm not going to hit anything, but if you two keep discussing my mood, I'm likely to change my mind."

Graham turned the volume up until the surround-sound speakers hidden around the room were blaring. He'd had enough of the chitchat and getting in touch with his feelings.

There was no mention of Sutton tonight, which was a relief. Brooks had his PI on the hunt for their father, and apparently there was still no news. Maybe they could just have a regular night like they used to. Something bland and boring. Graham never thought he'd wish for such a thing, but lately his life seemed to be heading in about twelve different directions.

His cell vibrated in his pocket. Setting his glass on the table next to his theater recliner, Graham slid the phone out and held it down to his side so his brothers couldn't see. The screen lit up with Eve's name. He wasn't going to reach out to her just yet. He wanted to leave her wondering when he'd be back, when he'd make a move. There was an ache in him that drove him insane and he wanted her to be just as achy, just as needy.

He quickly read her message.

Dr. McNamera November 17 9:00

That was all. Nothing more, nothing personal. The dynamics of their relationship had changed. Because he was apparently a masochist, he scrolled through their previous messages. Flirting, hookup times, codes for what they would do to each other once they were alone. He shifted in his seat as he recalled doing exactly those things.

It was late, but that didn't mean she wasn't at her office. She worked even on weekends, not that he could fault her because he knew that drive to stay on top of the career you'd worked so hard for. But he wanted to see her, needed to see her.

For the first time in…ever, Graham willed this movie to end. He loved spending time with his brothers, valued their special bond, but right now he had other plans.

Plans that involved Eve, a dark room and no interruptions from the outside world. He didn't want her to get swept away into the fear of being pregnant. He wanted her relaxed and he knew exactly how to make that happen.

Intending to make it through the next couple hours, Graham opted not to refill his bourbon. Two glasses were enough because he wanted his head on straight.

"You all up for more poker?" Brooks asked as the credits rolled.

"I need to get home," Carson replied, coming to his feet. "I don't have to spend my nights looking at you two anymore."

Carson had found love. Good for him. Graham wasn't jealous, he just didn't believe in such things. Still, whatever Carson and Georgia had together was genuine. The way they looked at each other, the way they were always looking out for the other was a testament to their deep bond.

"Can't say I blame you," Brooks countered. "You're a lucky man."

Brooks wanted that home life. He wanted the wife, the kids, all of that. Graham wanted to nail this case he was working on and get Eve to come around to seeing they didn't need to cool it in the sheets simply because they'd created a child. "I actually need to run an errand," Graham chimed in.

Both brothers turned to look his way. Brooks smirked. "Really? What's her name?"

Graham busied himself putting the remote away and taking his glass back to the bar, which was just off the theater room. His brothers followed him. No way were they going to leave him alone.

Empty glass in hand, he whirled around. "It's just work. Relax. I'm in the middle of a big case. That's all I can say."

They both stared at him, clearly not believing the lie. With a shrug, he turned to the bar and started stacking the glasses and returning the bottles to the shelves on the wall.

"I'm out," Carson said on a sigh. "I'd rather be home with Georgia than try to figure out what Graham is being so cryptic about."

Fine by him. One down. One to go.

From the corner of his eye, Graham saw Brooks eyeing him, arms crossed over his chest. The sound of Carson headed down the hall, the sound of his footsteps growing softer before eventually disappearing. Now that Carson was gone, Graham waited for the accusations from his twin.

"Whatever you're smirking about, get it off your chest," Graham finally said, turning to face Brooks.

With a shrug, he replied, "Nothing in particular. Just curious as to why you're rushing off. I'm sure you could do anything work related from here. I know you have your laptop at the ready at all times. And I'm sure you know whatever case you're working on like the back of your hand without having to look at any files."

Graham hadn't gotten to the top at such a young age by depending on anyone else. Every case, every file, every opponent in the courtroom was filed away in his mind. He knew every detail backward and forward. He studied his rivals and found their weaknesses so he could annihilate them when they came face-to-face. So Brooks was right, but no way was Graham going to admit such a thing.

"You don't have to know every detail of my personal life," Graham fired back. Okay, maybe that was harsh, but right now, he wanted to get to Eve. "Are we done here?"

Brooks blew out a sigh. "For now. I'll let you have your little secret, but all secrets come out eventually. Just ask Sutton."

The jab hit too close to home. Yes, Sutton's secret baby, aka Carson, had taken nearly three decades to come to the surface. Graham highly doubted Eve's secret would last three months. Soon both families would know that the Winchesters and the Newports were going to be bound together for life.

That thought had Graham reevaluating everything. Eve had every right not to put his name on the birth certificate. She had every right to fight him for custody. She'd lose, but that wasn't the point. The point was, he refused to let his child come into this world in the midst of a feud.

So now Graham had to show her who he really was. Eve had to see him as a compassionate, loving man who would do anything for his child. She had to see that working together was the best thing for all of them. Because he refused to allow any other man to come in and take away this little family. Love didn't have to be a factor. Graham held the power here, and he would get Eve to marry him, ensuring their child carried the Newport name. A marriage based on sexual chemistry was more than enough for him to rethink saying his "I dos."

And that was why Graham was even more eager to get to her house. Soon Eve would see just how perfect they were together.

Eight

Seven o'clock. Most nights she'd still be at the office, but it was Saturday so Eve had opted to come home. She really needed to cut out the weekends for a while. She was exhausted, and her doctor had told her to listen to her body. Well, she was listening and her body was telling her she needed to get rid of these heels and kill the suit. Yoga pants and a tee sounded pretty good right now. Oh, and a ponytail.

She rarely was off her game. Even at home she was always professional because she often did video meetings and had to look the part. Sure, the other day she had on yoga pants and bunny slippers beneath her desk, but she'd put on makeup, earrings and a suit jacket. Boom. She so owned this corporate world.

She'd nearly cried with relief after she washed her face and pulled her hair back. Now that she was comfortable, she had a little boost of energy…and an extremely empty stomach. She'd had an early lunch to work around meetings, but she seriously needed to keep some snacks in her office at work. Her assistant would've gladly gone and gotten her anything, but Eve had her assistant doing so much lately with the acquisition of the Australian company, Eve hated to even ask for a pack of crackers.

Maybe she'd lie in bed, gorge on food and watch a movie on Netflix. A date with herself? Sounded heavenly and completely relaxing. Just what the doctor ordered.

When someone knocked at the back door, Eve nearly cried. Only one person came and went via the French doors overlooking the outdoor living area. The door was conveniently located by the garage Graham used.

She peered down at her attire and shrugged. He'd seen her in her suits, in a ball gown and in her birthday suit, but he'd never seen her in sloppy, I-want-to-be-left-alone mode.

Circling the kitchen island and bypassing the breakfast nook, she reached the French doors. Only the soft glow from the motion lights illuminated Graham's broad frame, slashing a streak of light across one side of his face. His eyes pierced her straight through the glass. There was an intensity to this man that her body couldn't deny. She hated how, even now, especially now, she didn't want to deny him anything. But if she didn't watch out, she would end up hurt. Right now, she had to focus on her baby.

Flicking the lock, she opened one of the doors. Because she knew he wasn't just here for a quick visit, she stepped aside and let him in.

The second Graham was inside, she clicked the lock back into place. When she turned, his eyes raked her, as they always did. She shivered, but was too tired to even appreciate her instant arousal. There had to be some sort of stop button where this physical relationship was concerned. Shouldn't they focus on how to make this parenting thing work? The time for selfish desires and needs had come to an end.

"If you're here for—"

He held up a hand. "I'm not."

When he took a step forward, closing the gap between them, Eve waited for his familiar touch. But he simply held her gaze and offered a gentle smile. "I'm here for strictly innocent reasons."

Eve laughed, waiting for him to deliver the rest of the punch line. When he only quirked a brow, she sobered. "Innocent? Honey, you don't have an innocent bone in your body."

Honey? Had she seriously just used that term? Exhaustion had obviously stolen her common sense.

"I don't mean to be rude, but really. Why are you here?"

Graham took her elbow and guided her through the house. Her house. As if he owned the place. And she was allowing this to happen. Then he led her up the stairs, toward her bedroom, and pulled back the pristine white duvet on her king-size four-poster bed. Eve darted her eyes between the inviting bed and the confusing man.

"Okay, what's going on?"

Graham took her hand and ushered her into bed. "I had no plans until I got here. But now that I see you're practically swaying on your feet, we're going to relax."

"We?" Eve slid into bed because the temptation was far too great for her to fight.

"That's right." Graham picked up the remote, hit a few buttons. The flat screen slid up from the entertainment island that separated the bed from the sitting area. "I'm going to watch a classic with you."

Okay. So if she had all of this straight in her head, Graham had just appeared at her back door not looking for sex, but to watch a movie and…snuggle?

Eve continued to stare as Graham as climbed into bed beside her and began studying her remote. After several minutes of muttering under his breath—something about his law degree being useless—he finally figured it out. Instantly the room filled with music as the movie popped up, and Eve had to brace herself. He was legitimately here to watch a movie. They were in her bed…completely clothed.

"You're still staring and you're going to miss this opening," Graham said without looking her way.

Her gaze went to the large screen and she instantly recognized *An Affair to Remember*. It was one of her favorite movies. But how did he know? They'd certainly never discussed such personal things.

"Why are you doing this?"

Graham sighed, paused the movie and glanced her way. Those striking blue eyes pierced her heart. But she couldn't have her heart involved, not with him, not now. Her emotions were simply all over the place. She couldn't act on any temporary feelings.

"I love old movies. I want to do absolutely nothing right now but watch one with you. We both work too hard, and now we're having a baby. Maybe it's time we get to know each other."

Without another word, he took the movie off pause, turned the volume up and reached for her hand. The detail-oriented nerd in her wanted to know what was going on. Was this a date? Albeit a warped version of one. Was this some ploy to get her to fall for him? If so, he was doing a damn good job. Did he truly want to get to know her?

Eve attempted to concentrate on the movie, but between exhaustion and the way Graham's thumb drew lazy patterns over the back of her hand, she was having a difficult time.

What was Graham up to? The man was ruthless in a courtroom, if his reputation around Chicago was any indicator. He could've easily had her undressed and beneath him had he tried, because denying him was nearly impossible. Yet he seemed all too happy to lie here, hold her hand and do absolutely nothing.

Graham Newport was playing some sort of game and if she didn't figure out the rules soon, she was going to find herself on the losing side. And that was not an option because she'd end up hurt. Eve had been dealt enough by the hand of grief to last a lifetime and she wasn't looking for more.

Graham knew she'd fallen asleep within the first ten minutes of the movie. Her hand had gone lax beneath his and she even began to snore quietly. He found himself watching her and smiling. Okay, this little plan of his had backfired in a major way.

He'd come here for one reason—to start his plan of seduction. Getting her to trust him, to maybe even develop stronger feelings for him, was a must for making sure they came to a mutual understanding where their child was concerned. And when he asked her to be his wife, he was determined that she'd say yes.

Graham refused to get into a tug-of-war with her over the baby. He refused to allow his child to be a pawn in any family feud, let alone between him and Eve.

But the second she'd opened the door and let him in,

he'd seen just how tired she was. She was struggling to keep her eyes open. Was she not sleeping well at night? Was she not feeling well because of morning sickness? Was she working too hard?

Knowing Eve, she'd put 110 percent into her day as usual and then dragged herself home to rest in private. He knew she was trying to figure out what he was doing here, why he'd shown up and hadn't stripped her and made love to her right away. Every part of him wanted nothing more than to peel her out of her T-shirt and leggings. She'd looked damn good dressed down.

And that was a problem. Seeing Eve in an evening gown was heart-stopping. The way a killer suit hugged her hips nearly had him begging. But when she was just herself, makeup-free and wearing casual clothes, she was the most dangerous. He wanted to think this side of Eve was only for him, that she didn't expose this part of herself to anyone.

He shouldn't want to get more deeply involved with her, but he was a selfish bastard. He wanted all of her. She was the mother of his child and she was his. He didn't give up on anything he wanted, and he'd never wanted anything more than to be a father.

This realization hit him hard. Never before had he thought about having a child, yet now he could think of little else. He may not have had a father figure growing up, but he knew the love of a parent. He knew how to put his own needs aside to care for a child and make sure they had a secure life.

The movie had ended, and the room got dark. Graham turned off the TV, sliding the screen back into the island. Silence filled the room, save for Eve's soft snores. Pale light from the hall lamp gave enough of a glow for him to see. Graham reached across the bed and smoothed the silken strands of hair from her face. Instantly Eve startled awake. Her heavy-lidded eyes locked onto his.

"Sorry," he murmured. "I didn't mean to wake you."

Eve blinked and sat straight up against her mound of pillows. "I never make it through a movie on a good day, let alone when I'm already tired."

"Are you not sleeping well?" Concern had him scooting a bit closer. There was too much space between them, literally and figuratively.

"I'm sleeping fine. That's the problem. I want to sleep all the time. The doctor said that was normal in the first trimester."

A wave of relief washed over him. He knew absolutely nothing about pregnancies, so hearing any morsel of doctor's advice was comforting. He needed to start reading anything and everything he could get his hands on about this. He wanted to be able to connect with her, to comfort her, and somehow show her that he was there and she wouldn't be doing this alone.

"Maybe you should cut back a bit each day at work until this trimester passes." Her bored glare was all the answer he needed. Not that he thought she'd readily agree, but still. "You've only got a few more weeks. Then, when you're feeling better, you can add those hours back on."

"Can I?" she asked, her tone mocking. "I'm so glad to have your permission."

Raking a hand through his hair, Graham came to his feet and rounded the bed. "That's not what I meant and you know it. I'm worried about you."

"About the baby," she corrected.

"Fine. I'm worried for both of you." And he was.

Only a total jerk would ignore the mother's needs. "I want what's best for both of you."

Eve stared up at him. A red crease mark from her pillow marred the right side of her cheek, but her eyes were actually refreshed. Her ponytail had slid to one side of her head, random strands had escaped and hung down one side. Yeah, he knew nobody got this view of her, and part of him puffed up with conceit that he was the one here with her.

"I can't do this with you."

Confused, Graham lost focus on her sexy, disheveled look. "Excuse me?"

She waved a hand in the air. "This...whatever this is. Your attempt to get to know me or vie for some affection. I don't know what you're doing, but I'm not playing games now, Graham. We're having a baby—that doesn't mean we have to be a couple."

Why did those words feel like a slice to his...what? Heart? His heart wasn't supposed to be involved. But he sure as hell didn't like that she was so quick to put him on the back burner. That wouldn't work with his plan, not one bit. But he wasn't about to give up. He'd barely gotten started.

"Maybe I want to make sure we stay on the same track," he retorted. "Perhaps I want to stay friends with the mother of my baby so we can make this child's life as amazing as possible without turmoil."

"Are we friends?" she asked. "Seriously. We have amazing sex and we're both workaholics. That's about all we have in common. Can a friendship be built on that?"

Graham shrugged. "I've had friendships built on less."

Eve seemed to study him for a moment before her

eyes darted down to her lap where she toyed with the hem of her oversize tee. "It's getting late," she whispered.

If she thought he'd take that as a cue to leave, she didn't know him. Obviously that was the entire point of his being here. Why did this seem so forced? Why had everything seemed so easy up until very recently?

Because sex was easy. It was all the emotions that made the struggle real.

"Do you want me to go?" he asked, needing to hear her say it, but refusing to beg for anything. He eased a hip onto the bed next to her. "Do you want me to leave you alone and simply wait for texts about our child? Because you have to know that's not my style. I'm not a man who waits for anything. When I want something, I take it."

Her mesmerizing eyes slowly came up to his. "And what is it you want? The baby, I know. But we're a package, Graham. Don't you see that? I don't even know how we're going to make this work. You and I aren't together, our families hate each other and your brother is so angry and hurt, he's ready to destroy my father given any opportunity."

Tears welled up in her eyes and the sight was something Graham wished he never had to see. "Right now, all that matters is this child. Not your father, not my brother and not this fight. I don't want you worrying about this, Eve. It's not good for the baby."

She burst into tears. Full-on, hands-over-her-face sobbing. What had he said? Obviously the wrong thing when he was only trying to help. No wonder men and women never seemed to be on the same page. They weren't even in the same book.

Clearly words were getting him nowhere and he wasn't about to leave when she was so upset. Wrapping an arm around her, he pulled her against his chest as she continued to cry. Stroking her back, he attempted some comforting words, but he doubted she could hear them.

Moments passed and Graham had to wonder if there was something else that was upsetting her. Surely this wasn't just him. But with all the weight of everything coming down on her, she was bound to break. He didn't want her broken, but if she had to lean on someone, he wanted it to be him. No other man would be coming in here, not when she was carrying his child.

Eve wasn't weak, she wasn't vulnerable, yet right now she was having a moment. He wouldn't embarrass her by asking what he could do. She wouldn't want anyone coming to her rescue. He may not know much about her, but he recognized pride. Actions always trumped words anyway, so he'd show her how he cared instead of just talking about it.

Finally, Eve eased away, wiping at her damp cheeks with the back of her hands.

"Don't say you're sorry," he interjected when she opened her mouth.

"I'm not." She offered a soft smile. "You should've left me to have my meltdown. I can't believe you stayed."

"What kind of jerk do you think I am? I'm not just going to leave."

Closing her eyes, she blew out a breath. "I don't know what to think right now or what your angle is, but I don't think you're a jerk."

His angle? Simple. He wanted his child to be raised with the Newport name. He wanted her to willingly give him rights, and if he had to marry her to get them, then he would. Being around Eve was no hardship and his ache for her hadn't diminished in the slightest.

Before he could comment, her stomach growled. Graham laughed. "Hungry?"

She wrapped her arms around her waist as if to ward off any other sounds. "Actually, I was going to get something when you knocked. Then you guided me up here and the bed was so inviting. I haven't eaten since early lunch."

Graham came to his feet. "Stay here. I'll get something."

Eve rolled her eyes. "I'm not bedridden. I can make myself something to eat."

"I'm sure you can, but I'm here." Graham stepped back when Eve swung her legs over the side of the bed. "Stubborn, aren't you?"

Even with her red-rimmed eyes and pink-tipped nose, her smile was like a kick to his chest.

"A trait we both possess. Sounds like we'll have a strong-willed child."

Graham smiled. The idea of his child being strong, independent and a go-getter was absolutely perfect. A healthy combination of mother and father...he'd never given it much thought, but their child would be a perfect Newport.

Eve got to her feet and attempted to readjust her hair. Finally, she jerked the ponytail holder out and gathered up the fallen strands. In a flash, she had the mass of hair piled back atop her head.

"You don't have to stay," she told him. "I'm just going to make a quick sandwich and go to bed."

"You're trying so hard to get me out of here." He tipped her chin up and stepped in closer, so close the heat from her body warmed him. "I'm going to make sure you eat and then I'm going to make sure you're all settled in. We'll make small talk—we may even share a laugh. We can talk about the weather or we can talk about the baby. Up to you. But I'm not leaving, Eve. I'm going to be here, so you better get used to it."

"Is that a threat?" she asked with a soft smile.

He kissed her, hard, fast, then released her. "It's a promise."

Nine

Nine

Eve rolled over in bed, glanced at the clock and closed her eyes again.

Wait. She jerked up in bed and stared at the glaring numbers. How did it get to be so late? Sleeping in had never been an issue for her. She always showed up before anyone else and got a jump start on her day. At this rate, she was never going to make it into the office on time.

The sudden jolt of movement had her morning sickness hitting her fast. She rushed to the en suite bathroom and fell to her knees.

She'd had worse mornings, but still, she didn't like this feeling one bit. How could she remain professional if she was showing up late and looking like death?

Once she was done, she wiped her face with a cool, damp cloth and realized two things: one, it was Sunday so she wasn't late for anything. And two, there was a glorious smell coming from the kitchen and overtaking her home.

Surprisingly, whatever that scent was, it didn't make her more nauseous. If anything, her stomach was ready to go. This roller coaster of emotions and cravings was extremely difficult to keep up with.

Eve thought back to last night when Graham had made a simple grilled cheese sandwich and cut up an apple for her. Then he'd practically patted her on the head and sent her to bed, saying he'd lock up.

So, either he'd stayed and that was him in the kitchen, or one of her sisters was here. She highly doubted Nora or Grace had come by just to do some cooking, so she had to assume Graham had made himself at home.

Considering that she'd just tossed her cookies, so to speak, she opted to brush her teeth before heading down. By the time she hit the bottom steps, her mouth was watering. The magnificent aroma filled the entire first floor. Suddenly her belly growled and she had no idea how she could go from sick one second to hungry the next. Pregnancy sure wasn't predictable.

Heading down the wide hall toward the back of the house and the kitchen, Eve tried to figure out what to say to Graham. She'd seriously had a meltdown last night. He'd been so concerned about the baby, about her. But she hadn't been able to control those insane emotions.

Years ago when she'd thought herself in love, she'd have given anything for her boyfriend to have cared about her, about their baby. But she'd endured the first trimester and part of the second alone. Then she'd struggled through the miscarriage, the D & C, the grieving. All of it on her own. She'd pushed her sisters away because nobody could fix her broken heart. Nobody could bring back her baby and she wanted to be left alone.

Graham was most likely worried about his place in their child's life. He wasn't the type of man to sit back and let someone else raise his child. Still, the fact he'd stayed last night showed the type of man he was. He could've walked away.

So what did this mean? Did he want more than just shared parenting? Did he want to try at a relationship?

Good morning, shoulders.

Freezing midstride, Eve stared straight ahead to the sexiest cook she'd ever seen. She'd seen Graham countless times with nothing on, but finding him in just his jeans standing at her stove was like some sort of domestic porn. Seriously. This was calendar material. Forget the firefighters, sign Graham up. The way those back muscles flexed and relaxed as he did…whatever it was he was doing.

There was a man cooking in her house. The sexy, hot father of her baby was cooking in her house.

This sight alone was enough to make her want to strip and see if they could make use of that kitchen island, but she'd promised herself no more. She needed to focus on so many other things and her sex life was going to have to take a backseat for a while. What a shame, when she was facing such a delectable sight.

"You're just in time."

He didn't turn around as he spoke, just continued to bustle about getting breakfast ready as if this were the most normal thing in the world. As if he belonged here.

Eve couldn't move from the doorway. Between last night and this morning, she had no clue what Graham had planned next. Not one time did he try to get her undressed. Maybe he didn't find her as appealing as he used to. Perhaps pregnant women were a turnoff. Granted, it wasn't like she felt sexy at the moment.

No matter, she wasn't looking for more. At this point, her only hope was that she could keep the peace in her family when they found out she was carrying a Newport's baby.

"Why did you stay?"

Graham froze, plates in hand. Throwing a glance over his shoulder, he held her with his intense stare. "Because someone needs to make sure you're taking care of yourself."

"So you're my keeper now? I'm old enough to take care of myself."

She didn't mention the fact that he was younger than her. There was no need to state the obvious. But the fact that he'd stayed out of pity didn't sit well with her. Maybe she'd gotten her hopes up too high to think he'd stayed simply because he cared.

"I'm not saying you can't." He dished up some type of casserole and...was that fried apples? "It's the weekend. I wanted to stay and make you breakfast, so I did."

She wanted to argue, but the second she took a seat at the island and he placed that plate in front of her, she had no idea what they'd been on the verge of bickering about.

Eve stared down at her plate of food, which looked like it came from some cooking magazine—not the kind featuring light cuisine, either. Then she glanced at Graham, who was scooping up his own servings.

"You cook?" Okay, that was a stupid question. Clearly elves weren't involved. "I mean, this is more than just oatmeal or cereal for breakfast. Where did you learn this?"

Graham set his plate down and went back for two large glasses of orange juice. After putting everything on the island, he took a seat on a stool next to her.

"My grandma Gerty taught us all about cooking. It may have seemed like punishment at the time, but looking back I can see she did it out of love, and as a way to bond."

The wistfulness layered with the love in his tone told her this grandmother was one special lady. Eve pierced one gooey apple with her fork. The buttery, cinnamon sugar flavors exploded in her mouth. She prayed this food stayed with her. This was definitely too good to waste.

"Tell me about Gerty," Eve said, forking up a bite of some egg, sausage and cheese casserole. "Is she still alive?"

Graham swallowed and shook his head. "No."

That one word, full of sadness, had Eve pausing with her fork midway to her mouth. "Oh. Um…sorry. I didn't think."

Graham barely spared glance look her way. "No reason for you to be sorry. She passed away several years back. But she was like a second mother to us. Mom met Gerty at a coffee shop. Gerty was retiring, but she'd already taken a liking to Mom. The two were close and Mom moved in with Gerty because she needed help."

A single, pregnant woman. Eve's fork clattered to her plate as she thought of the parallel between Graham's mother's situation and hers. Did he see it? Is that why he was so adamant about helping her? Did he want to make up for the sins of some faceless man? Graham was so loyal, so noble where his family was concerned.

"Don't go there."

Eve jerked her gaze to Graham, who had shifted on his stool to face her.

"Don't let your mind betray you," he added. "I'm not pitying you because of my mother's circumstances. I'm sure she was scared being single and pregnant, but that's not why I'm here."

Resting her palms on the edge of the counter, Eve tipped her head. "Why are you here? What do you want, Graham? Just say it."

His aqua eyes sparkled, and his lips pursed just slightly, reminding her of what she'd been missing out on the past few days. "Maybe I want to get to know you more. Maybe I think you need to know me better, as well. We need to be strong together, for the sake of our baby and our families."

Eve couldn't agree more, but the way he looked at her said he wanted more than just pleasantries. Could she deny him? Probably not, but she did wholeheartedly agree with him that they needed to work together.

"Then you'll have to stop eye-flirting with me," she told him, resuming her amazing breakfast.

"Eye-flirting?"

"Yes." She stabbed another apple with her fork. "You look at me and I can see you undressing me in your mind, but you haven't made any attempt to do so. I can't figure you out, but I can't be on the receiving end of that stare anymore."

Eve froze midchew as Graham's fingertip slid along her jawbone. Quickly, she finished her bite so she didn't choke. Her body responded instantly and he'd barely touched her. Why did she have to still want him? Why couldn't she get him out of her system?

"I'll strip you right now and take you on this counter." He turned her head toward him, his eyes darting to her mouth. "Say the word."

Oh, she wanted to say the word. Any word. Anything that would turn this passion into action. But she had to think straight...didn't she? She'd told herself not to fall back into the pattern of sleeping with him. That would be all too easy...and all too amazingly delicious.

No. She couldn't. They couldn't work as a team to figure out how to deal with the pregnancy and their families if their clothes were always falling off.

"Oh, my word, that wind is…"

Eve and Graham jerked their attention to the back door where Nora stood, her hair blown around her face, her mouth wide, her eyes even wider. There was a toss-up as to who was more shocked.

"You've got to be kidding me," Nora finally stated, shaking her long hair away from her face.

There was no reason to deny anything. Seriously. What could Eve say? Graham was sitting right here, shirtless, and Eve had clearly just crawled out of bed. Denying anything at this point would only make Eve look like a fool and insult her sister's intelligence.

"Plenty of breakfast if you want some," Graham supplied with that darn sexy grin. Clearly he was going the hospitable route instead of the awkward one.

Eve couldn't help the laugh that escaped her.

Nora's eyes narrowed on Graham before she turned to Eve. "You think this is funny? I thought you two were done…whatever it was you were doing."

Eve started to stand, but Graham put a hand on her arm. "We're not done, as a matter of fact."

Eve cringed. If he said anything about the baby, there would be nothing to stop Nora from telling Grace. Eve really needed to be the one to tell her sisters…and not in front of Graham. This was definitely a private matter she needed to handle on her own.

"Eve, come on." Nora stepped into the kitchen, her eyes locked on Eve's. "They're trying to destroy Dad's name, his reputation. You of all people should get how damning that could be, not only to our family, but to the company. They think he's hiding secrets, but he's a dying man. Why would he keep secrets at this point?"

Nora had just wrapped up and delivered the crux of the entire situation in that one question. Why indeed? That the matter was out of her control made this whole pregnancy even scarier. There had to be a way to keep this baby safe from family backlash.

"You're not telling me anything I don't already know," Eve replied, purposely keeping her voice calm, though her heart was pounding hard in her chest. "Graham and I are keeping everything private." For now. "So this doesn't need to go any further." Also, for now. "Did you need something from me?"

Nora blinked, then shook her head. "Seriously? You're going to brush this off?"

"There's nothing to brush off," Eve corrected. Now she did slide out from beneath Graham's touch so she could stand and approach her sister. "What Graham and I are doing, or not doing, is really only our business."

Was she honestly going to put Graham above her sisters' feelings right now? Eve was dangerously close to relationship territory, to an area neither of them ever wanted to be. But he'd stood firm against Brooks regarding the media backlash; that much was obvious from the pullback in the coverage. Perhaps they had already crossed that line and that was something she'd have to think about later.

"Eve wasn't feeling well last night, so I stayed to make sure she was okay," Graham chimed in. "Then I made breakfast and was going to head home after we ate. Now that I know she's feeling better, I'm comfortable leaving."

The weight on her chest vanished as she realized he wasn't about to share their secret.

Nora gave him a suspicious look. "You mean you stayed and took care of her because…why? You care about her? Eve, come on. You have to see he's using you. He's using you to get closer to Dad."

The accusation hurt. She knew for a fact Graham wasn't using her. He wasn't. He wouldn't take what they shared and turn it against her. Just because he hated her father didn't mean he'd be so cruel to her. And she hated that her sister didn't think someone like Graham would want to be with Eve simply because he found her attractive.

"I'm not using her. In fact, I asked Brooks to retract the media statements he made regarding your father."

Nora's eyes narrowed once again. Eve couldn't blame her sister for being so skeptical. Eve would feel the same way if the roles were reversed. Nora wouldn't understand there was much more to Eve and Graham than met the eye. And Nora wouldn't understand because Eve didn't fully understand it herself.

Another wave of nausea swept over her and Eve swayed on her feet. She gripped the stool and closed her eyes. Instantly Graham had his strong hands around her waist.

"Eve? What?"

She squeezed her eyes tighter, willing the unwanted nausea away. She couldn't answer for fear of getting sick right here. She hoped staying still for just a moment would help…

"Eve, talk to me," Graham urged. "Is it the baby?"

"Baby?" Nora exclaimed.

Suddenly Eve's fear of getting sick wasn't the issue. Now her sister knew and there was nothing Eve could do to stop this train wreck.

Ten

Graham didn't give a damn about the slipup. And he could care even less if Nora was shocked. When Eve swayed and caught herself on the barstool, his protective instincts took over.

Scooping her up in his arms, Graham ignored her weak plea to put her down as he carted her over to the living area off the kitchen. Once he laid her on the sofa, he noticed her pallor and the sheen of sweat that dotted her forehead. He eased himself onto the sofa beside her and lifted her legs onto his lap.

"Get her a cold cloth," he ordered Nora without taking his eyes from Eve. What if something was wrong? Why did she look so damn pale?

Eve laid one hand on her stomach and the other over her forehead. "I'm fine. Just give me a minute."

Seconds later, Nora waved a washcloth in Graham's face. He used it to wipe Eve's forehead, her neck. He didn't like this helpless feeling one bit. He'd seen his grandmother and his mother grow weak and pass. Not that Eve was dying, but the thought that there was nothing he could do for her right now really pissed him off.

"Eve." Nora stood over the back of the couch and reached down to smooth a damp strand of hair from her sister's face. "Are you pregnant again?"

Eve groaned, muttering something Graham didn't comprehend because he'd homed in on the key word in Nora's question.

Again?

What the hell did Nora mean by that? When had Eve been pregnant before?

"I'm pregnant," Eve mumbled. "Don't tell Grace. I'll tell her."

"Oh, honey." Now Nora's voice took on a compassionate tone, one that Graham instinctively knew had everything to do with this former pregnancy. He was almost afraid to find out the details, but he would. "How far along are you?"

"Seven weeks now."

Graham listened to the sisters, but his mind was overloaded. A spear of unexpected jealousy hit him square in the chest. He had no right to be jealous of a faceless man who'd created a baby with Eve. Clearly they weren't together anymore. But still, Graham didn't want to think of her experiencing this with anyone else.

"Promise me," Eve was saying, her eyes pleading with Nora. "Don't say anything. Let Graham and me handle this. We want what's best for the baby, and our families have to come to some sort of peace."

Nora glanced at Graham before looking back down at Eve. "I promise. I know what it's like to be pregnant and unsure of what to do next."

Nora had been a single mother before she and Reid

had fallen in love. Graham didn't know much about Nora's circumstances, but it sounded as though she'd been alone and scared. Fortunately, Eve wouldn't be alone. Ever, if he had any say.

Eve started to sit up, waving her hand when Graham tried to ease her back down. "It passed. I'm fine. I'm just going to sit here for a bit." Looking over her shoulder, she asked, "What did you need this morning, Nora?"

"What? Oh, it's not important." Nora smiled, then wrapped her arms around her sister. "I thought we might go shopping for party costumes for Halloween, but we can go another day."

Again, Graham didn't like being left out of this little shopping trip. Didn't like being so easily dismissed as though he was replaceable.

"I'll feel fine in the afternoon if you want to wait."

Nora stood straight up and nodded. "Sounds good. Text me later. Reid doesn't want to go, so I'll just pick something up for him. But I was given a list of things he refuses to wear. Tights being at the top of the list."

"No Robin Hood for him, then." Eve smiled. "Thanks for understanding and keeping this to yourself. I know you have questions, but I'll address them. Just not now."

Graham watched the younger Winchester sister as she adjusted her cardigan and smoothed her hair back. "I promise to keep this all to myself, but if you need any help with doctor's appointments or someone to—"

"She's got someone," Graham stated. "Just be sure to keep that promise."

Nora pulled in a breath as if she wanted to let him have it, but Graham flashed her what he hoped was a charming smile. No way in hell was he letting anyone else care for Eve and his child. They may not be a couple, but she belonged to him now.

Closing her mouth without saying anything, Nora turned on her heel and left out the front door. Silence filled the spacious room. Eve's legs were still in Graham's lap, but she sat up with her arm stretched across the back of the sofa.

"We're going to have to tell your brothers now," she said, rubbing her head. "I'll have to talk to Grace and… this is just going to be a mess."

"This isn't a mess. If our families can't see that a child is more important than our rivalry, then—"

"Tell me more about Gerty." Eve's eyes held his. She reached down and took his hand.

"Excuse me?"

Eve glanced down, traced a pattern over his palm. "You seemed so happy when you were talking about her. You seemed nostalgic and that's a side of you I don't know."

Graham swallowed. She didn't know this side because it was the one that was most vulnerable. But he wanted her to fully know him, to gain her affection so that his plan would be flawless. In order for that to happen, he'd have to bare all his emotions where his past was concerned.

"Gerty was amazing." Because he couldn't sit still, he shifted from beneath her and went to the kitchen for her plate. After putting it on her lap, he set her juice on the side table. "She'd swat our hands with a wooden spoon if we cursed, then just as lovingly show us how to bake homemade bread. I've never known anyone like her."

Eve continued to hold on to her plate. Graham picked up the fork and got a small bite for her. When he lifted it to her lips, she kept her gaze on his as he fed her.

"When I fell off the monkey bars in the first grade, she came right to the school because she didn't want to worry my mom or disrupt her shift at the coffee shop. By the time Mom got home, Gerty had bandaged me up, given me ice cream for dinner, and we were watching *Casablanca*."

Eve smiled as he lifted another bite to her mouth. "You get your love of old movies from her."

Graham nodded. "I get many things from her. She would always say how she was just a waitress, but she took pride in her job. She told us to do whatever job we wanted, whether it be a janitor or a doctor. She wanted us to know that every job was important and to make sure we worked hard."

Graham recalled her harping on how important hard work was time and time again. No matter the career, they had to put 110 percent into it. She was a proud woman and Graham knew his mother had found a real-life angel just when she'd needed her. Or perhaps they'd needed each other, considering that Gerty's husband had just passed when she took in Cynthia.

Graham continued to feed Eve. He shared random stories about his childhood. Whatever popped into his mind, he shared. For once, he was completely relaxed. Surprisingly, he wanted Eve to be fully aware of where he came from. He didn't come from money. He'd worked his ass off to get where he was at the law firm.

After her plate was completely clean, he reached for the juice and handed it to her.

"That was amazing," she told him. "Feel free to cook for me anytime."

Graham stilled. He wasn't prepared to play house. He had no road map, no plan here. All he knew was the end result had to be that his child was raised as a Newport.

"I'm sorry," she told him, glancing away. "I didn't mean that the way it sounded."

"Don't be sorry."

Shaking her head, she put her plate and glass on the table before leaning back on the couch. "You may be able to keep those emotions hidden in the courtroom, but I can read you better than you think. I understand you don't want a relationship with me, or any type of commitment. I wasn't implying that."

Graham raked a hand over his face; the stubble on his jawline was itchy and annoying. "Neither of us is at a point in our lives when we can put forth the time and attention a relationship needs."

Eve nodded. "I agree."

"But that doesn't mean everything that happened before I found out you were pregnant is over. I can't just shut off my desire for you, Eve. If you want to cool it in that area, tell me now. I'll respect your wishes and I'll still do everything in my power to keep you and this baby safe and cared for."

He had to say what she wanted to hear. He couldn't scare her off this early. He couldn't even hint at what his true intentions were.

Eve pushed to her feet and started pacing. She stopped in front of the fireplace and turned her back to him. His eyes focused beyond her, on the photos she had arranged across the mantel. Every silver-framed picture showcased her family. The sisters, Eve and her mother, a young Eve on her father's shoulders. He didn't want to get into that aspect of her life. Graham couldn't afford to see Sutton as a loving father. Graham didn't give a damn about Sutton, save for the fact that he knew who Brooks and Graham's birth father was. Or he at least knew a name. The old bastard was keeping this information to himself and Graham would do anything to find it out.

But he wouldn't use Eve or his unborn child to get it.

"I don't know what I want," Eve finally said. "This passion clearly isn't going away anytime soon. But I need some space."

When she turned around, Graham had to force himself to remain seated. She didn't need him cutting her off, she needed him to be strong for her. But he wouldn't stay away long.

"Wanting you has never been a question," she went on. "But—"

"I know." And he did. Graham came to his feet, pleased when her eyes raked over his bare chest. Let her look, let her continue to want and need just as he did. If she needed him, then that would play right into his hand. "I'll give you space, Eve. But you need to understand, I'm not going away. I won't pressure you or point out that you're looking at me like you want to take the rest of my clothes off."

Eve rolled her eyes. "So arrogant."

"Accurate, not arrogant," he corrected as he slowly closed the space between them. "I'm going to check on you every day. I'm going to be involved with this pregnancy. But you're going to come to me on your own."

He now stood so close to her that his bare chest rubbed against her T-shirt.

She tipped her head back. "You're sure of that?"

Graham eased closer, his lips within a breath of hers. "Positive."

He brushed his lips against hers, not quite kissing her, but feeling her warm breath. The slight whimper that escaped her was reassuring, but he stepped back. Fisting his hands at his sides to remain in control, he counted backward from ten.

She wanted space? So be it. She'd see just how difficult ignoring this desire would be.

"I'll call you later."

Graham forced himself to walk away. After getting his clothes and letting himself out, he reevaluated the plan in his head. Carson and Brooks needed to know about the baby, but he couldn't tell them just yet. He needed to formulate a better strategy for dealing with the Winchesters that didn't involve obliterating Sutton, and in turn hurting Eve. He didn't want her hurt, he wanted her to be completely and utterly his. But he also wanted Sutton to divulge the name of his father before he died.

Damn it. There had to be a way to get everything he wanted and not hurt Eve in the process.

If Roman could find their birth father soon, Graham knew Brooks would ease off Sutton. Or if Sutton somehow found it in the deepest part of his dark heart to share the information he knew, that would be even better. But Graham feared the man would go to his grave with the secret.

Just like his mother had. Why hadn't she just told them? All Graham had ever heard was how their father wasn't in the picture and she didn't want to talk about him.

So here they were with no answers, other than that Sutton was Carson's father. But that was it.

Putting thoughts of Sutton out of his mind, Graham pulled away from Eve's house, already planning on how to gain her attention, to make her come to him. Because he wouldn't beg for any women...not even the mother of his child.

Eleven

Graham eased back in his chair and thanked God the case he'd been waiting on to go to trial was finally scheduled. This would be a slam dunk for his client, and another win for Graham and the firm.

Since she'd last seen him, he'd randomly texted Eve. He purposely didn't flirt, didn't get into anything sexual or do the whole pathetic what-are-you-wearing thing. Nope. He wanted to keep her guessing, because if she was guessing, then she was thinking about him and his next move. And if she was thinking about him, then her thoughts would travel to the bedroom all on their own.

But the wait was killing him. It had been too long since he'd touched her properly. The thought of having another woman didn't excite him in the least. Eve was the woman he wanted in his bed, or anywhere else he could get her all to himself.

He knew she was getting ready for her sister's upcoming costume party, but he still wanted to see her. She couldn't come to him fast enough.

"Mr. Newport." His assistant's soft voice came through the speaker. "You have a visitor."

Eve? No, that was ridiculous. She wouldn't come here, not after she'd exploded when he'd shown up at her office during business hours.

"Shall I send Carson in?"

Graham came to his feet and pressed the speaker button. "Yes. Thank you."

Graham's door swung open and Carson stepped inside, closing the door at his back.

"You have a minute?"

Graham gestured to the seat across from his desk. "Of course."

"I'll be brief." Carson remained standing, so Graham did, too. "I'm going to see Sutton this evening. He called me yesterday and wanted to meet. I've been hesitant, but his time is limited, so I'm going."

Graham stilled. "Alone?"

"I know you and Brooks want answers from him, so if you want to go, we can all meet there. That bastard thinks he can always get what he wants, but we're a team, so we're in this together."

Another encounter with Sutton? Why not. The more they pumped him for answers, the greater the odds he'd wear down and just tell them what they wanted to know.

"Is Brooks going?"

Carson nodded. "He's meeting me there."

Graham glanced at the files on his desk, the open emails on his computer screen waiting to be answered. Nothing was more important than another shot with Sutton. Their time was running out.

"What time?" he asked, turning back to his brother.

"Seven."

Graham gave a firm nod of his head. "I'll be there."

Carson pulled in a deep breath and shoved his hands in his pockets. "I have no idea what I'm going to say. It's still awkward for me, especially now that he's dying…"

Graham couldn't imagine the emotions Carson was dealing with right now. "Are you sure you don't want to take Georgia instead?"

"No. She understands the need for the three of us to be there. I want to help you guys get the answers you need, plus I want to see what he has to say."

Graham wondered what Eve would say if she knew he was going to see her father. She was protective of him, wouldn't want anyone going to him on his deathbed and pumping him for information. Still, Graham was going to try one last time. Who knew when the man was going to pass? Sutton may have still been getting the best care at his sprawling estate, but that was only because of his billions. He was too proud to be in some facility like everyone else.

Had Eve told her father about the baby? Doubtful, or Sutton would've called Graham to meet with him, as well. Was Eve planning on exposing their secret or was she hoping to avoid telling her dad?

"You okay?"

Graham blinked and focused back on his brother. "Yeah. Fine. I'll finish up here and meet you all over at Sutton's."

Carson let himself out and Graham hurried to finish up the work that needed his attention right now. Once he was done, he grabbed his cell and thought about firing off a text to Eve but opted not to. She didn't need to know what was going on. If Sutton wanted her to know, he could tell her. Graham wasn't putting himself in the middle any more than he already was.

Sutton's affairs were his business, but Sutton's affair with Graham's mom was clearly out in the open now. Considering that Carson wasn't much younger than Graham and Brooks, Graham knew the affair had started when he and Brooks were mere infants. There was no way in hell Sutton wasn't aware of the first name of their father at least. Why did the old bastard care enough to keep it secret? Any information he provided would go a long way to helping them discover who their father was.

But maybe they wouldn't like the answer. Maybe their father was fully aware of the twins he'd given up. Maybe he didn't want anything to do with them. Still, that was a risk Graham and Brooks were willing to take.

In the end, Graham texted Eve, asking if she'd found a costume for the party. Simple enough, but effective in keeping her on her toes and their lines of communication open.

As soon as he started to shut the lights off in his office, the cell vibrated in his pocket. He pulled it out and nearly sagged against the wall. The image of Eve dressed as some sexy goddess with a white wrap hugging all her tempting curves had him gritting his teeth and cursing himself for telling her he'd give her space. The little vixen was playing games with him. She wanted him begging. He was sure that was her angle.

But two could definitely play at that game and he never played without every intention of winning.

Sutton Winchester's house was a vast estate not too far from the offices where he'd once controlled the real estate world. Graham and Brooks moved in behind Carson as they were led toward the back of the house. The butler was solemn and said nothing as he gestured for them to follow. Not that Graham was expecting a warm welcome, but still.

He tried to take in the surroundings, tried to imagine Eve growing up in this cold mansion. There wasn't a thing out of place and it looked more like a museum than a place where children played.

Graham instantly thought of his penthouse and cringed. Not exactly a playground, but he would make damn sure his child had a fun place to be a kid even if he had to remove his wet bar and put in an indoor jungle gym.

How pathetic was this? He was already one-upping Sutton in his own mind in regards to parenting. Ridiculous.

The servant escorting them motioned toward a set of double doors. Carson thanked the man and threw a glance back at his brothers.

"We've got your back," Brooks stated. "Go in when you're ready."

Carson turned back around, placed his hands on the knobs and eased both doors open. Graham didn't know what he expected, maybe a gray-toned man lying in bed hooked up to machines keeping him alive. But the reality was Sutton sitting up in a plush chair with his feet up by the fire in what Graham assumed was the master suite. A thick, plaid blanket covered his lap.

Sutton was once a kingpin in the corporate world, but right now he looked to be someone's loving grandpa waiting for children to gather around for story time.

Actually, this was his child's grandfather, but Graham would rather forget that little fact and focus on the reason for their visit now.

"I was hoping you'd come alone," Sutton stated. "But I'm not surprised you brought your brothers."

Graham didn't reply. This was Carson's show…for now. Carson had received the invite and it was Carson who had the most to get off his chest. Graham and Brooks were most likely beating the proverbial dead horse. Okay, really poor choice of words, but he couldn't help what popped into his head.

"My brothers and I are a unit. You know all about family loyalty, right?" Carson mocked.

Sutton merely nodded, not answering the rhetorical question.

"I don't even know what to say to you," Carson admitted.

Graham exchanged a knowing look with Brooks. They both knew Carson was on edge, and it definitely cost him to admit it. The poor guy had been on the fence about whether to fully accept Sutton as his father, whether to approach him and listen to what the old man had to say. But they were here now and Graham was more concerned about Carson's feelings than anything else.

"Have a seat." Sutton turned his attention to the twins. "All of you."

Carson remained still, staring at his father. Graham moved first to take a seat on the sofa on the other side of the oriental rug across from Sutton. Brooks sat beside him and finally Carson took the last spot on the end.

Sutton shifted in his seat. Graham wasn't sure if it was nerves or if the old man was simply trying to get comfortable. Sutton wasn't the type to show his emotions, so Graham doubted he was feeling anything but smug. He'd called Carson to come, and he had.

"Why did you want me here?" Carson finally asked, breaking the silent tension.

"You're my son."

Graham snorted, ignoring Sutton's frown and quick, disapproving look.

"So you're expecting us to get to know each other now that I know the truth and you're sick?" Carson asked.

Sutton turned his face to the fire. Orange flames licked against the black stone. The Chicago air was cooling quite a bit, hinting at an early winter. Graham found it easy to focus on the weather, on the fire, on anything other than the fact he didn't want to be here. Oh, he wanted to be here if he was going to get a name, but the chances of that happening were about as good as Sutton recovering from lung cancer.

"What you decide to do is up to you." Sutton coughed, and that's when it was apparent how sick the man was. This coughing fit wasn't short and it wasn't quiet. Finally, when he was done, he turned back to Carson. "I wanted you to know that I truly loved your mother."

Brooks tensed beside Graham. Of course he'd bring their mother into the conversation. He'd pretend that he knew her well, that he was heartbroken to leave her. Sutton had left Cynthia alone and pregnant, just like he'd found her. Only this time she'd been pregnant with *his* kid and he hadn't known it. Still, a lowly waitress and outsider wouldn't have fit into his high-society world of luxury homes, cars and diamonds.

The atmosphere of anger and bitterness in this room enveloped them all. There was so much to be said, but at the same time they were dealing with a dying man… and Eve's father. The grandfather of Graham's baby.

Graham stared at Sutton and tried to imagine the man

from the picture on Eve's mantel. The man who held his daughter on his shoulders at some amusement park. Sutton may be ruthless, he may have had countless affairs, but he loved his children. Considering that he had been shocked by the news of Carson's paternity, Graham wasn't surprised he'd called Carson to his home. Sutton wouldn't sit back and just ignore his child.

But he had no problem ignoring his ex-lover's other children.

"If you loved our mother, then tell us the name of our father," Brooks stated. "You were with her long enough. She would've confided in you."

Sutton shook his head. "It's because I loved Cynthia that I won't betray her confidence. If she'd wanted you to know, she would've told you."

"Tell them." Carson's low demand shocked Graham.

"It's not my place, son."

Carson let out a humorless laugh, eased forward and rested his forearms on his legs. Hands dangling between his knees, he glanced toward Brooks and Graham. Trying to offer silent support, Graham nodded for Carson to go on.

"My brothers deserve to know their father," Carson said, looking back at Sutton. "They keep hitting dead ends. If you can help them—"

"I didn't call them here," Sutton interrupted. "I wanted to see you. I don't have much time, though my doctors keep telling me I'm a fighter. I'm realistic."

"All the more reason for you to tell us," Brooks stated. "You may be the only other person who knows. We don't even know if our birth father is aware of us."

Sutton simply stared back. He gave no hint of what he knew, no sign that he even cared if they were struggling. Graham never liked the man from his dealings with him in the corporate world. He'd been sneaky and underhanded. He kept secrets, even from his staff. Graham had actually seen one of Sutton's previous employees win a case against the old man, but that had been during Graham's internship so he hadn't had a hand in that win.

Graham knew Sutton wasn't about to give up the name, if he even knew a name. For all Graham knew, Sutton was just stringing them along. How had Eve turned out so loyal and honest?

Obviously Eve's mother had a hand in raising her daughter right and was smart enough to finally leave Sutton after years of unfaithful marriage.

"I want to make something clear," Sutton went on. "Cynthia was the love of my life."

Graham didn't want to hear this, didn't want to be subjected to more lies. But one glance at Carson made Graham realize that his younger brother wanted to know. Not that Carson was naive, but Carson was more prone to forgiveness than Graham or Brooks. So Graham remained silent, though he had plenty of thoughts racing through his mind.

Sutton's eyes didn't leave Carson. "I would've given anything to be with Cynthia. But my wife was so well connected in Chicago society, it would've been career suicide to leave her. Plus, she would've made life hell for Cynthia, and I couldn't allow that."

"Would you have made the same decision if you'd known about me?"

The underlying tone of vulnerability was something Graham had never seen from Carson. Graham's younger brother was a rock, he was always in control, but this little meeting was getting to him. Graham prayed Carson would hold it together.

"I would've gone through hell to be with my son."

Sutton's answer sounded honest. Graham fully believed the man would've sacrificed his marriage to Eve's mother. No doubt Sutton would've wanted a son to raise, to mold into his heir. But Eve had filled that role, and she was doing a remarkable job. Maybe too remarkable.

And just like that, his thoughts had once again strayed to Eve during this meeting. He'd be checking on her again when they left here...especially after that little picture she'd sent to torture him.

"I want to hate you," Carson muttered.

Graham glanced over in time to see Brooks give a manly, reassuring pat to Carson's shoulder. They were here for Carson, to support him. If he wanted to embrace Sutton as his father and live out these days happily ever after, then that's what they'd do. But Graham wasn't so willing to forgive the bastard.

"I know you do," Sutton agreed. "And you have every right. But I couldn't die, not without telling you that Cynthia meant the world to me and I regret not having been there for you."

Graham wasn't surprised that their mother had kept the baby from Sutton. She'd probably been scared of the backlash and it was just as easy to live with Gerty and raise her boys in secret as opposed to facing legal proceedings, which she wouldn't have been able to afford.

Silence filled the room. The fire continued to crackle, sending out wayward flickers and orange sparks. Graham glanced around the room. He thought for sure that he'd see pictures of Eve and her sisters here, but there was nothing. Images of Eve staring at pictures of her father on her computer flashed through Graham's mind. She'd been so eager to get those images uploaded and she'd scrolled through them as though they were her lifeline to her ailing father.

Graham didn't want Carson to give his loyalty, his love to Sutton, but this wasn't Graham's choice to make. Who knew what would happen if and when he ever found his birth father? Maybe Graham would find a jerk who knew about his kids and just didn't care. What then? Would Graham still forgive him or want to try to make a relationship with him?

"I don't know what to say, honestly." Carson stared at his hands dangling between his knees. "I'd like to visit you, maybe see you a little more and talk. For whatever time we have—"

"I'll take anything," Sutton said, a soft smile forming on his pale face.

Graham had only seen that smile in Eve's pictures. Apparently he reserved the emotion for his children. Graham was a bit jealous of how Carson's journey had ended; he deserved a dad, even if it was Sutton.

Brooks came to his feet and sighed. "I'm done here. Carson, stay as long as you like. I'll be outside."

Once Brooks was gone, Graham also stood. He approached Sutton, knowing this may be the last time he ever saw the man. He had no intention of ever coming back.

"I'm glad you're not my father," Graham said, leaning down just enough so only Sutton could hear. "But Carson is happy to finally know. If you have to fake affection, do it. He deserves a father who isn't a jerk."

"I love my son," Sutton said simply.

Graham nodded and straightened. It was so tempting to tell him about the baby. So tempting to get just one final jab in. But Graham wasn't that much of an ass and he'd never do that to Eve. He wanted a chance to show her what a good father he could be and harassing *her* father was not the way to go about that.

Graham turned to his brother. "I'll wait outside with Brooks. Seriously, take your time."

Before Graham had gotten outside, he'd fired off a text to Eve indicating what he'd do to her if he were to ever see her in that Halloween costume.

"That man can rot in hell for all I care." Brooks rested his back against one of the thick, white columns of the portico. "I'm happy for Carson, but damn it. That man is infuriating."

Graham stepped forward, shoving his hands into his pockets and hunching his shoulders against the chilly breeze. "Carson has been on the fence for a while now. He wants to forgive Sutton. I hate to come to the guy's defense, but he didn't know Carson existed."

Brooks jerked his gaze around. "Are you serious? You're going to stand there and make excuses for the guy? If Mom was the love of his life, as he claims, then he would've moved heaven and earth to be with her. And he damn well would give a portion of his estate to his biological son."

When Graham didn't reply, Brooks narrowed his eyes. "This has to do with Eve, doesn't it? You're still hung up on her."

He was the father of her child. Which was a few levels above being "hung up on her."

"I'm stating the obvious, that's all." Graham wasn't about to bring Eve into this discussion. She had enough on her plate without being further caught up in this battle. "Sutton and Carson need time to talk alone. You and I will only make things worse."

Brooks started pacing on the stone walk. "I need

Roman to come up with something concrete. I'm putting all my faith in him to find our father."

"I know," Graham said, hating how much this issue was controlling Brooks's life. "But it will happen. We can't run into dead ends forever. Something will turn up. Someone somewhere knows the truth."

Brooks snorted and jerked his thumb toward the house. "Yeah. He's in there."

Graham stared at the double doors. Sutton knew. Absolutely without a doubt he knew. But Graham refused to beg the man. He would find out on his own. He would not give Sutton any satisfaction in getting one up on him. Ever.

Twelve

Seven weeks pregnant and her body was already showing signs of change. Eve attempted to adjust her cleavage in the strips of fabric covering her chest. The white goddess costume had seemed like a good idea at the time, but now she felt very exposed.

Glancing in her floor-length mirror, she shivered as she recalled Graham's text. The man wasn't playing nice. He was trying to get her to give in and…well, she was having a difficult time recalling why she needed to stay away.

Oh, yeah. Someone had to be responsible and think things through right now. Someone had to step back and think straight. When he sent those messages, and there had been many, Eve found it more and more difficult to keep him at a distance.

She hadn't seen him for several days. Too many. The messages hadn't started out as flirty, but then she'd sent that picture and she'd opened up some sort of dam. He'd flooded her phone with messages that would've made her high-society mother blush.

With the cool, windy October weather, Eve would definitely need a coat this evening. Otherwise she'd freeze her butt off.

Eve glanced at the antique clock on her vanity and sighed. She was running late because insecurities over the changes in her body had her doubting her costume. But she had no plan B so goddess she was. Nobody would guess she was pregnant; of course Nora already knew, but she hadn't said anything yet. There was no reason for anyone to believe she was expecting, so worrying over her fuller chest was ridiculous.

Still, she feared that when the rest of her family found out, when her *father* found out she was not only expecting, but carrying a Newport child, there would be trouble. She'd already gotten a glimpse of things to come from Nora. Her family wouldn't be happy. Granted, she was going into this situation with her eyes wide open and not full of stars. Eve had lost a child before when she thought herself in love. Now her family would probably criticize her for making a mistake with another man who was all wrong for her.

Not that her baby was a mistake; the first person to even hint at that would have to deal with her wrath. No, her mistakes came in the form of choosing the wrong men. Clearly she had bad judgment.

By the time Eve pulled onto the Winchester estate, she was confident that she needed to tell her family. The sooner they knew about the baby, the longer they'd have to get used to the idea. After the party tonight, she'd tell Grace and their father when they were all together. It would be the perfect time. Not that there was a perfect time to drop a bomb like this. But there was no changing the fact that she was having a baby.

A baby. The thought thrilled and terrified her at the same time. She was still ten weeks away from the seventeen-week mark. She would feel so much better once she got past the hurdle that had left a hole in her heart during her last pregnancy. Eve honestly didn't know if she could bear another loss so great. She was already facing the inevitable loss of her father, but to add a second baby to the...

No. This baby was just fine. She wasn't going to even think that way... From now on she would have only positive thoughts. Her child was a Newport and a Winchester, which immediately equaled a fighter.

Eve pulled in behind Grace's car and grabbed her clutch and the present she'd brought for her father—a framed photograph. Sliding her phone into her purse, Eve headed toward the grand entrance. Her childhood home was nothing short of spectacular—Sutton Winchester would settle for nothing less than the best.

Instantly memories of growing up here flooded her mind. The house always looked like a museum, but there had been a toy room on the third floor where the kids were given free rein. She and her sisters had spent hours in there playing, dreaming, fighting...all the things close sisters did. They'd run around outside playing tag, chasing each other and fantasizing about being grown-ups. Seriously, growing up was so overrated. They should've enjoyed those carefree days a bit more.

Pulling her wrap tighter around her, Eve made her way to the door. Without knocking, she let herself in. The aroma of something spicy, maybe cinnamon, hit her. Definitely a hint of pumpkin, too. Whatever the cook had prepared—or Nora had had catered—smelled absolutely divine. And thankfully in the evenings, Eve was fine; she didn't have to deal with a queasy belly. So she was ready to have her fill of the party food, but not the wine.

Eve had just pulled her wrap off to hang it on the coat tree in the foyer when Nora came gliding down the hall. Eve put her wrap up and set her clutch and gift on the marble entryway table.

"You look gorgeous," her younger sister declared. "I knew this goddess costume would be so perfect for you."

Eve took in her sister's vibrant green historical ball gown. "Talk about stunning. Nora, you're glowing."

Nora beamed. "I know it's not what I bought when we were out, but then I saw this the other day and had to have it."

"So what is Reid?"

"Lucky." Eve glanced at Reid, who'd just stepped from the formal living space. He wrapped an arm around Nora's waist and kissed her cheek. "I'm damn lucky," he added.

Reid was dressed as a Civil War–era soldier, complete with sword dangling at his side. He and Nora looked as though they'd stepped out of a time machine. Eve was jealous of Nora's itty-bitty waist; no doubt she'd gone for the whole corset and all. Eve's hourglass shape was not long for this world.

"That you are," Eve agreed, giving her sister a wink. "How's Dad feeling today?"

"Good. He's even donned a bit of a costume for the occasion, though he said he'd stay in the study since his oxygen and everything is set up in there. Visitors are welcome, though."

Eve gripped the present beneath her arm and nodded. "I'm going to see him now before everyone else arrives."

"You doing okay?" Nora asked, keeping the question vague.

Eve glanced at Reid, who showed no sign of knowing anything. "I'm great. If you'll excuse me."

Eve made her way to the study. She hated thinking of her father being so sick that he was confined to one room, but she knew that if he truly wanted to move about the house, his caregivers would make it happen. Her father remained in the study more out of pride than anything else. There was a bathroom right off the spacious room and hospice care had set everything up to look like a master suite. Her father's old desk where he'd spent countless hours when he worked from home sat in the corner. Next to the desk was a large built-in shelf housing all of his favorite books.

As she walked down the hall, Eve took stock of all the memories. She hated the thought of his estate being split up when he passed. She wanted her childhood home to remain in the family, but that might not be possible. Who knew what would happen with Carson and how far his brothers would go to make sure he received his share.

Just the thought of Graham stirred mixed emotions within Eve. The ache she had for him kept growing with each day that passed without him, but on the other hand, she hated knowing he was one of the forces waging war against her father.

Pulling the framed picture from beneath her arm, Eve tapped lightly on the double doors and let herself into the study. The cozy fire welcomed her. Her father was actually in his chair beside the flickering flames. The last time she'd visited, he'd been sitting up in bed but hadn't felt like going much farther. To see him in a chair was such a surprise, Eve's eyes instantly filled with tears. The eye patch and pirate hat combined with his navy blue bathrobe made her laugh, though. He'd dressed up for the guests that would come through. If it weren't for the oxygen, she'd swear he was back to normal. But he'd never be himself again. He'd never be the man he once was and she was slowly coming to grips with the harsh reality.

"Look at this beautiful goddess who came to visit." He lifted a hand toward her. "Come on over. You look stunning, Eve. Just like your mother."

Of course she looked like her mother; everyone told her as much growing up. The honey-brown hair, the bright eyes, curvy figure. Eve had seen enough pictures of her mother in her younger years to know she was practically a clone. But Eve didn't want to discuss her mother right now. She wanted this evening to be fun, to be filled with love since the entire family would all be under one roof.

"What have you got?"

Eve flipped the frame around. "I had this made for you. It's from my visit the other day."

Sutton stared at the picture for several moments before finally reaching for it. With both hands, he gripped the sleek pewter frame and settled it on his lap. Eve waited, watching as her father continued to look at the faces staring back at him. Sutton with his daughters, an image that hadn't been captured since they were little.

"This means everything to me," he said, his voice thick with emotion. "You've always had such a good eye for photos."

Eve leaned against the side of the chair and laughed. "It was just a selfie, Dad. But I thought it turned out nice and wanted you to have something in your room."

He glanced up at her, his bushy brows drawn together. "You always know what to do. This is perfect."

"I'm glad you like it."

He looked at the image once more before turning his attention back to her. "Tell me about Elite. How are things going?"

The man was on his deathbed and wanted to know about business. He would probably die with his company—his baby—on his mind.

"We're doing great." Eve was thrilled with the direction they'd taken since she'd been placed at the helm. "We actually just signed on a Sydney office two days ago."

Sutton's smile spread across his face. "I knew you would take a great company and make it even greater. I'm so proud of you, Eve. You've not let anything stand in your way."

"I learned from the best," she declared, wrapping her arm around his shoulders as she settled a hip on the arm of his chair.

"Some women are cut out for husbands, kids, which is fine. But I knew you were the one to follow in my footsteps. You never had—"

"Let's not talk about work." She had to steer him in another direction. Because even though she hadn't wanted the whole family lifestyle once she'd gotten a taste of corporate world, clearly she wasn't going to be able to dodge it for long. "Nora said you were feeling pretty well today. You look good."

He started to laugh, but his robust chuckle quickly turned into a coughing fit. Eve rushed to the wet bar in the corner and refilled his water. She hated seeing him suffer even the slightest bit. For a man who was known to be a ruthless shark in the real estate world, he was now as weak as a baby. The vulnerable side of Sutton Winchester would only be known to his family, though. He'd never let outsiders see him in such shape.

Eve let him hold the cup while she took the framed picture and set it up on the table near the sofa.

"Thank you," he said after taking a few sips. "Damn disease."

Eve went back to his side and took his cup. She placed it on the small table next to him.

"You girls don't have to lie to me," he went on, taking her hand and squeezing it between both of his. "I know what I look like."

Eve kissed the top of his head. "Like my handsome father."

"You're going to find some man and charm him one day," her father teased. "Just make sure when you do that you don't leave my company in a bind."

As if she'd ever settle down and take the time to nurture a relationship. A global company and a new baby were definitely enough to keep her occupied. "I'll never leave Elite," she promised.

"I hate to bring this up—"

"But you will because you're honest," she joked. "Go ahead."

"I know that before all the questions came up about me being the Newport boys' father, you and Graham were—"

"Nothing," Eve interrupted. "We were nothing." And that was the truth. It was *after* the paternity test results came back that they tore each other's clothes off.

This conversation was entering dangerous territory, and that was putting it mildly. Guilt squeezed her chest like a vise. There was no way to avoid it much longer, but she wasn't going to tell anyone about the baby until after the party. No way was she going to ruin Nora and Reid's evening. There would be enough time to discuss it after the guests were gone and only family remained.

"I saw how he looked at you, Eve," her father went on. "Getting involved with a Newport would be the biggest mistake you could make."

Eve bit the inside of her cheek to keep from saying anything. What could she say? She could deny that she was involved, but that would be an obvious lie. She could even pretend they weren't going to be anything more than parents sharing a child, but since they were still flirting and she couldn't get him off her mind, it was only a matter of time before her control crumbled and they ended up intimate again.

Pulling her hand from her father's grasp, she leaned down once more and kissed his head. "I'm going to go see if Nora needs help since the guests should be arriving any minute. I'll be back in a bit."

To tell you I'm expecting a Newport's baby.

"You'd better," her father winked. "But keep in mind what I said, Eve. Graham and Brooks have an agenda. They think I know their father's name and they'll use any means necessary to get it. I wouldn't put it past him to use you to get to me."

Eve stilled. She'd never thought for a second that Graham was using her for anything other than a bedmate...and she'd used him right back. But did her father's words hold any truth? Nora had hinted at the same thing the other day. Was her family just being overly cautious or did they truly believe Graham would use her to get to Sutton?

No. Graham wasn't the type of man to play games. He was a lethal attorney and when he wanted something, he went straight at it. He wasn't the type of man to hide behind a woman and let her do the work.

Eve let herself back out into the hallway and pulled in a deep breath. Voices filtered through the house and it was clear guests had started arriving. Giving her cleavage one last glance in a mirror, she gave a mental shrug and headed toward the formal living room.

Grace, Nora and Reid stood near the mantel, talking and laughing. Grace was dressed as a sexy witch with glittery hose, a sparkly black hat and some killer black stilettos. Their guests were dressed in various fun costumes. Eve glanced around the room and saw an oversize Mrs. Potato Head—presumably the Mr. Potato Head by the wet bar with an appetizer in his hand was the spouse. There was another couple dressed as Vikings and a few others in glamorous gowns and masks. Some reminded her of Mardi Gras with their ribbons and gems.

Eve was stopped by Lucinda Wilde and Josh Calhoun. Lucinda was their father's main caretaker and had pretty much morphed into being one of the family. She and Josh had fallen in love recently and Eve smiled as the couple approached her.

"If there's a contest for best costumes, you two win hands down."

Lucinda smiled as Josh wrapped his arm around her waist. "Josh isn't one for dressing up, so he basically threw on things he already owned."

Eve gave him an approving nod. "The cowboy look works. And your saloon girl is perfect," she told Lucinda. "I could never pull that off, but you guys look so authentic."

"I'm here for the food," Josh joked as he tipped his hat down in a typical cowboy fashion. "And I'd use any excuse to have Lucinda dress up like this."

Lucinda gave him a playful swat. "Eve, you look amazing. This is such a fun party, and I think it's just what Sutton needs. He may come out later."

"Really?" Eve asked. "I hope he does. Everyone here loves him and I know it would do him good."

"I agree," Lucinda said. "I'm going to talk to him in a bit and coerce him to join the party. I even dressed him up."

"I saw," Eve laughed. "I love the pirate."

"It's all he would agree to."

Lucinda glanced around the room, pushing her curls to the side so they slid over one bare shoulder. "If you'll excuse me, I'd like to talk to Nora and Reid. They look great, too."

Eve watched as the two couples met in the middle of the room. They laughed and chatted. Eve stared for a moment too long because she caught Grace's curious look and quirked brow, silently asking if Eve was okay.

Eve pasted on a smile and gave a brief nod. Everything was fine. Seriously. Just because she was expecting a child by a man who was an enemy of her father, just because the two families would go ballistic once the pregnancy was revealed, and just because her father was dying…why shouldn't she be fine?

Thirteen

She needed air desperately. The more guests that filled the house, the more Eve felt as though she was suffocating. She'd spent over an hour smiling, making small talk and wondering if anyone noticed how she kept her water glass full and ignored the wine.

The Winchester mansion was vast, but still, the walls had been closing in on her.

Escaping out the back patio doors, Eve slid off her gold sandals and padded barefoot around the pool. The stones were cool on her feet and for once she welcomed the brisk breeze. She'd started getting so warm inside, but then her body temperature had been off lately. *Thank you, hormones.*

When an arm snaked around her waist, Eve gasped.

"It's me," a familiar voice whispered in her ear.

Her entire body tingled at the warm breath against the side of her face, the taut chest against her back. But as much as she relished the feel of Graham against her, fear gripped her. "What are you doing here?" she whispered.

"My invitation got lost in the mail."

Eve smiled, but quickly composed herself before turning in his arms. "You're—"

Words died on her lips when she realized he was wearing a mask...one of those Mardi Gras masks she'd seen a few of the guests wearing earlier. And a tux. Mercy sakes he had on a tuxedo and looked just as perfectly packaged as he had the night of the charity ball.

Graham slid the mask over his head and took her hand. Without a word he pulled her toward the pool house. A thrill of excitement rushed through her as Graham tried the knob and it turned beneath his palm.

He ushered her inside, closed the door and left the lights off. She waited for him to devour her, to run his hands over her heated body. But nothing. Her eyes hadn't adjusted to the darkness and she couldn't see him.

"Graham?"

"I'm right here."

His voice was close. The heat from his body had her shifting, hoping to brush against him...waiting for him to make contact somehow.

"What are you doing?" she asked.

"I told you, my invitation got lost in the mail."

Eve rolled her eyes, even though he couldn't see her. "No. What are you doing in here?"

Material rustled. Something, his sleeve maybe, brushed against the back of her hand then was instantly gone. Her body was wound so tight in anticipation of his touch. What was he waiting on?

"I wanted to see you," he said in that low tone that had shivers racing through her. "You sent me that picture and I knew I had to find a way to be at this party."

"Did anyone——"

"No. Nobody saw me. I even talked to a few guests, but no one caught on."

Relief washed over her, but was quickly replaced once again by arousal. "Are you…why are we…"

"Are you achy, Eve?"

That sultry voice filled the darkness. Her eyes were finally starting to adjust somewhat, but there were no outside lights coming in because the entrance to the pool house faced the back of the property. Damn it. She wanted to see him better, to touch him. What game was he playing?

"Have you thought of me these past few days?" he continued. "I know you have or you wouldn't be sending me pictures of you in that sexy costume. Did you think I'd come begging for you? I told you, you'd be the one begging."

She was damn near ready to do just that. "Is that why you're here? To get me to beg?" she asked, hoping her voice sounded stronger than she felt.

"I'm here because I told you I wanted to be your date."

Eve eased away from the door, only to stop short when she ran into Graham's hard chest. "So what are we doing in the pool house?" she asked, holding her hands up to steady herself. She couldn't stop herself from gliding her palms up the tux jacket toward his broad shoulders.

"Your call, Eve. I told you I won't be the one to make a move."

Why did life have to be full of so many tempting choices? Why was her greatest need the exact opposite of what she should be doing? But the lengths he went to in order to be with her was rather…oh, fine. It was flat-out arousing and exciting.

"You're quite cocky to come into my family's home," she told him, roaming her hands up toward his neck, her fingertips teasing that smooth jawline.

"Call it what you want, but there was no way in hell I was going to let some damn picture pacify my need for you."

He'd never admitted he needed her before. Granted he was talking in physical terms, but the words still sent a thrill of desire through her.

Eve leaned in until her lips barely brushed against his. "So you're here to give in after all? Dare I say, beg me?" she whispered.

With a groan, Graham snaked his arms around her waist and gripped her backside, pulling her flush against him. "Hell no. I'm not begging. I'm taking what I want, what you've teased me with, and I'm saving your pride so *you* don't have to beg."

Eve laughed. "So this is all for me?"

"I'm a selfish man, Eve. Never forget that."

His lips crushed hers as he backed her up a few steps to the door. She hit with a thud, but she barely noticed. With the way Graham's hands were wrestling the hem of her dress up her thighs, she couldn't concentrate on anything but the endless possibilities of what was about to happen.

"Never tease me again," Graham muttered against her lips. "Did you think I'd avoid you, knowing you looked like this?"

His mouth made a path down her neck, to the deep V of her dress. For the first time tonight, she was all too happy to be this exposed. Better access for Graham was exactly what she needed, what she ached for.

Eve arched her back, cupping the side of his face as he jerked the thick straps down her shoulders. The second her dress fell to her waist, Graham filled his hands with her bare breasts.

"If I'd known you weren't wearing anything beneath this, I would've intercepted you at your house before the party and we never would've left."

Eve gasped as his lips found her sensitive tip. "The dress…it has…um…"

"Yes?" he asked, a smile in his tone. "How close are you to begging?"

About a second.

"The dress has a built-in liner. No bra necessary."

"It's my new favorite."

When his hands trailed up the back of her thighs, Eve had to bite her lips to keep from crying out. He knew every single place to touch her and have her squirming. He knew she was on the brink of begging and he was practically gloating over it.

Time to turn the tables, so to speak.

Eve reached between them. The second she stroked her hand up his length, Graham let out a hiss.

"I'm not playing games, Eve."

She couldn't help but smile against his mouth. "You wouldn't have come here if you weren't playing."

She. Was. Killing. Him.

And his slow descent had started the second she'd sent that picture of her wearing the dress. But, seeing her in person, touching those curves, was absolutely everything he'd ever dreamed and fantasized about. Yes, he'd had her multiple times, but knowing she was carrying his child bumped up the sexual appeal. There was something so primal, so…damn it, *his*. She was his. That child was his. There would never be another man coming into her life, into their child's life. Not so long as Graham was around.

Maybe he'd come here to seduce her, most likely. But he'd intentionally decided to crash the party simply because he knew he could. He'd taken matters into his own hands.

Speaking of matters in hand…

"Take off your dress."

Eve stilled. "Here?"

"We can go back inside to the party to do this, but I'm sure your family wouldn't approve."

Graham backed away and waited until the rustling and soft swoosh of fabric indicated she was indeed bare for him. Closing the space between them, Graham wasted no time in grabbing hold of her and lifting her until her legs wrapped around him.

He eased over slightly so her back wasn't against the grooves in the door. But once he had her against the wall, he reached between them, unfastened his pants and kissed her. Hard. This wasn't a sweet encounter; he didn't have time for gentle touches and nurturing words. He was in this dark pool house with his own goddess for one reason only.

"Hurry," she panted against his mouth.

Clearly Eve was in here for one reason, as well. This was why they got along so well. Their needs, their wants were identical in nearly every single way. Convincing her to be his wife would be the easiest case he'd ever made.

The soft pants, the occasional groan from Eve were begging enough. Graham slid into her, smiling when her fingers curled around his shoulders and gripped tighter. The way she whispered his name as she threw her head back and closed her eyes only fueled Graham to move faster.

"It's been too long," he growled as he kept a firm hold on her hips. "Never again."

"No," she murmured, her eyes locking with his.

Graham couldn't go another day without touching her, let alone several. His stupid pride and the ridiculous game he'd played…it had backfired in his face. Now he was the one needing her, but damn if he'd admit it.

"I'm the only one, Eve." He didn't know why he needed to express this, but damn if another man would be keeping her bed warm. For now, she was his. "Say it."

Nodding, she gasped when he pushed harder. "The only one. Only you."

Feeling too vulnerable, way too close to the edge of exposing feelings he wasn't ready to come face-to-face with, Graham angled his mouth across hers once more. His hips quickened, and her knees tightened around his waist.

When her hands came up to frame his face, Graham ignored the tingle of awareness. He wanted it fast, hard, intense. Little sweet gestures weren't for him. They weren't for *them*.

Eve tore her mouth from his and squeezed her eyes tight.

"No. Look at me," he demanded. His eyes had adjusted to the darkness and he wanted to see as much of her as possible.

When her body convulsed, Graham could no longer hold back. He buried his face in the side of her neck, inhaling that familiar, jasmine scent. Holding tight, he waited until their bodies ceased trembling before he lifted his face. Her heart beat so fast against his chest, matching his own frantic pace.

"My family is going to wonder where I went," Eve murmured, breaking the silence.

Graham nipped at her lips. "Tell them you needed some fresh air."

"I don't even want to look in a mirror. They're going to wonder why I'm so messed up."

"Then leave with me."

Why had he said that? They weren't inseparable. But there was something about knowing they shared this baby…the bond was already too strong. Graham needed to rein things back in or he was going to find himself in a position he wasn't ready for.

Eve slid her legs from his waist. "We'll both pretend you didn't say that."

Once she was standing and had her balance, Graham stepped back and adjusted his clothes. He'd barely taken the edge off and if he stayed at this party, he was going to have to find a spare bathroom or walk-in closet to drag her into.

He pulled out his phone to use as a light, shining it on Eve. The instant the glow hit her face, she froze and blinked at him. But it was the tousled hair, the swollen lips and pinkened cheeks that held him captivated. There was no denying what she'd been up to and the thought of her putting that dress back on while looking so rumpled sent a jolt of desire through him.

"I can't see your face with that light in my eyes," she told him, holding up a hand. "But if I don't get back in there, my family is going to worry."

Angling his phone toward her body as she pulled her dress back up, Graham reached a hand out to help her. "I'm going in, too. I'm not going to leave."

"Why would you want to stay?"

Because he wanted to touch her, he wanted to catch a glimpse of her across the room…because apparently he was a masochist. Mostly because she was trying to push him away when she clearly didn't mean it, and he wouldn't let her.

"Because I can," he said simply.

Once she'd adjusted her dress, she pushed her hair back behind her shoulders. "I'm going to tell the rest of my family about the baby after the party."

He tightened his hold on his phone. No. He had to get her to agree to marriage before she told her family. They would instantly tell her what a mistake it was to be involved with him. They'd get inside her head and have her doubting.

"Are you sure that's a smart move? They already think I'm using you."

"Are you?"

He couldn't blame her for asking. Apparently they'd already gotten to her. "If you thought I was, you wouldn't be in here with me," he countered. He hadn't used her, not by any means. But now that she was having his baby, he would marry her to ensure that their child had a Newport name. A detail she didn't need to know.

Yes, he could've used her to get to her father, but he hadn't. Didn't that count for something?

"Regardless of what they think, they need to know," Eve continued. "There's so much worry with my father, fear of the unknown, and now with Carson finding out he's our half brother. My family needs to know exactly what they're dealing with. Besides, maybe this baby will be the bond that brings our families together and resolves this ridiculous feud."

Graham wasn't so sure of that, but if she wanted to

tell them, he'd support her…after that ring was on her finger.

"Let's wait a few days," he said, holding up a hand when she opened her mouth. "I want you to come away with me."

"What?"

Yeah, what did he mean? Where had that come from? He hadn't planned it. But now that he'd offered the trip, he had to admit it was a brilliant plan.

"We'll go away for just a couple days," he hurried on. "Nobody has to know, and when we get back, you and I can tell them."

"I'm telling them tonight, Graham. I've waited long enough."

Her inflexible tone told him this battle would be more difficult than he'd thought.

"I need to get back inside," she told him.

"I'm coming in, too."

Eve hesitated, but finally nodded. "Just keep your mask on until after the party, okay? I'd hate to have a scene with so many people here."

Graham would love nothing more than to cause a scene, but out of respect for Eve, he'd keep the mask on. He searched the floor, then found it. After sliding it back into place, he bowed toward her.

"You go on," he told her. "I'll be in later. You won't even know I'm there."

With her hand on the knob, she threw him a glance over her shoulder. "I'll know you're there. I'll feel you."

With those parting words, she was gone.

She'd *feel* him? Of course she would. And even across the room, he'd undoubtedly feel her, as well. The line he'd been teetering on, swearing he wouldn't cross it, was starting to waver. He was losing his grip and it was only a matter of time before he lost his balance and fell face-first into emotions he'd purposely dodged.

This entire situation was messy and if he wasn't careful, someone was going to end up hurt.

Fourteen

No matter how she mingled with the guests, no matter how many jokes Reid told her and no matter how many times she refilled her glass of sparkling water, Eve felt the presence of Graham just the same as if he'd come up and wrapped his arms around her.

Nora and Reid separated, but kept making eye contact with each other. Eve wondered what that kind of connection would be like. To look across the room and have your soul mate watching you. Silent communication passed between the couple. Whatever they were sharing, Reid gave a nod and Nora moved through the crowd toward the front of the formal living room.

"Those two are up to something," Grace whispered behind Eve's back. "They've been sneaking around all evening."

Eve caught sight of Graham across the room in the familiar mask. His face was turned toward hers, but she couldn't see his eyes. No matter, she knew they were on her. The connection across the room…it was just like Nora and Reid's.

No. She and Graham were nothing like her sister and Reid. Were they?

"That's what lovers do," Eve replied, not taking her gaze from Graham. She had to admit, the thrill of having him in her family home was exciting. For someone who was such a stickler for rules, lately she found herself not caring so long as she saw Graham.

No matter how she tried to shift her focus to the baby, to remain in control of her life, she kept getting pulled back into Graham's web. The encounter in the pool house shouldn't have happened, but she wouldn't change anything. How could she keep denying what they both wanted? They were having a baby together. That didn't mean they had to automatically stop seeing each other…did it?

Nerves fluttered in her stomach. She was anxious to get this night over with, to finally let her family know what was going on. If there was an issue, she'd deal with it, but she couldn't keep living this secret life. Keeping her affair hidden was difficult enough, but there was no way she'd be able to keep a child from her family. Soon, very soon, they'd see the evidence.

"Can I have everybody's attention?" Reid called. When only half the room quieted, he put his fingers to his mouth and whistled. Silence immediately settled over the space. "I'd like your attention."

"What's going on?" Eve asked her younger sister.

"No idea, but Dad was just wheeled in."

Eve turned around. Dr. Wilde was heading their way with their father. Sutton had his eyes on Eve and Grace, a smile on his pale face. The cancer had robbed him of his color, his dignity and his normal life. But here he was, attending the party in costume, giving his terminal illness the middle finger.

Eve glanced at Dr. Wilde, then down at her father when he pulled up beside her in his wheelchair and reached for her hand to give it a quick squeeze.

"Nora and Reid asked if I'd come in," he explained.

Reid cleared his throat, drawing Eve's attention back toward the front of the room. "As many of you know, Nora and I have been seeing each other for some time now. I've fallen in love with her, with her son, and I want to make things official."

Nora's wide smile was infectious. Eve found herself grinning, knowing what was coming. She clasped her hands in front of her mouth, mostly to prevent people from seeing her chin quiver. She was so emotional lately.

"I've asked Nora to marry me." Cheers erupted in the room. "I've also asked to adopt her son," Reid went on. Wrapping an arm around Nora's waist, he pulled her flush against his side. "She said yes and we plan to be married on Thanksgiving right here on the Winchester estate."

A burst of applause, and congratulations filled the room. Grace squealed and headed for the happy couple. Eve looked down at her father, who had actually teared up. Apparently she wasn't the only one with high emotions lately.

"You didn't know?" Eve asked.

"I had an idea. She asked if she could host a family gathering on Thanksgiving and I told her that would be great and just what the family needed."

Eve gestured to Lucinda, who was standing behind the wheelchair. "One of us will take him back in a bit. Go mingle."

With a simple nod, Lucinda made her way toward Josh. Eve gripped the chair and pushed her father toward Reid and Nora. Once Nora spotted their dad, she rushed forward, arms wide.

"I hope this is okay, Dad." She threw her arms around him before leaning back to search his face. "I wanted to surprise everyone, to ease some of the tension this family has been dealing with from the trouble with the Newports and your illness."

At the mention of the Newports, Eve searched for Graham, but couldn't find him. Surely he hadn't left. He wouldn't. Somewhere he was waiting for his chance to get her alone again.

"This is perfect, Nora," their father said. "I'm so happy for you guys and having the wedding here is an excellent idea."

Nora straightened and said to Eve, "I hope you'll stand up by my side."

Eve hugged her sister. "I wouldn't be anywhere else."

When Nora pulled away, she looked toward Eve's flat stomach, then back up into her eyes. "Everything okay?"

Eve simply nodded, not wanting to get into this now.

Dread filled her. No, she couldn't get into this now, or even an hour from now. This night belonged to Nora and Reid. The baby news would definitely have to wait, but for how long? As much as Eve would love to shield her child from the fallout, she knew she'd have to just tell her family and not worry about the timing. But telling them right now was definitely out of the question.

Stealing the night from Nora and Reid wasn't right.

A flash from the corner of her eye had her turning. The man in the striking Mardi Gras mask moved toward her. There was no way Graham could get this close to her family. He wouldn't purposely give away his identity, but still the idea of him getting within talking distance had Eve excusing herself from her sisters and father.

"You need to go," she whispered as she walked by him.

Eve kept walking, knowing he was right behind her. When they reached the foyer, Eve smiled at one of Nora's friends who was heading down the hall toward the bathroom.

Once the foyer was empty, Graham lifted his mask to rest it on the top of his head. With his back to the rest of the house, he stared down at her. He wasn't too concerned about the risk of being seen, not with the way he was standing.

"I can't tell them," Eve murmured. "Not tonight."

She hated this. Hated that such an innocent child, a child she loved with all her heart, was being kept a secret like there was something…dirty. A child should be celebrated, not hidden.

Graham's hands slid up her bare arms, his fingers curled over her shoulders. "I know."

He pulled her into his embrace and Eve willingly went. She hated leaning on anyone, but right now, they were a team, whether either of them wanted to admit it or not. And she had to admit, having Graham's arms around her felt…right. But that couldn't be. Nothing about having him here, let alone his embracing her as if he cared, was right. This affair had started as a whirlwind and they were caught up, that's all. There could be nothing more.

"Let's go away," he whispered into her ear. "We'll go to my cabin in Tennessee for a few days and relax.

Nothing will bother us, you can rest, and we can figure out a plan that will work for our child and our families."

Was that even possible? She'd give anything to be able to escape for a few days, to come to terms with everything and figure out a way to work with Graham. But if she went away with him, she knew what that meant...there would be more of what had transpired in the pool house.

Eve sighed and pulled back. "My mind is all over the place." She glanced over his shoulder to make sure they were still alone. "Let's go out onto the porch."

Once they were outside, she led him down to where the lights weren't shining right on them. The chilly air hit her hard and Graham instantly took off his black jacket and draped it around her shoulders. His familiar woodsy scent hit her, and the warmth from the jacket where it had hugged his body was just like having his arms around her.

"I keep battling myself where you're concerned," she went on, gripping the lapels closer together. "I want to keep my distance physically, but then I see you and—"

"I don't even have to see you to want you."

"Graham, we have to think of what's best here."

"I am." He leaned in closer, crowding her against the side of the house. "Right now, I'm thinking that escaping for a few days is exactly what we need. We would have time to talk without interruptions. I can fly the helicopter and nobody would have to know where you and I went. We'll both just say we're away on business."

Eve closed her eyes, giving the idea more thought than she probably should. "You make this seem so simple."

"Say the word and I'll make sure it's simple," he

whispered against her mouth. "All you'll have to do is pack a bag."

There was a reason Graham was one of the top lawyers in Chicago. The man could persuade anyone with that charm of his. He made his case so perfectly, so convincingly. Eve opened her eyes, meeting his bright blue stare.

"When do we leave?"

"You're leaving when?"

Graham held the phone between his shoulder and his ear. "Tonight."

Brooks laughed on the other end of the line. "Who is she?"

After placing a perfectly folded pair of jeans in his carry-on bag, Graham stood straight up and gripped the phone. "I said it was work related."

"We pretty much have the same mind and I know this urgency in your tone has nothing to do with work."

Hell, yeah, he was urgent to get Eve alone in his cabin. The obvious reason of privacy aside, Eve needed rest, she needed to relax and not worry about telling her family she was expecting. Now that Nora knew, Graham prayed she was too focused on her engagement to discuss Eve's condition. Graham had to trust her to keep her word. Plus, he had an engagement of his own to worry about. He wanted to get that ring on Eve's finger, and he'd use this trip to advance his case.

"I have a pressing matter that needs my attention," Graham said to his twin. "I'll only be gone three days."

"And this has to do with what case?" Brooks asked in a mocking tone.

"You know I can't discuss my client cases with you." Totally true. "Besides, I need to finish packing, so this conversation is over. Unless there's an emergency, don't contact me and I'll let you know when I get home."

"If I find out our father's name I'll sure as hell be calling you and you'll have to put your mystery woman on hold."

"If you find out our father's name, I'll be back," Graham promised.

"Wait…tell me you're not sneaking out of town with Eve. I thought you were done messing with her."

Graham turned toward his walk-in closet to grab some shirts. "I'm not messing around with anyone."

It was only partly a lie. Because he wasn't messing with her. He was the father of her child. That went well beyond messing.

"You're lying, but I'll let you off the hook because I'm on my way to meet Roman. He thinks he has a lead. I'll keep you posted."

"This late?" Graham asked.

"He texted me right before you called, so whatever he wants, it must be something important."

Excitement filled Graham as the possibilities swirled through his head. "Did he say what the lead was?"

"No. And he said it was minor, but at this point we're going to explore any option we have."

Graham would love nothing more than to find their biological father. Then maybe Brooks's vendetta against Sutton would ease up a bit and the tension would ease between their families. But that was doubtful, especially when Sutton discovered Eve was pregnant.

"Keep me posted," Graham told his brother before hanging up.

After tossing in the rest of his belongings, Graham zipped up the bag. He couldn't wait to get Eve to the cabin. She could take long bubble baths in the garden tub in the master suite that overlooked the mountains and just relax. He would make sure of it. He'd already called one of his staff members to have certain foods stocked. Eve wouldn't want for a thing these next few days.

The only look he wanted to see on her face was happiness. She was still so early in her pregnancy, and his goal was to get her to take her mind off her troubles because he knew she was worried.

Which left the question he'd had on his mind for days. What did Nora mean when she'd mentioned Eve's previous pregnancy? Graham didn't want to dredge up bad memories for her, but he also felt he deserved to know.

These three days could bring anything their way. But one thing was for sure: Graham wasn't going to let her get away without convincing her to marry him. This child would be a Newport. Added to that, merging the families in such a bold way would show everyone just how serious they were about ending this feud. But time was running out and Graham needed to act fast.

He grabbed his things and set the security alarm on his penthouse. After he swung by to pick up Eve, they'd be on their way to his cabin. Nothing would stop him from putting that ring on her finger. He may not have been looking for a family, but there was no way in hell another man would raise his child. And he'd yet to find anyone as compatible as Eve. No, they weren't in love, but what did that have to do with marriages these days anyway? Being an attorney, he'd seen the aftermath when people entered into holy matrimony solely on the basis of love. *No thank you.*

Graham was confident that by the end of this trip, he'd have Eve convinced this was the best decision for everyone. He knew what to say, how to get her to see his side. After all, he'd gotten her to agree to this trip in no time.

A little seduction, a little charm and she'd have that ring on her finger.

Fifteen

Fifteen

A cabin? Who referred to a sprawling five-thousand-square-foot log home as a cabin?

Being the real estate guru she was, Eve nearly laughed when she saw Graham's home away from home. The place was stunning and she hadn't even walked in the front door yet. It was after midnight, so she couldn't see the views. But the old lantern-style lights on the porch illuminated a beautiful facade and had her anxious to see the inside.

"I've got your bag."

Eve stood at the bottom of the stone steps leading up to the entrance. She'd forgotten all about her things once Graham had opened her car door and she'd seen the beauty of this place. All she wanted to do was take in each and every detail because she knew she'd never be back. She couldn't wait for sunrise. She'd bet money the views were spectacular.

"Ready to go inside?" he asked.

Eve blinked, glancing over at him. He held both bags and offered her a smile she knew she wouldn't be able to resist later.

Was she ready to go in? Was she ready to spend three days with a man she was falling for? Was she ready to let him fully into her life, into her heart? She'd made the decision last night after the party to come clean about her feelings. Graham needed to know. There could be no secrets between them, not if she wanted a chance at making this work.

"I'm ready," she told him.

The wide porch had sturdy wooden swings at each end that swayed in the gentle breeze. The warmer temperature here seemed so inviting and Eve already made mental plans to take advantage of those swings. She'd come to relax and she intended to do just that.

"I have the refrigerator stocked with your favorite foods," Graham told her as he set the bags at his feet so he could unlock the door. "I did a search on foods you couldn't have while pregnant, so no swordfish for you."

Eve laughed. "And here I was hoping you'd show me what you could do in the kitchen with swordfish."

That got a chuckle out of him. "I have something else planned for our meals."

The way he threw a sultry look over his shoulder told her he had more than dinner planned…not that she didn't know that already. Even after being with him so many times, she still anticipated their three days together. Something about being here, being so isolated from the outside, plus being so far from their families, seemed even more intimate. Yes, they were still sneaking, but for the next three days, they could be themselves.

Eve stopped short before she could enter the house.

After all they'd been through, this would be the first time they actually slept together. They'd both been careful about not sleeping over—that would've been another level they hadn't discussed. But here, she had to assume they were sharing a room.

Maybe not, though. Maybe he'd put her stuff in a guest room. If that were the case, then the feelings she wanted to reveal would be a moot point.

Eve knew one thing. By the end of this trip, they were going to have to have some serious plans laid out because she couldn't handle this emotional upheaval anymore.

The second Graham swung the old oak door open, Eve gasped. The open floor plan gave an immediate view all the way through the house. But that wasn't the extraordinary part. The opposite wall was nothing but a showcase of floor-to-ceiling windows overlooking the mountains and valleys. The lights dotting the landscape were so sporadic, so different from Chicago. There was space to breathe here, nature to explore. This was exactly the escape she needed from the city, from the chaos in her life.

As if pulled toward the beauty, Eve slowly crossed the open space. "Whatever you paid for this place was worth it."

Graham laughed as she passed him. "I had the same reaction when I first opened the door, too. I knew the asking price was high, but the second I saw that view, I knew this place would be mine."

Eve threw a glance over her shoulder. "And is that how things normally work for you? You see something you want and take it?"

He let the bags he was carrying fall to the floor with a thunk. "Always."

The intensity of his stare combined with his instant response had Eve turning back toward the million-dollar view. She already knew Graham was a go-getter; it was one of the qualities she found most attractive in him.

The way he'd been protective of her feelings, of her emotions during the party earlier had sealed the deal, though. She'd gone and fallen for Graham Newport, father of her child. Even if the baby didn't exist, Eve wouldn't have been able to stop herself.

But they *had* created a child.

A flashback to a time during her previous pregnancy when her belly had been slightly rounded hit Eve as she placed a hand over her stomach. She longed to feel a baby move beneath her palm, wanted to know there was a healthy child thriving inside of her.

Hands slid over her shoulders. "What are you thinking?"

Eve leaned back against Graham's firm chest. Did she open up to him? Did she fully let him in? If she wanted a chance at this, then yes. But not right now. She didn't want to start these relaxing days by dumping the darkest memories of her life right in his lap.

"Something to be saved for another time," she told him.

One of his hands came down to slide over hers. "No worrying. Remember?"

"I'm trying."

Graham spun her around, framed her face and kissed her softly. "Why don't you look around and I'll work on getting something to eat? I know you barely ate at the party."

She had picked at the appetizers, but then the encounter in the pool house had happened, then Reid and Nora's announcement and, well…here she was.

"More of your hidden kitchen talents?" she asked with a grin. "I am definitely on board with that."

"Then you're going to love these next few days. I plan on cooking for you every chance I get. I want a healthy baby, so I'm making sure his mama is cared for."

A healthy child. What she wouldn't give for that.

"You're going to spoil me and I won't want to leave."

Graham nipped once more at her lips. "That's the idea."

What? Did he mean…

Graham let go and went back to grab the bags. He headed up the stairs, leaving her staring after him as if he hadn't just dropped some veiled hint in her lap. Did he want to have her here longer than three days? Did he see their relationship as something more than physical? As something more than just sharing custody?

Hope blossomed inside her. Maybe this trip would be a turning point. Maybe letting him know exactly how she felt was just what they needed to move forward into a life together.

Graham froze at the edge of the couch where Eve lay on her side sleeping. He'd watched her from the kitchen as he cooked. She'd been sitting there reading a pregnancy magazine, then she'd stretched her feet out across the cushions. Now she was down for the count and the magazine had fallen to the floor.

Guilt slid through him. The ring he'd bought a week ago was in his room. He wanted to wait for the right moment to bring it out, to tell her he wanted their child to have his name.

They'd started out so hot for each other, and that hadn't changed. But the second Graham knew there was a child, he wasn't about to let anyone else get near what was his. This baby would have his name, no matter how he had to go about it.

But Eve's underlying defenselessness kept working its way further under his skin. When he wasn't with her, he was thinking about her—when he was with her, he didn't want to leave. He had never wanted a woman in his life permanently. Being married to his job was hard enough, but to try to sustain a relationship was damn near impossible.

For the first time in his life, Graham thought he actually wanted to try. Maybe he'd lost his mind. Perhaps he'd never had a chance where she was concerned. But no matter the reasoning or the path that led them here, Graham was tired of fighting this battle with himself.

Having Eve in his cabin, knowing she'd instantly loved this place the way he had only made him realize just how much they had in common.

He'd convinced her to come here immediately after the party. Maybe he should have waited until morning, but he was so afraid she'd start thinking and change her mind. So he'd whisked her off when she was exhausted. Sleep was exactly what she needed, and once she woke, they could start talking, planning.

Graham pulled the crocheted throw off the back of the sofa and placed it over Eve. Gerty had made this throw, and several other little items around the cabin. He'd wanted a piece of his past to be here. He'd wanted to hold on to the woman who had helped raise him and shape him into the man he was today.

Looking down on Eve's relaxed face, Graham couldn't help but wonder what Gerty would think of her. What would his mother think? No doubt both women would adore Eve. She was so easy to talk to. She may be president of one of the top real estate companies in

Chicago, but it was her charm, her charisma and her determination that would keep her on top.

Sutton didn't deserve a daughter so perfect. He didn't deserve her loyalty. Sutton had used Graham's mother, not bothering to care what happened to her because he had his wife to go back to when he was done.

Graham hated Sutton more and more each time he thought of how easy it had been for the mogul to end things with Cynthia. She'd been pregnant, not that Sutton had stuck around to find out. She'd already had twins at home and was expecting another child. With the income from waitressing, there was no way she could have survived on her own...or been able to pay for an attorney if she were threatened with a custody battle. And she hadn't taken a dime from him for fear he'd sue for custody. She wouldn't have been able to battle Sutton in court.

Graham didn't blame his mother one bit for not telling the tycoon.

Gerty had seriously been the biggest blessing in all of their lives.

Eve reminded Graham so much of his grandma. Both women were strong. They both clung to their determination to get them through rough times. And they were both stubborn to a fault.

Graham took a seat in the leather chair, propped his feet on the ottoman and laced his hands over his abs. He was perfectly content to watch Eve rest. This is exactly what he wanted her to do.

Now he just had to figure out what he really wanted. Asking her to marry him may give her false hope. But on the other hand, he wasn't so sure his goals in marrying her were quite the same as they once were.

There was no denying that when she woke up, and

once they started talking, the dynamics between them would change.

Graham just had to keep the upper hand and decide how much their lives were about to be altered.

Sixteen

Eve woke to blackness. There wasn't a single light on in the room. Where was she? She blinked a few times, sat up and quickly remembered. She'd fallen asleep on the couch in Graham's cabin.

The slightest glow from the porch lights filtered in through the windows. Eve sat up, turning her stiff neck from side to side. She didn't even recall lying down. She'd started reading a magazine, had gotten swept up by some article on how to make your own baby food, and that was the last thing she remembered.

Turning, Eve went still when she spotted Graham asleep in the chair across from her. His feet were propped on the oversize ottoman, his head tipped to one side. She wished there was more light so she could make out his facial features. Was he fully relaxed? When he'd fallen asleep in her bed, he always had those worry lines between his brows. Now that he was away, did he allow himself to completely let go?

Eve pulled at the throw caught around her legs. She hadn't put that there. An image of Graham covering her had a warmth spreading through her. The little ways he showed he cared couldn't be ignored. The way he cooked for her, opened up about his mother and Gerty, swept her away when life became too much…he was putting her needs first and she couldn't deny the tug on her heart.

Part of Eve wished they could just stay here forever. Ignore their families, ignore the entire mess with Sutton, Carson and the investigator Brooks had hired. Ignore the reality that her father was dying, that her sister was marrying the love of her life and everything was perfect for her. The entire family was thrilled for Nora, and Eve was, too. But there was still that fear that once everyone knew of Eve's pregnancy, she'd never be shown support. That she wouldn't experience such happiness. Her family wouldn't accept the fact that Graham was the father, and worse yet, that Eve had fallen for him.

Eve got to her feet, shaking out the throw. Moving around the ottoman, she started to lay the blanket over Graham. Instantly he gripped her wrist and pulled her down into his lap.

With a yelp, she fell right into the crook of his arm, her head to his shoulder.

"I thought you were asleep."

Graham adjusted her legs to settle them between his. "You thought wrong."

That low rumble vibrated from his chest. His fingertips trailed up her bare forearm. "How do you feel now?"

"Like I slept for days."

"Good. I want you to feel rejuvenated."

Eve relaxed fully against him. "I'm sorry I fell asleep when you were cooking. Did I ruin everything?"

"We can heat it back up whenever. It was late. You needed rest."

His fingertips continued to trail up and down her arm. When she shivered, Graham took the twisted blanket and gave it a flick to send it soaring out over their legs. He wrapped her tighter, in the blanket and his arms. Eve wasn't sure if this was some euphoric state from sleep or if this was really happening. Were they… snuggling? He wasn't trying to get her undressed, she wasn't straddling him and ripping his shirt off. They were just…doing nothing and it felt rather amazing.

"As much as I want you to relax and take it easy, I want to know something."

Eve stilled. "What?"

"About your first pregnancy."

Eve closed her eyes. She'd known the questions would be coming, and he deserved to know. He'd given her time to prepare and hadn't immediately asked when Nora spilled the secret the other day.

Eve was ready to tell him now—*needed* to tell him. There was still a part of her that had to heal before she could move on. Not that she could fully recover from the loss of a child, but talking about the pain with the man she'd fallen in love with would go a long way to preparing her for the next chapter of her life.

"I was in love once," she started, then realized that wasn't the right thing to say. "Actually, I thought I was in love, but I had just been blindsided by lust and charm."

Graham remained silent, but kept his firm hold on her. She appreciated the darkened room, the fact she didn't have to look him in the eye when she was telling him about this portion of her life. There was a deeper intimacy about letting him in this way.

"I met Rick in college," she went on. "The attraction was instant. We dated for six months. I thought he was the one."

The words sounded so cold, so lifeless when she said them, but there was no other way to tell this story. That period of her life was gone and she was only left with the emotional scars.

"I found out I was pregnant." She'd never forget how happy she was to tell Rick. "I thought we'd marry, raise our family and live happily ever after." Eve pulled in a breath, toyed with the edging on the crocheted blanket. "When I told him I was pregnant, he was done with me. Apparently he was interested in being married to Sutton's daughter, but not so much in having a child. No, wait. He was more interested in being married to money. I was nothing."

"I want to kill him."

Eve smiled. "I appreciate the offer, but he married into money, then his wife cheated on him with the pool boy. Clichéd, but I did a small victory dance."

Graham chuckled, squeezing her tighter. "I had no idea you had such a ruthless side. Remind me never to cheat on you with the pool boy."

Smacking his arm, Eve continued. "Anyway, I was about six weeks pregnant then. I was scared, but my family was so supportive. I knew I'd be okay. Losing the baby never even entered my mind. Not once."

Graham slid his hand over hers, their fingers lacing over her stomach. That silent supportive gesture had tears burning her eyes.

"Nora, Grace and I had already picked out names," Eve whispered, her throat full of emotions. "I knew I wanted the nursery decorated in gray and yellow no matter what the sex of the baby was. When I was seventeen weeks, I went in for an ultrasound. The doctor's office had a new machine, one that had top-of-the-line imaging. I was so excited to see that little face, to find out what I was having."

When her voice broke, Eve bit her lip. She wanted to hold it together. She wanted to show Graham that she was strong, but all those past emotions threatened to strangle her and end this conversation. Tremors racked her body as her eyes filled. There was no stopping the wave of memories and feelings as she relived the horrid day.

"Eve, don't—"

"No. I've come this far and you need to know." On a shaky breath, she continued, "The tech kept searching the screen and moving the device over my stomach almost frantically, and I knew something was wrong. Her face wasn't bright like when I'd first come in. At one point she excused herself and stepped out into the hall to ask someone to find the doctor. I knew. In my heart I knew something was wrong with my baby."

"What happened?"

"In simple terms, the cord came away from the amniotic sac. I don't know how far along I was when that happened. The doctor said my body still thought I was pregnant, so my uterus was still stretching." Eve sniffed, wiped at the tears on her cheeks. "I could've lost the baby a month earlier or I could've lost her that day. I honestly don't know. But I know I never want to live through that again. I can't."

"Oh, baby." Graham kissed the top of her head. "I don't even know what to say."

"Nothing can be said," she said. "People told me how sorry they were. They tried to say the right thing, but there isn't a right thing. I lost a piece of myself that day and the following days are a blur. I will never know that face. That's all I kept thinking. What did she look like?"

"She?"

Eve shrugged. "I don't know. I didn't ask. They had to perform a D&C the next day to remove all the tissue. I was getting prepped for surgery, wondering how things had gone from the highest mountain to the deepest pit I'd ever known, when the nurse had me sign a paper. It was a paper stating I gave them permission to dispose of any remains. *Dispose of.*"

"Eve, stop, please."

Tears slid down her face. "How could I sign a paper saying that was okay?" she asked, ignoring his plea. "This was my baby. I know I wasn't far enough along to have a funeral, but the wording was just so cold, so heartless. I'll never forget it."

Graham reached a hand up to wipe her wet cheeks, then smoothed her hair away from her face. "No more. Don't do this to yourself. I'm such a jerk for asking, but I thought I deserved to know. I should've thought of your feelings."

"No." Eve shifted in his arms to face him. "You did deserve to know. I wanted to tell you, but I didn't want to kill our mood here. I want you to know everything about me."

"I don't want you hurt," he murmured against her lips. "I can't stand it, Eve. Never again will you hurt like that."

Reaching up to cup his face, Eve tipped her head back. "I hope I don't. I hope this baby is delivered full-term and healthy. I'm so afraid of how my family will react, how your brothers will take the news. I can handle quite a bit, but I won't let our child be in the cross fire."

Graham slid his thumb along her bottom lip. "Nobody will harm you or our child so long as I'm in the picture."

"And how long will that be?" she dared to ask.

In lieu of an answer, Graham kissed her gently. Eve instantly opened to him. He never had to ask, never had to persuade her. She was always ready for more contact, more of anything that had to do with Graham. He'd listened to her, he'd hurt for her and he was trying to make her forget if only for a short time.

When his hand trailed down to the hem of her shirt, she shifted. Without words, without the usual rush and frenzy, they were undressed and somehow ended up settled right back in the chair.

Eve rested a knee on either side of Graham's hips. "I love you."

She didn't mean to let loose with the words, but there was no holding them back.

"Eve—"

"No." She held a finger to his lips. "I don't need anything said in return. I've been completely open with you tonight and I wanted to get it all out. I needed to. Now show me how you were going to make me forget the rest of the world."

Graham couldn't get those words out of his mind. She loved him. Loved. Him.

No other woman, save for his mother and Gerty, had ever uttered those words to him before. He wasn't sure what to do, what to say. Had she not cut him off, what would've come out of his mouth in reply?

As he put breakfast together the following morning, Graham tried to pull himself together. This was what he'd been waiting for. She'd fallen in love with him and now all he had to do was make this relationship more official.

But after all she'd shared before her declaration of

love, he didn't feel right about using her state of vulnerability to complete his plan. He needed to see what happened today, when they could talk more, explore the area together and just be themselves. Maybe...

What? Nothing had changed. He still wanted this child to have his name.

His cell vibrated on the counter. Brooks's name lit up the screen. Graham slid the casserole into the oven and answered his phone.

"Hello."

"Roman has a major lead. He thinks he has a name, but he's going to make a quick trip before he tells us to be sure."

Could this be it? After all this time could they have found their father?

Since Eve was still in bed where he'd left her, Graham put his phone on speaker so he could start cutting up the fruit.

"How soon will we know?" Graham asked, pulling out various bags of produce from the refrigerator.

"He's heading there today. Hopefully soon."

Graham slid a knife from the block on the counter. "I'm going to be nervous all day."

"Me, too," his brother said. "You ready to tell me where you are?"

"I'm at the cabin."

Brooks made a humming sound, one that mocked Graham and made him sorry he'd even admitted that much.

"With?" Brooks asked.

"None of your concern."

"It's my concern if you're sleeping with our enemy's daughter."

Graham glanced over his shoulder, thankful to see

the living area still empty, which meant she was still in bed. "I'm with Eve, yes. But—"

"What the hell, man? What are you thinking?"

Graham didn't get a chance to reply before his brother went on. "Are you using her to try to get to Sutton?"

Graham slid the knife through the mango. "No. I wouldn't do that to her."

"Then what are you doing?"

Graham swallowed, deciding now was as good a time as any to come clean. "We're having a baby."

The explosion of cussing had Graham dropping the knife to the counter and taking the phone off speaker. "Calm the hell down," he barked.

"How long have you known and how could you keep something like this from me?" Brooks demanded.

"We kept our personal lives from everyone," Graham explained, leaning against the counter. "Between you, Carson and her family, we just wanted—"

"What? To mess around and not get caught?"

Basically.

"How'd that work out for you?"

Graham raked a hand through his bed head. "Listen, we're figuring things out and we needed to get away from the city."

"Sutton is not going to like this."

"No, he's not, but there's nothing that can change the fact." Graham stared at the stairs to the second floor, wondering how long she would sleep in. "I'm going to ask her to marry me."

"Are you a complete moron?" Brooks yelled. "Can you just slow down and think this through?"

"I have." Graham turned around and checked the casserole in the oven. "This baby is a Newport and will be raised as such. I'll do anything to make sure my child has my last name."

"So you love her?"

Graham shut the oven door again. "Love has nothing to do with it. The baby is what I'm concerned with."

When he turned back around, he froze. Eve stood on the other side of the kitchen island. All color had drained from her face as she clutched her silk robe together. The hurt in her eyes gutted him. He'd promised her no more pain, but he'd delivered a hell of a punch.

"I'll call you later," he told Brooks, ending the call without waiting for his brother's reply.

"Don't make excuses for what I wasn't supposed to hear," she told him, tipping her chin. "I'm flattered you want to marry me, but I think I'll decline. You see, I already made a fool of myself for one man I conceived a child with. I don't intend to do so again."

Graham started to step forward, but when she held up a hand and squared her shoulders, he stopped. The sheen in her eyes, the fact that she was fighting back tears, told him he'd completely ruined everything.

But he wasn't going down without a fight.

"Marriage isn't a terrible idea, Eve."

"For us? It's a terrible idea."

"Why?"

Crossing her arms over her chest, she pursed her lips as if choosing her next words carefully. Damn, she looked beautiful this morning. With her tousled hair, bright eyes, face devoid of any makeup, Eve was stunning. And she was pulling away. He couldn't let her end what he'd worked so hard to complete.

"I told you I loved you," she started, blinking away the tears. "I meant it. I didn't expect the words in return if you weren't feeling the same way. I understand.

But to know you only want to marry me because of our baby, it's just so archaic. Did you think I'd keep your child from you?"

Graham didn't care what she wanted. He took a step toward her. "I didn't know what would happen, Eve. All I know is I'm going to be a father and I can't miss that. I can't."

Emotions he hadn't fully grasped came rushing at him. "I grew up without a father," he went on, still slowly closing the gap between them. "I've wondered for the past thirty-two years who my dad is, if he wanted me, if he even knows I exist. It's an empty void that I may never fill."

He stood so close now, Eve tipped her head back to look up into his eyes. The need for her understanding was so great, he had to find the right words. Any charm or wit he normally used to get his way wasn't possible here. All he could do was hope for the best when he opened up with complete and total honesty.

"Do you understand what I'm saying?" he asked. "I can't let my child grow up without me. I don't want another man raising what's mine."

Eve's jaw clenched as she closed her eyes and pulled in a breath. "Do I look like I have men lined up outside my door?" she finally asked, glaring back at him. "Apparently you don't know me at all. And all I hear is how you want to give this child a name and treat him or her like your property. That's not how this works and that sure as hell isn't how a marriage should work."

"Eve—"

"No."

She backed away and held out both hands. Just as she did, she started to sway. Graham reached for her, but she pushed him away. She held her stomach with one hand and covered her mouth with the other. Alarmed, he waited to make sure she wasn't going to get sick or pass out. He was a complete ass for…well, everything. He remained close, though, in case she needed him. Not that she'd take his help now.

Moments later she pulled herself together and smoothed her hair from her face. "I'm going back to Chicago as soon as I call my pilot to come get me. Elite has a private helicopter at our disposal."

"I'll take you."

She was going. There was no stopping her. She'd erected walls he couldn't penetrate, not when she was so angry, so hurt. But he'd continue to chip away because he wasn't lying. There was no way he'd let his child grow up without a father.

"I'd rather call my pilot," she told him.

Eve turned on her heel and headed toward the stairs. Graham couldn't take his eyes off her. He silently pleaded for her to understand where he was coming from, why he was so adamant about marriage.

With her hand on the post, she turned to look over her shoulder. "You know what's sad? I thought you brought me here because you cared about me. I was naive enough to think you might have stronger feelings for me, that you wanted to get closer to me. Not because I was pregnant, but because of me."

Graham couldn't breathe, couldn't move.

Eve dropped her head between her shoulders, her grip tightening on the post. "You were using me all this time. I should've listened to my family when they first told me to stay away from you. But I defended you."

Now she turned to face him, her cheeks pink from tears, from anger. Graham hated himself at that moment. He hated the way he'd portrayed himself, the way he'd let her down when he'd promised that no one would hurt her again. He'd destroyed her. Destroyed the light in her eyes, the smile she so freely gave.

"I won't keep you from your child." Her voice shook, her chin quivered. "But I won't marry you, and from here on out, we're nothing to each other."

Without another word, she went up the stairs. Graham listened as the bedroom door clicked shut. The gentle sound seemed to echo through the spacious house. It symbolized everything that had just happened. She'd put a barrier between them, and as he stood on the outside, he couldn't help but wonder how the hell he could ever fix this.

Seventeen

When he left her alone to pack, and then leave the cabin, Eve was even more hurt. She shouldn't have been surprised, but she was. He'd given up. Clearly he only wanted the child and she was an absolute fool to have believed otherwise.

But what hurt the most was that she still loved him. Well, she loved the man she thought he was. He'd been so caring, so amazing these past couple of weeks, but one overheard phone call had revealed the truth.

Eve had been home only a day, but she'd called her sisters and her father for a family meeting. Dr. Wilde had told Eve that Sutton was resting, but he was having a good day and to come on by. Grace and Nora were meeting Eve at the Winchester estate.

As Eve stood outside the front door, she fought back her nerves. Had it only been two nights since she was here for a party? A party announcing her sister's engagement. A party Graham had crashed, and then he'd taken her...

No. There would be no more thinking along those lines. Whatever they'd shared in the past was best left there. Their affair had started out so fast, so intense, there was no way it could've lasted or even morphed into something with deeper meaning. Eve cursed herself for getting so caught up in romanticizing the secret of it all.

Gathering up her courage, she let herself in and headed straight to her father's study. Grace and Nora were already there. Grace adjusted the throw on her father's legs and Nora glanced up, catching Eve's eye. A soft smile from her sister was all Eve needed to get through this. Having Nora here was a huge help since she already knew.

Grace glanced up when Eve shut the door. "Is everything okay?" she asked. "You sounded strange on the phone."

Eve met her father's questioning eyes. "I'm fine, but I have something I need to tell you all."

Grace straightened, taking hold of their father's hand. "You're scaring me. Are you sick, too?"

"What? No." She hadn't meant to scare them. "I'm pregnant."

Silence. Not a word was said as her sisters and father just stared back at her.

"I'm at seven weeks," she went on, in a rush to fill the dead air. "The doctor has assured me that everything looks great, but I'm scared." There, she'd said it. "I need your help and support, no judgment, please. I can't deal with it right now."

"Because Graham is the father?" Grace asked.

Eve bit her lip in an attempt to battle back the emotions. Afraid to speak, she merely nodded.

"He didn't say a word when he was here the other day," her father chimed in. "Does he know?"

Eve moved farther into the room. "What? He was here?"

"With Brooks and Carson."

Eve's mind spun. He'd been to see her father and hadn't said a word. The betrayals kept on coming. He'd been sleeping with her, telling her everything she wanted to know, but sneaking to see her father behind her back.

"Was he pressuring you?" Eve demanded as she eased a hip onto the side of the bed.

"I actually invited Carson here," he stated. "I wanted a chance to tell him I'm sorry, to see if there was a possibility of connecting now that I know for sure he's my son. I didn't want to die without him knowing that I loved his mother, that I would've fought had I known he existed."

Eve listened as her father exposed his emotions. She'd never heard him this passionate about anything other than business. Sutton Winchester was one of the most prominent, powerful men in Chicago and he'd been deprived of raising his own child.

Was that truly what Graham had thought she'd do? Had she ever indicated she'd be so heartless? He'd been determined to marry her, so much so he'd swept her away on a trip away from everything she knew. She'd been easily swayed because she honestly thought he cared about her, when in reality he was softening her, getting her to fall for him, all so he could convince her to marry him.

"Wait, has he pushed you away?" Grace asked.

"No." Eve took her father's other hand. "He...it's complicated. I don't want to go into the details, but—"

"Complicated? You two were on the same page when I saw you the other morning."

Eve glanced at Nora, who had pulled up a chair by their father's bed. Grace and Sutton both turned to Nora.

"She knew?" Grace asked.

Nora shrugged, sending Eve an apologetic glance. "I happened to stop by her house when Graham was there making breakfast for her."

"Things have changed since then," Eve explained. "All I need right now is for you guys to know I won't let Elite down. I'm 100 percent committed to the company and—"

"This baby comes before any company."

Eve stilled at her father's words. He'd never said anything like that. He was loyal to his family, yes, but he always put business first. Always.

"I can handle both," she assured him.

"I'm sure you can." He turned his hand over and held on to hers. "But I want a healthy grandbaby. I want you to take care of yourself. We have enough staff that can assist you, so put some of the burden on them. That's my greatest regret—not having been there more for my kids."

Eve glanced to her sisters, who had both started tearing up.

"When you're faced with the end, you start thinking about the beginning," he went on. "And if I could go back, I'd definitely put some work off onto my assistants so I could be with you all more. Learn from my mistakes, Eve. Take care of yourself."

"That's what I've been telling her."

Eve jerked at the familiar voice behind her. Graham stood in the doorway with the butler right behind him.

"I tried to stop him, Mr. Winchester," the poor man explained.

"It's fine," Sutton replied. "Close the door and leave us."

Eve continued to stare at Graham, who hadn't taken his eyes off her. "What are you doing here?" she demanded, coming to her feet. "You can't just barge in here—"

"I can. And I did."

Eve didn't risk looking behind her to her sisters or father. The tension in the room had multiplied, threatening to take over.

"I don't want you here," she told him, pulling her cardigan tighter around her. As if such a simple gesture could keep any more pain from seeping in.

"I realize that." His tone softened as he inched closer. "I know I hurt you, but the moment you left I knew I wasn't finished."

Eve didn't have much energy for a battle. The past forty-eight hours had been hellacious at best.

"Then say what you want to say and get out."

He'd reached her now, but didn't touch her. "I meant I wasn't finished with us."

Eve stared into those striking eyes that had first drawn her in. "There is no us. If that's all, then leave."

"Do you two want to go outside for privacy?" Grace asked from behind Eve.

"No," both Eve and Graham said at the same time.

"I don't care who hears me," he went on, keeping his eyes locked on hers. "When you left yesterday I knew I had to take drastic measures to get you back. So, if I have to make a fool of myself in front of your family, then so be it."

Eve didn't want to hear it, though she wouldn't mind

him looking like a fool considering she'd been played for one.

"I'm not discussing the baby's last name. I know that's all you care about." Eve stepped back because being this close, knowing she still loved him but couldn't touch him was agonizing. "If you'll excuse me, I'm visiting my father."

Eve had just turned away when Graham's soft, "I love you," hit her hard.

Frozen in her steps, she looked to her sisters, her father, to see if she'd heard correctly. And saw three pairs of eyes wide with shock staring back at her. Yeah, he'd said that.

Eve looked back over her shoulder, her heart aching more than she'd ever known possible. "That was cruel," she whispered as tears clogged her throat. "Throwing those words around won't make me marry you."

Graham reached for her, turning her to face him fully. "I'm not proposing. I love you, Eve. I want to be with you. Not for the baby, for you."

If he'd said those words two days ago she'd have believed him. "Revelation has certainly come at a convenient time."

His hands curled around her shoulders as he stepped in closer. Her entire body brushed against his, as if she needed the physical reminder of how much she'd missed his touch.

"Nothing about us has been convenient," he told her. "I didn't want a child, a relationship, but now I can't live without either. I don't want to try. I know I hurt you, I know I destroyed everything we'd started building, but I'm asking for another chance."

Eve couldn't say anything. What was there to say at

this point? He was a shark in the courtroom because he knew the exact thing to say at precisely the right time.

If she even thought he was serious, she'd wrap her arms around him and start fresh. But she knew better. Graham was only looking out for his best interests where the baby was concerned.

"You need to go," she whispered.

The muscle in his jaw clenched as he nodded, dropping his hands from her shoulders. "I'm not giving up, Eve. I love you. I've only had two women in my life who heard those words from me."

His mother and Gerty.

Eve turned away from him and went back to her father's bedside. She listened to Graham's footsteps as he left the room. Once the door was closed behind him, Eve couldn't stop the emotions from washing over her.

"I hate him," she sniffed. "I'm sorry you had to see that."

Her father reached for her, tipping her chin up so she could look him in the eyes. "I'm not sorry at all. I saw a man who loves a woman. I saw a man who stood in the same room as his sworn enemy and didn't give a damn what anyone else thought."

"He's only saying those things because he wants to marry me so the baby will have his name."

"The baby can have his name without marriage," Grace pointed out. "He could fight you for custody in court and probably win, if that's the way he wanted to go about it."

Eve knew all of this. She wasn't stupid, wasn't ignorant when it came to laws. But she had been blindsided and refused to let Graham have another swipe at her.

"I'll agree he didn't go about things the right way,"

her father said, swiping a tear from her face. "But men are fools when they're in love. Most of the time they don't even know it until they've lost someone."

Eve knew her father was referring to Cynthia. There were no secrets about the fact that Eve's parents didn't love each other. Eve fully believed that her father was in love with Graham's mother at one time. But he'd let her go.

"I can't let him back in," she whispered.

"You can't let him out," Nora countered. "He loves you, Eve."

Eve met the eyes of her family. "Are you all defending him?"

Sutton smiled. "I'm just as shocked as you are, but I want my daughter and grandchild to be happy. When I saw the way he looked at you, the way he didn't care how he laid his feelings on the line, I knew he loved you. Any man who is that strong and passionate is exactly what I want for you."

Eve couldn't believe what she was hearing. "You want me to forgive him? Just like that? It's that easy?"

When her fathered smiled, wrinkles formed around his sad eyes. "I want you to follow your heart. I don't believe Graham will give up and that has everything to do with his feelings for you. Grace was right. He could fight you in court, where things would get ugly if he only wanted the child to have his name. I don't think he realized how much he cared for you until you left."

Eve shook her head. "I can't just take him back. Right now, I only want to be here with you guys. I want to visit and laugh and... I don't know. Pick out nursery themes."

"I'm thrilled that's your attitude," Nora said, reaching over to squeeze Eve's shoulder. "This baby will be perfectly healthy and come home to a beautiful room and a family who loves her."

"Her?" their father asked, raising his brows.

"I think Eve is having a girl, too," Grace laughed. "Another Winchester girl? That has a nice ring to it."

Eve didn't care about the sex, she just wanted a healthy baby. Now more than ever, she wanted that happiness in her life. She prayed her father would live long enough to see her child, but the odds were against them.

For now, though, she wouldn't dwell on the sorrow. She'd live in the moment.

Later she'd deal with the ache…and she'd deal with Graham.

Three days had passed since she'd seen Graham… since he'd exposed himself before her family. But he'd texted her. He'd checked on her, asked if she was eating, joked that he'd send over some of the fried apples she loved. He didn't tell her he loved her again, didn't pressure her to meet him or to make a decision regarding this relationship they'd thrown up in the air and left hanging.

He'd genuinely been…well, caring. And she was positive this wasn't some game to him. He wasn't using her. Eve realized that if he'd wanted to use her all along, then he would've tried to use her to get closer to her father. If he was that sure her father held secrets about Graham's past, then he could have easily used his charms and sneaky maneuvers to find out what she knew. Or have her find out what her father knew.

He'd done neither. When they were together, he'd avoided the topic. It had taken Eve two restless, sleepless nights to replay their last seven weeks. There were no red flags, nothing other than an intense affair and unexpected emotions.

Now she stood in the lobby of his building, clutching a photo, more scared than she'd ever been in her life. This was the biggest risk she'd ever taken, but this could also be the greatest thing to ever happen to her.

By the time Eve reached the top floor and stood outside the only door in the hall, she was a little more under control…until the door swung open and Graham stood there in a pair of running shorts, beads of sweat running down his chest.

"Doorman told me you were on your way up," he explained. "I was on the treadmill."

Eve still didn't say anything. Now that she was here, all the speeches she'd rehearsed vanished from her mind. The picture in her hand crinkled, drawing her attention to the reason she needed to gather up that Winchester courage.

"I, um…can I come in?"

Graham stepped back, opening the door wider. The second she passed by him, she was assaulted with that sexy, sweaty, masculine scent. She wanted this to be easy, didn't want a messy reunion…if he'd take her. They'd been through so much already, Eve wasn't even sure a relationship was possible.

Eve crossed the spacious entryway and stepped down into the living area. Her eyes were fixed on the skyline.

"I never got to appreciate the view in Tennessee," she muttered. "I was numb when I left."

When he said nothing, Eve turned, only to find he'd moved in closer behind her.

"I was still numb when I saw you at my dad's house," she went on. "But then I realized you didn't have to be there. You could've let me go, could've waited and fought me."

His intense stare hit her as fiercely as his words. "I'd never fight you, Eve."

"I'm tired," she whispered. "Tired of worrying, tired of questioning and tired of wondering what we're doing."

Graham reached for her, pulling her into his arms. She didn't care that his chest was damp with sweat. All she cared about was that he didn't seem to have changed his mind.

"Put it all on me," he murmured against her ear. "Every fear, every worry, give it to me. I want to be everything for you, Eve."

She eased back, hope spreading through her. "Can our lives be that easy? Can we make this work?"

"I'll do anything to have you in my life, Eve. Anything. Not just the baby, but you." He framed her face with his strong hands. "I've never loved a woman the way I love you. I've never wanted to. But we fit, Eve. We get each other and I can't imagine life without you."

Sliding the black-and-white image between them, she held up the picture for him to see. "This is for you."

Graham took a step back and stared at it. It was a sonogram of their baby. His eyes instantly misted as he slowly reached for the glossy image.

"I didn't think you'd had the appointment yet."

"I called the doctor for a favor." Eve smiled, unable to stop herself as she saw how in love Graham was with this child already. "I wanted to give you this. I wanted you to know that we are both yours if you'll have us. If you can forgive me for doubting you, for doubting us."

His eyes instantly sought hers. "There's nothing to forgive. I'm the one who nearly ruined the greatest thing that's ever happened to me. I won't ask you to marry me. But know that the second you want to, I'm ready."

Eve started to say something, but he held up his hand.

"Because I love you both. I want to build a life with you, raise all the babies you want."

"My father defended you," she told him.

Graham looked shocked. "He did?"

"I know you think he has a secret about your father, but this disease, it's changed him. I—I'll go with you if you want to ask him. He won't lie to me."

Graham pulled her in once more. "I have everything I need right here. I won't put you between your father and me. Besides, Brooks has a lead with the investigator."

Eve pulled back. "That's great."

Graham smiled. "Roman is out now searching and he's pretty sure he has the name we've been searching for."

"Oh, Graham. Are you excited?"

"I am." He kissed the top of her head. "But not nearly as excited as I was the second I knew you were here to see me. Don't leave. Stay with me."

Eve leaned up on her tiptoes to kiss him. "Maybe we should start with a shower and then talk."

Graham set the picture down on the accent table and scooped her up into his arms. "That's the best idea I've ever heard."

* * * * *

BACK IN THE ENEMY'S BED

MICHELLE CELMER

For Mike and Trevor

One

Grace Winchester didn't get nervous.

As the youngest of the Winchester daughters, she may have had a privileged and pampered childhood, but as an adult she was no spoiled heiress. She'd worked damned hard building her fashion-design business, and she was a well-known and respected activist for women's rights. In a world where men dominated, she'd trained herself over the years to believe that there wasn't *anything* she couldn't do.

Okay, so there was *one* thing.

She couldn't say no to her father.

The closest thing to royalty in Chicago, Sutton Lazarus Winchester was not the sort of man who took no for an answer. One stern look from those piercing green eyes and people fell in line. But with all the recent scandal surrounding their family, and Sutton's failing health, lately she could see the worn-away edges on his harsh manner and hoped that he would take pity on her. Just this once, because what he was asking of her was truly her worst nightmare.

"Daddy, I don't want to do this."

Her father, sitting like a king on his throne at his massive teak desk, in his equally massive office in the Winchester estate, didn't even look up from the laptop screen. He'd been ill for months, sometimes barely strong enough to climb out of bed. But today was a good day. He even had some color in his hollow cheeks. "We all do things we don't want to, Princess. It's called life."

She felt herself being reduced to the whining and stubborn adolescent who would stomp her foot and huff when her parents told her no. Which honestly hadn't been all that often. She was the baby of the family, and with a bat of her ultra-long super-dark lashes most everyone gave her what she wanted. But what he was asking her to do now? When he'd said the words, they shook her deep to her core.

Roman Slater is coming to speak to me and I want you here.

Roman Slater, owner of the top private investigation firm in the Midwest, Slater Investigation Services, and the one man on the face of the planet whom Gracie swore never to speak to again. Roman Slater, who'd swept her off her feet and promised to love her forever, then betrayed her and her family in the worst way possible. And not just once, but *two* times.

All of her life people had used Gracie to get to her father, but she'd thought Roman was different. She'd thought he'd truly loved and trusted her. And she had trusted him with not only her family, but her heart.

Big mistake.

"I don't understand why I need to be in the meeting," she told her father, and if she were hoping for an explanation, she didn't get it. Sutton Winchester never justified his demands, or explained himself. He'd never had to.

"You're staying," he said, an edge of impatience in his tone. It was the voice he used when she was pushing her luck.

The reality of the situation began to sink in. In only a few minutes Roman would be standing there, in the flesh, in her father's office. So many mixed feelings buzzed through her brain she felt dizzy and disoriented. Instinct was telling her to run and hide, and though she knew that it wasn't physically possible for her heart to sink, it sure felt as if it had. It was currently somewhere south of her spleen.

Earlier in the day, before her father summoned her home, life had been good. In fact, it had been great. Her new line of purses was flying off the shelves in every boutique in every major city in the United States, and the new fashion app she'd recently created was now on smartphones and tablets all over the world. So other than not having any time for a personal life, and being a tiny bit lonely, she couldn't complain. Now it felt as if her world had been thrown totally off axis.

Why did it have to be her? Couldn't her sister Eve take her place? She was the CEO of the family business, Elite Industries, the multimillion-dollar real estate giant Sutton had founded. The business that Roman had recently, under the direction of Sutton's mortal enemy, Brooks Newport, tried to take down in a scandal of epic proportions.

If there was a competing royal family in Chicago, the Newport brothers, Brooks, Graham and Carson, were it. The Newport brothers were self-made millionaires with axes to grind. Brooks in particular had made it his mission to crush Sutton, run his business into the ground, and ostracize Gracie and her sisters, Nora and Eve. Which had nearly slammed the brakes on the intense love affair between Eve and Graham Newport, Gracie's future brother-in-law.

And Roman had helped him orchestrate the entire media smear campaign against their family. As if he hadn't betrayed her family enough already. Seven years after the first scandal he'd been involved with, in which the Winchesters had been exonerated of any wrongdoing, he was coming back for more. But once again Brooks's outrageous claims had no basis in reality, and in the end had only made the man look like the petty and greedy power-hungry narcissist that he was.

"After all the lies Brooks and Roman spread about us, why take a meeting with Roman at all?" Gracie asked her father. "Have you forgotten the way he dragged our family name through the mud? *Twice!* And the horrible things that they said you did this time?"

If she had been hoping for outrage, she didn't get it. In fact, Sutton didn't so much as bat an eyelash. "I haven't forgotten," he said.

Gracie adored her father, but she wasn't blind to his faults. And he had more than his fair share. He'd lived large most of his life. He was a narcissistic, arrogant, womanizing jerk, who drank, smoked and lived hard, but he would never sink so low as to commit date rape.

And four of the five illegitimate children Brooks had accused him of fathering were a genetic mismatch. Carson, however, had tested positive, proving beyond a shadow of a doubt that he was Sutton's illegitimate son. Gracie and her sisters were still reeling from the news that they had a half brother. Sutton's numerous romantic affairs were no secret. But Gracie had strong suspicions that his relationship with Cynthia Newport had been more than an affair. She knew that her parents' marriage had been one based on financial compatibility more than love, but it still hurt to think that Sutton had been in love with someone other than their mother, Celeste.

But enough already. She was tired of the rumors and conjecture. Sutton was dying and Gracie just wanted him to be able to go in peace.

Not only had the scandal affected Sutton's failing health, but the risk to their company had been profound, and they were in jeopardy of losing several multimillion-dollar accounts if the attacks on Sutton's reputation didn't stop. Eve had managed to keep the company on an even keel, but now that she was pregnant with Graham's baby, things were even more complicated.

And this whole mess was thanks to Roman and what Grace considered to be his less-than-impressive PI skills. When she thought of all the pain he had caused, all the suffering and humiliation he had subjected them to, anger lit a fire in her belly.

She would choose anger over shaky nerves any day.

"What if Brooks sent him here to dig up more dirt?" she said, hoping to talk some sense into her father. "So he can finish the job and destroy our family."

Sutton folded his hands on the desk in front of him and looked up from the computer screen with the same clear green eyes she saw every morning in the mirror. For a sixty-five-year-old, he'd been in impressive physical shape until his lung cancer diagnosis earlier this year. Now his poor health was undeniable. Though he was a true fighter, the cancer had spread to his lymph nodes and there was nothing that his team of doctors could do. It was only a matter of time.

Today, thankfully, was a good day. Some days lately, he could barely make it out of bed.

"Roman didn't request to see me," Sutton said. "I asked for this meeting."

It took a second or two to process what he'd said, then her jaw nearly came unhinged, right along with her temper. And she did something that she never, *ever* did. She raised her voice to him.

"*Why* would you do that, Daddy? After all the family has been through, how could you even think of letting that man in our home?"

"It's something I need to do," he said firmly, and there was a softness in his gaze, a look of resignation in his eyes that broke Gracie's heart. Sutton never showed weakness. She had never once seen him cry, or lose his composure, and rarely had she seen him truly angry. But this look of defeat was more than she could take.

She felt her own anger, and what little was left of her resolve, fizzle away. She had to remember that her father had very limited time left on this earth. Weeks. Months. No one could say for sure. If meeting with Roman meant so much to him, what choice did she have but to respect his wishes? Her pride be damned... and her nerves, because although Gracie Winchester never got nervous, right now her heart was thumping against her kidneys and her palms had begun to sweat.

The sudden rap on the door nearly startled her right out of her Manolo Blahniks and she automatically reached up to check her hair, which she had smoothed into a tasteful chignon that morning. Suddenly she found herself wishing she'd worn it down. Though she had no clue why.

As her father's assistant opened the door, Gracie nervously smoothed the front of her Versace skirt, then folded her hands behind her back, so no one would see them trembling.

"Roman Slater to see you, sir."

Gracie felt as if the room was spinning around her. Her heart was pounding hard, and that irrational urge to run was back, but her knees were so weak she would never make it to the door.

Or out the nearest window.

"See him in," Sutton said, and Gracie stood frozen, trying not to hyperventilate.

The assistant stepped back and with a sweeping motion of her hand invited the family's worst enemy into their most sacred domain. Gracie held her breath as the bane of her existence strolled through the doorway, as though he didn't have a care in the world.

Wearing all black, he cut an impressive figure in tailored slacks, a dress shirt unbuttoned at the neck and a sport coat that showcased his wide shoulders, thick arms and narrow hips. All designer label.

So different from the Roman of their youth, the jeans-wearing, T-shirt-sporting college student who never gave a hoot about fashion. But now, as owner of a multimillion-dollar company, he had to look the part. And he did, except maybe for the hair. His dark locks were a touch too long, and a little too rumpled, but somehow it worked.

She waited for the anger to crash over her like a suffocating wave, for the resentment to turn her blood to acid and eat its way through her veins, but she felt something so unexpected it took a minute to identify the emotion.

She felt...*relieved*.

Several years after Roman had betrayed her the first time, he'd gone missing on a military mission, and had been rumored to be dead. It had ripped her to pieces, even after the way he'd betrayed her. At the time, she would have given anything to have him back. Anything to change what had happened, because her leaving him was the reason he'd joined the military in the first place.

She'd thought that maybe if she had forgiven him and they had stayed together he would still be alive.

The guilt had eaten her up for months, until she'd heard on the news that he and several of his fellow soldiers were still alive and being held in a POW camp in the Middle East by an Al Qaeda offshoot. And most likely being subjected to unspeakable forms of torture. Though she had been weak with relief to know that he was alive, had he been dealt a fate *worse* than death? Would they torture him, then kill him anyway? The possibilities had kept her up nights, and robbed her of her appetite. She'd lost ten pounds in a week, and felt so tired and depressed she could barely do her job. So she'd stopped watching the news reports and reading updates in the papers. She'd pushed him as far from her mind as she could, though there hadn't been a day since then that she didn't think of him at least once.

Eventually Roman and his teammates had been rescued. When she knew he was alive, and safely back in the US, she'd felt a soothing sense of peace. She'd felt as if she could finally let go of the resentment. They were, in a sense, even.

Which was a horrible way to look at it. Her broken heart and sullied reputation couldn't hold a candle to his weeks of torture. She wouldn't wish that upon her worst enemy.

Which, come to think of it, he was.

Because recently Brooks, with Roman's help, had launched his campaign to destroy not only her father, but Gracie and her sisters as well, and that familiar old hatred had come oozing back like burning tar in her soul.

Yet here she was feeling relieved to see him?

What the hell was wrong with her?

"Roman," Sutton said, slowly rising from his seat to shake his adversary's hand, and Roman's hesitation to take it underscored his hostility.

"Sutton," he replied, contempt clear in his tone.

"You remember my daughter Grace," Sutton said and Gracie's heart sailed to the balls of her feet.

Roman turned and his soulful hazel eyes sliced through her like hot knives.

Roman had always been beautiful. Now he was a Greek god, with his wide jaw and broad shoulders. His nose had been broken at some point, and he had scars on his face. One started at his temple and bisected his left brow, coming dangerously close to his eye, and another jagged line ran across his forehead and disappeared under his dark hair. Some women might have been put off, but she thought it only enhanced his sex appeal.

Then she thought of how he'd gotten them, and that there were probably others she couldn't see, and felt a shaft of guilt.

"Grace," he said, his deep voice strumming her nerve endings, making something primitive and completely irrational stir in her belly.

Attraction.

Uh-uh. *No way.*

No normal, well-adjusted person would be physically attracted to someone who tried to ruin her life.

He reached over to shake her hand, and without thinking, and purely out of habit, she took it, regretting the move instantly. But it was too late now.

He grabbed on firmly, and she gripped his much larger hand just as tightly. It was as if they both felt they had something to prove. It was almost amusing in its absurdity, and she wondered what he would do if she challenged him to an arm wrestle.

Roman's eyes taunted her. Dared her to say something snarky. Dared her to pull away first. She wouldn't give him the satisfaction.

She met his challenge, chin in the air, praying he wouldn't call her bluff…and sighing quietly with relief when, with the ghost of a smile, he finally let go.

Imagine that. Apparently even he had limits.

Roman turned to her father, exasperation and impatience oozing from his pores. He clearly was not there by choice. "So let's cut to the chase, Sutton. Why am I here?"

Sutton sat back down, his movements slow and precise to lessen the profound pain he suffered on a daily basis now, then gestured to one of the two chairs opposite his desk. "Relax. Have a seat."

One dark brow rising slightly, Roman folded his arms across that ridiculously wide chest, as if to say, *Yeah, right.* "Just tell me what you want. You said you have important information regarding a client of mine. Who?"

Gracie couldn't deny being curious herself. What was her father up to? And why hadn't he run it past her beforehand, so she didn't feel so left in the dark? Did it maybe have to do with something other than business? Something personal?

"I understand you're still looking for the natural father of Graham and Brooks Newport," Sutton said.

Unimpressed, Roman shrugged. "I am. So what?"

"I may be able to help you."

"Help me?" Roman said, with a deep and incredulous laugh. One that Gracie felt deep in her bones. "Is that some kind of joke? You've repeatedly fought me in my investigation, throwing up roadblocks every chance you could. Now you're saying you want to *help*? I don't buy it."

"I don't blame you for your hesitation, Roman, but for the sake of your clients you should listen to me. I have information that could help them."

Looking skeptical, but intrigued, Roman narrowed his eyes and said, "All right, what information?"

"I can't tell you."

One of those laughs rumbled in Roman's chest and he shook his head. "I'm finished with your games, Sutton."

"It's not a game. I can help them, but I have to speak

to them directly. I've been thinking a lot about this since they came here with Carson."

"So why am *I* here?"

"I'd like to set up a meeting with them. As soon as they're both available. Together."

Gracie blinked with surprise. He wanted to invite his mortal enemy here, into their home? And they'd actually already met once before? Had the cancer treatments begun to compromise his brain?

"Graham and Brooks aren't on the best of terms right now," Roman said. "As Graham's future father-in-law you should know that."

"I do. That's why I called you. I'm confident you can make them see reason."

Roman didn't look so confident, and Gracie had to side with him on this one. Graham's secret relationship with Gracie's sister Eve had made things very tense between the brothers. Now that Graham was going to have a child by Eve, he'd eased up on the Winchesters, but Brooks continued to pursue his vendetta against them, leading to fights between the brothers. And Brooks was trying to drag Carson into the mix by insisting he fight for what was rightfully his: a full quarter of the Winchester fortune. However, if Graham and Brooks knew Sutton was now willing to talk regarding their real father, whose identity had eluded them for years, perhaps they would put their differences aside.

"Why not tell Graham and have him pass the information on to his brother?" Roman asked. "If it's legitimate, Brooks will listen."

"No," Sutton said. "I have to do it here, in my office, with both of them."

"Why, Daddy?" Gracie hadn't meant to say that out loud and the sound of her own voice surprised her. It seemed to startle Roman, as well. He looked her way.

Sutton gazed up at her with what could only be described as tenderness, and said quietly, "It's just something I need to do."

The vulnerability in his eyes melted her. And forced her to do something she'd thought she would never have to again. Talk to Roman.

She met his icy gaze and swallowed past the lump building in her throat, struggling to find the anger and resentment she'd felt before he walked through the door. Did he have to look so hard and cold and intimidating? Maybe he'd learned that in the military. Because the Roman she knew had never looked at her like that before. She could barely remember him even raising his voice to her when they argued, which they hadn't really done all that much come to think of it. Their relationship had been pretty easy. Right up until the moment it wasn't. When she learned of how he'd betrayed her.

She had screamed at him then, and the worst part was that he never screamed back. He had only stood there looking remorseful, taking full responsibility for what he had done.

Though he had never actually said the words *I'm sorry*, his remorse had been clear on his face. And it wouldn't have made a difference if he had. There were no words to make up for his betrayal and all the hurt he caused. And if her father wanted this meeting, he was going to get it.

She could be snarky, but she knew Roman well enough to know that attitude wouldn't work. She shoved down her pride as far as it would go and tucked her tail firmly between her legs. She was doing it for Daddy.

"You know that my father isn't well. If this is something he needs to do I want to get it done. What will it take to get you to help?"

Her father touched her arm and said firmly, "Thank you, Princess. But let me handle this."

Two

Princess?

Really?

Roman resisted the urge to roll his eyes. He wasn't the least bit surprised to see Gracie pleading Sutton's case. She always had been, and always would be, a slave to her father's demands. A dedicated daddy's girl. Roman had learned that one a long time ago, the hard way. When it came to her loyalty, Sutton and her two sisters always came first.

Though it did look to Roman as though the old man didn't have much time left. The weight loss, the gray pallor. Roman had watched it happen to his own father when he was only fifteen, then five years later to his mother. Roman could see that Sutton Winchester was knocking on death's door, and didn't doubt that the man's excessive lifestyle had ultimately been his undoing. The skirt chasing, heavy drinking and high-stress business dealings had taken their toll.

Which was why Roman didn't feel a bit sorry for him.

Sutton turned to Roman and asked, "Will you arrange it?"

Yeah, right. Who the hell did Sutton think he was, asking *anything* from Roman? He didn't owe the man a damned thing. "Um…no. I won't."

"I'll pay you," Sutton said, and Roman's hackles went up.

The idea of taking the old man's money made him sick to his stomach. He shook his head and said, "Not gonna happen."

"What do you want? Just name it."

He opened his mouth to tell the old geezer that he had nothing to offer that Roman could possibly want, when something stopped him. He glanced over at Gracie, who was doing her best not to look at Roman. He remembered all the times in the past that Sutton had tried to sabotage Roman's relationship with Gracie, because he never considered Roman—a military brat—good enough for his precious daughter. But Roman had come a long way since then. Now Sutton needed him, and clearly he had nothing to lose.

He glanced over at Gracie, casually eyeing her up and down. "How about an hour alone with your daughter."

Gracie blinked, then blinked again, and asked in an incredulous tone, "To do *what*, exactly?"

He let a slow smile curl his lips. "Whatever I want."

She opened her mouth to speak but nothing came out. He had rendered the great Grace Winchester speechless. That was a first. And it gave him more satisfaction than he'd ever imagined it could.

"It was a joke," Roman said. "I just want to talk."

"But I don't want to talk to you," she replied, glancing nervously toward her father. Would Sutton really do that to her? Knowing Roman and Gracie's complicated past, would he really force her to speak with him?

"I'll give you fifteen minutes with her," Sutton said, cementing in Roman's mind what a bastard the man really was, selling out his own daughter.

Gracie gasped and said, "Daddy!"

She looked to Roman with pleading eyes.

"Forty-five," Roman said, ignoring her.

"Twenty," Sutton countered without missing a beat.

Un-freaking-believable.

Grace just stood there, her mouth hanging open, as if she couldn't believe this exchange was really happening. That she was being bartered like property.

"Thirty and not a minute less," Roman told Sutton. "And that's my final offer. Otherwise, you're on your own, old man."

Knowing how vain Sutton was, the "old man" comment had to stick in his craw, but he never let it show. He considered it for less than ten seconds before he said, "We have a deal."

Wow, the man truly had no scruples or decency. Gracie had offered to help, but considering her wide-eyed stare, Roman doubted this was what she had in mind. The question was, would she really do it?

Maybe Sutton had no scruples, but Roman did. "What do you say, Grace? Thirty minutes to catch up?"

Roman could see that she wanted to say no. But Sutton broke into a coughing spasm that paled his skin and stole his breath, and Grace winced.

She laid a hand on her father's shoulder until the spasm ceased then said gently, "Of course I'll do it."

"I'll see what I can do," Roman said. "But I can't promise that Graham and Brooks will cooperate."

"If anyone can get them to agree, you can," Sutton said.

An actual compliment? Wonders never ceased.

Roman turned to Grace and grinned, and the patience and compassion she showed her father evaporated before his eyes. He could feel the tension and her hatred for him radiating from every pore. And he deserved it for his boorish behavior, but if this was the only way to get Gracie to talk to him, so be it.

"When would you like your thirty minutes?" she said through clenched teeth.

"Right now works for me," he said with a grin, feeling smug about the whole situation. He hadn't been looking forward to his meeting with Sutton and had originally told him no. It had taken some convincing to change his mind and now he was glad he had. And if Sutton thought that having his daughter there would soften Roman up, he was wrong.

Well, maybe not *totally* wrong.

He had half suspected the old man would pull something like this, but when Roman saw Gracie standing there in her father's office it was still a shock.

"We can talk in the library," Gracie said stiffly, her back ramrod straight as she spun around and led him out of the room, her entire being vibrating with anger and hatred for him.

Considering what her family had been through recently, who could blame her? But she had it all wrong this time. And she owed him a chance to explain his role in the recent scandal involving her family. How it was not his intention, or even his fault, that her family was caught up in scandal.

Not this time anyway.

Her spiked heels clicked against the marble floor as she led him to the library, where they used to spend many a Sunday morning stretched out on the sofa in the sunshine, their bodies intertwined, reading the paper. Back when they were dating, of course, when she was in college and still lived at her father's estate. Roman had been fresh out of college and working his first job as a fledgling private investigator, quickly moving up the ranks of the firm.

But he had been too smug and gung ho for his own good and consequently had made the biggest mistake of his life. He'd begun investigating officials and politicians with suspected ties to the mob and Sutton's name had come up. Gracie, who had been interning at Elite Industries at the time, was implicated in making some computer files disappear and helping Sutton launder money. Roman had confronted her and she'd sworn that it wasn't true, that her father would never work with the mob and she certainly wouldn't do anything illegal. He had wanted to believe her, but he was young and stupid and the evidence had looked so overwhelming that he hadn't trusted her. By the time he had realized his mistake, it was too late.

And he'd paid for it.

The pain and anguish in her eyes as she'd berated him for his betrayal were almost more than he could take. And he had deserved each and every harsh word.

He would have done anything to take it back. To go back in time and relive the past. But knowing she would never forgive him, that he didn't even deserve her forgiveness, Roman hadn't even tried to apologize. He'd ruined his career and made more than a few enemies in the mob. For his own safety he'd had to leave town.

After denying his military roots for so long, and with nowhere else to go, he'd joined the army and started a new life for himself. Started over. But his capture, and torture, and resulting PTSD, had brought to a close that phase of his life, as well.

Once again he had pulled himself up and started over, never accepting for a second that he would be anything but successful. His former training in black ops and status as a war hero had brought in the business at first, but his impeccable performance and record of success in solving cases had kept the customers calling. The firm had grown to proportions and experienced a level of success that even he hadn't imagined.

And this time, when it came to Gracie and her family, he'd done nothing wrong. He'd been doing his job, and doing it well.

Gracie ushered him into the library and shut the doors behind them. It looked just as it had seven years ago. In fact, nothing of the Winchester estate that he'd seen so far today had changed at all.

Roman strolled to the huge bay window that looked out over the grounds. Mostly bare trees swung testily in the cool wind blowing off the lake, their colorful leaves fluttering to the lawn, where workers hurried to gather them up.

"So what is this all about?" Gracie asked from behind him. He turned to her and she did not look happy. And her mood wasn't likely to improve.

"As I said, I just want to talk."

She folded her arms and glared at him. "What if I don't want to talk to you?"

Didn't seem like she had much of a choice. He slowly and deliberately crossed the room to where she stood, his eyes never leaving her face, and stopped in front of her at a distance that was probably just a bit too close for her comfort. So that she had to look up to meet his eye. Even in her gargantuan heels.

"Sweetheart, all you have to do is listen."

It took a lot to make Grace Winchester squirm, but he was sure he had her panties in a twist right now, but she held her ground. Her confidence and competence had fascinated Roman from the day they were introduced by a mutual friend in college. She had been young and pretty, sharp as a whip, ridiculously smart and motivated, and he had been instantly drawn to her. The first time he talked to her, he could see that she felt it too—that tug.

He had always been a practical, logical person, but there had been nothing logical about his feelings for this woman he had barely known at the time. She had turned his whole world upside down. Back then she was confident, driven and full of energy. And he'd wanted her. Badly. He'd had no idea who she was until weeks later when, scanning the society pages, he happened to see a photo of Gracie and her sisters with Sutton taken at some charity event. Being a navy brat, he'd lived in bases all over the world. He'd had no clue about high-society Chicago.

He and Gracie had grown pretty close by then, and

knowing she'd held that back from him had hurt his feelings and had him questioning their friendship. He'd confronted her, and her explanation for the deception had broken his heart. She'd shrugged, as if it was no big deal, and said, "People use me to get to my father all the time. When someone shows interest in me, I have a process. I had to know if you were really who you said you were."

"And you think I am?" he'd asked, hoping she'd say yes.

She'd smiled and said, "Yeah, I do. Thanks for being a *real* friend."

In that instant, he'd realized he could never be with her. He'd wanted to. More than she ever could have imagined. But friendship was the only thing she'd really needed from him. Someone to always have her back, and help keep away those people who would try to take advantage of her. And it had been shocking to see just how many there were. That's when he genuinely understood her caution, and the realization had cemented them firmly in the friendship zone. If they were to get into a romantic situation that didn't work out, he knew it would end their friendship. Then who would watch out for her? Who would be her "true" friend?

It wasn't a chance he had been willing to take. Not then anyway. But later, after he graduated, things changed. And by then it was too late to change back.

"I want to explain what happened," he told her.

Her voice ice-cold, she said, "You mean how you tried to destroy my family. *Again*."

It was the "again" that got him, and the hint of pain layered just beneath the anger in her voice. The last thing he'd wanted to do was hurt her. "Brooks hired me to investigate and I was doing my job."

She huffed. "Sure you were. By making up lies and spreading rumors about us. Just like the last time. I know my father isn't perfect, but to accuse him of date rape?"

"That wasn't me. I had no intention of accusing him of anything until I had the facts. But Brooks was pushing me for an update so I told him what information I already had. I told him that it was unsubstantiated, and I needed more time to investigate. Brooks didn't want to wait. I was just as shocked as everyone else when he went public."

Roman hadn't known that Brooks had been planning to take all that unverified evidence to the local media until it was too late. Unfortunately his brother Graham hadn't realized either that Brooks's only goal had been to take Sutton and his family down, even if his allegations were based on rumors and lies. But by then there was nothing Roman or anyone else could do to stem the flow of speculation and accusations. The damage was already done.

Definitely not Roman's fault.

"It's not as if you have a history with this sort of thing," Gracie said, her tone dripping with resentment as she propped her hands on her very sexy hips, lifted her chin high and met his gaze. As if to say, *Here I am. Take your best shot.*

"I've made terrible mistakes," he told her, and his candor made her blink with surprise. But he believed in taking responsibility for his actions, no matter how hard it might be. "I know I've caused you and your family unspeakable pain. And I've had to live with that. But I swear to you that I didn't have any knowledge of Brooks's plan and had nothing to do with it. I was just doing my job."

"Give me *one* good reason why I should believe you."

"I don't have one." If he were her, he probably wouldn't believe him, either.

She didn't seem to know what to say, when in the past she'd always had strong opinions about pretty much everything.

"Now I want to ask you a question," he said.

She shook her head. "Nope. That was not part of the deal. I'm only supposed to listen, remember? It's just like you to go back on your word."

A direct hit. Clearly she was giving him no slack. That was more like the Gracie he knew.

"Answer it, don't answer it, that's up to you," he said. "I just want to know why you let Sutton do that to you."

Her brow wrinkled with confusion, and her curiosity won out over her stubborn nature. "Do what?"

"Belittle and disrespect you."

She instantly went on the defensive, looking outraged by his accusation. "He didn't. He loves me."

"You're so used to it you don't even see it," he said, shaking his head sadly. Sutton was a textbook sociopath. Roman wasn't sure if he was even capable of genuine love. He was too narcissistic.

"See what?" she snapped.

"Let's put it this way. You have a name and it isn't *Princess*."

Gracie rolled her eyes in exasperation. "It's a term of endearment. Not an insult."

"Not during a business meeting," Roman said, and

she felt her resolve falter. Okay, so it did annoy her a little when her father called her *Princess* in certain situations. Especially in business meetings. But that was just his way.

"And that's not half as bad as the way he just bartered you like property to get what he wanted," Roman said.

Ouch. He hit a raw nerve with that comment, and it took everything in her not to wince. He was right. What her father had done to her today was beyond humiliating. And inexcusable. But she didn't believe he was intentionally disrespecting her. He was just used to getting what he wanted.

And how does that make it okay? an annoying little inner voice asked.

Simple. It didn't. There was nothing okay about the way he'd treated her, so why *did* she put up with it? He would have never done such a thing to Gracie's sisters. But then again, they wouldn't have tolerated it. Had she been so enamored, such a devoted daddy's girl, that she let him walk all over her? That he took advantage of her devotion?

The idea made her sick to her stomach.

She could blame it on his illness but she would only be lying to herself.

"No one deserves to be disrespected that way," Roman said, and she recognized his tone. She'd heard it a lot near the end of their relationship. He was *angry*. But not *at* her.

He was angry *for* her.

She had no idea what that meant, or how she should take it. Or even what she should say in response. *Thank you? Mind your own business?*

After all this time why did he even care anymore? Was this some sort of trick or manipulation? Was he using her to get to her father again?

"You should have told us *both* to go to hell," he said, sounding genuinely mad. And he was right, she should have, so why hadn't she? Why had she...

Her thoughts came to a screeching halt.

Wait a minute. *Roman* had been the one to suggest the bargain in the first place. Was that not disrespectful, as well? Who was he to judge her father? Or her.

Her temper flared and her blood simmered in her veins. "Could you be more of a hypocrite? Are you forgetting that *you* started it? *You* put me in the hot seat."

"I did," he admitted, looking unapologetic. "And it was wrong. Absolutely. But I honestly didn't think he would do it. I thought he would throw me out on my ass. I would have if it was my daughter."

Ouch, another direct hit. Damn him. And he was right. If she were ever to have a child, she could not even imagine putting him or her in such a compromising position. "So why didn't you just walk away? You didn't want to help him in the first place so I'm sure it would have given you a lot of satisfaction to leave him hanging."

"It would," he agreed. "But it gives me *more* satisfaction to know that I talked to you, and you listened. That was all I wanted."

"Why?" she said, then immediately regretted the question. Maybe she didn't want to know why. Because the look in his eyes...

It was the one he always got right before he kissed her. And they were standing so close that if he wanted to, he would barely have to lean forward...

"On second thought I don't want to know," she said, taking a small step back, hoping he wouldn't notice. But of course he did.

His eyes sparked with mischief. "Are you afraid you might like what I have to say? Or are you just afraid of me in general?"

Pretty much all of the above. She didn't even want to go there, but as he stepped a little closer, invading her personal space, her feet felt glued to the floor.

"I have no reason to be afraid of you," she said, cursing the slight wobble in her voice.

"I came here at your father's request for one reason, and one reason only," he told her, leaning in just a little, and she braced herself for what she already knew was coming. "Because I thought I might see you."

Damn, that was what she was afraid of.

His wry grin said he was having too much fun torturing her. And it *was* torture to be so close to him and not be able to put her hands on him. How had this happened when a few minutes ago she hated him? Well, maybe not hated. That was a very strong word. And for all their troubles, sexual attraction had never been one of them. Not even at the end.

Obviously, not even now.

The first year they'd known each other their relationship had been deeply rooted in the "just friends" category. And he truly had been her best friend. However, that had never doused the fires of a heart-melting crush. But he'd never shown an interest in her physically, so she had been convinced she wasn't his type. Until one night after a horror-movie marathon, as they were hugging goodbye at his apartment door. She had pushed up on her toes to kiss Roman's cheek, and he had leaned forwrad in that exact second to kiss hers. She had tilted one way, and he the opposite, and somehow their lips had collided.

And oh. My. God.

The kiss had gone from zero to sixty in an instant. Roman had groaned and tangled his fingers in her hair, pulled her close. Then they couldn't stop kissing, and before she knew what was happening she was off her feet. He carried her to his bedroom, where they ripped at each other's clothes, falling into a tangle on the unmade bed. The sex was even better than she had imagined it would be. And boy, had she imagined it a lot. He had more than exceeded her expectations.

They'd made love half the night, and fallen asleep in each other's arms. She'd been sure the next morning the disappointment would come. He would blame it on the bottle of wine they had shared, and ask her if they could go back to just being friends. And she'd known it would break her heart, and seeing him with another woman would destroy her, but she couldn't imagine losing his friendship.

But he had told her he loved her instead. That he had *always* loved her, and wanted her, and she'd nearly wept with relief. After that they'd been inseparable. She'd loved him with all of her heart.

Then he had betrayed her.

Three

Those warm fuzzy memories from their past turned to ice in her veins. Was he here not really to explain, but to turn her against her own father? His weapon this time wasn't lies and accusations. This time it was truth. And the truth did hurt. A lot.

But why should she trust anything he said to her?

Something in Roman's expression changed. "Did someone open a window? It just got chilly in here."

"I see what you're doing," she said, backing away from him. "You're trying to turn me against my father."

A shadow passed across his face and the temperature dropped another ten degrees. "Is that really what you think?"

She had offended him. Well, tough. "You've tried it before."

"As someone who lost both of his parents at a very

young age, I would never intentionally put a wedge between a parent and a child."

"You told me my father was working with the mob! How did you think I would feel?"

"I said that I *suspected* he was. And I only told you that to keep you safe. And you didn't believe me anyway."

"And I was right. There were no mob ties, were there?"

He shook his head. "No."

"And I wasn't laundering money for him, either. Or destroying evidence. Was I?"

That made him wince a little. "No, you weren't."

"After all this time I still can't believe you would accuse me of that," she said. "I thought you knew me better."

"I didn't accuse. I asked."

"You suspected, and that was just as bad. The idea that you believed I might be capable—" Emotion rushed up to block her airway, making it impossible to finish her sentence. It was taking all her strength to hold back the sob that was working its way up.

She would not cry. He wasn't worth it.

She thought she'd put all of these feelings to rest, but here she was raw and bleeding again.

She was *not* going to cry.

"I made a mistake," he said, "and not a day has gone by since then that I haven't regretted it."

He was making it worse, being so reasonable. Admitting he was wrong. And if she didn't get a grip, she was going to go all girly on him. She was not a crier. The last time she remembered shedding a tear was the day of Sutton's cancer diagnosis. But here she was fighting back a waterfall.

He needed to go now.

"Your time is up," she said, not even looking to the clock to see if thirty minutes had passed. Or was it supposed to be twenty? She couldn't even remember. She just wanted him gone. And she hated herself for letting him get to her. For letting herself care at all. She was stronger than that. And smarter. "You have to leave."

He didn't look at his watch as he nodded. Apparently he had said all he came to say. "I'll let myself out."

Maybe he could see that she was hanging on by a very thin thread and was kind enough to spare her dignity.

She watched him cross the room to the door, noting a slight catch in his gait, as though he was favoring his left leg. He stopped on the threshold, his broad shoulders nearly filling the frame, and turned back to her. She held her breath, waiting, feeling an overwhelming sense of anticipation.

"Seven years ago, I thought I could keep the nature of my investigation from you. That alone was wrong. And when you did find out I should have trusted you when you said you weren't involved. But I was young and arrogant and I screwed up. I know I never apologized for what I did, but only because I didn't think you would ever accept it, or that I even deserved your forgiveness. But I'm saying it now. I'm sorry, Gracie."

Her heart melted. She wanted to run across the room, throw her arms around his neck and tell him that she forgave him, that she would *always* forgive him, but she had to keep her head on straight. She was caught up in the moment, in his tender honesty, and knew she would regret letting him off too easy. Besides, she didn't even know if she *did* forgive him, or if she believed he had nothing to do with the latest scandal. She didn't know what to think, so she chose her words carefully.

"I appreciate that," she said, which got her a wry, slightly crooked grin.

"I get it," he said. "You'll accept my apology in your own good time. I understand, and I'm in no hurry."

She had no idea what to say, but it didn't matter because he turned and then he was gone.

Feeling relieved, grateful, and painfully disappointed for some silly and irrational reason, Gracie collapsed into a leather chair and exhaled deeply, waiting for the flood, giving herself permission to cry. To sob her heart out if that was what she needed. But the damned tears wouldn't come.

What the heck was wrong with her?

She didn't feel sad, or hurt, or even angry with him. She wasn't sure *what* she was feeling right now, other than confused.

She had anticipated this day for seven years, and it had gone absolutely nothing like she'd imagined. She'd always envisioned him being cocky and unapologetic. Someone she would love to hate, and keep on hating. But this?

This was way worse than the anger. Or the nerves.

She thought about what Roman had said, about her father disrespecting her. And she hated how right he was. And hated herself even more for letting Sutton do it to her. For turning a blind eye for so long. She deserved his respect. She had *earned* it. But maybe he didn't even realize the way the things he did affected her. And instead of walking around with a big chip on her shoulder, she could just tell Sutton how she felt. Maybe he would apologize and promise not to do it again. It would be an amazing gift, because the great Sutton Winchester did not apologize for anything. Ever. But in his fragile condition did she want to risk upsetting him, or possibly putting a wedge in their relationship? He had so little time left.

No, she had to say something. If he passed away tomorrow she would spend the rest of her life feeling this unresolved resentment. That wasn't what she wanted.

Rising from the chair, she smoothed the front of her skirt, took a deep breath and walked back to her father's office. She rapped on the partially open door and peeked inside. Sutton was still sitting at his desk. He looked pale and exhausted. He should be in bed resting, but it was just like him to push himself to the limits and tire himself out.

She rapped softly on the door again. "Daddy, can I have a word with you?"

"What is it?" he snapped, not even looking at her.

She winced a little. That wasn't a good sign. He'd been going through some severe mood swings lately. Most likely a result of the cancer now growing in his brain. "I wanted to talk to you about what happened with Roman."

His eyes never left the screen, as if she wasn't even worth his time, and it hurt. A lot.

"What about it?" he said.

As her hands began to tremble, she realized that this was going to be harder than she'd anticipated. But she pulled herself up by her bootstraps, raised her chin and said in a semistrong yet slightly shaky voice, "It was wrong what you did."

In her life she couldn't recall ever telling him he was wrong about anything, and he clearly didn't like it.

The savvy and ruthless businessman looked up at her with eyes as cold as icicles. "And what did I do?"

The question was, what had *she* just done? He was obviously not feeling well. He looked so pale. Maybe she should have just kept her mouth shut.

Her voice trembling a little, she said, "I didn't want to talk to Roman and you shouldn't have forced me."

"We all make sacrifices, Princess."

Sacrifices? Shouldn't that have been *her* choice? "You didn't even ask me if it was okay. It was disrespectful and cruel."

He muttered a curse under his breath. He was mad at her, and she felt herself backing down again the way she always did. "I've had a long day and I'm tired." He sighed. "I don't have time for this nonsense."

He thought her feelings were nonsense? Was that seriously how he felt about her?

He's not well, she reminded herself, holding her tongue. He was dying. Wasting away. For a man like Sutton, to lose his faculties had to be the highest form of humiliation.

So what was his excuse for the other twenty-six years before his diagnosis? that annoying little voice asked. But after what she had been through with Roman today, she didn't have the energy or the will to make it an issue. If it weren't for the pile of designs on her drawing table at the office, she would go home, crawl into bed, hide under the covers and stay there until her dignity returned. But that just wasn't her. She was a fighter.

"I'll leave you alone," she said, backing away from his desk.

"I'm not through with you yet," he said testily, stopping her in her tracks. Then he closed his eyes and rubbed his temples, and she wondered if it really was either the cancer in his brain or the treatments making him so temperamental.

She swallowed her pride and in the calmest voice she could manage, said, "Yes?"

"I need you to do something for me." He gazed up at her and the softness was back in his eyes. "Please."

It was the *please* that got her. That melted her into a puddle. And every bit of resolve went out the window that she herself had wanted to jump through earlier. "Of course. Anything."

"I need you to start seeing Roman again."

It took a second for the meaning of his words to settle in, and when they did her jaw nearly hit the desk. There was no way he meant what she thought he meant. After what she had just said to him? "Seeing him where?"

"You're going to date him." It was a demand, not a request, and she was so stunned, she couldn't form a reply. Now Sutton was pimping her out?

Finally she managed, "Wh-what if he doesn't want to see me?"

"He's clearly still attracted to you, and I need to know what he's up to."

Still attracted to her? Oh no he didn't. He did not just suggest...

Sutton glanced up at her and did a double take. She must have looked as horrified as she felt.

"I'm not asking you to *sleep* with him," he said, though his tone suggested he would have expected her to do it had he asked.

Or maybe she was being overly touchy under the circumstances. He wasn't necessarily in his right mind.

"Just take him out a few times. You used to be good friends. He'll open up to you," Sutton said.

What did he think she was, a spy or something? A female James Bond?

She couldn't deny the lure of spending time with Roman. Purely out of curiosity, of course. Just to see what he was like now, and how much he had changed. But this was crazy. "Daddy, I don't know if I can do that. You know I'm not a good liar."

"So don't lie," he said, and when she frowned his gaze softened. "Princess, I don't have much time left and I don't want to spend it embroiled in another scandal. Brooks is still determined to take us down and I think Roman is helping him."

"He said he's not."

Her father's brows lifted. "And you trust him?"

She sighed. Of course not. What reason would she have to? He'd lied to her before. Why would she assume that he would be honest about anything? She was smarter than that.

She shook her head. "No, I don't."

He held his hand out and she took it. His skin felt papery thin and so cold. He had aged so much in the past few months, and it broke her heart.

He squeezed. "I need to know what to expect, Princess. You're the only one I trust. I need you to do this for me."

And the guilt train pulled into the station. This was how he got her every time, and as much as she wanted to, as always she couldn't say no.

"Okay," she told him. "I'll do it."

"Do you have a date for the Welcome Home fund-raiser this weekend?"

She rarely took dates to charity functions, but a social interlude in a very public place sounded like a good idea. Though Roman had always hated formal affairs, and having to wear a "monkey suit." But Welcome Home was an organization to assist wounded vets and their families, and being a wounded vet himself, he might make an exception.

"I'll ask him to join me," she said, then added, "but only as a friend. I will not lie to him, or lead him on in any way. And if he says no, I'm done. I won't beg him."

"Trust me, Princess," he said, with that rare tenderness in his eyes. "He isn't going to say no."

How in the hell had he ended up here?

Roman sat in the back of the limo, watching the lights of Chicago whiz by through the tinted window, but the view inside the vehicle was the one getting him all hot and bothered.

Gracie was seated opposite him, with one tanned, shapely leg peeking out from the slit of an apricot silk evening gown. She was on her cell phone, speaking fluent French. She'd always had great legs, but they hadn't come from hours of working out in the gym. She was one of those naturally thin women who could eat whatever they wanted and whom other women loved to hate.

Roman wasn't fluent in French, but he knew enough to understand that it was a business call. After several minutes she said goodbye and slid her phone into her clutch.

"Sorry about that," she said.

"That's okay," he told her, lowering his gaze to the leg playing peekaboo with her gown. "I've just been sitting here enjoying the view."

She shot him a look dripping with exasperation. *"Really."*

He grinned and gestured out the tinted window. "The view of the city," he said, though she knew damn well what he was really looking at. And he couldn't help but notice that she made no attempt to cover her leg.

She *liked* that he was looking. And he liked that she liked it. Clearly the past seven years had done nothing to douse his desire for her. The musky scent of her perfume enveloped him like a warm blanket, heating him to the core. It was the same brand she'd always worn. Her silky hair, pulled up in a mass of blond curls, revealed a long, slender neck he would love to kiss, and diamond-studded ears he was dying to nibble on. As a young woman she'd been cute and spunky with a mischievous glint in her eyes. Now, at twenty-seven, she was a knockout. And despite all the time that had passed, and all the discord between them, he still felt a familiarity and a closeness that puzzled him.

"So, are you ready to tell me what all this is about?" he asked her.

"All what?" she asked innocently, but he could see her squirm a little. She had always been a terrible liar. Which made what he'd put her through seven years ago even worse. Though she had never given him a reason not to, he hadn't trusted her, and he'd paid the price.

"Tonight," he said. "Your text was very…elusive. I was surprised when I got it."

"I was a little surprised that I sent it."

"Didn't get enough of me the other day, huh?" he asked with a grin, which seemed to make her even more uncomfortable. "Or you just couldn't get a date."

"Just to be clear, this is *not* a date. This is two acquaintances sharing a ride to a social function. And as I already explained, since it's a fund-raiser for wounded vets, I thought you would be interested in attending."

He shrugged, shooting her a knowing smile. "If you say so."

"Some of the most influential people in the state will be there. You'll make good connections."

"You sure this nondate has nothing to do with the fact that you wanted me to kiss you in the library the other day?"

She blinked. "When did I say that?"

He grinned. "Sweetheart, you didn't have to. It's been seven years, but I can still read you like a book."

"I seriously doubt that," she said, but her eyes told a different story. Like maybe she worried that he was right. "I'm not the same naive, trusting woman I was back then. And *don't* call me *sweetheart*."

"How about Princess? Can I call you that?"

She glared at him.

He shrugged. "Sorry, *Gracie*. I thought you liked terms of endearment."

"But that's not why you said it. You're not nearly as charming as you think you are."

"But I *am* charming," he said, waiting for a kick in the shin.

She rolled her eyes instead. "I know you *think* so."

"Honey, I *know* so."

She let the *honey* comment go. "Funny, but I don't recall you being this arrogant."

He grinned. "And you're as stubborn as you ever were. Just like my sister."

"How is April? I seem to remember that she was getting married."

Yeah, and Gracie was supposed to be his date, but he'd screwed that up. "She's living in California with her husband, Rick, and their twin boys, Aaron and Adam."

Gracie softened into that gooey-eyed look that women got whenever children were mentioned. "Oh my gosh! Twins?"

"Yep. She has her hands full."

"How old?"

"They'll be a year on Christmas Day," he said, hearing the pride in his own voice. He'd never imagined himself ever having children, so he spoiled his nephews any chance he got. He had held them both just minutes after their birth, so there was a close connection. He would lay down his life for them. And for April—not that she needed his protection. She was one of the most competent women he'd ever known.

"I was in town visiting for the holidays when she had them. Her husband was deployed at the time so I went through the entire labor with her. It gave me a whole new respect for mothers."

"Do you see them very often?"

"We Skype weekly."

"She was always such a great person," Gracie said with genuine affection in her voice.

Four years his junior, it had been exceptionally difficult for his sister when they lost their parents. And even harder for him to be away at college while she grieved alone, though she'd been taken in by a close family friend. He'd considered dropping out of school until she finished high school, but she wouldn't let him. She did visit him often, though, and she had taken to Gracie instantly. They were only a year apart in age and were both strong, capable women, though they couldn't have been any more different in their interests. April was a rough-and-tumble tomboy capable of drinking any man under the table, and she chose the armed services over college, marrying young. Gracie hadn't been interested in marriage—at least not until she finished school—and they had never really talked about a family. He wondered now if she had ever considered it. Her ambition to be a fashion designer had always been her main focus. From what he'd seen in the media, she was a raging success, and her philanthropy was legendary.

"Is she still in the navy?" Gracie asked him.

"She and her husband both," he said. "They're both stateside right now, but tomorrow, who knows?"

"It must have been difficult for her when you were a POW."

"It was." At the mere mention of his capture that familiar sense of dread worked its way up from someplace deep inside him. But he instantly shoved it back down. It had taken intense rehabilitation to heal the physical trauma of his ordeal, and even longer to conquer the PTSD that had tortured his soul. To this day he still suffered nightmares, and occasionally woke in a panic, drenched in a cold sweat, his mind convinced he was still in the Middle East. But he was back to being a fairly centered and functioning human being. Giving in to his demons had never been an option, and he'd fought like hell to be well again.

Though he was usually pretty good at hiding his emotions, and burying the anguish, Gracie's pained look said that after all these years, she could read him just as well as he'd read her.

For several seconds she was quiet, her eyes locked on his, then asked softly, "What was it like?"

The question threw him for a second. Aside from group therapy, and private sessions with his therapist, Roman had never spoken of his experience as a POW. Not even with his sister. No one ever asked. The physical scars pretty much spoke for themselves.

But despite their rocky past, he knew Gracie would never judge, or question his fortitude or bravery. He wasn't sure how he knew, but he just did, that despite everything that had happened between them, she genuinely cared.

So he talked.

Four

"The first few months after my rescue were almost unbearable," Roman told her. "I couldn't stop thinking about the men who didn't make it out alive. The ones who were killed in front of me, in cold blood. The survivor guilt was worse than the actual torture. I would have given my life for any one of those men. The scars will never go away, but I've made peace with myself. It wasn't easy, though."

She gazed over at him, her eyes filled with pain and regret. "I used to feel as though, because of everything that happened between us, if it hadn't been for me, you would have never joined the military in the first place. Like, maybe if I wasn't so hard on you…if I could have forgiven you…" She shrugged. "It doesn't make a whole lot of sense, I know."

The idea that she felt guilt over his leaving both surprised and disturbed him. "Gracie, my joining up had nothing to do with you. I screwed up. I was arrogant and cocky and I messed with the wrong people. Even if you had forgiven me I wouldn't have stayed because then your life would have been in danger, too. Besides, the military is in my blood. I fought it for a long time, but it's where I was meant to be."

What she didn't realize was that if it hadn't been for her, he may not have even survived the torture. Picturing her face, believing that if he endured he might see her again, had given him a reason to live as he watched his fellow soldiers die, picked off one by one as the rest had been forced to watch. One of those men had been his closest friend. A husband and father of three. To this day Roman would still give anything to switch places with him. But all he could do now was make sure that the man's family was taken care of financially. He'd set up a trust for them in their father's name. Even that hadn't assuaged the guilt, but it made it easier to live with the pain.

He leaned forward, closing the gap between them, and took Gracie's hand. It was so small and delicate compared to his own. And she didn't even try to pull away. "Trust me when I say you were better off staying away from me. And you hold no responsibility for my mistakes. I was the one who turned my back on you. I didn't trust you. I was young and stupid and arrogant. It was my fault."

The limo pulled up to the Metropol hotel where the fund-raiser was being held but she didn't let go of his hand or break eye contact. The driver steered the car into the parking structure to the VIP entrance underground. When they stopped, an attendant opened the door but Gracie just sat there looking at Roman, then she squeezed his hand.

"Roman, when I heard the false reports that you were killed, I thought I couldn't feel any worse. Then I learned of your capture, and the torture…" She paused and took a deep breath. "I know that it was nothing compared to what you were going through, but I want you to know that I thought about you and prayed for you every day."

Deep down he knew that. Maybe that was why he still felt such a strong bond to her. "Gracie, that means more to me than you could ever know."

Gracie had helped plan more charity functions than she could count, and she had to admit that the Welcome Home decorating committee had seriously outdone themselves this time. Red, white and blue tulle swirled tastefully overhead, garnished with American flag balloons and crepe streamers. The tables had been draped in white linen with blue cloth napkins and red rose centerpieces. The decor screamed patriotism and valor. And in the center of it all against the back wall a slideshow of the wounded warriors and their families the foundation had assisted played on a huge screen.

The crowd was a who's who of Chicago, with a handful of Hollywood personalities mixed in. From where she stood she could see Roman mingling with the other guests. He looked damned fine in a tux, and the slightly rumpled hair coupled with the battle scars made him look rugged and a little dangerous. Yet somehow he fit right in.

One of the tallest and biggest men there, Roman had turned heads the minute they walked through the door. She felt an odd sense of pride to be there with a man whom she considered to be by far the sexiest, most gorgeous in the room. Only they weren't there together, she reminded herself. Not in a romantic way. She had no claim to him, nor did she want one. Though she couldn't deny that a tiny part of her, deep down inside, wished she did.

Okay, maybe it wasn't so tiny. And she hated herself for it. For being so weak. And irrational. For wanting a man who did her and her family so wrong. But her body kept betraying her.

Roman glanced her way, saw her watching him, and a sly grin curled his lips. He said something to the man he'd been speaking with then headed her way, and her heart shifted wildly in her chest.

When he took her hand in the limo she'd just about melted into a puddle on the leather seat. She'd wanted to pull away, and scold him for being so personal, but she just couldn't make herself do it. It was hard enough to fight the desire to launch herself into his arms and hold him.

But he wasn't hers to hold.

Though as he came up next to her, sliding her hand back into his would have felt as natural as breathing.

Damn him.

"See something you like?" he asked, a suggestive lilt in his tone. One that she was sure was meant to rattle her cage. And it worked.

She gestured randomly in the direction he'd come from, sighed wistfully and said, "Yes, but I think he's married."

Roman threw his head back and laughed. "You're a terrible liar."

Yes, she was, and he knew her too well. She had to fight the irrational urge to lean in close, so that their arms touched.

Back in the old days Roman had never been shy about physical affection in public. He'd always held her hand, no matter where they were.

When she started college she hadn't had a whole lot of sexual experience. Too many times she'd been deceived by men who were only interested in her money and family name. Trust had been a difficult concept to grasp back then. And though she had sacrificed her innocence to one of the men before Roman, she had never surrendered her heart. Sex had been something fun to do, but not emotionally satisfying. She had never come close to connecting emotionally to anyone the way she had with Roman. When they'd finally crossed the line from friends to lovers, she'd been so ready, and so desperately in love with him, making love had been truly magical.

And she had the sneaking suspicion that it still would be, not that she would ever find out.

"Are you having a good time?" she asked him.

"Better than I thought I would. I'm not big on large crowds."

"Then why did you come?"

"I couldn't let the most beautiful woman here show up without a date."

She glared at him, though a smile hovered just below the surface. "This is *not* a date."

He shrugged. "So you keep saying."

She heard someone call her name and looked away from Roman to see Dax Caufield, the newest addition to the state senate, making a beeline for them, flashing that renowned campaign smile. Dax was a typical politician, but a decent guy. She had no doubt that with his good looks and charm he would eventually work his way up the Washington food chain. Though she didn't agree with all of his politics, in a world where lies and half-truths were almost expected, he seemed to be a genuinely good and honest man who believed in his positions. He could be a little overbearing, and a touch arrogant, but that usually went along with the territory. He always struck her as honest and morally sound, so much so that for a short time, for his current state senate seat, she had been an assistant campaign manager. Working behind the scenes, using her experience as an event planner, she'd arranged most of his local speaking engagements and fund-raising events, though it had been the volunteers who did the majority of the work. If there was one thing she excelled at, it was delegation. And because Dax was so popular and well liked, finding people to help had never been an issue.

Still, though he was very attractive and charismatic, he couldn't hold a candle to Roman.

"Grace!" he said, beaming as he gave her a hug and a kiss on the cheek. "I'm so glad you could be here!"

"I wouldn't have missed it," she said, and turned to Roman. "Roman, this is State Senator Dax Caufield. He sponsored this event."

"Roman Slater," Dax said, vigorously shaking Roman's hand. "It's an honor to meet you. I've heard good things about you. And let me say thank you for your service."

Roman nodded, but didn't smile. He was typically rather gregarious but something in his eyes said Dax had rubbed him the wrong way. She was curious to know why, since Roman didn't even know him.

Dax hooked an arm around Gracie's shoulders and told Roman, "This woman is a godsend. She was indispensable during my campaign and she helped to plan this event. I don't know what I would have done without her."

"I think you may be exaggerating a little," Grace said with a smile. "But I did what I could to help."

"It's a privilege to have a true war hero with us tonight," Dax told Roman.

"Every soldier is a hero," Roman said sharply. "And deserves the same honor."

His tone took Gracie aback, but before the situation could get awkward, or escalate, someone called to Dax and he turned his attention to Gracie, his smile never wavering. "I'd like to speak with you later about a few ideas I had for the foundation. In the meantime work your magic."

Gracie smiled. "You know I will."

He winked, then said to Roman, "Have a good time."

When he was gone, Roman said, "I don't like that guy."

Puzzled, Gracie asked, "Why?"

Frowning, he shrugged. "Just a feeling. And what did he mean by work your magic?"

"Let's just say that I have a gift for fund-raising."

Roman looked around. "Then you've got your work cut out for you. This is quite the guest list. Is there anyone here who isn't rich and famous?"

"Not at ten grand a ticket."

His brows tipped upward. "Is that what I'm paying to be here?"

"Not exactly. I pulled some strings."

For the next half hour or so Gracie introduced Roman around and word spread fast of the "genuine" war hero in their midst. At one point she completely lost track of him, only to see him later on the dance floor with a very popular and very young Hollywood starlet. They were talking and laughing, and she was looking as if she wanted to eat Roman up as a midnight snack.

A wave of jealousy gripped Gracie so intensely she felt like throwing up.

What was wrong with her? She had no right to be jealous. She had no right to feel anything at all. She knew for a fact that Roman was single, so it only made sense that he would socialize and flirt. And it wasn't as if he was there as her real date. She'd said it herself: they were only there as acquaintances.

But knowing that didn't make her feel any better. In fact, it only made her feel worse.

Roman glanced over and caught her watching before she could avert her eyes. So when she did look away, it appeared as if she was trying not to get caught staring. Which of course was exactly the case.

She just couldn't seem to win tonight.

"Hey, you!"

She turned to find her sister Eve approaching with a dazzling smile filled with so much love and affection it warmed Gracie's heart. While Gracie favored their mother's side of the family, Eve was a Winchester through and through. Tall, athletic and elegantly beautiful, Eve had the trademark Winchester green eyes and a dazzling smile. Her hair was perfect, her makeup flawless, and her dress sleek and stylish. No one who didn't know her would guess that underneath the glamorous facade lurked a ruthless businesswoman. Nor would they know that despite her svelte figure, she would soon be trading her sleek size-zero wardrobe for maternity clothes, which had inspired Gracie to consider a designer maternity line of her own. "Hey back, beautiful! You're positively glowing."

Eve hugged her and air-kissed her on each cheek. "And you look lovely as always. Is that dress one of your designs?"

Grace shook her head. "It's Armani."

As much as she loved her own fashions, to wear them to a function for charity felt arrogant and tacky, as though she was a walking billboard for herself. She was proud of her accomplishments, but too humble to be so forward and flashy.

"How have you been feeling?" she asked Eve.

"Pretty good. A little queasy in the mornings, and I've been tired, but I can't complain."

Gracie gazed around the room looking for her soon-to-be brother-in-law. Though he and Eve had been through a rough time, it had only brought them closer together, and made their love for each other and their commitment to their relationship that much stronger. In a way she envied her sisters for finding the loves of their lives. Had it not been for Roman's deceit, she might be married with a family of her own. She'd dated casually over the years, but always made building her business her main priority. She'd always just assumed that when the right one came along, she would know. She would feel that spark of excitement and attraction.

The one she'd felt the first time she laid eyes on Roman all those years ago.

But she hadn't even come close.

"Is Brooks here?" she asked her sister.

"He was called out of town on business. But he'll be back for the party at the children's hospital site Sunday. Everyone's excited to see the progress being made on the construction."

"I really hoped that Nora and Reid would be here, so I could thank him." Reid Chamberlain, her future brother-in-law, owned the hotel and had graciously donated the ballroom for the night, as well as posh rooms to the foundation's most generous out-of-town guests.

Eve put a hand on Gracie's shoulder and then asked in a hushed voice, "How are you holding up, baby? Are you all right?"

Holding up? The question struck her as odd, since Eve knew that Gracie loved formal functions. Especially fund-raisers. Schmoozing with the wealthy and divesting them of their inheritances and trust fund money were skills she excelled at. "Fine, why?"

"It must be difficult seeing Roman here. I didn't even know he was on the guest list."

Oh, *that*. She winced a little. How was she supposed to explain this one?

"I suppose it's fitting considering his military status. And his financial success. He's certainly made a name for himself in the past two years. It's hard not to be impressed."

It was very impressive, but for Gracie not at all surprising. She'd always known that someday he would be an incredible success. He had been as driven and dedicated to his studies and his career as Gracie. It was one of the reasons they had connected so instantly in college.

"He actually wasn't on the guest list," she said.

Eve's brow wrinkled with confusion. "Oh. He came as someone's guest?"

"Um, yeah." Gracie hoped she would leave it at that.

But of course she didn't. "Whose?"

"Well…"

Eve folded her arms, narrowed her eyes and flashed that don't-screw-with-me look Gracie had seen countless times growing up, and said in a motherly voice, "Gracie…?"

She had no choice but to fess up. "Me. He came here with me."

Her outrage made Gracie wince. *"Why?"*

"It's not what you think. It's not a date. We aren't back together, or getting back together. It's just business."

"Considering the way he's looking at you right now, I find that a little hard to believe."

Gracie looked over to where Roman was now speaking with one of Hollywood's most well-known power couples and an Illinois state representative. But his eyes were on her. He smiled and winked.

Oh hell. Why did he have to go and do that? Especially in front of her sister.

"I rest my case," Eve said.

Gracie turned back to her sister. "The truth is, Daddy asked me to bring him."

Eve closed her eyes and sighed deeply. "Oh, honey, what is he making you do now?"

Apparently even her sister thought their father's

overreaching was inappropriate. "He thinks Roman is up to something and he asked me to…well…"

Eve regarded her pensively. "To what?"

"He was hoping I might be able to find out what Roman is up to. Since he and I were so close before."

Eve was not happy. "Who the hell does he think you are? James Bond?"

"That's exactly what I thought, but he guilted me into it." As usual. "He said he can't take another scandal."

Eve took her hands. "Honey, I know Daddy is very sick, and his time is limited, but you don't have to do this. Not if it's upsetting to you. There are other ways he can get what he needs. After everything Roman put you through…"

"It's really okay," Gracie said, and realized that she meant it. "He and I have unresolved issues. Maybe it's time we clear the air. And let go of the past."

"So do *you* think Roman is up to something?"

That question had been hounding her all night. "I don't know. He takes full responsibility for the problems he caused us seven years ago, but says that he had nothing to do with spreading the rumors about Daddy's alleged illegitimate children in the media this time around. That Brooks acted on his own with information that Roman warned him hadn't been verified. Has Graham mentioned anything?"

Eve frowned. "We don't talk about Brooks. And they don't talk to each other right now. Graham is still furious with him. But if you want my personal opinion…"

Boy, did she ever. "Please."

"Be careful."

Her sister was right, but as Gracie glanced Roman's way and their eyes met, and she felt that tingly anticipation, she wondered if she was already in way over her head.

Five

After making a full sweep of the ballroom and securing commitments for very generous sums from donors, Gracie found an empty seat with a view of the dance floor and settled back to have a drink. Her third of the night, which was her absolute limit. She was scanning the room to see where Roman might be when she felt a tap on her shoulder. "Would you care to dance?"

Gracie looked up to find Roman standing beside her, and like a dummy said, "Dance?"

"It's what those people over there are doing," he said, gesturing to the dance floor with that wry grin. "I hold you, we sway."

"I know what it is," she said, trying not to smile. He was only making it worse, poking fun at her like that. And she liked it far too much for her own good. The drink was making her feel fuzzy and loosening her inhibitions. Which couldn't have been worse.

She set it down on the table beside her.

"I'm just not sure I want to."

"If I recall, you loved to dance."

"Are you sure you have room on your ticket?" she asked, since as far as she could tell he had danced with practically every young, single woman here tonight.

"What's the matter, Gracie? Are you jealous?" he asked with a playful look that melted her.

She rolled her eyes. "As if."

He leaned in close, the whisper of his breath caressing her ear. "You know you're the only one I really want to dance with."

Why did he have to say things like that? To have him hold her hand had been tantalizing enough, but the idea of being that close to him, and the feelings it would stir up, terrified her. But he was so handsome and charming that when he offered his arm she took it and let him lead her to the dance floor, knowing that the second he pulled her into his arms she would both regret and love it at the same time.

She really shouldn't have had that third drink.

Feeling his huge hand on her lower back, she braced herself as he eased her in close. Much closer than those other women he'd danced with. And as her breasts brushed against his wide chest she felt her nipples tingle and harden. His grip on her hand was gentle yet firm, and as her other hand came to rest on his biceps, she could feel the hard muscle underneath his tuxedo jacket.

Roman had always been a big guy, but now? There was just so much of him. And it felt good.

Way *too* good. Too much like the old days when keeping their hands off each other had been impossible. Her thigh brushed his and against her will she could feel herself relaxing in his arms. Roman had always been a good dancer, and his injuries didn't seem to have changed that.

As if reading her mind, Roman said, "I seem to recall us doing this a time or two before." He paused, his eyes snagging hers, and then added, "Although not with quite so many clothes on. And not vertically."

Her knees went weak and her cheeks burned. He had to go and remind her, didn't he? Making love with Roman had never been anything but wonderful. They connected in a way that she never had with anyone else. Not before and not since. They would spend hours in bed lying naked together alternating between kissing and making love and just talking. Touching him, running her hands over his body, had always been a favorite pastime that never grew old.

Apparently not even now.

"You're pushing it," she warned him, feeling dizzy from the musky scent of his aftershave as the rest of the world faded into the background, until it felt as if it was just the two of them there in the ballroom.

"It's the truth," he said. "I know you haven't forgotten."

She wished she could, but what they'd had together had been pretty unforgettable. "Stop trying to seduce me."

A grin tilted the corners of his beautiful mouth. "Is that what I'm doing?"

She cursed the wobble in her voice as she said, "I told you that this isn't a date."

The deep baritone of his voice strummed across

her senses and his breath tickled her cheek. "So, no good-night kiss at your doorstep?"

"I picked you up," she reminded him.

"No kiss at mine?"

Since the limo had fetched him at his office, she had no idea where he even lived. Not that it made a difference either way. "No kissing *anywhere*."

"Not even a little one on the cheek?"

It would never stop at just her cheek. And one taste of his lips would destroy her self-control. She was on shaky ground as it was.

His eyes grew dark with desire. "But we were *so* good at it."

She couldn't argue there, and denying it would be a waste of time.

"This is business," she told him, scrambling for a safe topic to explore, one he couldn't turn into a sexual innuendo. "Have you talked to Graham and Brooks about meeting with my father?"

"Did Sutton tell you to ask me that?"

Well, no, not specifically, so it wasn't a lie when she said, "I was just curious."

"But he did ask you to bring me tonight. He wants to keep tabs on me."

To say no would be a lie, and she was a terrible liar. He would see right through her.

"Why would you think that?" she asked instead, answering his question with a question of her own.

He laughed. "So that's a yes."

She blinked. "I didn't say—"

"You didn't have to. I can still read you like a book, Gracie."

Damn him. What was she supposed to say now?

The hand resting on her lower back slipped an inch or so lower and her heart skipped a beat. "Look me in the eye and tell me Sutton didn't put you up to this."

She couldn't do it. She couldn't look him in the eye and lie, and if she looked away he would have his answer. She didn't know what to do.

Curse her damned guilty conscience.

The arm around her tightened and Roman's look went from playful to serious in a heartbeat. "I don't care, Gracie. It doesn't matter why we're here together. Just that we are."

He'd obviously known all along that she'd had ulterior motives, and the fact that he wasn't angry, or at least a little upset with her, meant…what? That he wanted her? Well, that was pretty obvious. The question was, what did she want?

The song ended and she pulled away, out of his arms. And thankfully he let her go. If he had resisted, even a tiny bit, or asked her to dance again, she would have been toast.

"I have people I need to speak with," she said. "But thank you for the dance."

He didn't say a word. He just smiled.

And she ran.

Well, her four-inch heels prevented her from *actually* running, but she did bolt. Right for the bar. Screw her three-drink limit. She needed a strong one right now. She was lusting after a man who only three days ago she'd hated with a passion almost as hot as her desire for him.

One more drink turned into two as she mingled and talked up the wealthiest of the guests in attendance. She ignored Roman, but she could feel his eyes on her.

He had her in such a state she found herself at the bar asking for drink number six. And at some point she went back for drink number seven. Which was a very bad idea. By eleven o'clock she was feeling more than a little tipsy. She was fatally attracted to him, and her defenses couldn't be much lower. What the hell had she been thinking?

In an attempt to dull her senses, she'd only amplified her desire and left herself more vulnerable than ever.

Stupid, stupid, stupid.

Dizzy and a little disoriented, she made her way to the ladies' room to freshen up. She sat in the lounge for several minutes to collect herself and guzzled a bottle of water, hoping it might dilute the effects of the alcohol, but when she stood back up she felt more unsteady than ever.

What was she supposed to do now, stumble around the ballroom like a drunken fool?

What the hell had she gotten herself into?

Hating herself for being so careless, she left the ladies' room as gracefully as she could. Roman was waiting for her a few feet from the door, holding his coat and her wrap.

"I had a feeling you would be ready to leave," he said and she could have cried she was so relieved.

"Yes, please."

She braced herself against the wall as he slipped her wrap around her shoulders and put on his coat. He slipped his arm through hers, presumably so that she wouldn't fall over, and led her to the elevator.

"You know what happens when you have more than three drinks. Were you trying to get hammered?"

Yup, he had been watching her. That he knew her so well should have bothered her, but it didn't. Other than her wounded pride, there wasn't much of anything bothering her right now.

"I'm not hammered," she said, but her mouth couldn't seem to make the words come out just right.

"Liar."

Yep, she was lying.

They took the elevator down to the parking level and she leaned against him, his hard body keeping her upright, but as the doors slid open, and she took a step, she stumbled.

"You're going to break a leg in those heels," he said.

"Am not," she argued, stumbling again, clutching his arm for balance. In a flash of movement that left her dizzy and disoriented, he scooped her up into his arms. She let out a startled squeak and wrapped her arms around his neck. "I can walk."

"Barely," he said, sounding amused. He carried her to the limo and helped her inside. Then he disappeared. She looked around, confused. Was he sending her home alone?

He was back several seconds later carrying her clutch and one of her shoes. She looked down and saw that her left foot was bare.

Huh. She hadn't even felt the shoe fall off.

He climbed in and sat across from her. "Lose something?"

"Thanks," she said, as he dropped her things on the seat beside her.

The limo started to move and she closed her eyes.

Bad idea. The interior of the vehicle began to spin

around her. She clutched the edge of the seat and opened them again, but it didn't help much.

Roman regarded her sternly. "You're not going to be sick, are you?"

She shook her head, which made the spinning worse. "I may be a *little* drunk."

"You think?"

The seat shifted underneath her, but then she realized it was her body shifting and righted herself. "No, that's a lie," she said, her words slurred. "I'm definitely hammered."

"Are you sure you're not going to be sick?"

"I'm not sure of anything right now." This time, when she closed her eyes, she didn't open them again.

After a night of strange, vivid dreams about Roman, Gracie woke slowly the next morning, a drum pounding in her temples, wondering how the heck, and when the heck, she had gotten home. Her throat was dry and her tongue felt thick and as she pried her eyes open and took in her completely unfamiliar surroundings, she realized she *wasn't* at home. She was…

Where the hell was she?

She blinked the sleep from her eyes and sat up in bed, the movement sending a shaft of pain through her head. Nothing looked familiar.

She spotted a sheath of apricot silk draped over a chair across the room. It was the dress she'd worn the night before. And then she realized that all she had on were her strapless push-up bra and matching panties.

Oh God, what had she done? And where the *hell* was she?

She closed her eyes against the raging pain in her

skull and groaned, trying to piece together what had happened last night. The last thing she remembered was Roman carrying her to the limo. Everything after that was pretty much a blur.

Had he taken her home with him?

At the foot of the bed lay a pair of pajama bottoms and T-shirt big enough to fit two of her, and on the bedside table sat a glass of water and two pain-reliever tablets. At least, she was guessing that's what they were. They could have been poison for all she knew, but death right now would be a welcome reprieve from the pain.

She gobbled them down and chugged the entire glass as she glanced around the room. It was decorated in earth tones with splashes of color here and there. The room was neither masculine nor feminine, which told her it was probably a spare. Through an open door she could see the bathroom, and guessed that the closed door next to it was a closet.

She pushed herself to get out of bed and change when what she really wanted to do was lie back down and sleep off the pounding in her head. The T-shirt hung down to her knees and thankfully the pajama bottoms had a drawstring because otherwise they would have been around her ankles. She looked out the window to a very cushy subdivision of midsize homes on decent-size lots. She had no clue where it was geographically. It looked cold and dreary out.

She didn't doubt that Roman could afford a much bigger home, in a much swankier neighborhood, but he had never been into appearances. He had always been a practical man, and she could see that hadn't changed.

In the bathroom she found a toothbrush still in the package and an unopened tube of toothpaste. And when she looked in the mirror she cringed. Her hair was a disaster, sticking every which way, and her mascara was smudged around her eyes. She looked like a deranged raccoon.

She found a hairbrush in one of the drawers and did what she could to her tattered blond locks and used the washcloth hanging on the towel rack to fix her face.

Honestly it wasn't much help. Her excessive behavior was clear in her baggy eyes and pale complexion.

Oh well. Roman had seen her in worse shape than this before.

She brushed her teeth and refilled the water glass two more times, drinking more slowly. She didn't feel sick, but she didn't feel great, either. If she hadn't already barfed—and oh did she hope she hadn't—it was still a possibility.

With no hope of looking even halfway decent, she opened the bedroom door. The scent of coffee led her down the stairs to an open-concept living and dining room and a functional kitchen.

She found Roman lounging on a leather sectional wearing a long-sleeved camouflage thermal shirt and black running pants, his bare feet propped on a familiar-looking coffee table. He was reading the newspaper and a football game played on the flat-screen television across the room.

"Do I smell coffee?" she said.

He glanced up at her and smiled. "You do. The last time I checked on you, you were stirring so I made a fresh pot."

He'd checked on her. How sweet was that? Not that she needed to be checked on. She was used to living alone. But still…

"Would you like a cup?"

"Please. A really big one." She needed the caffeine to shake the blazing headache.

He eyed her questioningly. "Think your stomach can take it?"

"If I don't have a cup, my head might explode. Unless you have something more direct, like an IV."

He laughed, the deep baritone strumming across every nerve in her body. Even in her compromised state it made her already-wobbly knees knock a little harder. "Have a seat," he said, pushing up off the couch. "One black coffee coming right up."

She took a seat on the other end of the couch from where he'd been sitting, her body sinking into the plush leather, and watched him as he pulled a mug down from the cupboard over the coffeemaker and poured.

"Did you see the pills I left you?" he asked.

"Yes, thank you. And the things in the bathroom."

He carried the cup to her. "Hungry?"

At the thought of food, her stomach turned and she shook her head.

Bad move.

Her temples screamed and she told him, "One thing at a time."

The superstrong brew burned her tongue, but it tasted amazing. Definitely what she needed. This wasn't the first time he'd nursed her through a hangover. Not even close. And he still knew just what to do. How to make her feel better. And he still cared after all this time.

"So, what happened last night? Aside from me getting drunk?"

He sat back down, taking up so much space it was

ridiculous. When had he gotten so…wide? His biceps bulged against the sleeves of his shirt and his thighs were ridiculously muscular. "What do you remember?"

"After we left the hotel? I vaguely recall the limo ride, and after that, nothing. Why did you bring me here instead of taking me home?" Or maybe she didn't want to know.

"I did take you home, but without the passcode I couldn't get you into your apartment. The doorman wasn't much help."

She winced a little at the idea of Dale, the night doorman, seeing her that way.

"How did I end up out of my dress?" she asked.

"You don't remember?"

Cautiously she said, "No."

"Damn," he said, shaking his head, a frown cutting deep into his brow. "Sex that wild, I was sure you would remember."

She gasped, her eyes went wide and her heart stalled in her chest. "We did not!"

"Relax. I'm kidding," he said with a chuckle. "Nothing happened."

Was that disappointment she just felt? Nah, it couldn't be. Besides, if she was going to sleep with him she would like to actually remember it.

If? Oh my God, there was no *if.* She wasn't going to sleep with him. Ever.

Yeah, Gracie, you just keep telling yourself that.

"So why did I wake up in my underwear?"

"I helped you out of your dress and into bed. In the dark, so I didn't see anything."

She narrowed her eyes at him. "Really?"

He grinned. "That's my story and I'm sticking to it."

He was so lying.

"Not that I haven't seen it all before," he added.

True, and her body hadn't changed much in the past seven years. But his sure had, and what she wouldn't give to see him out of his clothes.

"You did try to jump me on the limo ride home, though," he said, and then added with a grin, "Still limber as ever."

Six

"I did not!" Gracie said, looking scandalized. And she was sexy as hell wearing his clothes. She was sexy wearing anything, but seeing her in the oversize shirt stirred up distinct memories. Though he preferred to see her wearing nothing at all.

"Oh yes you did," he told her. She had climbed into his lap and tried to kiss him, and as much as Roman had wanted to kiss her back, he would never take advantage of any woman in such a compromised state. If she was going to kiss him—and he didn't doubt that she would—she was going to be sober. And *she* would come to *him*. "I practically had to beat you off with a stick."

She glared at him.

He laughed. "Okay, I'm lying about the stick part, but you did put the moves on me. You were all hot and bothered."

"I'm sorry," she said with a wince.

Sorry? Last night had been the most fun he'd had in ages. The best part had been watching Gracie watch him dancing with all of those young, beautiful women, knowing she was crawling out of her skin with jealousy.

And the worst part had been watching that Dax character ogling her. That guy had his sights on Gracie, and not just for her philanthropic abilities. Roman had watched him watching her, and could tell the state senator had known as well as Roman that she'd been overdoing it on the drinks. So when Gracie left the ballroom, and Dax followed her, Roman had followed him. He'd never cared much for politicians, and that man had bad news written all over him, so Roman wasn't surprised to find him hovering around the general vicinity of the ladies' lounge.

Rather than allowing Gracie to find herself in a compromising position—and he'd had no doubt about the senator's intentions—he'd collected their coats and headed for the lounge hoping Gracie hadn't already been caught up in the man's web. Dax was still standing there looking irritated and impatient, glancing at his watch. When he saw Roman approach he'd flashed a phony smile.

"Roman!" he'd said, as though they were old friends. As if.

"Seems like a man in your position wouldn't want to be caught hanging out around the ladies' room," Roman had told him.

Dax had laughed, but there was an uncomfortable edge to his voice when he said, "Just taking a breather."

They both knew that was bullshit. And Roman had

never been one to sugarcoat the truth. "This breather wouldn't have anything to do with the fact that Gracie is in there, would it? Or that she's drunk?"

The man's smile had wavered and he'd puffed out his chest. He'd known he'd been busted. But Dax stood several inches shorter than Roman, and was in what could only be considered average physical shape. Roman could take him out with one solid crack to the jaw. Not that he would hit anyone unprovoked, but damn would it have felt good to knock that smug smile off his face.

"Are you her keeper?" Dax had asked him.

"Try me and find out," Roman had said, and his words had taken Dax back a step. As Roman had assumed, he was all talk.

He'd held both hands up in defense. "I just wanted to be sure she made it home safely. But clearly she's in good hands."

Yeah, the only hands she would have anything to do with that night. And when she'd stumbled out of the lounge a few minutes later Roman had gotten her the hell out of there.

"I never get that drunk," Gracie said now. "Not off four drinks."

Is that what she thought she'd had? Damn, she must have been worse off than she realized. "Hate to tell you, sweetheart, but you had more than four."

She frowned. "I did?"

"I saw you hit the bar at least six times."

Her eyes went wide again "*Six?* I did not!"

"Oh yes you did. You were knocking them back like a woman on a mission."

"Why didn't you stop me?"

"Because you're stubborn as hell and you wouldn't have listened. Knowing you, it probably would have made you drink more."

Her pained look said he was right.

"What did you eat yesterday?" he asked her. He couldn't even count how many times in the past he'd had to remind her to eat, and sometimes go so far as to force-feeding her. She'd always been so busy and he doubted that had changed much.

She gave it some thought. "Breakfast. *Maybe?*"

"Maybe?"

"It was a busy day."

"You didn't eat at the fund-raiser?"

She shook her head. "Please tell me I didn't make a fool of myself."

"No, but that Dax character had his sights set on you. I don't like him."

"I worked on his campaign. He's a decent guy."

"A decent guy who wants to get in your pants. Or panties. And by the way, you look good in pink lace."

She narrowed her eyes at him. "I thought you said it was dark."

"It was, but I see really well in the dark." She had been so out of it, he'd had to carry her into the house and up the stairs. And with the light streaming in from the hallway, it hadn't left a whole lot to the imagination.

"Would it be too much to ask for a ride home?" she asked. "Or I can take a cab. Honestly I don't even know where I am."

"You're not going anywhere until you get some food in your stomach," he said.

"I'm not quite there yet. My head is still pounding and my stomach feels iffy."

"Then sit back and relax. How about a cold compress for your head?"

"Are you sure you don't mind? If you have things to do…"

"It's Saturday. There's nothing that can't wait."

"I usually work Saturday," she said. "And Sunday. Mostly on charity stuff."

Clearly they shared the same work ethic. "Not today. Today you're going to relax."

"I guess I could stay for a little while," she said. "And the compress couldn't hurt."

"Lie down and make yourself comfortable. I'll get it."

He pushed himself up off the sofa and the effort made his left leg, which was more titanium than bone, ache. He had been in bad shape when he and his men had been rescued. His femur, which had been shattered in one of many beatings, had become infected. Had it been a day or two longer he probably would have lost his entire leg from the hip down. A week and he would have gone septic. The rescue had come just in the nick of time.

After several surgeries and months of rehabilitation he still walked with a limp, and was in near constant pain, but he was alive.

He grabbed a compress from the freezer and carried it back to her. She was stretched out, her hands folded across her chest, eyes closed, snoring softly.

He very gently set the compress across her forehead and she didn't rouse. If she was anything like him she didn't get more than five or six hours of sleep a night, so every moment of rest counted and he didn't wake her. Or climb on the couch beside her—which would have carried the very real risk of getting slapped. Instead he went upstairs to take a shower. And considering the ache in his groin, it would probably be a cold one.

Despite his attraction to her, she was a Winchester, and the running feud between himself and her family would always be there. Gracie was very close to her sisters and parents, who all despised him. He'd seen the expression on Eve's face last night when she looked over at him. Indignation. Raw and fresh. They would never accept him, and he would never do anything to alter their family dynamic.

But if it was just sex…

The only problem was that with Gracie, it had never been *just sex*.

Roman shaved, showered and pulled on a pair of boxer briefs. Having lived alone for so long, it hadn't occurred to him that he should have shut the bedroom door. Not until he heard a breathy "Oh my God" and looked up to see Gracie standing in the doorway.

"You have tattoos," Gracie said, her eyes so fixed on the ink branding his arms that she barely noticed he was in his underwear.

Okay, yeah, that was a lie. She'd noticed. And though he'd always been in great shape physically, now? He was ridiculously buff.

On his enormous left biceps, spanning from the edge of his shoulder to the crook of his arm, he had a very scary-looking skull and crossbones. The skull wore an army helmet, and the bones were actually military rifles. The right biceps bore a flowing American flag with red barbed wire for stripes.

She wanted to touch them. His biceps and his wide shoulders. And every other inch of his body.

"You like tattoos?" he asked, though the words barely made it through the fog that had settled in her brain. And he didn't look the least bit scandalized that she was seeing him this way. He'd never been shy about his body.

He had nothing to be shy about.

Transfixed, she nodded. But the real treat was when he said, "There's more," and turned.

An American eagle in flight spanned the entire width of his back, the tips of the bird's wings flirting with the edges of his tattooed arms. In its razor-sharp talons it clutched a banner that said Death Before Dishonor.

She couldn't stop a very breathy-sounding "wow" from escaping her lips.

Wearing a slightly crooked smile, he looked back over his shoulder at her. "See something you like?"

Did she ever. The bird was so lifelike she imagined she would actually feel the silky softness of the feathers if she touched Roman's back. Then he was getting closer, but he wasn't the one moving. Her feet were carrying her across the room to where he stood, then her hands were reaching out.

She felt possessed. And she was—by lust. By a need so intense her breasts ached and her heart pounded. She flattened both hands against his skin at the level of the eagle's breast and she could swear she felt Roman shiver. She slid her hands upward, across the wings to his shoulders.

"Gracie," he said, in a voice gravelly and low. "If you keep that up…"

He didn't have to finish his sentence; she knew exactly what he was going to say, and she was already too far gone. Now that she had touched him she couldn't stop. The ache pulsed downward and settled between her thighs and she could feel herself getting wet. His skin was hot and smooth against her palms as she slid them upward across the eagle's wings.

Over his shoulders.

Down his arms.

He moaned softly and uttered her name, and all she could think was *mine*. She wanted him, and nothing was going to stop her from having him this time.

She wrapped her arms around him and pressed her cheek to his wide back, threading her fingers through the thick, crisp hair on his chest, his hard nipples tickling her palms.

His head fell back and he cursed under his breath as she hugged herself close to his body, but it wasn't close enough. She wanted to crawl inside of him, be a part of his being. A part of his soul.

He had always been a part of hers. Maybe that was why his betrayal had hurt so much.

"Last warning," he told her. He was still holding back, but he was wasting his time. She dragged her nails down his chest to his stomach, gently, so it was barely more than a tease, then slipped her hands under the waistband of his shorts. He groaned as she wrapped one hand around his erection. He was solid and hot in her hand. She stroked him, gently at first, then she squeezed.

With a throaty growl he spun her around to face her, then wrapped his arms around her and lifted her right off her feet. She wrapped her arms around his neck and her legs around his hips, and when their lips met and their tongues tangled in a desperate kiss, it felt just like it had that first time so many years ago.

They fell onto the bed, Roman on top of her. He grabbed the hem of her T-shirt and pulled it up over her head. She moaned as he buried his face in her cleavage and tugged the cups of her bra down.

"You're so beautiful," he said, teasing the tip of one breast with his tongue, then nipping just hard enough to make her gasp. After all this time he still knew what to do to drive her crazy. He did the same to the other side, then he unfastened her bra with an adept flick of his fingers, pulled it off her and tossed it somewhere over his shoulder. Then he kissed her again, the hair on his chest tickling her nipples in the most tantalizing way.

She yanked his shorts off over his hips and used her feet to push them down his legs, desperate to feel him inside her. There was a fire building at her core, an ember burning hot on the verge of igniting.

He rose up on his knees, stripping her out of her pants and underwear in one swift motion, and grabbed a condom out of the drawer of the bedside table. Tearing the packet open with his teeth, he wasted no time rolling the condom on. Then he was back on top of her, his weight sinking her into the covers. He teased her first, sliding his erection against her. She was so slick and sensitive she probably could have climaxed just like that. But then he stopped, pulling back slightly. If he stopped now she was afraid that she actually might die from the ache building inside her.

She grabbed his muscular backside, and though she had never been one to beg she said, *"Please, don't stop."*

He grinned down at her, eyes glazed, his lids heavy. "Not a chance in hell."

His eyes locked on hers as he slowly entered her, giving her just an inch or two before pulling back again. Slow and gentle and sweet. But she didn't want slow. She needed him inside her now.

Digging into his buttocks with her nails, she thrust her hips upward against him. She cried out as he sank as deep as he could go. Roman moaned and buried his head in the crook of her neck as he cursed and told her with gritted teeth, "Slow down."

But she couldn't. She didn't want to slow down. She arched up to meet each of his thrusts, slipping easily into the rhythm they had mastered so long ago, their bodies so perfectly in sync it was almost as if they were one person.

Across the room, in the mirror above his chest of drawers, she could see their reflection. She lay beneath him, her legs hooked tightly around his hips, his muscular backside flexing with every thrust. It was the hottest, most arousing thing she had ever seen, and her muscles instantly began to coil and tighten. He must have felt it, too. He groaned and tunneled his fingers through her hair, kissed her hard as she reached a crest of pleasure that left her weak and breathless.

Moaning as her muscles gripped and pulsed around him, Roman was only seconds behind her. He picked up speed and pressed his forehead to hers, eyes squeezing shut as every muscle in his body tensed. "Gracie," he moaned as he climaxed, holding her so close and so tight she could almost feel the pleasure coursing through him.

Shuddering and gasping for air, they lay like that,

wrapped in each other's arms, their bodies still intimately joined. And though she tried to fight it, feelings of affection threatened to overwhelm her.

This was just good sex, she told herself. No, not good sex. Fantastic sex. Mind-blowing, earth-shattering, out-of-this-universe sex.

But still just sex.

Then he lifted his head and looked deep in her eyes, teased the tip of her nose with his own and smiled, and her insides went all gooey again. But not gooey enough to say or do something she would later regret.

She was a woman who kept her heart carefully guarded and locked up tight. He used to have the key, but it would do him no good. It had taken so long for her broken heart to repair itself that the lock had rusted shut. And she refused to let anyone, especially him, break it again.

Besides, even if she wanted it to be more, even if she could someday forgive and trust him again, her family never would. Sure, he was charming and funny and great in bed, but he had given her no reason to trust him. And far too many reasons not to.

Seven

Grace stood with her sisters amidst the crowd at the construction site of the new children's hospital, shivering under her cashmere coat. The reception for donors was set to begin in just a few minutes and she had serious mixed feelings about being there. After all, the Newport brothers were naming the hospital after Cynthia Newport. The woman with whom her father had had an affair and an illegitimate child. But Carson was her half-brother, and Eve was engaged to his brother Graham, so how could she not be there for them? The project was being funded almost entirely by the Newports.

She turned to scan the crowd to see many familiar faces. Nash Chamberlain and his wife, Gina. And of course Georgia and Carson. Even Dr. Lucinda Walsh and Josh Calhoun were in town. Brilliant cancer specialist that Lucinda was, Gracie and her sisters had hoped that she would remain their father's caretaker for the duration of his illness, but her love for Josh had taken her from Chicago to his dairy farm in Iowa, where, Gracie had heard, she was taking over the oncology department at a local hospital. Josh, with his long hair, rugged good looks and cowboy hat, was a quintessential cowboy.

"Of course they had to pick the coldest day of the year for this," Nora said, pulling her collar up against the bitter cold wind that poured in through openings that would soon be windows. "The windchill has to be ten below zero."

Eve pulled out her phone and checked. "Close, fifteen degrees."

"I feel warmer already," she joked.

"Have you talked to Mom?" Nora asked Eve.

Eve frowned and shook her head. Despite their parents' divorce, and their father's very public reputation for womanizing, the news that he had fathered a child with Cynthia Newport had hit their mother, Celeste, pretty hard. It had also been difficult for her to accept that Eve was in love with Graham, and that her grandchild would have the Newport name.

"She'll come around," Nora said, wrapping her arm around Eve's waist and giving her a squeeze.

"I know," Eve said, clearly holding back tears. "It still hurts, though."

Of the three sisters Eve was by far the toughest of the bunch, but Gracie had the feeling her hormones were out of whack from her pregnancy and making her weepy.

"I'm sorry," Nora said. "I shouldn't have brought it up."

"It will all work out," Eve said, but not with her usual confidence. "It will just take time."

There was a moment of silence, then Nora asked Gracie, "So how did the fund-raiser go Friday? I'm sorry I couldn't be there but the wedding plans have me chasing my own tail."

"It was great," she told her sister, but it was the memory of Saturday that was making her feel all warm and toasty under her coat.

Nora frowned. "That's it? Just *great*? No juicy gossip to share?"

"Honestly the whole night is kind of a blur." She glanced over at Eve, who was looking straight ahead with a wry smile on her face. Had she said something to Nora about Gracie being there with Roman? And the fact that she'd gotten drunk.

If she had, or if someone else had mentioned it, Nora didn't let on.

"Did you meet your fund-raising goal?" Nora asked her, and Gracie wished she would just let it go.

"I haven't talked to Dax yet, so I'm not sure."

Nora looked at her funny. "I thought you would be all over it Saturday."

She'd been all over something, but it wasn't fund-raising.

"It's a busy time for me at work," she said, hoping Nora would drop the subject. She didn't want to think about the fund-raiser or work or anything else. She didn't even want to be here today. Where she wanted to be was back in bed with Roman. And at the same time, the reality of how quickly and effortlessly they had reconnected scared the hell out of her. This was not a good idea, this thing they had started. It had never been her intention to sleep with him. Not that it wasn't some of the best sex she'd ever had in her life. But they had crossed a line, and she was afraid that she would never be able to cross back over it to where she was before. She wasn't even sure if she wanted to go back, and that was probably the scariest thing of all.

She wanted to trust him, and believe that he had nothing to do with the recent smear campaign targeting her father, but that didn't erase what had happened seven years ago. He had taken responsibility for his mistake, and his time in the service went a long way to prove his character. She wished she could just let it go, but it still lingered there somewhere in the back of her mind. She wasn't sure if that residual little sliver of doubt would ever completely go away. And that lack of trust would eventually become their undoing.

Or maybe she would get over it and they would live happily ever after. If that was even what he wanted. Or what she wanted. Was she obsessing over something that he might not even want? Was she assuming things that had no basis in reality?

It was all so confusing.

"Well, if it isn't the Winchester girls," someone said from behind them and they turned to see Brooks Newport, smug as usual, walking toward them.

"Oh great," she heard Eve mutter under her breath, but not quietly enough.

Brooks, with acid in his voice, said, "Sorry, I didn't catch that."

Gracie was typically nonconfrontational, and tried

to stay out of family spats, but she was feeling particularly snarky today. "Grow up, Brooks."

Her sisters both turned to her, looking as if they couldn't believe that had come out of her mouth. Brooks looked a little taken aback himself, but he recovered quickly.

"So the spoiled little heiress has a voice."

"She does," Gracie said, and though she had never been comfortable using profanity, she calmly, but forcefully, said, "and she's sick of your bullshit intimidations. This is a special day for your family and your inability to behave like an adult does a great disservice to your brothers and disrespects your mother's memory."

He obviously didn't like being called out as the immature, narcissistic ass that he was. "Your father is the one who disrespected my mother," he said smugly, with a top-that look.

So she did. "And that makes you no better than he is."

Brooks blinked, and she could see that the comment stung. Well, good. She hoped it would make him stop and think about his actions.

She could see the wheels in his head spinning, but before the situation could escalate further, Carson appeared at his brother's side.

"We're getting ready to start," he told Brooks.

Brooks looked at Gracie and her sisters, as if he wanted to say something more, but then turned and stalked away.

"Everything okay here?" Carson asked his half sisters.

"Fine," Gracie said. "Brooks was just being Brooks."

Carson shook his head sadly. "I wish I knew why he's so bitter. I understand his anger toward Sutton, but there's no reason to drag the three of you into it. I'm sorry if he upset you."

"I think I speak for me and my sisters when I say we're over it," Gracie told him.

"You're my family," Carson said. "I don't want Brooks's behavior to have a negative impact on that."

"Brooks's behavior has no bearing on our connection to you," Nora told him. "Family is family."

Gracie figured that they had proved that by accepting Carson as their sibling, despite the extramarital affair that was responsible for his existence. Sutton's actions were in no way Carson's fault, and it wasn't fair to blame him for their father's poor judgment.

"I have to go," Carson said. "Maybe we can talk more afterward."

When he was gone, Eve looked at Gracie and asked, "Wow, what's gotten into you today?"

Riding on the edge of a guilty conscience, Gracie asked, "Was it wrong of me to stand up to Brooks?"

Nora laughed. "Heck no. He expected you to defend Sutton, and when you didn't he had no idea what to say."

"You blindsided him," Eve said. "And it was thoroughly amusing."

Gracie's phone buzzed with a text. She pulled it out of her pocket and saw that she had a message from Roman. She was almost afraid to open it on the chance that he would say their encounter had been a mistake, and there was just too much bad blood between them to make even a sexual relationship work. Because she saw no harm in occasionally having a warm body to cozy up to on cold nights. She had needs and Roman was pretty damned good at fulfilling them.

Occasionally.

Her heart pounded as she punched in the code on her phone and the text popped up on the screen.

Dinner at my place? Then a little dessert?

She couldn't suppress the smile curling her lips. She'd been worried for no reason. He obviously was still interested. As excited as she was, and as much as she wanted to see him, she had the distinct feeling that her life was about to get very complicated.

With the guarantee that Sutton was about to reveal information about the identity of their real father, Roman finally talked both Graham and Brooks into a meeting with the dying tycoon. Which was how, the following Friday, Roman found himself back at the Winchester estate. Once again against his will and better judgment. He just hoped that Sutton would actually deliver this time. According to Grace he hadn't been out of bed in days and she was worried that the cancer, or the treatments, or a combination of both, had begun to affect him mentally. She'd been visiting him daily, and he'd been alternating between being himself, sinking into a deep depression and experiencing fits of irrational anger at the drop of a hat. She said it was a little like Jekyll and Hyde.

Roman didn't even know why he had to be there. When he'd asked Sutton, all he'd gotten back was a very cryptic *To keep the peace.* But if tempers flared and Graham took a shot at his brother, it wasn't Roman's responsibility to stop him. As far as he was concerned Brooks could use a little sense knocked into him. And though Brooks was nothing more than a thug in an expensive suit, he was still a client—and a very lucrative one at that—and Roman was under contract to find their birth father. As far as he'd found, it was as though their mother, Cynthia, in the time before she moved to Chicago, hadn't existed.

Gracie had wanted to join them but her father had forbidden it, and of course she'd backed down instantly. It had always fascinated Roman, the control her father had over her. Gracie on her own, in any other element, was one of the toughest, brightest, most capable women Roman had ever met. She'd certainly never taken any crap from Roman. But bring Daddy into the picture and her backbone mysteriously dissolved.

She'd certainly been aggressive Saturday morning. And Saturday afternoon, and most of Saturday night. He drove her home Sunday morning so she could get ready to attend the hospital reception, then she came back Monday evening and he'd made her dinner. He had talked to her every day since then, but they hadn't seen each other since she left Monday night.

Clearly the fire that burned between them seven years ago had never gone out. But he could feel her holding back. And he understood. He couldn't say for sure that he was still in love with her. But he couldn't say that he *wasn't* in love with her, either. Not that it mattered. She'd made it clear that it was just sex to her. That she could never trust him with her heart again. But they could still be friends.

Friends with benefits. He could live with that.

When he arrived at the Winchester estate Brooks

and Graham were already there, and he was surprised to find Carson, their youngest brother, and Sutton's recently confirmed son, standing by his bedside. Sutton held the meeting in his personal suite from his bed. Though Roman had thought he couldn't look much worse than the last time he saw the man, he'd been wrong.

Brooks and Graham stood far from each other, at opposite ends of the room.

"It's about damned time," Brooks snapped at Roman as Sutton's nurse showed him into the room, then reclaimed her seat just outside the door. According to Roman's Rolex he was a minute early.

"Forgive my brother," Graham apologized, looking both irritated and resigned. "I've yet to find anything to kill the bug that crawled up his ass."

The comment earned him a glare from Brooks. Hell, maybe they would come to blows.

Roman took a spot at the foot of the bed between the two men. Just in case.

"Now that we're all here, let's get started," Sutton said, his voice so weak Roman had to strain to hear him. He was sitting propped up by a mountain of pillows, which Roman suspected was the only thing holding him upright. It reminded him of Gracie in the limo on the way home the other night, and he instantly wanted to smile.

Graham moved to his future father-in-law's side. "Roman tells me that you have information about our father."

"I do."

"I'm a little confused as to why I'm here," Carson

said. "I know who my father is. I have no relation to the man you're looking for."

"This concerns your mother, too," Sutton told him.

"So out with it," Brooks snapped, completely insensitive to his rival's fragile condition.

"You all know that I'm a man of my word. Once I've made a promise I will not break it," Sutton said.

"Which is why you never promise anyone anything," Roman told him and Sutton shot him a vague, wry smile.

"But I did once, a long time ago. A promise that until recently I intended to take to my grave." He looked from Brooks to his brother. "One I made to your mother."

"Your word means nothing to me, old man," Brooks ground out. "Just tell us what you know."

"First you have to give me your word that what I am about to tell you will never leave this room." He looked to Roman. "All four of you."

"This is business," Roman said. "I would never divulge to anyone information I obtained in a private meeting with my clients."

Sutton looked to Graham. He nodded and said, "Of course." Then Graham gave his brother a look that seemed to say, *Do it or else.*

Brooks grudgingly nodded. "You have my word, as well."

"First I want you to know that your mother was an amazing woman. I had never met anyone like her. And I haven't since."

"And when was that?" Brooks asked.

"She was pregnant with the two of you," Sutton said. "Pregnant and alone working as a waitress in a café I went to occasionally. She'd only been working there a week, and she spilled a drink in my lap. She apologized profusely, then broke down in tears, so afraid that she would lose her job..." He smiled vaguely and faded off, as if lost in thought. To anyone who didn't know what a coldhearted and brutal businessman he was, they might think he was just an average sentimental old man.

"And?" Brooks snapped after several seconds, which earned him another look from Graham. Roman couldn't deny feeling a little irritated, too. It was obvious that Sutton was in poor shape. Still Brooks couldn't cut him a break, which said a lot about his integrity. As in he had none. The man lay dying in front of him, confessing a secret he'd once intended to die with, and Brooks couldn't see past his thirst for revenge. His need to conquer.

But Sutton didn't even seem to notice. Or didn't care.

"Let the man speak," Graham said with a warning tone.

Carson laid a hand on his father's shoulder and in a patient voice said, "Go on, Sutton."

Sutton blinked rapidly and snapped back to the present. "I could see the desperation in her eyes, and that she was carrying a child, or as I later discovered, two children. I left her a generous tip, and couldn't stop thinking about her. When I went back a week later she was working again, and I found that I was happy to see her. But she looked so tired and stressed, as if she carried the weight of the world on her shoulders.

"She thanked me for my generosity the week before. She wouldn't admit it then—she was too proud—but she had been about to lose the room she was renting and that tip was enough to pay her rent for another month. That was before her coworker Gerty took her in. I hung around for a while, until her shift ended, and I invited her to have dinner with me.

"She hesitated of course, worried I had ulterior motives, but I think hunger won out over her pride. And she ate like she hadn't seen real food in months. It gave me so much satisfaction to help her."

"Why do I find that hard to believe?" Brooks said, but Sutton went on as if he hadn't even heard him.

"I inquired about her pregnancy, and she confessed to me that she hadn't told the father of her unborn twins about the pregnancy before moving to Chicago from Texas to start over. The long hours on her feet were difficult, but it was the only job she could find. But she said that now, since her pregnancy had begun to show, her boss was making noise like she would no longer be an asset. She knew it was only a matter of time before she was fired."

"Isn't that illegal?" Carson asked.

Sutton shook his head. "Not back then. But I admired her courage and fortitude, so I offered her a job." His eyes belied the affection he felt, and maybe still felt, for Cynthia Newport.

"As your *mistress*?" Brooks asked.

"As my secretary. She had no experience. She couldn't even type, but I knew that she would learn and she did. And what started out as a friendship became something more. I helped her as much as I could after you and your brother were born. But we had to keep our relationship a secret."

"Which is how Carson came to be," Graham said, looking to his younger brother.

Brooks glared at Sutton. "That's what womanizers do."

Sutton faced him, looking almost apologetic. "It was more than an affair. We were deeply in love. Your mother was my soul mate. I would have done anything for her. I wanted to divorce Celeste and marry her, but back then I was still under my father-in-law's thumb. He threatened to ruin me financially, and keep my daughter and my unborn child from me. Cynthia couldn't bear to watch that happen. We knew that as long as we were together Celeste's family would never let us be happy. So we were forced to go our separate ways.

"When she discovered she was pregnant with Carson she said nothing, would never confirm that he was mine, so I tried to forget her. I distracted myself with work, and women who meant nothing to me, thinking it would ease the need to be with her. But it never did. I always told myself, maybe someday... Then she died and I lost my chance."

"You claim to have loved her, but you didn't even come to her funeral," Brooks said.

"I couldn't," Sutton said. "It would have caused a scene, and I couldn't do that to her."

Carson shot his brother a look and told Sutton, "I understand."

"The day your mother and I parted ways, she made me promise something, something I had to swear I would take to my grave."

"Yet here we are," Brooks said smugly. "And you claim you're a man of your word?"

"Enough!" Carson snapped at his older brother, and Brooks actually backed down.

Sutton looked so sad when he said, "I don't have much time left, Brooks, and I don't want her secret to die with me. Our personal feelings aside, as her sons, you should know who your mother really was, and what she sacrificed for the two of you. It's all I can do to honor the memory of the woman I never stopped loving."

"What do you mean who she really was?" Graham asked, his brow knit.

"Your mom wasn't who you thought she was. Her real name was Amy Jo Turner."

Eight

The brothers all looked taken aback. "She moved here from Cool Springs, a small town in Texas."

"Son of a bitch," Roman muttered, shaking his head. With the truth out it all made sense. He'd always suspected that Cynthia Newport was an alias, but he could never be sure and his investigation had proven inconclusive. "That explains why I couldn't find anything on her before she moved here."

Sutton's nod seemed to take extreme effort. "She had no choice."

"Why would she change her name and lie about where she's from?" Brooks asked, sounding a little less cocky this time. "Was she a criminal? On the run from the law?"

"She was on the run, but not from the law. She was trying to get away from her father, your grandfather."

Graham frowned. "Why?"

"He was an evil man. A violent and sadistic alcoholic. She told me about the beatings and the emotional abuse…" He shook his head, wincing, as if the words were too painful to speak. "He was a monster."

"She had scars," Graham said. "Physical ones. I remember asking her about them and she brushed it off, said something about being clumsy. I think deep down I knew it was a lie. Maybe I didn't want to know the truth."

"She wasn't clumsy. But she did get careless, and found herself pregnant. She knew he would beat her. Two of her classmates turned up pregnant the previous year, and her father told her that if she ever got herself knocked up, he would take care of the 'problem' himself, with a fist to her stomach. Then he would kill the man who'd violated his daughter.

"She knew that he would do it. For everyone's safety she knew she had to leave. But she couldn't just disappear. She knew he would try to find her. And kill her."

"Jesus," Brooks mumbled as the color leeched from his face, the reality of the situation finally sinking in. "What about her mother?"

"She left when Cynthia was five. She couldn't take the beatings and the abuse any longer."

"And she just left our mother with him? Why?"

"She didn't have a choice. He would have never let her take Cynthia away. And she feared that if she tried, he would kill them both."

"So our mother changed her name," Graham said.

"She did more than change her name. As far as everyone in Cool Springs is concerned, Amy Jo Turner went for a swim in Whisper Lake and never came back out. They found her belongings on the ground at the water's edge, and though they never did find a body, she was assumed dead."

Carson shook his head in disbelief. "Our mother faked her own death?"

Sutton nodded, looking sallow and tired. And so sad.

Knowing the man's reputation as a shameless womanizer, the depth of emotion he was showing in regard to Cynthia blew Roman away. He could hardly believe it, but he actually felt sorry for the man.

"She had no other choice," Sutton told them.

"So what about our father?" Graham asked. "Do you know who he is?"

Sutton shook his head. "She never told me his name, but I know that he lived in the same town. And she told me once that you boys look just like him. I don't doubt that with this new information, Roman will be able to track him down."

As long as Roman had known Sutton, that was the closest thing to praise he'd ever gotten from him.

"Does he even know we exist?" Graham asked.

"She never told him about her pregnancy."

At least now Roman knew why Sutton wanted to keep Gracie out of this meeting. Sutton's dalliances were legend in Chicago. But it would have been awkward, explaining in front of his own daughter how he'd not only cheated on her mother, but had been in love with Cynthia.

As if reading his mind, Sutton looked over to Roman and said, "My daughters can never know about this."

So what the hell was he supposed to tell Gracie when she asked Roman about the meeting? Did Sutton expect him to lie to her? Or would she accept that what was said was confidential? That it was official business and as such he couldn't break privilege. He was a man of his word. Once he made a promise, he would not break it. He'd learned that lesson too late to save his relationship with Gracie, but it was a mistake he would never make again.

Either way, he couldn't tell her.

The brothers were eager for answers, and Roman was eager to finally solve the mystery, but when the other men left, he hung back, hoping to have a word with Sutton alone.

"You have something to say to me?" Sutton asked him when he didn't leave.

Roman stood at the foot of the bed, feet spread, arms folded across his chest. It was an intimidation tactic, and one he did automatically, because he knew that despite being so ill, no one could intimidate the great Sutton Winchester.

"That was good what you did for them," Roman said.

"I didn't do it for them," the older man said, looking so weak and pale Roman worried he might drop dead right there. "I did it to honor Cynthia and her legacy. I couldn't let the truth of who she was die with her."

"You really did love her," Roman said, finding that hard to imagine.

"I've loved deeply, and I lost her. But that was my fault. I never should have let her go, but I did and I've had to live with that. I was torn between being with the woman I loved and losing my family, who I loved just as much. Though I haven't always been good at showing it."

"Yeah, about that. Kudos on the reconnaissance mission you sent Grace on."

He folded his hands in his lap. "You disapprove?"

"That's putting it lightly."

"Everything that I do, every decision I make, is for the good of the family name," Sutton said.

He really was a selfish bastard, wasn't he? Though Roman really should be thanking Sutton. His actions had brought Roman and Gracie back together.

Which, come to think of it, was probably the worst thing he could have done if he wanted Roman out of the picture. Sutton had never approved of him before the first scandal, and he sure as hell never would now. But Sutton had seen Gracie's reaction to Roman that day in his office. She was clearly shaken. Hell, there was no reason for her to even be there, other than to rattle Roman's cage. So why would he take the chance that Gracie and Roman might reunite? Wouldn't he want them as far apart as possible?

And what did that mean exactly?

Roman heard a soft snore and realized that Sutton had fallen asleep.

Dude, it doesn't even matter. Sutton was dying, and Gracie had set very clear parameters for their relationship. They would go back to being good friends, like before, with the added bonus of incredible sex.

What man in his right mind would turn down a deal like that?

Roman didn't call Gracie after the meeting. Which she took to mean that he couldn't talk about what had been discussed. She understood confidentiality agreements. Every one of her employees was required to sign one. The fashion industry was rampant with espionage and backstabbing. It was the nature of the business.

Whatever had happened in there, her father didn't want her to know about it, but she couldn't deny that she was dying of curiosity. Yet she felt torn between wanting the truth and wondering if she was better off in the dark. All she did know for sure was that her father had divulged the information necessary for Roman to continue his search for Graham and Brooks's father. Eve had called to let her know. She just didn't know what that information was.

She had decided that if Sutton wanted her to know, he would tell her. Which was why when Roman picked her up later that evening she didn't bring it up. It would only put him in an uncomfortable position, and she wanted this to be a good night. Though they had spoken on the phone every day since last Sunday, neither had had time to see one another. They'd both been too busy to take the time away from work.

But tonight was all about them. He was taking her to one of the hottest new restaurants in downtown Chicago. And one of the priciest. And he must have been in some sort of hurry because he was driving like a maniac, whipping around corners and going over the speed limit.

"You know that the restaurant isn't going anywhere," she told him, clutching the door as he took a turn at high speed.

Roman glanced her way, a wry grin on his face. "What's the point of having a sports car if you can't have fun with it?"

"There is a fine line between fun and idiocy," she said, knowing that he had always been a thrill seeker, and fearless, which was probably why he had done so well in black ops.

He whipped around a curve in the road while she held on for dear life. "I'd like to get to dinner alive if it's not too much trouble."

With a smile he slowed and downshifted. Why did she get the feeling he was trying to rattle her chain? And why, deep down, did she kind of like it?

"You used to love going fast," Roman said.

"Then I grew up."

"That's too bad. The Gracie I knew liked to take risks."

She couldn't help but feel defensive. "I've taken tons of risks. My business plan was aggressive, and extremely risky. I invested everything I had into my clothing line."

"I'm not talking about financial risk. Money doesn't count. Money isn't *real*. If you lose it you can always earn it back. A real risk is the possibility of losing something priceless."

She didn't mean to say them, but the words just popped out of her mouth. "Like when you lost me."

She expected a snarky reply or a witty comeback; instead he nodded, eyes forward, voice low, and said, "Yes, just like that."

His words dripped with so much regret her heart hurt. What was wrong with her? She had been looking forward to this night all week. Why was she trying to sabotage it?

"I'm sorry," she said.

"Don't be. It's the truth."

"I know, but—"

"Gracie," he said, reaching over to take her hand.

"Don't worry about it. Not a day goes by that I don't think about what I did and regret it. I would take it back if I could. But all I can do now is move forward."

"I want to let it go," she said. "I want to be over it. I want to trust you."

"And you will when you're ready." He gave her hand a squeeze then let go to shift. "Just let it go tonight, so we can have a good time."

"Okay," she said, but still felt lousy for bringing it up in the first place. It was against her nature to hurt people, and when she did, she always felt awful. She was sure that right now she felt far worse for saying what she'd said than he had hearing it. Or maybe not.

They pulled up to the restaurant, a seafood and steak house that was receiving rave reviews, and the valet opened her door. Roman handed over his keys and they walked inside.

It would have made her night if he had taken her hand as they walked in, but friends didn't do that sort of thing. She couldn't be seen with him in public, looking so close and intimate. She could just imagine the chatter and gossip that would surely follow. Honestly it would be better if they weren't seen in public together at all. The last thing she wanted was for this to get complicated.

The hostess greeted Roman by name and took their coats, then led them immediately to a table in a dimly lit enclosed patio away from the chatter, with a stunning view of Lake Michigan. The night sky was clear and the surface of the choppy water shimmered in the moonlight.

A candle illuminated the cloth-covered table, and rose petals lay scattered across the surface. Champagne sat chilling in a silver bucket beside it, and a single long-stem rose lay across her napkin.

Simple and elegant, and it stole her breath. This kind of gesture was the last thing she had expected from a "friend."

Just getting the reservation must have been a feat. She knew for a fact that they were booked months in advance, and anyone getting in on a few days' notice had to have some pull. And they were sitting in the absolute prime seats of the establishment.

Roman had pulled out all of the stops and she had nearly ruined the night with her big mouth, by making him feel bad for something he already clearly regretted. Though she hated to admit it, there were times when bits of her father came out in her own personality. She loved him, and respected him as a businessman. But as a person, he'd done nothing but let her down, and served as a terrible example of how a man should be. Which was probably why she'd been so attracted to Roman. He couldn't have been more different than Sutton in practically every way.

Their waiter, a youngish and very attractive guy—probably a college student—appeared immediately. He greeted Roman by name, offered them each a leather-bound menu and poured the champagne. Without even looking at the menu Roman ordered what had always been her favorite appetizer. Though she considered herself a modern and independent woman, knowing that Roman still knew her so well, she didn't mind that he'd ordered without asking what she wanted.

"To new beginnings," he said, toasting the night with a gentle clink of the delicate crystal flutes.

She took a sip then set her glass down. "I'm curious. How did you get a reservation here?"

"You're not the only one who knows people," he said with a grin, opening his menu. "What are you in the mood for?"

A slow smile curled her lips and he didn't even have to ask what she was thinking.

His eyes growing dark with desire, he said, "Sweetheart, that's dessert."

"Grace!"

Hearing her name being called, she turned to see Dax approaching their table. Roman frowned. Though she was sure he hadn't meant to, Dax had just killed what had been a very special, and very sensual, moment. Dax had called her a dozen times that week, on both her work and private lines. She'd had her assistant take a message, or let it go to voice mail, as her week had been too busy to get caught up in another one of the "projects" he always seemed to have on the back burner. Usually she didn't mind his enthusiasm. She'd enjoyed working on his campaign. But it seemed that the more time she devoted to his causes, the more he expected from her.

"I was beginning to worry when you didn't get back to me," he said, all but ignoring Roman, who she could see was not at all happy with the rude interruption. And neither was she. Normally she would have risen and greeted Dax with a platonic hug, or air-kissed him on each cheek, but this time she stayed put.

But he was being a typical self-centered, pushy politician, she supposed.

"I've been very busy," she told Dax, her irritation growing as he placed a heavy hand on her bare shoulder and gave it a squeeze.

"I have some ideas I need to run past you for an event I'd like to sponsor."

"This is a very busy time for me," she said, hoping to brush him off. "Call my assistant. Maybe she can squeeze you in after the holidays."

His smile never faltered. "I have a better idea. We'll meet for dinner tomorrow night. I'll pick you up at seven."

Was he asking her or telling her? Either way, the answer was no. "I'm busy tomorrow."

He wasn't swayed. "All right, Sunday, then."

What the hell was wrong with Dax? He was almost acting as if they were an item. Or as if he was deliberately trying to piss off Roman, and sabotage their evening. And Roman was seriously pissed off. His jaw was tense, and she could see that he wanted to interject. He glanced at her questioningly and she shot him a look that she hoped said, *let me handle it*.

Turning to Dax, she was firm, but polite. "Dax, I don't mean to be rude, but I just want to have a quiet evening with a friend. Call my assistant and I'll see what I can do."

He gave her shoulder another firm squeeze and she fought the urge to shrug his hand off, or bat it away. It wasn't like him to be so forward. Not with her anyway. Maybe Roman was right and Dax had set his sights on her. But she wasn't interested. Not even the least little bit. Sure, they had seen each other socially a few times, and had worked together, but she had never led him to believe she had any romantic intentions. If that's what he thought, he couldn't have been more mistaken.

"We'll talk next week," he said. He didn't ask, he

all but demanded. And she didn't justify it with a response. She just wanted him to leave.

When he finally removed his hand, the ghost of his touch made her feel so…icky. And he walked off having never even acknowledged that Roman was there.

So much for his respect for a *true* war hero.

"I'm so sorry, Roman. I'm not sure why Dax just did that. If I didn't know better I would say that he was jealous. Or trying to make you jealous."

"You know what I think," he said, sounding irritated.

She did, and she was beginning to believe he was right. "If he's looking for something beyond a professional relationship, I'm not interested. And if he thinks that kind of behavior is appropriate in any way, he had better start looking for a new volunteer."

"Good," Roman said, sounding relieved. "I don't trust him."

Right now, neither did she. "I could see that you wanted to say something to him."

"Oh, you have no idea," Roman said. "Let's just say that he's lucky he left when he did."

"Well, thank you for letting me handle it."

"I didn't feel like it was my place," he said. "As your friend."

She could swear he almost sounded hurt. Or disappointed. They had agreed to this arrangement. Did this mean he wanted more? Or was she just imagining things?

And if he did want more, how did she feel about that? Maybe she wanted more, too, if she could shake off her apprehension? He had been nothing but honest and up front with her, and had never made any excuses for his betrayal seven years ago. And she now truly believed that he had nothing to do with the recent slurs against her family. He was a good man, and a good friend. So why was she clinging so firmly to that last shred of resentment?

Just let it go and enjoy the night, and what you do have together, she told herself. *Don't overthink it. Keep it simple.*

"I don't want this to ruin our evening," she said.

"Neither do I."

She lowered her voice and added, "Just so we're clear, the only one getting into my panties is *you*." She paused, then said, "Though that could be a problem tonight."

"And why is that?"

She leaned forward, flashing him a sexy grin. "Because I'm not wearing any."

Nine

Roman was pretty sure Grace was kidding when she made the crack about not wearing panties. She was using it as a way to dispel the tension of the senator's rude interruption. Whether it was true or not, it worked.

Dax could have potentially ruined their evening, but Gracie didn't let that happen. She seemed just as disgusted by the senator's unnecessary intrusion as Roman was. And she finally seemed to be seeing the man for who he really was: a narcissistic, manipulative creep who had more on his mind than campaigns and fund-raising. After his stunt last Friday at the fund-raiser, Roman didn't want him within a hundred yards of Gracie.

He hoped she meant what she said and this would be the push she needed to stop working with Dax altogether. Roman had done a little digging, and asked around, and though he hadn't found anything out-wardly corrupt in the senator's dealings, the general consensus seemed to be that the man was as crooked as they come—just very good at hiding it.

And though Roman tried not to let it show, he was jealous. When the senator put his hand on Gracie's shoulder Roman had caught himself clenching his fists. He didn't condone violence, but if they hadn't been in a crowded restaurant, his natural instinct to protect her would have left the senator with a broken hand.

But he'd let it go and they were able to eat and talk and enjoy each other's company the way they used to. He wanted to reach across the table and hold her hand, but he had to settle for a discreet game of footsie. But she took it a step further when she nudged out of her shoe and slid her foot up his leg. He nearly choked on his lobster when she slid her foot up his thigh and used her toes to play around in his crotch. He shot her a look, and she'd replied with a wicked grin. She was playing with fire and loving the hell out of it. Which only turned him on more. He slipped his hand under the table and stroked the arch of her foot and a fire lit in her eyes.

By the time they finished dinner, and the waiter asked if they wanted dessert, the only thing he had a taste for was her. He paid the bill and they waited im-patiently as the valet brought the car around. Her back was to the valet stand, and there was no one around, so he reached up under her coat and copped a quick feel for a panty line, but couldn't find one. She smiled up at him and said, "Told ya."

When they were in the car, she took his hand and guided it under her dress.

Nope, definitely no panties that he could feel. Just soft, smooth skin, and she was already moist with arousal.

He cursed under his breath, his crotch tight.

"Are you as turned on as I am?" she asked.

"You tell me," he said taking her hand and guiding it to his zipper, hissing out a breath as she stroked him through his slacks.

"Drive," she said. "Fast."

She didn't have to tell him twice.

If it hadn't been for the fact that he had to shift gears, he would have kept his hand between her legs, but he tried to behave. Her, not so much. She leaned over and kissed him and he got so carried away the car behind him had to honk to get his attention when the light turned green.

Her place was closer by a good twenty minutes so he drove there. And rather than wait for the elevator, they took the stairs up to her fourth-floor loft. With her spiked heels slowing her down he got impatient at the second-floor landing. So he lifted her up, tossed her over his shoulder and carried her the rest of the way. It must have been a huge turn-on because they barely made it through the door before she shoved his coat down his arms and tugged at his belt. She unfastened his pants, shoved him against the door and dropped to her knees right there in the foyer. He groaned as she took him deep into her mouth, but he was so fired up he couldn't stand it for more than a minute or two before he had to stop her. Taking his own pleasure before hers was not, and never had been, an option.

When they made it to the bedroom she pulled her dress off and he discovered that not only was she not wearing panties, she didn't have a bra on, either. Just a pair of silky thigh-high stockings. Black, his personal favorite. With her tousled hair and flushed skin she looked like something out of a sexual fantasy. He had planned to make love to her, slow and sweet, but that clearly wasn't going to happen. Not this time.

So instead he shed the rest of his clothes, picked her up and tossed her onto the bed. She tried to pull him down on top of her, but he pinned her arms at her sides and buried his face between her thighs. She gasped and arched upward, curling her fingers into the covers. She was sweeter and more delicious than anything on the menu at the restaurant. And she was so turned on it couldn't have been thirty seconds before she moaned and shuddered and thrust her hips up as she shattered. She barely had time to catch her breath before she was up on her knees, pushing him onto his back.

He was hoping to take things a little bit slower but she was a woman on a mission. There was no stopping Gracie as she climbed on top of him, taking him deep inside of her. And it felt so damned good he didn't want to stop her. She was so hot and wet he had to dig extra deep to find the will and the control not to lose it instantly.

Head back, eyes closed, lost in her own world, she rode him hard and fast, bracing her hands on his chest, digging her nails into his skin. He gripped her hips, tried to slow her down, but it was already too late. He could feel the coil of pleasure pull tight in his groin, until it was almost too much to take, then let go in a hot rush.

He rode out the storm, and when he opened his eyes

Gracie was smiling down at him. And all he could say was "Wow."

She laughed. "I'll take that as a compliment."

"Did you make it in time?"

She smiled and nodded.

"I tried to hold back."

"I know you did, and seeing you lose control made me lose control." She settled down on his chest, her skin hot against his. "That was incredible."

Yes, it was. But every time with her, no matter how they did it, was incredible. Fast, slow, he didn't care. As long as he was close to her. "I didn't really do much."

"Sometimes it's okay to just lie there and enjoy it," she said. "Let me do all the work."

He could live with that. "Well, it was the perfect end to a perfect evening."

Her laugh was a wry one. "Oh, but we're not done. Not even close. In fact…"

She got that devilish gleam in her eye, the one that said she was up to something. "I'll be right back," she told him, jumping off the bed and bolting from the room, then called over her shoulder, "Don't go anywhere."

Yeah, right. Like he had the energy to move. He could barely *breathe*.

He closed his eyes, trying not to fall asleep. He hadn't done any of the work, so why was he so wiped out?

"I'm back," she said several seconds later.

He opened his eyes and lifted his head.

She stood in the doorway, naked and flushed and sexy as hell, those damned thigh highs hugging her perfect legs just right. Holding a bottle of chocolate syrup in one hand and a can of whipped cream in the other, she grinned as she said, "How about a little dessert?"

The following Monday, Gracie sat at her drawing table in her studio, trying to sketch out a few pieces for next year's fall line, but she couldn't concentrate. Typically the view of the Chicago skyline out the long stretch of floor-to-ceiling windows was all she needed to inspire her, but it wasn't working today.

Today, she couldn't keep her mind off Roman.

He was all she seemed to think about lately. And not the way a friend should be thinking about another friend. Her feelings for him seemed to be spiraling out of control, and as much as it scared her, she'd never felt so alive and happy in her life. Or more conflicted. Why is it the two always seemed to go hand in hand?

Hard as she tried to stick to the friends-with-benefits arrangement, her heart would have no part of it. And she'd gone and done exactly what she promised herself she wouldn't do. She'd started to fall in love with him again. And she was pretty sure, knowing Roman the way she did, that he was falling for her, too.

It wasn't logical. It wasn't even sane. And to call it complicated didn't adequately describe what they would be getting themselves into if they took the next step.

A knock on her studio door had her looking up from her half-finished sketch. When the door opened and her sister Eve popped her head in, Gracie smiled.

"You busy?" Eve asked.

"Actually your timing is perfect," Gracie said, tossing her pencil onto her drawing table. "I could use a break."

Eve crossed the room to look over Gracie's shoulder at the sketch she'd been trying to complete. "Nice."

"Thanks."

"It still blows me away at times how talented you are. You definitely got all the artistic talent in the family. I still draw like a third grader."

"What brings you to my side of town?" Gracie asked.

"Oh, I just thought I would stop in and say hi."

Gracie frowned. Eve was a very busy woman. She never just stopped in. If she went out of her way to drop by, she had a good reason to be there.

"Is everything okay with Sutton?"

"I talked to his nurse earlier and she said he's having a rough day, but he's stable."

"So what is it?"

"What is what?" Eve asked, going for a nonchalant look and failing miserably. "Can't I pay a visit to my baby sister?"

"Nope. You pretty much always have a reason. You might as well just tell me what it is." Though she was pretty sure she already knew what was bothering her sister.

"I'm worried about you, Grace."

"Worried about what?"

"You and Roman."

"Roman and I are friends."

"He almost ruined us."

"It was a long time ago, and he had nothing to do with the recent accusations. That was all Brooks."

"So what you're saying is, you trust him?"

"I do," she said.

Her sister eyed her cautiously. "Completely."

"Yes," Grace said, with not even a hint of reservation, and realized it was true. She really did trust him.

"Are you in love with him?"

Again there was no hesitation in her reply. "Yes, I'm in love with him."

Eve's troubled look didn't bode well, so Grace tried to explain.

"I know it probably doesn't make much sense to you. Hell, it doesn't make much sense to me, either. All I know is that everything inside me is screaming that he and I are supposed to be together. And though he's never come right out and said it, I think he feels the same way. We're just so…*good* together. I don't know how else to explain it. Even knowing that it could cause discord in the family, I still want him. And need him."

"I want you to be happy, Grace. We all do. And though I do have my reservations about Roman, I trust *you*, and I think that over time, after he proves himself, we'll learn to trust Roman, too. I just don't want to see you get hurt again."

"It's a chance I'm willing to take."

Eve took a deep breath and nodded, looking relieved. "Good. I guess I needed to hear that from you. I needed to see how sure you are. Because if you were still having reservations I had every intention of talking you out of seeing him, before you got in over your head."

Honestly she was already in over her head that first day in Sutton's office.

"There is something else I wanted to talk about," Eve said. "Daddy and I spoke last night and he's made the decision to change his will to include Carson."

Carson may have been a Newport, but he was just as much a Winchester. He was their brother, which gave him just as much right to the Winchester fortune as her and her sisters. The actions of his parents were in no way his fault, and as such it would be wrong to hold that against him.

"It's the right thing to do," Grace said.

Eve smiled and nodded. "I figured you would say that. I had my reservations at first, but I think you're right."

"How does Nora feel?" she asked, though Gracie was sure she already knew. Nora cared deeply about people, and had never taken any interest in money or power.

"She feels the way you do. I guess I was the only holdout. But he is our brother. Our blood. My only concern was that Brooks would use him to get what he wants, but now that I've gotten to know Carson I don't think that will happen. Graham said that Sutton's willingness to help them find their father, and the kindness he showed Cynthia in her time of need, has Brooks rethinking his priorities, and letting go of the bitterness."

"I know it's our legacy, and we should honor that, but in the end, it's only money."

"Guess we'll just have to hang in there and see what the future brings," Eve said.

Though her future was still hazy, one thing Gracie knew for sure was that hers would be a happy one.

In the world of private investigation, after months of dead ends there was nothing more satisfying than solving a case. And thanks to Sutton and his burst of conscience, less than a week after their meeting with the Newport boys, Roman now knew the identity of Graham and Brooks's father.

And the only thing more satisfying than solving the case was delivering the good news to the client.

Roman arranged a meeting for Wednesday morning, telling the brothers that he had information, and nothing more. This was news he wanted to deliver in person.

As he'd expected, the men showed up right on time. Roman's secretary showed them into the conference room at exactly 10:00 a.m. They walked in together looking anxious, and not at all as though they wanted to kill each other this time. Roman suspected that learning the truth about their mother had reminded them of the common ground they shared, and they had begun to repair their relationship. According to Gracie, who had talked to her sister Eve, Brooks had been very humbled by the truth and had begun to reevaluate his priorities, and his opinion of the man who'd essentially saved his mother's life.

Roman rose from his chair at the head of the table and shook both men's hands before he said, "Have a seat, gentlemen. Can I interest either of you in a beverage? Coffee? Water?"

The brothers declined with a shake of their heads, and rather than sitting on opposite sides of the table, sat side by side.

"So, you said you have information," Brooks said. "What do you know?"

Roman slid the file across his desk. "Your father's name is Beau Preston. He owns a horse ranch in Texas called the Lookaway."

"That was fast," Brooks said, looking as if he thought it was too good to be true. He opened the file so he and his brother could both read it.

"Cool Springs, Texas, is not a big place," Roman told them. "Once we knew where to look, and what to look for, the information was right there. It took some time, though, because the town doesn't even have a website."

"There isn't much here," Graham said.

"Unfortunately the town hasn't yet progressed into the digital age, so details are hard to come by. I wasn't sure how deep you wanted me to dig. I can get you more, but I'll have to send someone there, and in a town that small it won't be a covert operation. If there's a stranger there asking questions, word will probably spread fast. I wasn't sure if that's the way you want this to go down. Do you want your father to learn about you from the grapevine, or from his sons?"

Graham turned to his brother. "It's up to you, Brooks. This is your obsession."

"Are you saying you don't want to know?"

"No, I'm saying that this means more to you than it does to me. Do I want to know more? Absolutely. But I think that he should hear the truth from you or me, and not as gossip. And knowing how much this means to you, I think you should be the one to go."

The cocky real estate mogul looked more like a confused little boy. "To be honest, I'm not sure what I want to do. I've waited so long for this, and now it all seems to be moving so fast."

"Maybe you're just afraid of the truth," Graham said. "If this man knows nothing about us, he might not be thrilled to know that he has two illegitimate sons.

We honestly have no idea how he'll react. Personally I need a little time to prepare myself for whatever happens. Good or bad."

Brooks's confusion couldn't be more obvious. "I've been so focused on finding him, I guess I haven't given much thought to the next step. Or considered that he might not want to see us."

"Take some time to think about it," Roman told him. "Beau Preston has lived in Cool Springs his entire life, and he owns a lucrative business. As a horse breeder he's well-known for his champion bloodlines. I doubt he's going anywhere."

"I think this is something that my brother and I should discuss in private," Graham said, rising from his seat to shake Roman's hand. "Thank you for not giving up on this and solving the case. It means so much to us."

"Don't thank me. If it hadn't been for Sutton, I would still be spinning my wheels."

Looking shell-shocked, Brooks rose and shook Roman's hand. Maybe this would bring him some peace, and he would finally be able to let go of the irrational anger and hatred he'd held for the Winchester family. With Brooks it was hard to say.

Now that he and Gracie were exploring a relationship, Roman was happy to put the whole matter to rest, before he found himself sucked into the middle of another scandal. Because he knew that Brooks, despite his humbled state, could turn on a dime with a renewed thirst for revenge. Roman supposed that all they could do was wait, and time would tell.

"Will I see you at the wedding next Thursday?" Graham asked him.

"Wedding?" Roman said, unsure of what he was referring to. Next Thursday was Thanksgiving, but he and Gracie hadn't yet discussed spending it together.

"Nora and Reid's," Graham said. "I just assumed, since you and Gracie…" He paused and said, "I'm sorry, did I speak out of turn?"

If Gracie wanted him there, she hadn't said so. She still needed time, and he understood that. It was a slow process gaining back her trust. But it would happen. Because as far as he was concerned, they were meant to be together.

"Don't apologize. What Gracie and I have is very… complicated."

After the men left, Roman sat there for several minutes thinking about his relationship with Gracie, and that maybe they needed to have a talk. He was in no hurry. He was fine with letting their relationship progress naturally. Maybe he just needed to know that they did have a future together.

They had spent the entire weekend together, and even carved out time for lunch together yesterday. He'd met her at her office and she had introduced him around to the junior designers on her staff. He didn't know a whole lot about the fashion industry, but he was impressed with what he saw, and her employees seemed to have the utmost respect for her. And from the looks of it, she was wildly successful. But he always knew that she would be.

He considered calling her just to say hi, then changed his mind. She was probably busy, and he had meetings to prepare for. They would talk later that evening. They did every night. Usually for an hour or more. And they were usually both still at work wrapping things up for the night. Like him, she was a work-aholic, and typically hung around the office long after her employees went home for the night. Though he was sure that he would work less and delegate more if he had something, or better yet *someone*, to come home to.

As Roman was leaving the conference room, his secretary, Lisa, stopped him in the hallway.

"You got a call while you were in the meeting," she said.

"From who?"

"A Special Agent Crosswell, from the FBI."

Roman frowned. *The FBI?* What could they possibly want from him? "Did he say what he was calling for?"

"No, but he asked that you get back to him right away. He said it was an urgent matter. I left his contact information on his desk."

"Thanks, Lisa."

She eyed him quizzically. "Anything I should know about, boss?"

"I'll let you know as soon as I do."

She smiled. "Fair enough. I'm leaving to run some errands and pick up lunch. Would you like me to bring you back something?"

He was too distracted now to eat. "No, thanks."

He went to his corner office. He'd bought the company from a college friend who after a decade in the business decided the life of a PI wasn't for him. What had started as a three-office, four-employee operation was now a thriving business in a swanky downtown location. The agency took up an entire floor of the building and he now employed over three dozen people. And he still couldn't keep up with all the business coming his way. Unless things slowed down, he would have to look into expanding again. It was as if everything that he'd ever wanted in life was being dropped at his feet.

Well, almost everything. With Gracie it was a little more complicated.

He called the number Lisa left him and got the agent's voice mail. Annoyed and curious as to what he wanted, he left a message, then sat back to wait for a return call, going over a list of potential new clients.

Not five minutes later, the agent called back, and as he answered Roman felt an unusual sense of apprehension. "Roman Slater."

"Mr. Slater, my name is Rudy Crosswell. I'm a special agent with the FBI's fraud division. I was hoping you would be willing to meet with me this afternoon."

Well, you didn't get much more direct than that. "In regard to…?"

"I'd rather speak to you in person. Could we set something up?"

"Am I being investigated? Should I have counsel?"

"No, sir, nothing like that," he assured Roman. "The truth is, we need your help."

Well, that was good to know. His afternoon was booked, but this being the FBI, he felt it took precedence. "Can you be here at four?"

"Actually I was hoping you could come to the field office. It's a matter of the utmost secrecy."

Now Roman was really intrigued. "I'll work it in."

They decided on a time and when Lisa returned two hours later Roman asked her to cancel everything on his schedule for the afternoon. When he arrived at the field office Agent Crosswell met him in the lobby at the metal detector. The man was middle-aged, and looked to be ex-military with a graying buzz cut and serious eyes. Roman had to surrender the firearm he always kept strapped to his ankle and the knife from his inside coat pocket. Then the agent handed him a guest badge and led Roman through an open area crammed with cubicles and bustling with activity to his office in the back. The fact that he had an office said that he was fairly far up the ranks.

Roman's suspicion that he was military was confirmed when he saw the medals displayed in the agent's office, including a Medal of Honor and a Purple Heart. Otherwise the room was small, plain and a little outdated with its '90s-era furniture.

"Please have a seat," he told Roman.

Roman sat in one of two uncomfortable-looking chairs. "When did you serve?"

"Gulf War," he said, sitting at his desk, which was as clean and organized as the rest of the room. Another military trait. "I'll get right to the point. And what I'm about to tell you doesn't go past this office."

"Of course."

"I'm heading up a task force investigating political corruption on the state level. I need someone to do some outside digging."

"On who?"

"Dax Caufield."

Son of a bitch. Roman knew there was something not quite right about the senator, which made Gracie's affiliation with him that much more disturbing. "You think he's corrupt."

"I *know* he's corrupt. I just can't prove it yet. Two months into office it was rumored that he was taking bribes from business lobbyists in exchange for his support on key legislation. But he's smart, and hasn't left a paper trail. The case is weak at best. We're fairly sure we can get him on misuse of campaign funds, though. And that's where you come in."

Roman didn't like where this was going. "Why me?"

"Considering your past experience with political corruption, and your current connections, you're the perfect man for the job."

"What connections would those be?" he asked, afraid he already knew the answer.

"Grace Winchester."

Ten

Shit. This was the last thing Roman needed. He rose from his seat, which was just as uncomfortable as it looked, and told Agent Crosswell, "I'm sorry, but I can't help you."

The agent leaned back in his chair, nonplussed. "You may want to rethink that."

"Why?"

"Because as far as we know, she could be involved. She could be hiding evidence."

No way. Knowing Grace the way he did, Roman didn't believe that for a second. Besides, he'd gone down this road before and he'd lost the only thing that mattered to him. He would not take that chance again. "She would never do that. If she does have evidence, I'm betting she doesn't know it."

"An undercover operative learned from a source

that she may be in possession of files that would prove
the misappropriation of funds and even the bribery we
suspect him of."

If they had undercover people working this, it was
clearly a serious investigation. He didn't want to see
Gracie implicated. She had been through enough in
the past few months. "I can tell you right now that she
isn't hiding anything. She worked on his campaign
because she believed in his politics. She would never
knowingly hide evidence. Going after her would be a
waste of your time."

"She may not know that she has the evidence, but
we've learned that the senator thinks she does and that
she may know something she shouldn't. If she isn't
working in collusion with Senator Caufield—and that's
the theory we're leaning toward—our concern is that
he will do anything to get them back from her, and
keep her quiet if necessary. Meaning that she could
be in serious danger."

The idea of Gracie getting hurt made his heart beat
faster. If she truly was in danger he had to listen to
what Agent Crosswell had to say.

Roman reclaimed his seat. "You're sure about this."

Crosswell nodded. "Without a doubt."

"What do you need from me?"

"We need to get to those files before the senator can.
Do you have any idea where they might be located?"

With a shrug, Roman said, "Not a clue, but I can
ask her."

"No. Absolutely not. If she suddenly drops out of
sight, Senator Caufield will know something is up. We
can't take the chance of the investigation going public.
We have too many man-hours invested in this to blow

it. The senator cannot know that we're investigating him. Whatever you have to do, Miss Winchester cannot know about it."

"And if I tell her?"

"I can charge you with impeding a federal investigation."

Great. It was his past coming back to bite him in the ass. If Gracie was truly in danger his first instinct was to take her as far from Chicago as he could, if that's what it took to keep her safe. But there was no way Gracie would agree to that. Not without knowing why.

Dax had obviously had Gracie completely snowed. Then Roman thought of something that nearly made his heart stop altogether. "The senator has been trying to set up a meeting with her."

"We know. You can't let that meeting happen. If she gives him the files, our investigation is over. Or worse, she could be charged as an accomplice."

Jesus, how did he keep getting into these impossible situations? "This is emotional blackmail."

"I know. And I'm not unsympathetic."

His sympathy wouldn't stop his and Gracie's relationship from crashing and burning. "I can't lie to her."

The agent leaned forward, his expression serious. "Mr. Slater, if it's her life on the line, can you afford not to?"

Gracie came home from work early after a surprise call from Roman that afternoon. Though they typically didn't see each other on weeknights, he'd said he missed her and offered to bring dinner over. The truth was, she missed him, too, and seeing him only on the weekends just wasn't cutting it anymore. And it would give them an opportunity to talk about their relationship.

There was no question in her mind that she loved him, and she wanted them to be together. And she was fairly certain that he wanted the same thing if it felt as right to him as it did to her.

She had just gotten out of the shower and was still wrapped in a towel when her sister Nora called. With her wedding barely a week away she was scrambling to make last-minute preparations. Normally Gracie would have helped with the arrangements but she had just been too busy with work, and the proposed date had been too close for Gracie to arrange for time off. But Nora, sweet as she was, had been understanding.

"Reid and I took Declan for the final fitting on the tuxes," Nora told her. "He looks so adorable."

Declan, Nora's son from her first marriage, was a precocious two-year-old with curly ginger hair, adorable freckles and striking blue eyes. Nora's fiancé hadn't been open to taking on another man's child at first, which had worried Gracie and Eve, and especially Sutton. But Reid proved himself to be an amazing father and the three couldn't be happier.

"I wish there was something I could do to help," Gracie told her. "I know you have your hands full."

"I'm fine. For once in your life I want you to just enjoy a family event instead of feeling like you have to run it."

But that was what Gracie did. She helped people. She sacrificed her own time to make the lives of others easier. "Well, if there's anything you need me to do—"

"There isn't," Nora insisted. "You are a guest at this wedding and I want you to act like one. Which reminds me, are you planning to bring a date? I'd like to have the final list ready by tomorrow. And I've heard a thing or two…"

Of course she was talking about Roman.

"Would it be a problem if I brought someone?"

"Honey, of course not."

Gracie frowned. Maybe she just didn't understand who Gracie would be bringing. "Seriously, I can bring *anyone*?"

Nora laughed. "Why are you beating around the bush? If you want to bring Roman that's fine. I think it's better than fine."

Huh? "You do? After what he did to our family…"

"That was a long time ago, and Eve explained that he had nothing to do with this last scandal. He's human, Grace. Everyone makes mistakes. Everyone deserves a second chance. And it's obvious that he makes you happy. There's a light in your eyes that I haven't seen in ages. I'm not saying that he doesn't have to prove himself, but I do think he has potential."

Her relief at hearing that left her weak in the knees. "I'm in love with him again."

"Again?"

What was her sister implying? That Gracie hadn't really been in love with Roman before? "I'm not sure what you mean."

"I'm curious, Grace. How many men have you dated seriously in the past seven years? Just a rough number."

Nora already knew the answer to that. Gracie had used work and her charity obligations as an excuse to avoid dating, but the truth was, no man had come along whom she'd been interested in dating more than once or twice. She always compared them to Roman.

"None," she told her sister.

"Exactly."

She wasn't sure what her sister was trying to say. "Meaning what?"

"Is it possible that maybe you never *stopped* loving him?"

Leave it to Nora to speak her mind and tell it like it was. And of course Gracie had considered that. "At this point, I'm not really sure. I just know that I feel good when I'm with him. We just…fit. The thought of letting him back in then losing him again terrifies me. Maybe it's not so much that I don't trust him. Maybe I don't trust myself."

"I know all about loss, honey, believe me. When I lost Sean I thought I would never recover."

Nora's husband and childhood sweetheart, Sean O'Malley, had died fighting in the war in Iraq. He'd given his life saving other soldiers. Gracie hadn't forgotten how devastated Nora had been to lose the love of her life. The only thing that had kept her going was her son, Declan. And she'd sworn that she would never give her heart to a man again. But here she was, now happily engaged, deeply in love and about to get married. People did get second chances.

Maybe it was now meant to be, and seven years ago just hadn't been their time.

"Your only other option is to not try," Nora said. "Is that what you want?"

No, not trying wasn't an option at all. They had something good. Something special. "I can barely imagine my life without him in it. I've never been able to talk to anyone the way I can talk to him. He accepts me for who I am. He sees past the Winchester name

and appreciates me for *me*. He always has. In a couple of weeks he's gone from being my mortal enemy
to my best friend. How do you give up on something
like that?"

"Simple. You don't. You give it your all, and you
fight for what you want. And you don't stop until you
have no fight left in you."

Nora was right. Gracie needed to fight for them.
And the truth was that so far, she hadn't even had to
fight all that hard. Everything just seemed to be falling
into place. It was almost too easy. But easy was good,
and she planned to enjoy it.

"Yes," she told her sister. "I'm bringing Roman to
the wedding."

Nora sounded genuinely pleased when she said,
"Wonderful! I'm so happy for you, Grace."

Her doorbell rang. "Speak of the devil. Roman is
here. I have to go."

"If I don't talk to you before then, I'll see you next
Thursday. Love you!"

"Love you, too!" Gracie hung up, slipped a robe on
and scurried to the door. Roman was early. He wasn't
supposed to be there for another half an hour, but she
didn't care. She couldn't wait to see him.

She pulled the door open, ready to throw herself into
his arms, and was surprised to find not Roman standing there, but Dax Caufield.

Before Gracie could say a word, Dax walked right
in without invitation, and for a second she was too
stunned to say or do anything. He'd been blowing up
her phone and nagging her assistant since Friday, after
Gracie had seen him at the restaurant. But to show up
uninvited at her home?

"Dax, what are you doing here? And how did you get in?"

He avoided her question entirely. With a smile that didn't quite reach his eyes, he shrugged out of his coat and said, "You've been avoiding me, Grace."

She instinctively pulled her robe tighter around herself. She'd always felt comfortable with Dax. He'd been to her place a dozen times before when they'd worked on the campaign and she'd never thought twice about it. But something about this surprise visit, and the vibe she was getting from him, felt very wrong. She made a mental note to have a serious talk with her doorman. She didn't care if it was the president there to see her, he should have called up. "As I told you the other night, I've been very busy."

He took a seat on the couch, making himself comfortable. "You don't look busy now. Let's talk."

Who the hell was he to tell her if she was or wasn't busy? Why was he acting like this? "This is not a good night for me."

"I won't take too much of your time," he said. "I promise."

He already had taken too much time. And he was making her uncomfortable. She didn't like the way he was looking at her, and the fact that all she had on was a thin silk robe.

"You could offer me a drink," he said, crossing one leg over the other, settling back as if he was planning to stay a while.

He was trying to intimidate her, she realized. He was bullying her. She'd seen him do it before, never to her but to his political enemies during the campaign.

She hadn't cared for it then, and she really didn't like it now.

"Dax, I'm going to have to ask you to leave."

With a sigh he leaned forward, clasping his hands together. "Grace, I can't do that."

She went from uncomfortable to downright uneasy. He was actually refusing to leave her home?

"Grace, I have a problem and I need your help."

"What kind of problem?"

"There are people out to get me. They're trying to ruin me, Grace."

Well, of course there were. He was a politician and it was a cutthroat business. And what did he think she could do about it? "Who is trying to ruin you?"

"People who don't like my politics. Who think there's no place for a straight shooter in the senate. They tried to buy my vote, and when I refused they set out to ruin me."

Unless he had something to hide, it shouldn't have mattered who was after him. "How can they do that if you've done nothing wrong?"

"That's why I need all the files you have from the campaign. It's the only way to prove my innocence."

That made no sense. "You have copies of everything."

"You're going to have to trust me on this, Grace. I need you to hand over everything you have."

That was the problem, wasn't it? She *didn't* trust him. Not anymore. He wasn't acting like himself, and it was scaring her a little. "Dax, I'm sorry, but I don't have backups of anything."

"Grace," he said, rising from the couch. "We both know that's not true."

She took a step back, not just intimidated, but actually scared. "Dax, you have to leave right now."

He took a step toward her. Casually, but there was a darkness in his eyes that made her heart beat faster and her breath hitch.

"I really need your cooperation. It's a simple request."

She held her ground, but her knees had started to knock. "I can't give you something I don't have."

"We can do this now. You can hand over the flash drive and we can be done with it, or I can send someone to get it for me. And my colleagues are not as patient as I am. It's up to you, Grace."

Colleagues? He was threatening to send someone to do what? Rough her up?

Who the hell was this man?

"If you don't leave now I'm going to call the police," she told him, squaring her shoulders, struggling to hide the tremble in her voice, wishing she had her cell phone. If she could record his threats…

"That's not advisable, Grace. You would be wise to cooperate."

Screw that, and screw him. With a surge of courage that came from somewhere deep inside of her, she walked past Dax and grabbed the cordless phone off the coffee table. She punched in 911, and with her finger hovering over the button to connect the call, said firmly, *"Get. Out."*

Dax shrugged and shook his head, as if he were disappointed in her, then grabbed his coat. "Don't say I didn't warn you."

He strolled to the door, casually pulling his coat on, and without looking back, walked out. She ran to the door and locked it behind him. That was when the reality of what had just happened hit her full force, and she started to shake from the inside out. What could ever possess Dax to treat her that way? To bully and threaten her.

She felt betrayed and used and so stupid for not seeing sooner what he was really like.

And why were her copies of the files so critical? They were no different from his. At least, they shouldn't be.

Something was up, and she had the feeling that it had nothing to do with his innocence. If people were out to get him there must be a damned good reason. And she wanted to know why.

She collapsed onto the couch and sat there for several minutes, trying to calm down, stuck somewhere between grief and fear and hurt. The sharp rap on the door several minutes later nearly had her jumping out of her skin. Was that Dax's colleague already? Was he there to rough her up?

It took all her courage, but she got up and with shaky knees walked to the door, checking the peephole this time.

It was Roman. She went limp with relief. She threw the door open, hurled herself into his arms, knocking the bag of food he'd brought right out of his hand, and started to cry.

Eleven

"Gracie, what's wrong?" Roman asked, holding her tight, though he was pretty sure he already knew the answer.

She buried her face against his chest and sobbed, clinging to him like he was her lifeline, trembling all over.

He walked her backward into the apartment and shut the door behind them. When he'd pulled onto her street he had seen a man, one who'd looked an awful lot like Dax Caufield, leave her building and climb into a limo, but he'd been too far away to tell for sure.

Now he knew.

He wanted to know what had happened, if Dax had hurt her, but she was in no shape to explain. So he held her tight until the sobs subsided and she stopped trembling.

"Are you okay?" he asked, holding her away from him and cradling her face in his hands so he could see her eyes, which were all red and puffy.

"I am now," she said, sniffing and wiping the tears from her cheeks. "Dax came by."

His heart skipped a beat. He should have gotten there sooner. He should have gone straight to her when he left the FBI. To protect her. But there had been no way to know Dax would be so bold as to show up at her apartment. "Tell me what happened."

She told him how Dax had arrived unannounced and harassed her, even threatened her, for the flash drive from his campaign. That he would flat out threaten someone of Grace's social standing disturbed Roman more than anything. Dax was either running scared and desperate and making mistakes, or so arrogant he thought he was invincible.

"Did you give him the flash drive?" he asked her.

"I told him I didn't have them."

"Do you?"

She nodded. "In my file cabinet. Something isn't right, Roman. He has the same copies of everything that I do. Why is this so important that he would threaten me? I thought he was a decent guy. How could I have been so wrong?"

"I'm sorry," he said. He didn't know what else to say. At this point there was nothing else he *could* say. He was bound to secrecy by the FBI. His hands were tied. "Maybe it would be better if I held on to them for you. Just to be safe."

She shook her head firmly. "I refuse to let him intimidate me. I'm going to go over every single one of the files and see what it is he's so anxious about."

That was not a good idea. Roman didn't know what was in the files and he didn't want to take a chance on her seeing something she shouldn't and putting herself in even more danger. "Maybe you shouldn't." And he couldn't even explain why he was saying that.

"Roman, I have to. I have to know what's going on."

He knew that once Gracie set her mind to something, changing it was next to impossible. But he couldn't let her do this alone. "Then would you at least let me look at them with you?"

She seemed relieved. "Of course. Maybe you'll see something I would have otherwise missed."

"Get dressed and pack a bag," he said.

She frowned. "Why am I packing a bag?"

"Because you're staying with me until we sort this out." There was no way he was taking a chance and leaving her alone. He had friends in the security business. If necessary he would hire someone to shadow her when he couldn't be there.

"I can't let him scare me out of my home. If I keep the door locked—"

"Gracie, the sort of people we're talking about won't be stopped by a locked door. And they won't hesitate to hurt you if they don't get what they want."

Gracie looked so confused and hurt when she said, "I didn't even know that he had connections to people like that. Maybe he really doesn't, and he was just trying to scare me."

Roman seriously doubted it. He'd done a bit of digging and talked to a few people after his meeting with the FBI. Everyone agreed that while Dax had a stellar public persona, he also had a dark side, and reputed connections to some very bad people. Not just corrupt public officials and businessmen but the mob, as well. But no one as of yet had been able to prove it. "I'm not taking that chance," he told Gracie. Agent Crosswell had forbidden him from telling her about the investigation, but he couldn't stop Roman from protecting her. "Now pack some things. We're leaving."

Grace had only lasted an hour or so before the adrenaline rush of being threatened by a man she thought was her friend left her completely drained of energy. Roman had tucked her into his bed, then sat at his desk and got back to work. By 5:00 a.m., he had a pretty good idea of why the senator was so hot to get his hands on Grace's files. After comparing them to the documents on public record, there were major inconsistencies.

Until the senator got what he wanted, or the FBI nailed Dax for his crimes, Gracie would continue to be in danger. And Roman would do anything necessary to keep her safe. Even if he had to do it covertly.

The only way to put an end to this was to hand over everything she had to the FBI. The quickest way would be to make copies of the flash drive, and Gracie would never be the wiser. But while he could view the information on his computer, the flash drive was locked with a code and couldn't be duplicated or altered in any way. The only way to prove the senator's guilt was to take the original flash drive and hand it over to Agent Crosswell. But Roman would have to do it behind Gracie's back. Meaning he would be forced to lie to her.

Just like before.

The realization had been like an arrow through his

heart. This was supposed to be their second chance. But it was the only way to keep her safe.

"Good morning," he heard Gracie say, and looked up to find her standing in his office doorway, wrapped in a blanket, her hair tousled from sleep. "Have you been up all night?"

He nodded, wondering what the hell he was going to do next.

"Did you find anything?"

He'd given this a lot of thought, and he'd made a choice, one that could save Grace's—and his own—ass.

"Nothing," he told her. "I found nothing at all."

Confused, Grace said, "Nothing? Are you sure?"

"I'm sure."

She drew in a deep breath then blew it out. "Well, then, what was the big deal about him getting the flash drive?"

"I don't know, Gracie."

"Do you think I should just give them to him?"

"Hold off a while," Roman told her, looking as confused as she was. "There's clearly something shady going on and I want a little more time to dig. I'll keep the flash drive and you're going to stay here just in case."

"For how long?"

He got up and crossed the room to where she stood, putting his arms around her. "I wish I could answer that."

This was crazy. When and if she ever moved in with Roman, she wanted it to be the next step in their relationship, not some twisted obligation to keep her safe.

It wasn't right. "I could stay at my father's estate. That place is like Fort Knox."

Roman tipped her chin up so he could look in her eyes. "Is that your way of saying you don't want to be here with me?"

"No, of course not. I just...I don't want to inconvenience you."

He dipped his head and kissed her gently, and her heart melted on the spot. "You could never be an inconvenience to me, Gracie."

She laid her head on his chest and held on tight. "Maybe this is a bad time, but there's something I think we need to talk about."

"Something bad?"

"No, just something that's been on my mind."

"Can it wait till I take a shower?"

She stroked the side of his face with her palm. It was rough with beard stubble. "Of course. Would you like me to make you breakfast? Or did you want to get some sleep first?"

"No time for sleep," he said. "I'm used to pulling all-nighters so it's not a big deal. And I would love some breakfast. Give me fifteen minutes."

While Roman showered, Grace threw on her robe and headed to the kitchen. Considering he was a man, his refrigerator and cupboards were insanely well stocked with, for the most part, healthy foods. But he'd always taken good care of himself, exercising regularly and eating well. He did have his weaknesses, though, two being bacon and eggs.

She opened the fridge and found a slab of thick-sliced bacon, a half-empty carton of eggs and a jug of orange juice. From the pantry she pulled out a loaf of raisin bread, which had always been a favorite of his in the mornings. That she remembered his habits was a comfort somehow.

She found the pots and pans she needed and got to work. She had skipped dinner last night, and though she didn't have much of an appetite now, she knew that she needed to eat. But it would be difficult with the huge knot twisting her insides. It was still a little surreal the way Dax had spoken to her, and threatened her. She'd thought for sure that Roman would find something incriminating in the files.

She had hoped she would wake up this morning and it would all make sense. Now she was more confused than ever. She was tempted to give Dax the flash drive and just be done with the whole thing, but intuition told her to wait and let Roman dig deeper. She trusted him, and she knew that if anyone could figure this out he could. And if she really was in some sort of danger, he would keep her safe. Despite all that they had been through she had never once doubted that he would sacrifice his own life to save hers.

There had been an incident back in college, when they were still just friends. They had been studying at the university library for finals and he was walking her back to her sorority house when a strung-out-looking guy, not much older than them, pulled a gun on them and demanded Gracie's purse and Roman's wallet. Without hesitation Roman had stepped in front of her. Whatever the guy had been on, his hands had been shaking and he'd been visibly agitated. Roman had spoken to him in a very calm and rational voice and done as he'd asked, handing over the requested items. As soon as the guy had them, he'd run off. He was never caught, and it had been a pain in the butt having to replace everything in her purse, but Roman's cool head and quick thinking had saved them from further trouble.

Still, she hated that she *needed* someone's protection. It was just all so confusing and disturbing, but she trusted Roman to do the right thing.

When he walked into the kitchen fifteen minutes later he was freshly showered, clean-shaven and dressed for work in black slacks and a black cashmere sweater, carrying a black blazer that he hung over the back of a chair at the kitchen table. "Something smells good," he said.

"Bacon, eggs sunny-side up, raisin toast and juice. And of course coffee." She had the feeling they were both going to need it. "Have a seat."

He took a spot at the table while she fixed their plates, and he asked, "What did you want to talk about?"

Here we go, she thought, and the knots that had begun to loosen in her belly cinched tight again. What if she poured her heart out to him, and he rejected her? What if to him this was just a fling? What if he was content being single and on the market?

But what if he wasn't?

She served the food and sat down, taking a deep breath for courage. "The last few weeks have been wonderful," she said.

He nodded and smiled, but his eyes were serious. "I think so, too."

"Despite everything that's happened between us, I feel as if we've really reconnected."

"I feel that way, too."

She was so nervous the smell of the eggs was upsetting her stomach so she pushed her plate away. Why couldn't she just say it?

"Obviously something is on your mind that you're hesitant to talk about," he said. "Whatever it is, good or bad, I want you to tell me." He reached across the table and took her hand. "If that's what *you* want."

For a big tough guy he was so damned sweet sometimes.

She swallowed her fear, and her pride, and said, "I know we agreed on our friends-with-benefits arrangement, but everything feels different now. I feel different. But before I get in any deeper I need to know if you feel the same way. If you think we have a future together. I know it's only been a few weeks, and I don't want to rush you—"

"Yes."

She blinked. "Yes?"

"Yes," he said, still holding her hand, and the affection in his eyes was so nakedly honest her heart shifted in her chest. "I see us having a future together. I want us to be together. That's all I've ever wanted, Gracie. Hard as I tried to forget you, I never could. You're a part of me. I know there's bad feelings, and it will take time, but not being with you isn't an option anymore. We can just take it one day at a time."

She was so relieved, and so happy that she'd had the courage to ask.

"I can do that," she said. Hell, in the past she had waited two years for their relationship to bloom into something more than friendship.

"I do have one more question," she said. "What are you doing for Thanksgiving?"

"I was kind of hoping someone would invite me to Nora and Reid's wedding," he said with a grin.

His smile warmed her from the inside out. "Would you be my date?"

"I would love to," he said, pressing a kiss to the back of her hand, then letting go. "But right now I have to eat and get to work."

"This early?" she said, feeling disappointed. She had been hoping they might have a little time to fool around before he left.

"My day is booked solid. How about you?"

The truth was, she had more work than she could handle. They were obviously both workaholics, but she was sure they could make that work. "I'll probably shower and get to the office early, too."

"Not gonna happen."

"I have to go to work."

"And you will, but I'm sending a car for you. It will take you to and from work, or anywhere else you need to go. I don't want you going anywhere alone. Understand?"

"You don't think that's excessive?"

"Not at all. A threat is a threat."

"But if there's nothing on the flash drive—"

"This is not negotiable," he said firmly. "We're not taking any chances."

"Maybe I should take a look at that flash drive again and see if there's something you missed. I know that campaign like the back of my hand."

"Actually I was going to take them with me to work. I want to make a few inquiries and take another look at them. Besides, if the senator really is determined to get them, his 'associate' will never get past my building security. They'll be safest there."

"Should I maybe call the police? Like you said, a threat is a threat."

"They're going to want proof. I hate to say it, but it's your word against a state senator's, and you might not be taken seriously. He has connections. It might only make the situation worse."

Roman was probably right. Dax was extremely well liked. And well connected. "It's just so frustrating that he can get away with that. That he can threaten and bully me with no consequences. I did so much for him. I really believed in him. I feel so betrayed, and so stupid for not seeing who he really is."

"You could only see what he let you see. He's a politician, and sadly most of them will say or do anything to appeal to the base and get elected. And they'll do anything to avoid a scandal. This is why I stay away from clients with political motivations."

"I'm sorry you had to be dragged into this. I'm pretty sure this will be the last time I venture into the political realm."

Roman got up and put his plate in the sink, then shrugged into his blazer. "What time should I have the car pick you up?"

"You know, I could have one of my dad's limos take me where I need to go."

"Is his driver trained to kill a man with his bare hands?"

Boy, he really was serious about keeping her safe. "Um…well…"

"I didn't think so. So don't bother arguing, it will be a waste of time."

"How long do I have to live like this?"

"Hopefully not long. Let me make some calls today, and do some digging. I'll update you when I get home tonight. In the meantime I want you to talk to the security detail at your office. Let them know that there could be a problem, but don't go into any detail."

"What should I tell him exactly?"

"Just tell him that you've gotten threatening phone calls, and he needs to watch for anything suspicious."

"Okay," she said, the whole situation still feeling so surreal. Like something she would see on one of those true-crime shows.

"I have to go, but I'll call you later. And call me if you need anything."

She rose from her seat to kiss him goodbye. "I will, I promise. And thank you for everything."

"You don't have to thank me." He kissed her gently and stroked her cheek with the backs of his fingers. "I will move heaven and earth to keep you safe."

She smiled up at him. "I know. And I should be ready to leave by eight."

"I'll make sure the car is here by then. And *be careful*."

"I will. Have a good day." She almost said *I love you*. It was on the tip of her tongue, but she held it in. *One day at a time, take it slow, no pressure.*

Now that she knew where she stood, and that they were headed in the right direction, that was good enough for her. She trusted Roman with her life, and now she trusted him with her heart.

Twelve

As soon as Roman was in his car he called Agent Crosswell and left a message. The guilt of having to lie to Gracie was eating him alive. He loved her, he wanted to be with her for the rest of his life and this deception was killing him. But he couldn't risk her getting hurt or, almost as bad, going down as an accomplice. He'd come so close to telling her the truth, but he just couldn't. Hell, for all he knew the FBI could have his place bugged. It wasn't unheard of. And if this thing was going to end, he had to turn the flash drive over to them. He had no other choice. But before he did, before he would even take them to the FBI building, he and Agent Crosswell were going to sit down and talk, and put together some sort of deal to protect Gracie from any form of legal retribution or liability.

There was no doubt in Roman's mind that the senator had committed fraud, and Roman would not let Gracie get sucked into what had the potential to be an epic scandal. That was the last thing she needed. As a key player in the senator's campaign she would definitely feel some backlash. There was no way to avoid that. And at some point she would probably have to testify at trial, unless the senator took a deal. But Roman doubted he would. He was too arrogant to believe he would ever be found guilty. But this house of cards he'd built was about to come down.

Roman would insist that it be made clear, unequivocally and with no question, that Gracie was in no way involved in the senator's illegal dealings. Because it was often people in her position who went down as the fall guy. And the senator was just the sort of man to throw someone else under the bus to save his own ass and not think twice about it.

The more he learned about the man, the more troubling the situation became. Roman knew that Dax must have friends in high places, but he had learned the misconduct was further reaching than even he'd imagined. And as badly as he wanted to see the senator go down, his main priority was making sure Gracie walked away unscathed.

If Gracie wasn't given full immunity, the FBI would never see that flash drive.

When he got to work he made the car arrangements for Gracie, hiring a fully armed driver whom he spoke to personally. Knowing there would be someone to watch her back took his stress level down considerably. Then, at 8:30 a.m., Agent Crosswell called him back.

"We need to have a meeting," Roman told him.

"You have what I want?" he asked.

"We talk first."

There was a long pause, as if the agent were thinking it through, then he said, "Fair enough. One o'clock, my office."

"I'll be there," Roman said. The flash drive was already locked away in his office safe, and wouldn't be coming back out until he had everything that he needed from the FBI. And as soon as he was able, he would come clean with Gracie and hope she understood why he had to lie to her. That he was doing it to protect her. Because this time he had no doubt in his mind of her innocence. That he'd believed she could be guilty of anything seven years ago still haunted him. He'd betrayed her, and though he had moved on, the guilt had never completely gone away. But he would spend the rest of his life making it up to her if that was what it took. And he hoped that she could eventually forgive him. Until then he wasn't going to push. Like he told Gracie, one day at a time.

The meeting with the FBI went well, and Crosswell agreed to a deal giving Gracie full immunity. Roman also insisted that her name be kept out of this for as long as humanly possible. Still, he knew that there would be no way to completely avoid the fallout. They made arrangements for an agent to pick the flash drive up at his office later that afternoon, and of course he showed up right on time, dressed as a delivery man. Handing them over, knowing he was deceiving Gracie, was one of the hardest things Roman had ever had to do. But he just kept reminding himself that he was doing it for her safety. Because when this blew

open, it wasn't just Dax who would be going down.
Some very prominent officials would be shoved into
the spotlight, not to mention local authorities and their
mob connections. But if the FBI was going to make
their case, he hoped they would do it soon, because as
long as Dax suspected her of having that flash drive
she would be in danger. Hell, even if she turned them
over to him, and he suspected her of knowing the truth,
he might do something drastic to silence her. Something that would surely look like an accident. Roman
had seen it before. And he knew that the longer he had
to lie to Gracie, the worse the damage would be when
the truth came out.

Roman had a hell of a time concentrating the rest
of the afternoon. He must have texted Mark, Gracie's
driver/bodyguard, a dozen times to check up on them.

Mark, an ex-marine, finally had enough, and late
in the afternoon, sent him a terse text:

Relax boss, I've got it.

Roman didn't make it home until almost eight, and
the limo was still in the driveway, which alarmed him.
The security system at his home was top-of-the-line,
so he hadn't asked or expected Mark to stick around
after she was home for the night, but when he walked
into the house they were sitting at the kitchen table
eating pizza. Gracie had a beer, and Mark, ever the
professional, was drinking a bottle of soda. She had
exchanged her work clothes for a pair of leggings and
an oversize sweatshirt. With her hair pulled back in a
ponytail, she looked just like she had back in college.
As soon as she saw him, Gracie smiled and stood

to greet him. "Sorry we started without you, but I was starving."

He walked over to her and she threw her arms around his neck and kissed him. She tasted like tomato sauce and beer. "Did you have a good day?"

Hell no, not even close. "I had a busy day."

She shrugged and said, "I guess busy is good. I was just telling Mark that my new purse line is doing fantastic. They're flying off the shelves. We're going to make record profits this quarter."

"That's great," he said with a smile, wishing he could share her enthusiasm.

Mark finished his soda and stood. "I'm going to head out. What time tomorrow, ma'am?"

"Gracie," she said. "And let's say seven thirty if that's okay. I have an early meeting to prepare for."

"I'll be here."

"A word?" Roman asked Mark, who nodded. "I'll be right back," Roman said to Gracie over his shoulder as he left.

When they were outside, Mark said, "I hope you don't mind that I stayed. She offered pizza and I was hungry."

"I don't mind, I just saw the limo still here and thought the worst. So there was no trouble today? No sign of anyone following you?"

Mark shook his head. "Nothing. And I have to say, that's one hell of a great girl you've got there."

Roman couldn't suppress a smile. "She is."

"When you told me who she was I expected her to be snooty or arrogant. I was wrong. I told her that my eight-year-old daughter is really into fashion and she offered to give her a tour of her offices. I didn't expect that."

Roman had learned over time that people were just people. Heiress or not, Gracie was still a good person who cared deeply for others. "She is something special," he said. And he had to go in there and lie to her face. Because she was going to ask him about the Dax situation, and he had no information to give her.

"Hang on to that one," Mark said, opening the driver's side door.

He was trying. When he went back inside Gracie was clearing their plates from the table.

"Are you hungry?"

"I had a bite to eat at the office." The truth was he hadn't eaten all day. Not only did he have no appetite, but when he thought about lying to her he wanted to barf.

"Did you make any progress on those files?" she asked, putting the plates in the dishwasher.

Shit.

"I didn't," he said, which technically wasn't a lie. "But I put some feelers out and I'm waiting to hear from a few people."

Again, technically not a lie.

"Tonight I'd really just like to crash on the couch and watch TV."

"Sounds good," she said. "But first, can we talk about something?"

He had no idea what she wanted to talk about, but still his heart dropped. "Of course. What's up?"

"Roman," she said, walking over to him, tilting her chin up so she could look him in the eye. "There's something I have to say to you. Something I've wanted to say for a while now, but I... I just had to be sure."

"Okay," he said, heart in his throat, expecting the worst.

She cradled his face in her soft hands and looked him in the eye. "I forgive you."

A knife plunged through his heart couldn't have stung more, and though he was happy and relieved to hear the words, they were bittersweet. And he couldn't stop himself from what he said next. He took her hands and held them tight, looked deeply into her eyes and told her, "I love you, Gracie."

With misty eyes she smiled and said, "I love you, too," twisting the knife that much deeper.

He wrapped his arms around her, wishing he never had to let go again.

He had the love of his life back. He was finally right where he wanted to be. And now, due to circumstances completely out of his control, there was a pretty good chance that he could lose it all.

Gracie and Roman never did watch TV that night. They never even made it to the couch. They fell into bed together instead, and made love way past their bedtime. The way they had pretty much every night since.

In the following week Mark became a familiar fixture in her life. She hated that the driver had to be there, and as far as she knew there had been no nefarious activity, but if Roman thought it was necessary, she wasn't going to argue. But he hadn't made any headway to speak of on the files and she was getting impatient. If she didn't know better she might think he was stalling, but that ended tomorrow. She was going to ask him to bring the flash drive home so she could look at what was on it.

Home. That was an entirely new concept for her. When Roman gave her the all clear, would she be able to go back to her place? Would she be happy not seeing him every day, waking up to his smile and his messy hair? Would she feel alone without him to cuddle up to in bed? She had been at his place only a week yet somehow it felt like a lifetime.

And what if he asked her to stay? She'd been back to her place twice with Mark to pick up a few things. Well, more than a few actually. All of her makeup, hair products and toiletries were in Roman's bathroom. Half her wardrobe was hanging in the closet in the spare bedroom. Other than her furniture, she was practically moved in already. And it couldn't have felt more natural or more comfortable.

That didn't ease her nerves the day of her sister's wedding. This would be their first outing as a couple, and her entire family would be there. She thought her sisters would be okay; it was her mother and Sutton she was worried about. She wanted her sister's wedding to be perfect.

"I need help," Roman said, stepping into the bathroom, where she was putting the finishing touches on her makeup before she slipped into her gown.

He was dressed in his tux, and he looked so hot and sexy, she almost asked him to take it back off again. But they were already running late. They were supposed to be at Sutton's estate in less than an hour.

Roman held his bow tie out to her. "I've always

sucked at these," he said, tugging at his collar. "I hate these damned monkey suits."

She tied a perfect knot, then stepped back to look at him. Perfect, other than the slightly rumpled hair. But that was just Roman. And it was getting long enough that he was due for a trim. She was so used to his hair that way, that when she saw photos of him with a military cut he was barely recognizable.

But still hot as hell.

"You look good," she said as he gave his collar another tug.

"Are you almost ready?" he asked her.

"Almost." She stepped over to the mirror and grabbed a bottle of hair spray, giving her updo another light misting. "Could you help me into my gown?"

Because the guest list was mostly family and good friends, she'd chosen to wear one of her own designs, a floor-length off-the-shoulder beaded dress the exact same color as her eyes. And it weighed a ton.

"What do you need me to do?" he asked.

"Zip me please." She pulled the dress down off the hanger and stepped into it. It took effort to get it up over her bosom and she knew that by the end of the night, lugging around the extra weight was going to wear on her.

He fastened the zipper and she turned to the mirror to see the final effect. Not half bad.

"You look beautiful," Roman said, stepping up behind her. He wrapped his arms around her middle and nibbled her shoulder. "Taste pretty good, too."

"And you smell delicious."

"Looking like you do, you might upstage the bride."

Not a chance. Having designed Nora's dress herself, Gracie knew her sister would be a knockout.

She turned in his arms and kissed him softly, so he didn't end up wearing more of her lipstick than she was. "I think I'm ready."

The way she was feeling right now, with so much happiness deep in her heart, she could take on the world.

Thirteen

By the time Gracie and Roman put on their coats and got into the limo her father had sent to fetch them, they were really late. It was windy and cold and lake-effect snow had begun to fall, making the surface roads slippery, adding more time to their drive.

When they finally made it to her father's estate the limo pulled up to the front steps and a valet opened the door.

They stepped into the foyer, which was a wonderland of draped pink and white tulle and a mix of pink and white blooms. In the foyer alone there had to be thousands of flowers, so she could only imagine how the rest of the house looked.

"Wow," Roman said under his breath. "That is a *lot* of pink."

She elbowed him playfully.

Her mother was the first person Gracie saw as she slipped out of her coat and handed it to an attendant.

Celeste saw them and eyed Roman coolly.

"So," Roman said. "She's clearly not happy to see me."

Gracie had wondered how she would take the news of her and Roman's reunion. Now she knew: not very well. "Give me a few minutes alone with her," Gracie said.

"Would you like a drink?" he asked.

"Not just yet. I need to pace myself."

"So, no more than four?" he teased.

She laughed. "Well, maybe five."

She crossed the foyer and Roman headed for the bar in the great room. Her mother opened her arms and gave Gracie a warm hug and an air-kiss. Celeste had always been beautiful, tall and lithe and graceful. But tonight she looked positively radiant.

"Mom, you look great!"

"I feel great," she said. "You look beautiful. Is the dress one of yours? It's lovely."

"It's mine. Have you seen Nora yet?"

"I was up there earlier for pictures. And Gracie, you've outdone yourself this time with her dress. It's absolutely stunning. And Eve's dress, oh my goodness. That's beautiful, too. Have I ever told you how talented you are, and how proud I am of you?"

"A time or two," Gracie said with a smile. Her mother had always been one of her biggest supporters. She'd raised her to be independent and think for herself. In part, Gracie guessed, because Celeste's parents had made most of her decisions for her. Like marrying Sutton.

"How was your trip?" Gracie asked.

Her mother lit up like a firefly. "Exactly what I needed."

"You look very happy."

With a coy smile, she said, "I have reason to be."

Could it be...? "Mom, did you meet someone?"

Her smile gave it away. "He's Italian. And ten years younger than me. And the sex?" She fanned her face and Gracie resisted the urge to put her fingers in her ears and sing, *la la la la la*. But she was so pleased to see her mother happy she didn't care. At sixty, Celeste was still young and vigorous.

Though her parents never had a great marriage, her mother had still taken the divorce and, more recently, the news of Carson's paternity hard. There was so much residual bitterness. Gracie had worried that being here would bring all of that hurt and turmoil back up to the surface on what should be a happy occasion.

"Your father doesn't look well at all," her mother commented. "It's obvious he hasn't much time left."

"I know," Gracie said, her heart aching a little at the thought of losing him. He wasn't a great *man*, but he had been a good father. It broke her heart to know that he wouldn't be there for her wedding, or to see his grandchildren if she had any. That was something she and Roman needed to talk about eventually. And speaking of... "So I guess you probably heard about me and Roman."

At the mention of his name, her mother's smile faded. "You know how I feel about him. About the hell that he put you through."

"I know, but I've forgiven him for that and we've

moved forward." It had felt so good to say the words, to finally let go of the past and start fresh.

Her mother's lips dipped into a frown. "I don't trust him."

"But *I* do, and that's all that matters."

"You'll have to give me time to get used to this. Don't expect me to immediately welcome him with open arms just because you do."

The truth was, Gracie didn't really care what her mother or anyone else thought, because it wasn't their decision, or their business.

"I should probably go say hello to Daddy," she told her mother. "We'll talk more later."

"Of course," Celeste said, looking a little hurt. But Gracie was so happy and she didn't want anything to spoil her day.

As she walked through the house she saw so many familiar faces. Though a Thanksgiving wedding was a little unconventional, everyone from the guest list seemed to be there. Carson and Georgia stood chatting with Gina Chamberlain, and Graham was at the bar with Roman. She had heard Brooks would not be attending, though out of courtesy he had been invited. Eve and Nash, as maid of honor and best man, were likely upstairs getting ready. But there were countless other friends and extended family, all of whom she would get to eventually, but as Nora had told her, she was a guest at this wedding. She would leave the formal greetings to the wedding party. This being her second marriage, Nora had chosen to keep it small and intimate. But Nora being Nora, she fretted over leaving her sister out. Gracie had been in the wedding party at Nora's first wedding, though. She just wanted her sister to do what made her happy.

After the ceremony in the arboretum, a sit-down turkey feast would be served in the ballroom, which hadn't been used in Grace couldn't remember how long, and there would be music and dancing afterward. When she was a child they used to have elaborate holiday celebrations with all of their friends and family, but as she and her sisters got older, and their parents' marriage got rockier, the parties had been few and far between.

She found her father sitting in his wheelchair, nurse at the ready, amidst a group of business associates.

When he saw her approaching, he smiled. Despite her mother's observation, Gracie thought he looked pretty good today. He wasn't so pale, and he still looked dashing in a tux.

He shooed away the men and waved her closer.

"Princess, you look beautiful," he said as she leaned down to kiss his cheek.

"And you look handsome as usual."

"You know, after so many years of wearing a suit I actually miss my robe and slippers," he joked, and it was so nice to see him in good spirits. She'd been so busy at work lately she hadn't had much time to visit with him. She needed to make more of an effort.

"Are you still planning to walk Nora down the aisle?"

He nodded, a look of determination on his face. "If it kills me."

"Daddy, don't say that."

"I'm kidding. I'll be fine. I'm feeling good today."

She could see it, and she was so relieved. She had

worried that he might be too ill to even attend. But he was tough, although much softer around the edges now and much more sentimental.

"Are you still at Roman's?" he asked her. The last time she'd seen her father she explained the entire situation, not sure if he would even remember the conversation. But apparently he had.

"I am. Until he thinks it's safe for me to go home."

"I never liked Dax," he said, frowning. "I never trusted him."

"I still can't believe I was so wrong about him. I feel so stupid."

"Don't," her father said, taking her hand. His felt cold and frail. "You see the good in people. It's your gift."

Some gift. In this instance it could have gotten her seriously hurt. Or possibly even killed.

For a fleeting second she thought about Roman, and how she had trusted him, too. But that was different.

Wasn't it?

A bell rang, alerting everyone that it was time to move to the arboretum for the ceremony. Nash appeared to wheel Sutton to the spot where he would meet Nora.

Roman stepped up beside Gracie and offered his arm, smiling so sweetly and looking so handsome she couldn't doubt him. She just needed to let it go and let herself be happy.

She took his arm and they found seats in the arboretum in the family section up near the front. A few minutes later Reid took his place beside the reverend, looking dashing in his tux and so happy. And maybe a little nervous, too. Nash stood beside him.

Soft music played as Eve walked down the aisle, followed by Nash's niece, Phoebe, who sprinkled pink and white rose petals over the satin runner while her twin brother, Jude, watched anxiously from his mother's lap. Declan was next, looking adorable and debonair in his tux, carrying the pink pillow with the rings.

When the wedding march began everyone stood and turned, and when her sister appeared, Gracie's breath caught. In cream silk, with her pale complexion, Nora looked like a living porcelain statue. Her dress was simple but elegant and fit her perfectly. Gracie couldn't help but give herself a pat on the back.

"You've outdone yourself," Roman said softly, making her smile.

Sutton moved slowly, bracing himself against his daughter, but held his head high. And when he gave her away to Reid Gracie could swear there were tears in his eyes.

The ceremony was short but heartfelt, and when Declan got restless and wanted Mommy, Nora and Reid held him together as they spoke their vows. And when they kissed, he kissed them, too. It was probably the sweetest thing that Gracie had ever seen. They were truly a family united by love, and for a moment Grace wanted that so badly for herself it almost hurt. That would be her and Roman someday. Getting married, having a family. Growing old together. She knew it beyond a shadow of doubt.

The reception afterward truly was a feast, but the guilt chewing a hole in Roman's gut made it almost impossible to eat. He found himself wishing there was a family dog he could slip his dinner to, the way he had when he was a kid. When Gracie asked him if something was wrong, he told her the whiskey he'd drunk earlier had upset his stomach. Her look of sympathy, and her offer to go find him an antacid, nearly did him in.

He would drink himself into a stupor if he thought it would help, but he'd never been one to use alcohol as a crutch. He knew too many soldiers who turned to drinking to deal with their PTSD and he refused to go there. But at times like this it was tempting.

After dinner they mingled, but Roman noticed that Sutton, back in his wheelchair, didn't look so good. Maybe a little bit of Grace was rubbing off on Roman. He could hardly believe he had sympathy for the man, considering what a son of a bitch he'd always been. Sitting alone with his nurse at his side, Sutton looked so old and frail and sullen. He was too weak to even dance with Nora. And Roman felt compelled to do something.

What the hell.

Roman walked over to Sutton, nudged his nurse aside and said, "You look like you need a breather."

The relief was clear on Sutton's face. "My suite," he said, so Roman pushed him there, and strangely enough no one seemed to notice or care. The shark was gone, reduced to nothing more than…a goldfish. A sick, helpless old man. But Roman knew that he would never be forgotten. He'd made his mark on the world, and no one could ever take that from him. But clearly he was ready to throw in the towel. Ready to let someone take over his legacy. He had groomed Eve to be the shark that he'd once been, but with her softer side, she would rule the family business with compassion and heart. And she would never have to live with the regret that was so obvious in Sutton's expression. He'd lived large and fast, and burned out before his time. Roman hoped that if nothing else, Sutton's children had learned from his mistakes.

Sutton ordered his nurse to take her seat in the hallway, and when the door was closed and they were alone, he told Roman, "Thank you."

"Don't thank me. I needed a breather, too," he said, brushing his thanks off, realizing that it was actually disturbing to see such a powerful man reduced to this. What a terrible way to go.

"Help me into bed?" Sutton asked, surprising Roman again.

Without a word Roman helped him undress and change into his pajamas. He was too weak to stand so Roman literally had to lift him into his bed.

"I'm tired, Roman," he said, as he settled back against the pillows. "I'm tired of fighting."

"I understand," Roman said, and he did. There were times, as a POW, when he'd been tempted to give up, to let the enemy win, but he'd kept on fighting. But his enemy had been radical Al Qaeda soldiers. Sutton's enemy was cancer, and it was eating him from the inside out.

"I know you do," Sutton said, then asked, "Have you heard from Agent Crosswell?"

Roman was stunned into silence, and Sutton just smiled. "I may be a sick old man, but I still have connections. After what Dax Caufield did to my daughter..." He shook his head and frowned, as if he couldn't bear to think about it. "I knew he was crooked, but I also knew that eventually he would be exposed for who he really was. I never thought he was dangerous. Especially not to Grace. When I heard what happened I took matters into my own hands and made a few calls."

"No, I haven't heard from him," Roman said. "But I'm hoping to soon."

"You love my daughter."

The question caught him off guard. "Yes, I do."

He always had.

"And I trust that you'll keep her safe."

"I lied to her," he said, the words coming out of nowhere. "I lied to her again."

He expected Sutton to be angry, but instead he said, "Yes. But you did it to keep her safe."

That didn't make it right. "She may not see it that way."

"Roman," he said. "I love all of my children equally. I may not show it, but I do. But Grace? There's something special about her. She always sees the good in people. She always gives people the benefit of the doubt. God knows she's done it for me. She will forgive you."

Roman wasn't so sure. "I lied to her."

"You didn't have a choice."

No, but that still didn't make it right. "I have to tell her the truth."

"You will, when the time is right. And she'll forgive you, and give you another chance. Because that's who she is."

Again, Roman wasn't so sure about that.

"When you get home tonight, turn on the news."

Sutton obviously knew something he didn't. "Why?"

The old man's smile was devious, and for an instant he looked like the Sutton he used to be. "As I said, I still have my connections."

Without elaborating, Sutton closed his eyes, and in an instant he was asleep, leaving Roman to wonder if they had arrested Dax today, or were planning to.

He left Sutton sleeping and headed back to the ballroom, but Carson, on his way to the den, told him, "Roman, you have to see this."

Roman followed him, joining a large group of the wedding guests gathered around the television. It was tuned to the news, and the banner across the screen screamed State Senator Arrested on Fraud Charges.

And sure enough, there was Dax on the screen being led away from his home in handcuffs. The relief Roman felt left him weak. He could finally talk to Gracie and tell her the truth. And he could stop worrying about her safety.

He saw Gracie standing over by the bar, a drink in her hand, and she waved him over.

"Is this really happening?" she said, looking dazed.

"It's really happening." And it was about time.

"I knew something was up, but I never expected this."

Clearly no one had if the shocked expressions and low hum of incredulous chatter were any indication.

"Does this mean I'm safe now?" she asked Roman, looking so hopeful it made him feel about an inch tall.

"I hope so." Things would be dicey, and he was sure that she would be getting a visit from the FBI. Which meant he had to tell her the truth, before she heard it from someone else. So he said, "We need to talk."

She frowned. "Right now?"

"Yes, right now."

Fourteen

Something in Roman's voice, in his troubled expression, put her instantly on edge. Shouldn't he be happy that this mess was finally going to be over and she could get her life back? And why did she get the feeling that he knew something she didn't?

"We can go to my room," she said. Like her sisters she still kept a room at the estate, so she led Roman there.

When they were inside with the door closed, she asked him, "What's going on? I couldn't help but notice that you didn't seem at all surprised by the news report. Or relieved."

"I knew this was coming," he said. "I just didn't know when."

A feeling of dread started in her heart and trickled downward into her belly. "How did you know?"

He sat on the edge of the bed, wearing a look of pure misery, which only made her feel worse.

"I've been working with the FBI," he said.

And he hadn't told her. Her heart started to thump. "How long?"

"They contacted me the day before Dax came to your place. They knew that he wanted the backup flash drive, and they wanted to get their hands on it first."

She closed her eyes and took a deep breath. Oh no he didn't. He couldn't have. "You found something, didn't you? In the files that first night."

Eyes lowered, he nodded.

"So you lied to me."

He nodded again.

She felt eerily calm as she asked him, "And where is the flash drive now?"

"I turned it over to the FBI last week."

So he hadn't really been going through the files looking for evidence. That was just another lie.

He could not be doing this to her again. Not now. Not after she had forgiven him, and given him her heart. He just couldn't.

The dread grew exponentially, sucking her into a place so dark and foreboding she wanted to disappear.

"They didn't give me a choice. You were going to be implicated in the case. I gave them the flash drive in exchange for your immunity."

She blinked, then blinked again. "Because you thought I was guilty."

His head shot up. "No! To protect you."

"Why would you have to protect me, and make a deal for me, if you knew I hadn't done anything wrong?"

"Gracie," he said, reaching for her.

She stepped back, repulsed by the thought of his hands on her. It was seven years ago happening all over again. "Don't touch me."

"It wasn't like that," he said, standing. "You have to believe me. I was just trying to keep you safe."

"I don't," she said, aware that she had started to tremble. "I don't believe you. And I don't trust you. I won't trust you ever again."

"If you'll let me explain—"

She had only seen him look this crushed once before: the last time he'd betrayed her. "No. There's no excuse you could give me that would justify you lying to me. You doubted me. Again. I'm finished."

"Gracie, please—" He reached for her again, touched her arm and she ripped it away.

"Get out," she said.

She could feel it coming on, the total collapse of her soul. She was crumbling from the inside out. She wanted to scream at him, and pound his chest with her fists, make him *feel* how much he'd hurt her. But at this point why bother? It was over. For good. And with that realization, the last of her will fizzled away. She just wanted to hide. She was so cold and empty she just wanted to curl up in bed, close her eyes and sleep until the ache in her heart went away. But she had the feeling that this time his deceit ran so deep, the pain would never go away. This was her so-called "gift" of seeing the best in everyone biting her in the ass again. She'd believed in Roman when he said he loved her, and had given him the benefit of the doubt when deep down she'd felt as if something wasn't right. And once again she'd been burned.

"Gracie, please talk to me," he said.

She shook her head. There was nothing to talk about. It was over. "Roman," she said, her voice eerily calm, "I want you to leave, and I never want to see you again."

Unable to even look at him any longer, she crossed the room and stepped into the bathroom, shutting the door and leaning against it, her heart pounding so hard and fast she felt light-headed and sick. So sick that she dashed to the commode, barely making it in time before she lost her dinner.

She sat on the floor, still in her gown, waiting for the tears to come, but she was so dead inside she just felt numb. The perpetual optimism was gone, and in its place something dark and cold took over, making her determined to hold on to and protect her heart, and never let another man hurt her again.

Gracie had an amazing dream. It was her and Roman's wedding, and they were so happy and in love, but as she slowly woke and opened her eyes and realized where she was, the memory of last night came rushing back with an intensity that made it hard to breathe. She couldn't even scrape together the will to lift her head. She'd been depressed before, but right now she felt utterly destroyed. And that was when the tears started, and they didn't stop again for three days. She spent the entire holiday weekend in bed, sleeping, crying and hating herself for trusting him. She couldn't eat, couldn't concentrate and on Monday when she should have gone back to work, she called in sick.

When she finally worked up the will to get out of bed and charge her long-dead cell phone, she was bombarded by dozens of text messages and voice mails. But none from Roman, which made her feel both relieved and heartsick. An Agent Crosswell from the FBI and a federal prosecutor had left several messages. As a player in Dax's campaign, of course she would be questioned and probably asked to testify. Just one more mess brought on by her "gift." Or her curse as she'd now begun to see it.

Tuesday she finally ventured downstairs to the kitchen for a bite to eat, barely able to choke down a bagel with cream cheese. The wedding decor had been replaced with holiday decorations that would be up till the first of the new year. But she couldn't enjoy it.

She was headed back upstairs, when she passed her father's nurse, who looked surprised to see her.

"Miss Winchester, I didn't know you were here."

"How is my father?" She'd been so wrapped up in her own problems she hadn't even thought to check up on him.

"The wedding took a lot out of him. He's mostly been sleeping. He feels better today, though."

"I should probably go say hello."

"I'm sure he would like that. Your visits always cheer him up."

"Take a break and I'll sit with him awhile," Gracie said.

With a frown, the woman asked her, "Are you okay?"

She must have looked absolutely awful. She hadn't eaten or showered in days. She hadn't even looked in the mirror. She was too ashamed to face her own reflection.

"I'm fine."

"There have been a lot of calls since Thursday. Mostly from reporters."

Well, that was no big surprise. They had been calling her, too. But she didn't want to talk about it, or even think about it. "Thank you for the warning. I'll call if I need you."

She went to her father's suite, knocking lightly before opening the door and peeking inside. He was sitting propped up in bed working on his laptop. When he saw her, he smiled. "Princess, I didn't know you were visiting today."

He obviously had no idea that she'd never left. And as she drew closer to his bed, his smile began to fade. "Princess, what's wrong?"

With an ache that was all consuming, she sat beside him, laid her head in his lap and cried while her father stroked her hair. And it was exactly what she needed.

When she was all out of tears, he handed her a tissue and she wiped her eyes. "I suppose you probably heard what happened," she said. "How stupid I've been. How he betrayed me again. I should have listened to you. I should have trusted you when you said he was no good for me."

"But you went with your heart instead."

She nodded. "You must be pretty happy that it's over."

"On the contrary. I think you're making the biggest mistake in your life."

His words took her aback. "But…"

"Be quiet and listen. Do you know why I insisted you attend that initial meeting with Roman, and why I asked you to get close to him?"

"To avoid another scandal."

"There wasn't going to be another scandal. I knew that Brooks was working alone to discredit me in the media, and that Roman had no part in his twisted revenge plot."

Gracie frowned. "I don't understand. Why did you make me do it, then? Were you trying to torture me?"

"I was trying to make you see what I've seen all along. That you still loved him."

What? "But...you don't even like him. You never did. You always tried to come between us."

"I was jealous."

His words stunned her. "Jealous? Of what?"

"Princess, since the day you were born, you were a daddy's girl. You wouldn't go to sleep at night if I wasn't there to tuck you in. Despite all of the horrible things in my life you still saw the good in me. I didn't want to lose you to someone else."

Is that how he really felt? Did he really love her that much? She could hardly imagine him so vulnerable. "Daddy, you could never lose me. You're my father. I'll always love you."

"I didn't see it that way. And I was wrong." He took her hands in his. "I don't want you to make the same mistake that I did. I let the love of my life go, and I never stopped regretting it."

She didn't have to ask who. She'd heard the rumors. "Cynthia Newport."

He nodded, looking so sad. "I tried to fill the void, but I was never able to let her go. Learn from my mistakes. Don't do that to yourself. Talk to Roman. He loves you."

Her father didn't understand. "He lied to me. That's not love."

"He was protecting you."

"He thought I was guilty."

"No, he was fighting to prove that you weren't. You have no idea what you got yourself into. As a part of Dax's campaign, you were implicated in the fraud. You could have been prosecuted. Roman made a deal with the FBI. Your flash drive in exchange for full immunity."

"So why didn't he just tell me the truth? When the FBI called, why didn't he tell me?"

"He couldn't."

"He didn't trust me."

"It wasn't about trust. He was under the thumb of the FBI. What they did was nothing shy of blackmail. He couldn't tell you, and if he did you could have both been prosecuted. He couldn't take that chance."

Through the darkness in her soul a dim shimmer of light appeared. She thought about the way Roman had taken care of her and protected her when he thought her life was in danger.

"He loves you, Princess. Don't you see that? He did what he had to, knowing that when he told you the truth he could lose you forever. But it was a chance he had to take. He loved you so much, and wanted you to be safe, so he took the gamble."

And lost. But she hadn't even let him explain. She had been so wrapped up in her own pain she couldn't even make herself listen.

The dim light grew a little brighter. "How do you know all of this?"

"He confided in me Thursday night."

She blinked. Roman had confided in Sutton? His

mortal enemy? It was almost too far-fetched to believe. And if he really had done it just to protect her...

Once again, a flicker of hope broke through the gloom. Was it possible that this wasn't really the end? Shouldn't she at least give him a chance to explain?

He squeezed her hand. "Talk to him, Grace."

She had been pretty awful to him Thursday night. "What if he doesn't want to talk to me?"

"He does."

"How do you know?"

"I just do. I know that over the years I've expected a lot from you, and I'm asking you now, for the last time, to do one more thing for me."

"What, Daddy?"

"I'm asking you to trust me."

When he said it like that, with so much love in his eyes, how could she tell him no?

Fifteen

For five days following the wedding, Roman barely existed, trapped in his own personal hell. The hell he had created. Again. He hadn't eaten or slept. He hadn't been back to work. He'd basically wandered around the house in a daze, trying to figure out a way to fix this, and coming up with nothing.

Sutton had been wrong about her forgiving him. And as every new day passed, he knew it was less and less likely that he would ever hear from her again. In his efforts to protect Gracie he'd hurt her so deeply that she had completely shut him out.

It hadn't been the first time, but it would definitely be the last. She was clearly done with him. She wouldn't even let him explain, and he didn't blame her. Why would she?

He needed to pack her things so he could send them

to her, but he hadn't been able to make himself do it. Everything was exactly as she'd left it, and there wasn't a square inch of his home that didn't remind him of her. It didn't even feel like home anymore. Not without her there. She'd left her mark indelibly on his entire world. He would have to sell his house and move if he was ever going to have a chance of forgetting her. But he doubted even that would work.

But at least she was safe, and protected from prosecution. At least he had given her that. And she would never know how much, and for how long, he had loved her. It hadn't even been clear to him until he lost her.

Around two his doorbell rang, and for a second he felt an actual sliver of hope that it might be her, but that was just him living in a fantasy world. She was gone. Out of his life. And the sooner he accepted that the better off he would be.

But when he opened the door, he was sure that he was hallucinating from lack of sleep, because that couldn't possibly be Gracie standing there on his porch. She looked up at him, her face expressionless, as if she were waiting for him to say something.

All he could come up with was "Back for your things?"

Without warning she launched herself at him so forcefully he stumbled backward, and when she wrapped her arms around him, Roman was so stunned that for a second he didn't even hug her back.

Now he knew he had to be hallucinating. But when he pulled her close to him, she couldn't have felt more real. He buried his face in the softness of her hair and breathed her in.

Yep, she was definitely there. The question was why.

"I'm sorry," she said, holding on tight. "I'm so sorry."

Wait. What?

She was sorry? That made no sense. He must have misheard.

He peeled her away from him and held her at arm's length, managing a dumbfounded-sounding "What?"

"I said I'm sorry."

Was this some kind of sick joke she was playing on him? "What could you possibly have done to be sorry for? I'm the one who's sorry. I lied to you."

"And I loved you, and that I trusted you, then I didn't even give you a chance to explain. I was so angry and so hurt that all I cared about was protecting myself. I didn't even think about you and how hard it must have been keeping that from me. And the risk you took to keep me safe."

He wanted to pinch himself to make sure that he was actually awake.

"I wish I could take credit for realizing what I was doing, but it took a talking-to from my father to open my eyes."

Wait a minute…it was Sutton who'd saved his ass?

Looking crushed, she said, "I let you down and I'm sorry."

"You think you let me down?" he asked incredulously. Maybe *she* was the one hallucinating. "*I* let *you* down."

She shook her head. "No, you didn't. You probably saved my life. I was just too stupid to see it. But I see it now, and I'm begging you to give me another chance."

She was the one begging? "Gracie, I should be begging you. And I would have, but I didn't think…I just assumed you would never want to speak to me again."

"Like the last time," she said, and he nodded. "This is different. I know that, deep in my soul. You're my forever. My home."

He cradled her face in his hands and kissed her softly. "And you're mine. You always have been."

She gazed up at him with a smile. "So does that mean you'll give me a second chance?"

"Yes, of course I will," he said, pulling her into his arms. And a third and a fourth and a fifth chance. Anything to keep her in his life, because she was his everything. "I want to spend the rest of my life with you. I want to marry you, and have a family with you. It's what I've always wanted."

"Me, too," she said. "And if that's a proposal my answer is yes."

He grinned. "Sweetheart, when I formally propose you'll know it. I'm pulling out all the stops. I want to do this right."

She deserved the best, and that's what he would give her. And though he'd thought for sure that he'd ruined it, she was giving him another chance, too. A second chance at the love of a lifetime.

* * * * *

THE TEXAN'S
ONE-NIGHT STANDOFF

CHARLENE SANDS

To my very talented editor, Charles Griemsman,
who is also a wonderful person and someone
I call friend. Thanks, Charles, for all you do!

One

Brooks Newport swiveled around on the bar stool at the C'mon Inn, his gaze fastening on the raven-haired Latina beauty bending over a pool table, challenging her opponent with a fiercely competitive glint in her eyes. With blue jeans hugging her hips and a cropped red plaid blouse exposing her olive skin, the lady made his mouth go dry. He wasn't alone. Every Stetson-wearing Texan in the joint seemed to be watching her, too.

His hand fisting around the bottle, Brooks took a sip of beer, gulping down hard. The woman's moves around the pool table were as smooth and as polished as his new Justin boots.

"Five ball, corner pocket," she said, her voice sultry with a side of sass, as if she knew she wasn't going to miss. Then she took her shot. The cue ball met its mark and sure enough, the five ball rolled right into the pocket.

She straightened to full height, her chest expanding

to near button-popping proportions. She couldn't have been more than five-foot-two, but what she had in that small package was enough to make him break out in a sweat. And that was saying something, since he'd come to Texas for one reason, and one reason only.

To meet his biological father for the first time in his life.

He'd spent the better part of his adulthood trying to find the man who'd abandoned him and his twin brother, Graham in Chicago. Sutton Winchester, his bitter older rival and the man Brooks thought might be his biological father turned out not to be his blood kin after all. Thank God. But Sutton had known the truth of his parenthood all along, and the ailing man, plagued by a bout of conscience—or so Brooks figured—had finally given up the information that led to the name and location of his and Graham's father.

Brooks would have been speaking with his real father at Look Away Ranch in Cool Springs right now if he hadn't gotten a bad case of nerves. So much was riding on this. The trek to get to this place in time, to solving the mystery surrounding the birth of the Newport twins, as well as his younger brother Carson, would finally come to fruition.

So, yeah, the powerful CEO of the Newport Corporation from Chicago had turned chicken. Those bawking noises played out in his head. He'd never run scared before and yet, as he was breezing through this dusty town, the Welcome sign and Christmas lights outside the doors of the C'mon Inn had called to him. He'd pulled to a stop and entered the lodge, in need of a fortifying drink and a good night's rest. He had a lot to think about, and meeting Beau Preston in the light of day seemed a better idea.

He kept his gaze trained on the prettiest thing in the joint. The woman. She wielded the pool cue like a weapon and began wiggling her perfectly trim ass in an effort to make a clean shot. He sipped beer to cool his jets, yet he couldn't tear his gaze away. He had visions of bending over the pool table with her and bringing them both to heaven.

Long strands of her hair hung down to touch her breasts, and as she leaned over even further to line up her shot, those strands caressed green felt. She announced her next shot and *bam*, the ball banked off the left side and then ricocheted straight into the center pocket.

The whiskered man she was playing against hung his head. "Man, Ruby. You don't give a guy a chance."

She chuckled. "That's the rule I live by, Stan. You know that."

"But you could miss once in a while. Make it interesting."

So her name was Ruby. Brooks liked the sound of it, all right. It fit.

He had no business lusting after her. Woman trouble was the last thing he needed. Yet his brain wasn't doing a good job of convincing his groin to back off.

The game continued until she handed the older guy his vitals on a silver platter. "Sorry, Stan."

"You'd think after all these years a man could do better against a teeny tiny woman."

She grinned, showing off a smile that lit the place on fire, then set a sympathetic hand on the man's shoulder and reached up to kiss his cheek.

The old guy's face turned beet red. "You know that's the only reason I endure this torture. For that kiss at the end."

Her deep, provocative chuckle rumbled in Brooks's

ears. "You're sweet for saying that, Stan. Now, go on home to Betsy. And kiss your sweet grandson for me."

Nodding, Stan smiled at her. "Will do. You be good now, you hear?"

"I can always try," she said, hooking her cue stick on the wall next to a holly wreath.

Stan walked off, and Ruby did this little number with her head that landed all of her thick, silky hair on one shoulder. Brooks's groin tightened some more. If *she* was any indication of what Cool Springs was like, he was quickly gaining an affinity for the place.

The woman spotted him. Her deep-set eyes, the color of dark cocoa, met his for a second, and time seemed to stop. Blood rushed through his veins. She blinked a time or two and then let him go, as if she recognized him to be an out-of-towner.

He finished off his beer and rose, tossing some bills onto the bar and giving the barkeep a nod.

"Hey, sweet doll," a man called out, coming from the darkest depths of the bar to stand in front of her. "How about giving me a go-round?"

Ruby tilted her head up. "No thanks. I'm through for the night."

"You ain't through until you've seen me wield my stick. It's impressive." The big oaf wiggled his brows and crowded her against the pool table.

She rolled her eyes. "Pleeeze."

"Yeah, babe, that's exactly what you'll be crying out once we're done *playing*."

"Sorry, but if that's your best come-on line, you're in sad shape, buster."

She inched her body away, brushing by him, trying not to make contact with the bruiser. But the jerk grabbed her arm from behind and gave a sharp tug. She struggled to wiggle free. "Let go," she said.

Brooks scanned the room. All eyes were still on Ruby, but no one was making a move. Instead they all had smug looks on their faces. Forget what he'd thought about this town; they were all jerks.

The muscles in his arms bunched and his hands tightened into fists as Brooks stepped toward the two of them. He couldn't stand by and watch this scene play out, not when the petite pool shark was in trouble. "Get your hands—"

The words weren't out of his mouth before Ruby elbowed the guy in the gut. "Oof." He doubled over, clutching his stomach, and cursed her up and down using filthy names.

Crap. Now she was in deep. The guy's head came up; the unabashed fury in his eyes was aimed her way. Brooks immediately pulled his arm back, fists at the ready, but before he could land a punch, Ruby grabbed the guy's forearm. The twist of her body came so fast, Brooks blinked, and before he knew it, she'd tossed the big oaf over her shoulder WWF-style and had him down for the count. As in, she'd laid him out flat on his back.

Someone from the bar groused, "No one messes with Ruby unless she wants to be messed with."

Apparently the oaf hadn't known that. And neither had Brooks. But hell, the rest of them had known.

She stepped over the man to face Brooks, her gaze on the right hook he'd been ready to land. "Thanks anyway," she said, out of breath. Apparently she wasn't Supergirl. The effort had taxed her, and he found himself enjoying how the ebb and flow of her labored breaths stretched the material of her blouse.

He stood there somewhat in awe, a grin spreading his mouth wide. "You didn't let me do my gladiator routine."

"Sorry. Maybe next time." Her lips quirked up.

Behind her, the bartender and another man began dragging the patron away.

"Does that happen often?" he asked her.

"Often enough," she said. "But not with guys who know me."

He rubbed at his chin. "No. I wouldn't imagine."

He kept his gaze trained on her, astonished at what he'd just witnessed. Her eyes danced in amusement, probably at his befuddled expression. And then someone turned up the volume on the country song playing, and his thoughts ran wild. He was too intrigued to let the night end. This woman wasn't your typical Texas beauty queen. She had spunk and grit and so much more. Hell, he hadn't been this turned on in a long, long time.

A country Christmas ballad piped in through the speakers surrounding the room. "Would you like to dance?" he asked.

She smiled sweetly, the kind of smile that suggested softness. And he would've believed that if he hadn't seen her just deck a man. A big man.

Her head tilted to the left, and she gauged him thoughtfully.

He was still standing, so that was a plus. She didn't find him out of line.

"Sure. I'd like that, Galahad."

"It's Brooks."

"Ruby."

She led him to the dance floor and he took over from there, placing his hand on the small of her back, enfolding her other hand in his. Small and delicate to big and rough. But it worked. *And how*, did it work.

He began to move, holding her at arm's length, breathing her in as they glided across the dance floor.

"I thought you were in trouble back there," he said.

"I gathered."

"Are you a black belt or something?"

"Nope, just grew up around men and learned early on how to take care of myself. What about you? Do you have a knight in shining armor complex or something?"

He laughed. "Where I come from, a man doesn't stand by and watch someone abuse a lady."

"Oh, I see."

"Apparently I was the only other guy in the place who didn't know you could handle yourself."

She was looking at him now, piercing him with those cocoa eyes and giving him that megawatt smile. "It was sorta sweet, you coming to my rescue." Was she flirting? *Man, oh man.* If she was, he wasn't going to stop her.

"I was watching you, like every other guy at the bar."

"I like to play pool. I'm good at it," she said, shrugging a shoulder. "It's a great way to blow off steam."

"That's exactly why I stopped into the bar myself. I needed to do the same."

"You get brownie points for not saying the obvious."

"Which is?"

Her lips twitched and she hesitated for a second, as if trying to decide whether to tell him or not. "That you know a better way to blow off steam."

Her raven brows rose, and he stopped dancing for a second to study her. "You must drive men wild with your mouth."

She shook her head, grinning. "You're sinking, Brooks. Going under fast."

"I was talking about your sass."

She knew. She was messing with him. "Most men hate it."

"Not me. It's refreshing."

He brought her closer, so that the tips of her breasts grazed his shirt and the scent of her hair tickled his nostrils. She didn't flip him over her shoulder with that move. She cuddled up closer. "So far, I have two brownie points," he said. "What can I do to earn another?"

Her gaze drifted to his mouth with pinpoint accuracy. Air left his chest. A deep hunger, like none he'd experienced before, gnawed into his belly.

"You'll think of something, Galahad."

The stranger's lips touched hers, a brief exploration that warmed up her insides and made her question everything she'd done since setting eyes on this guy. Usually she wasn't this brazen with men. She didn't flirt and plant ideas in their heads. But there was something about Brooks that called to her. He had manners. And he knew how to speak to a woman. He seemed familiar and safe in a way, even though they'd never met before. He wasn't hard on the eyes either, with all that blond hair, thick and wavy and catching the collar of his zillion-dollar shirt. He was as citified as they came, even if he wore slick boots and sported five-o'clock stubble. As soon as she'd spotted him at the bar, she knew he didn't belong. Not here, in a dusty small town out in the middle of nowhere. Cool Springs wasn't exactly a mecca of high society, and this guy was that and then some. His coming to her rescue, all granite muscles and fists ready to pummel, was about the nicest thing a man had done for her in a long while.

Trace came to mind, and she immediately washed his image from her head. She wasn't going to think about her breakup with him. He was six months long gone, and she'd wasted enough time on him.

Instead she wrapped her arms around Brooks's neck and clung to him, her body sizzling from the heat surrounding them. He began to move again, slower, closer, his scent something expensive and tasteful. Her nerves were raw. Something was happening to her. Something unexpected and thrilling. Her life was too predictable lately, and it was time to change that.

His mouth found hers again, and this time the kiss was hot enough to brand cattle. A fiery mix of passion and lust, making her forget she didn't kiss strangers like this, on an open dance floor with half the town watching. But Brooks didn't let up, and she couldn't pull back or move away. It was that good.

She played with the curling ends of his hair.

He slid his hands lower on her back.

She tucked herself into him.

He groaned and kissed her harder.

The music ended and she hardly noticed.

She stared into his blue eyes.

He gave her a smile.

Her body was shaking.

He was trembling, too.

"What now?" he rasped. "You want another dance?"

She shook her head. "I need air."

He took her hand and led her off the dance floor and out the door of the C'mon Inn. Clouds shadowed half the full moon, and the bite of December air should've cooled her down. But Brooks kept her close to his side, his body shielding her from the cold. Any shivering she was doing was caused by the man beside her and not the dropping winter temperature. He led her around back, where a bench made of iron and wood sat unoccupied near a walled garden. "Would you like to sit?" he asked, and before she could answer, he took a seat and reached for her, giving her the option of where on the bench she wanted to plop down. She chose his lap.

His satisfied smile was her reward, and she wrapped her arms around his neck. "You're beautiful, Ruby. You probably hear that all the time." His hand grazed her neck as he held her hair back to nibble on her throat. Then his tongue moistened her skin as he laid out a row of sensual kisses there. Her insides went a little squishy from his tender assault. Whatever this was, it was happening fast. His rock-hard erection pressing against her legs told her he was as turned on as she was.

"Not really. I tend to scare men off." By her own choosing, she warded off men's advances before giving them half a chance. She'd been waiting around for Trace, hoping he'd come back to her, but that hadn't happened. And now she found pleasure in this man's arms. She didn't know a thing about him, other than her instincts said he was a decent man.

"Little ole you," he whispered softly before claiming her lips again. The taste of alcohol combined with his confidence was a sweet elixir to her recent loneliness. His mouth pressed hers harder, and the tingles under her skin bumped up another notch. "You didn't scare me off."

"Maybe that's why I'm here with you."

"I like the sound of that." The rasp in his voice intensified.

They stopped talking long enough to work up a sweat. Sharp and quick tingles ran up and down her body, and her breaths came in short bursts. She was aware of him at every turn. His well-placed touches made her tremble. His kisses swamped her in heat. Brooks wasn't far behind. His passion swept her up, and the proof of his desire strained the material of his dark pants. She arched her body in a curving bow, craving more, wanting his hands on her everywhere. Under her cropped shirt, her nipples tightened, and an ache throbbed below her waist.

Finally Brooks touched her breasts, and the beauty of the sensation purred from her lips. "Oh, yes."

Low guttural sounds surfaced from his chest, groans of pleasure and want as his hands moved over her body, palms wide, so he could grasp every inch of her. He flattened her erect nipples, followed the curve of her torso and dipped down lower to her hips. He ran his hands along her legs, up and down her thighs, and from under her jeans she felt the burn on her skin.

Laughter coming from patrons leaving the inn rang in her ears.

Brooks stopped and listened.

The sounds became softer and eventually ceased. Thank goodness those people weren't coming back here.

"Ruby, honey. I'm not one for public groping." He hesitated a second. "I have a room."

She bit down on her lower lip, his taste lingering on her mouth. It helped her make the decision. She wasn't ready for this to end. "Take me there."

Ruby drove him wild and crazy with want. Yeah, he'd been without a woman for several months, but this woman was more than he'd ever dreamed of. This woman, he couldn't have even imagined. She was the hottest female he'd met in his life, and she was exactly what he needed to…ah, hell, *blow off steam*. Her flipping that oaf on his back had been just the beginning. From then on, every word that came out of her mouth, every tempting gesture and coy smile, had been perfect. Brooks had it bad for her. Suggesting taking her to his room had been brash. Insane, really, since he'd known her less than an hour.

No one messes with Ruby unless she wants to be messed with.

Apparently he'd made the grade. 'Cause he was messing with her, and had her full approval.

He scooped her up from the bench, and she automatically wound her arms around his neck as he climbed the outside staircase that led to his room. She was petite and lightweight, and it wasn't a struggle to carry her up the stairs in his arms. Darkness concealed them for most of the way. Once he slid the key card into the lock and shoved the door open with a hip, he moved inside and set her on her feet. She still clung to him.

Lord have mercy.

They were finally alone. Brooks's deep sense of decorum kicked in big time. He knew what he was dealing with. She wasn't some floozy who staked men out in a bar. She wasn't an easy piece who'd consider him another conquest. He could tell that from the warm glow in her eyes now, from the way all the men at the bar respected her, from the way she'd chosen *him* and not the other way around. For all those reasons, he wasn't going to take advantage of the situation.

He brushed a kiss to her lips. "Welcome."

As antiquated as the inn was, at least the place was clean. There was no flat-screen television on the wall, no wet bar or cushy king-size bed for added luxury. Nor was there a spacious wardrobe closet or a sunken bathtub or any of the things Brooks was accustomed to. Ruby strolled over to peer out the back window. From where he stood, the view was hardly noteworthy or attractive: just a vast amount of unincorporated land. The lack of illumination was actually a plus since there was nothing to see out there. "I've never been inside one of these rooms," she said.

"I figured."

She whirled around. "You think you've got my number, Galahad?"

"Maybe. I know you don't do this."

Her bright laughter ended with an unfeminine snort. "You'd like to believe that, right?"

"I do believe it. So, why me?"

She glanced out the window again, gazing into the darkness. "Maybe I like you. Maybe it's because you came to my rescue—"

"Which you didn't need."

She continued, "You came to my rescue with no thought of the danger to your own hide."

He took a step toward her. "Are you saying I couldn't take that guy?"

"Hold on to your ego. I'm only saying that you're the one I want to be with tonight. Can't we leave it at that?"

He nodded and inclined his head toward the door. "We were about to combust out there. That's never happened to me before."

"So, you're saying you don't like losing control and decided to slow down the pace?"

"What I'm saying is, you deserve better than that."

She smiled, and the natural sway of her body as she walked toward him fueled his juices. "There, you see? Things like that are exactly what a girl wants to hear. So, what did you have in mind?"

Her scent filled him up, and the shimmering sheet of dark, straight hair falling off her shoulders gave him pause—was he crazy to slow things down?

Her eyes were on him, warm and soft and patient.

"A drink, for starters?"

Another survey of the room had her gaze landing on the amber bottle of whiskey he'd brought from Chicago sitting on the bedside table. "Okay."

He grabbed two tumblers and poured the whiskey. The very best stuff. He'd figured he would need some fortification before meeting his biological father, but he'd never thought he would entertain a lady with it.

Standing before her, he offered her a glass. "Here you go."

She eyed the golden liquid. "Thanks. What should we drink to?"

"To unexpected meetings?"

She smiled. "I'm glad you didn't say 'to new beginnings.'"

He wouldn't. He wasn't in the market for a lover or a girlfriend. And apparently, Miss Ruby—he didn't know her last name—wasn't looking for a relationship, either. She'd dropped enough hints about that tonight. Somebody must've hurt her along the way, but Brooks couldn't delve too deeply into her past. He wouldn't want anyone prying into his, and tonight was all about the present, not the past or the future.

He touched his glass to hers, and a definitive clink sounded in the room. "To unexpected *pleasant* meetings."

She gave him a brief nod and then took a sip, taking time to relish the taste before swallowing. "This is pretty amazing stuff. It surely didn't come out of any minibar."

He was surprised she would notice the quality. "Are you a whiskey expert?"

"Let's just say I know good whiskey when I taste it."

She took a seat on the bed and continued to sip. He sat beside her, enjoying her quiet company. His heart was still racing, but he was glad he'd toned things down some. She wasn't a woman to be rushed. And he wanted to savor her tonight, in the same way she was savoring her whiskey.

"Tell me," she said, "aren't you afraid that I'll come to my senses and walk out on you?"

"I don't think you're a flight risk, Ruby. So, no. But if you think better of this, I would respect your decision. When I make love to you, I want you to be sure and all in."

She smiled, and her eyes drifted down to the amber liquid in her glass. "You don't mince words."

"You don't, either."

She nodded, and her soft gaze met his stare. He reached out to touch her face with a sole finger to her cheek. She gasped, and a warm light flickered in her eyes.

"What do you want, Ruby?"

"Just a night," she whispered, breathy and guileless. "With you."

He sensed she needed it as much as he did. To have one night with her before his life would change forever.

Taking the glass from her and setting both of their drinks down on the nightstand, he cupped her face with his hands and gazed into her eyes. "One night, then."

"Yes," she said. "One night."

And then he pulled her up to a standing position so they were toe-to-toe, her face lifting to his. He peered into warm, dark eyes giving him approval and then slowly lowered his head, his mouth laying claim to hers.

Their night together was just beginning.

Two

Brooks's touch was like a jolt of electricity running the course of her body. One touch, one simple finger to her cheek, one slight meshing of his whiskey-flavored lips with hers, was giving her amnesia about the other men in her life. Men who'd trampled on her heart. Men like Trace, who'd taken from her and hadn't given back. Trace, the man she'd waited for all these months. She squeezed that notion from her mind.

Her time to wait was over.

Brooks's giving and patient mouth didn't demand. Instead, he encouraged her to partake and enjoy. She liked that about this man. He wasn't a player of women. No, her gladiator and presumptive keeper of her virtue was a man of honor. He didn't take. He gave. And that's exactly why she'd decided to come to his room tonight.

She placed her trust in him.

He wasn't asking her to bare her soul. But she would bare her body. For him.

Her fingers nimbly played with the tiny white buttons on her blouse until the material slipped from her shoulders, trapping her arms. Cool night air grazed her exposed skin.

Brooks's sharp intake of breath reached her ears. "You're unbelievably beautiful."

He worked the sleeves of her blouse down her arms until they gathered at her wrists. He held her there, mercilessly tugging her closer until her bra brushed his torso. "Yeah, I like you in red." He stroked her hair and then snapped the silky strap of her bra.

"It's my color," she whispered, and he smiled.

"I won't disagree."

He nipped at her lips then, several times, until his mouth claimed hers again. The kiss swept her into another world, where the only thing that mattered, all that she felt, was the pleasure he was giving. His tongue plunged in and met hers in a sparring match that ignited a fiery inferno within her. Whimpering, she ached for his touch. Finally his fingers dipped inside her bra to caress her nipples. Everything unfolded from there—the pleasure too great, the sighs too loud, the hunger too strong.

He worked magic with his mouth while his hands found the fastener of her bra. Within seconds, and none too soon, she was free of her blouse and restraints. Her breasts spilled out into his awaiting hands, and the small ache at her core began to pulse as he touched, fondled and caressed her. She was pinned to the spot, unwilling to move, unwilling to take a step, his invisible hold on her body too strong. Her nipples stood erect and tightened to pebble hardness. Aching for more, she leaned way back and was granted the very tip of his tongue dampening her with moisture.

"Oh, so good, Brooks."

His outstretched palms bracing the small of her back, he answered only with a low guttural groan.

And once he was through ravaging her, he brought her up to eye level, drinking her in from top to bottom. Shaking his head, he fixed his gaze on the full measure of her breasts. She had a large bust for a petite woman and this time she didn't mind having a man's eyes transfixed on her. "I can't believe you," he muttered. "You're not real."

The compliment went straight to her head.

Brooks was a city dude, a man who didn't fit in her world, yet here she was, nearly naked with him and enjoying every sensual second of it.

"I'm very real," she breathed, closing the gap between them and lacing her arms around his neck. His erection stood like a stout monument, and there was no missing it. "And I want more."

"Whatever the lady wants," he said, running his hands up and down the sides of her body, his fingertips grazing the sides of her breasts. Another round of heat pinged her as anticipation grew.

He turned her around, came up behind her and slowly grazed the waistband of her jeans with his hands. His powerful arms locked her in, and his mouth was doing a number on her throat while his long fingers nudged her sweet spot. She murmured her approval, and lights flashed before her eyes. He stroked between her thighs, and a cry ripped from her throat. And then he was pulling the zipper of her jeans down, slowly, torturously, his erection behind her, a thrilling reminder of what was to come.

"Kick off your boots," he whispered in her ear.

Goose bumps erupted on her arms.

Her legs were a mass of jelly.

She kicked her boots off obediently, and then his index

fingers were inside her waistband, gently lowering the jeans down her legs. She stepped out of them easily. "Red lace panties," he murmured appreciatively. He cupped one cheek, fitting her left buttock in his palm. He stroked her, smoothing his hand up and over, up and over. "Oh, man," he muttered, the heat of his body bathing her.

From where she stood with her back against his chest, she felt his body shudder. Quickly she turned around. The room was dimly lit with a sole lamp, and they were cast in shadow, but there was enough light to see a deep, burning hunger in his eyes.

"Lie down on the bed," he told her.

Her heart was pounding like a drum, beating hard, beating fast. He was a man who took control. She wasn't one to obey so easily, but there was a look in his eyes telling her to trust him. She did as she was told and lay on the queen bed, naked but for the panties she wore.

His gaze roamed over her body, slowly, the gleam in his eyes filled with promise.

"Galahad?"

"Hmm?"

"Having second thoughts?"

He laughed at her, giving his head a shake. "Are you kidding me? You have no idea…"

"What?"

"…how turned on I am. I'm trying to keep from jumping your bones, Ruby."

She glanced at the flagpole erection bulging in his pants. "What if I want you to jump my bones? Isn't that why we're here?"

He squeezed his eyes shut. "Yeah, but… I want this night to last."

She rolled to the side and leaned on her elbow. His eyes sought the spill of her hair touching her breasts.

"Come to bed, Brooks. I'm a big girl. I can take whatever you have in mind."

"Doubtful, honey. What I'm thinking…"

She grabbed his hand and tugged. He landed on his butt in an upright position on the bed. "Do it, Brooks. But first take off your clothes."

He grinned. "How did I get so lucky?"

"Judging by the cut of your cloth, you were probably born lucky." She was guessing.

He grunted. And that was all the reply he gave her.

Sitting up on her knees, she helped him lift his shirt over his head and pull off his boots between kisses. Her hands sought his chest, all powerful and rippled with muscle, smooth and hard, like the planes of a solid board. She reveled in touching him, her fingertips toying with his flattened nipples.

That move landed her on her back, her arms locked by one strong hand above her head. "Two can tease," he said.

And then he was pulling her panties down and touching her where she'd prayed he'd touch. Her body instantly responded, and soft moans rose from her throat. She undulated with each stroke of his hand, each caress of a fingertip. He kept her pinned down, covering her with his body, the soft flesh of his palm applying pressure at the apex of her thighs.

"I'm… I'm going to lose it," she moaned, the pleasure unbearable.

"Don't fight it, honey," he rasped.

And then she shattered, and spasms wracked her lower body in beautiful jolts that electrified her body. Her hips were arched, and she didn't remember how they got that way. Slowly she lowered herself and finally opened her eyes to swim in Brooks's deep blue gaze. He watched her carefully, a satisfied smile on his lips as he unzipped his pants and removed them.

"Your turn," she said.

He shook his head. "Our turn."

And then he fitted a condom on his erection and moved back over her.

His hands molded her breasts. His kiss went deep, his tongue delicious and probing. "Tell me when you're ready, sweetheart," he murmured before kissing her again.

She ran her hands through his longish blond hair, her fingers curling around the locks at the back of his neck. Then her gaze drifted to his eyes. "I don't think I'll ever be more ready."

He made a caveman sound, raw and brash, and then braced her in a protective way to roll them over on the bed. She found herself on top of him. "Set the pace, Ruby. I don't want to hurt you."

She bit the corner of her lip. Sure, she was petite, but Galahad worried that he was too big for her small frame. She could actually fall for a guy like this. She gave him a nod and straddled his thighs. "You won't hurt me," she said, fitting herself over his shaft, tossing her head back and shuddering from the feel of him inside her.

Then she began to move.

Spooned against Brooks's large frame, with his arm resting possessively around her torso, Ruby slowly opened her eyes. It was past midnight and she'd promised Brooks she'd stay the night with him. She didn't doubt her decision but instead smiled as he snuggled her closer and brought his hand to rest just under her breast.

"Are you awake?" he whispered, his breath warm on her neck.

"Just," she answered. "I dozed."

"Me, too. I haven't been this relaxed in a long time."

"Had a lot on your mind lately?" she murmured.

"You have no idea. But I don't want to talk about that right now."

His hand made lazy circles around her breast, his fingers feathery light over her nipple. Her body heated instantly. He had the ability to make her yearn, and the longing was potent. His leg moved over both of hers, and she was locked to him now, the soft flesh of her thighs meeting with legs of steel.

"I don't want to talk at all," he said, fisting her hair and planting kisses at the back of her neck. "Do you?"

"No." Oh God, what he was doing to her? Her body flamed. She was going up in smoke. "Talking is overrated. Not when we could be doing better things."

Ruby had never given herself so freely before. She'd never really been the *bad* girl, and everyone who knew her well knew that for a fact. She'd had only three relationships in her twenty-six years, and only the last one had really meant anything to her. The *last* one had hurt her.

She'd been in love.

Or so she'd thought.

But tonight with Brooks was different. It was all about having a man appreciate her. Give to her. Excite her and make her feel like a woman.

He rolled over on top of her, careful of her small frame, his hands bracing the bed on both sides of her head. She gazed into his deep blue eyes. "I want you again, Ruby."

Ruby smiled. "I want you, too."

He nodded and let go of a deep breath. "I was praying you'd say that, honey."

He bent his head and touched his mouth to hers. Already the taste of him, the firmness of his lips, seemed familiar and welcome. She'd never see him again. She wasn't in the market for a man. But Brooks would leave her with a good memory.

And then his mouth moved from her lips down her chest toward her navel, streaming kisses along the way. Her hips lifted; she was eager and willing, waiting. She didn't have to wait long. He touched his tongue to her center and suckled her sweetest spot. She whimpered and moved wildly as his mouth performed magic. It was a torturous, beautiful few minutes of pleasure. And when she was on the brink, ready for a powerful release, he rose over her and joined their bodies. Oh…it was bliss, the best of the best as he moved inside her. And then, moments later, his eyes darkened, his body stiffened and every sensation between them intensified. He moaned her name, an utterance of pleasured pain, and then he broke apart at the seams. It was enough to turn her inside out, and she, too, shuddered with an incredible release.

"Wow," she said once her breathing returned to normal.

"Yeah, wow," he said, keeping her close. He kissed her forehead, stroked her hair and tucked her body into his.

She closed her eyes and waited for the exquisite hum of her body to ease her into sleep.

Brooks tiptoed back into the room, holding two cups of coffee and a white paper bag filled with muffins and buttered biscuits from the café at the inn. There wasn't a croissant to be had in this hokey Texas town, and he liked that about this place. Clean, simple and… He glanced at Ruby asleep in the bed, her hair smooth black granite against the pillow. Beautiful. Yep, Cool Springs left him with a good impression.

The mattress groaned as he sat down.

"Is that coffee I smell?" a soft, sultry voice whispered from the other end of the bed.

"Can't fool you," he said, turning to find Ruby coming to a sitting position. "Leaded and dark as mud." Apparently that's how they made coffee in Texas. He showed her the two cups.

"I think I love you," she said, reaching for one. She'd worn one of his shirts to bed. The thing hung down to her knees and covered most of her up, but she still looked sexy as sin.

Her lips pursed as she blew on the rising steam.

He shook his head and talked down his lust. "Got biscuits, too, all buttered up, with honey."

"I adore you even more," she said. He handed her one and she wasted no time. She took a big bite, chewed with gusto and then took another bite.

"You've got an appetite."

"I had a busy day and *night*."

He joined in, sipping coffee and digging into the biscuits. "Maybe I should've taken you out for a nice big breakfast."

She shook her head. "This is perfect," she said, reaching for the bag from his hand. "What kind of muffins did you get?"

"Banana and blueberry. So, you wouldn't want to go out for breakfast with me?"

She chose blueberry. "It's nothing personal, but showing up somewhere public at this hour will cause talk. You know what they say about small towns. All of it is true. And you don't owe me anything, but I appreciate your gallantry."

"Just call me Galahad."

"I do." She laughed before putting her teeth into the muffin.

He laughed, too, and was sorry he had to leave Ruby behind. She wasn't like most females he'd met, and he had a feeling she wasn't going to put up a fuss about saying goodbye.

He wasn't entirely sure he liked that idea, but he had a new life waiting for him. His emotions were keyed up, and he was too damn confused to add a woman to the mix.

They drank coffee and chatted quietly about nothing in particular. And after they'd taken their last sips, Brooks rose from the bed and began packing his belongings. "Sorry, but I have to hit the road soon. I have an important meeting."

Ruby rose from the bed and padded over to him. "Brooks," she said.

"Hmm?"

She stood before him, her expression unreadable. "Don't forget your shirt."

Slowly she began undoing the buttons, her nimble fingers working one after another. Once done, she shrugged out of the shirt, and it fell easily to her feet. His gaze fastened on a beautiful body in red lace. "Ruby," he said, sucking in oxygen and pulling her into his arms, her skin smooth and her muscles toned under his fingertips. "I wish I could postpone my meeting."

"No problem." Her eyes were soft and warm. He was never going to forget that particular deep cocoa color. Who was he kidding? He was never going to forget *her*. That was for damn sure. "I've got a busy day myself. I'll take a shower. You'll probably be gone by the time I get out."

Like a fool, he nodded. That was the plan. He had to leave. Now.

He claimed her lips one last time, putting all of himself

into that kiss. Then, mustering every ounce of his will-power, he turned away from her. But a thought struck, and he reached into his pocket to pull out a business card. "In case," he said with a lift of his shoulder, "I don't know, if you want to talk. Or need me or something." He set the card on the bedside table.

By the time he turned back around, she had disappeared into the bathroom.

"Goodbye, Brooks," she said just as the door was closing.

The lock clicked.

He closed his eyes. It was time to get on with the rest of his life.

Three

Brooks pulled into the gates of Look Away Ranch, his gaze drawn to the size and scope of Beau Preston's horse farm. The animals grazing freely in white-fenced meadowlands had a majestic presence. They were tall, their coats gleaming in browns and blacks and golds. Brooks didn't know much about horses, but even an amateur could tell by looking at them that these stallions, mares and geldings were top-notch.

He smiled at the notion that the apple didn't fall far from the tree. If what he'd been told by Roman Slater, the PI he'd hired to find his biological father, was true, then Brooks's drive to succeed above all else must've been in his blood. Because Look Away Ranch had all the makings of hard-earned success, much like his very own Newport Corporation.

He, Graham and Carson had worked their asses off for years in order to create one of the leading real estate and land development companies in the country. He was proud of what they'd accomplished, coming up the real estate ranks in Chicago and becoming genuine competitors of Sutton Winchester's Elite Industries. Winchester was their biggest rival both professionally and privately. And Brooks had done his very best to take the ruthless older man down, more for personal reasons than professional.

For a time, Brooks had believed that the now ailing Sutton fathered him and his twin brother Graham. The knowledge only fueled his desire to destroy the man he believed abandoned his mother in her time of need, when she was pregnant. It turned out none of that was true. But paternity tests had revealed that his baby brother, Carson, was indeed Sutton Winchester's biological child. Sutton and his late mother, Cynthia, had history together. She'd been his secretary once, and they'd had a love affair.

He hoped his true father, Beau, would fill in the rest of the blanks. After years of wondering and months now of tracking the man down, Brooks was ready to meet the man who'd fathered him.

He pulled up into the portico-covered drive that circled the stately ranch house and killed the engine. A man was waiting on the steps. Brooks's first glimpse was of a tall rancher, his hair once blond and now dusted with silver, dressed in crisp jeans and a snap-down Western shirt. He immediately approached, marching down the steps, his gait extremely similar to his twin brother's and probably Brooks's as well. Warmth swamped his chest.

He was out of the car quickly, walking toward the man whose blood flowed through his veins. They came face-to-face, and Brooks took in the blue eyes, the firm jaw and the hint of a wicked smile bracing the man's mouth. "Beau?"

Tears welled in the man's eyes. His lips quivered and he nodded. "Yes, son. I'm Beau Preston. I'm your father."

His father's legs wobbled, and Brooks grabbed his shoulders to steady him. As emotion rocked him, Brooks's own legs went numb, too. Then his father broke down, sobbing quietly and taking Brooks into his big, sturdy arms as he would a little boy. "Welcome, son. Welcome. I've been searching for you for a long time."

A few seconds later, Beau backed away, wiping at his tears. "I'm sorry. I'm just so happy, boy. Come inside. We have a lot to talk about."

"Yes, I'd like that," Brooks said.

They walked shoulder to shoulder into the house.

"Forgive me for not showing you around just yet," Beau said.

"I understand. We have a lot of catching up to do."

But Brooks noticed things about the rooms he walked through, the sturdy, steady surroundings, dark wood floors polished to a mirror shine, bulky wood beams above and wide-paned windows letting the outside in. The wood tones were brightened by the red blooms of poinsettia plants placed in several of the rooms, and his nostrils filled with the holiday scent of pine.

His father led him into the great room, which contained a giant flat-screen television, a corner wet bar, and tan and black leather couches. He got the feeling this was his father's comfort zone, the room he relaxed in after a long, grueling day. "Have a seat," the older man said. "Can I offer you coffee or iced tea? Orange juice?"

Brooks had had morning coffee with Ruby. A slice of regret barreled through him that he'd never see her again. He sat down on a tan sofa. "No thanks. I'm fine."

"You found the place okay?" His father took a seat facing him, his gaze latching onto Brooks and gleaming as bright as morning sunshine. All of Brooks's apprehension over this meeting vanished. Beau was as glad they'd found each other as he was.

"Yep, didn't have any trouble finding Look Away Ranch. It's pretty amazing, I have to say."

"What's amazing is that you're finally here. And look at you, boy. You're the spitting image of me when I was your age."

"There are two of us, you know. But Graham wanted to lay back and let me make the first contact with you. We didn't want to overwhelm you and, well...we have questions. He thought it'd be easier for you and me to speak privately before he joins us, since I was the one hell-bent on finding you."

His father rubbed at the back of his neck, a pained look entering his eyes. "I have to explain. I didn't know about you boys in the beginning. I didn't know your mama, Mary Jo, was carrying my babies when she ran away from Cool Springs. And once I started receiving anonymous notes and photos, I wasn't sure any of it was true, but as the photos kept coming, I saw the resemblance. It was unmistakable, and I moved heaven and earth to find Mary Jo. To find you boys."

"It's weird to hear you call my mother Mary Jo. As far as we knew, Mom's name was Cynthia Newport."

He shrugged a shoulder and got a faraway look in his eyes. "Mary Jo and I were desperately in love. She must've been scared out of her mind to run from me the way she did. That son of a bitch father of hers..." He paused to gauge Brooks's reaction. "Sorry, I forget he's your grandfather. But he was mean to the bone. Mary Jo was convinced if he found out she was seeing me, he'd kill both of us. I tried like the dickens to calm her down and tell her I'd protect her, but she must've panicked when she found out she was pregnant. God, I keep thinking how desperate she must've been back then. Alone in the world and carrying twins, no less. She wouldn't have run off if she wasn't terribly frightened of the consequences. That's all I can figure. She must've thought her daddy would beat the stuffing out of her, and harm her babies, if he ever found out the truth.

"I didn't know she'd changed her name and started a new life. I surely didn't know she was with child. But I want you to know, to be clear, I searched high and low for her in those early days. Trouble was, I was searching for Mary Jo Turner, not this...this Cynthia Newport person."

"I understand. I don't fault you for any of this. I've, uh, well, I'm just now coming to terms with all of this myself. I must admit, I was a bit obsessed with finding you."

"I'm glad you never let up, son."

Brooks gave him a nod. "Mom, she was a survivor. She did whatever it took to keep me and my brothers safe and cared for. She hid so many things from us during our lives. But Graham and I and our younger brother, Carson, who has a different father, don't blame her for any of it. We had a good life, living on the outskirts of Chicago with our Grandma Gerty. That woman befriended Mom when she was at a low point, and she took all of us in. She let us live with her in a modest home in a nice neighborhood, and she helped get us through school. We were a family in all respects. My brothers and I always looked upon her and loved her as if she was our real grandmother. I have a sneaking suspicion she was the one sending those updates and photos to you."

"Sounds like a wonderful woman." Beau sighed as he leaned farther back in his seat. "If she was the one, then I owe her a great debt. I'd long believed that your mother was gone to me forever, but just knowing you boys were out there somewhere gave me hope. I wish like hell Gerty would've just told me where to find you, but your mama probably held her to a promise to keep the secret."

"Grandma Gerty died about ten years ago."

"That's about when the updates stopped coming. It makes sense," his father said, "as much as any of this makes sense." He laughed with no real amusement.

"Grandma Gerty had a keen sense of duty. She must've believed in her heart she was doing the right thing. She only wanted what was best for my mom."

"I'm sorry Mary Jo isn't with us anymore. We were so young when we were in love, and…well, I have fond memories of her. Such a tragedy, the way she died."

"The aneurism took us all by shock. Mom was pretty healthy all of her life, and to lose her that way, after all she'd been through…well, it wasn't fair." Brooks took a second to breathe in and out slowly. After composing himself he added, "I miss her like crazy."

"I bet you do. The Mary Jo I remember was worthy of your love. I have no doubt she was a wonderful mother."

"Do you know what ever happened to my grandfather?"

"Still kicking. The mean ones don't die young. He's in a nursing home for dementia patients and being cared for by the state of Texas. I'm sorry, son. I know he's your relation, but if you knew how he treated your mama, you wouldn't give him a second of thought."

Brooks closed his eyes. This part was hardest to hear. His mother had never mentioned her abuse to him or any of her children. She'd shielded them all from hurt and negativity and made their lives as pleasant and as full of love as she possibly could. She'd come to Chicago hell-bent on changing her circumstances, but those memories of her broken youth must've haunted her. To think of her as that young girl who'd been treated so poorly by the one person who should've been loving and protecting her burned Brooks like a hot brand. "I suppose I should visit him."

"You can see him, son. But I'm told he's lost his mind. Doesn't recognize anyone anymore."

Brooks nodded. Another piece of his family lost to him. But perhaps in this case it was for the best that his grandfather wouldn't know him. "I'll deal with him in my own way at some point."

"I'm glad you agreed to stay on at the ranch awhile. You're welcome at the house. It's big enough and always open to you. But when we spoke on the phone, you seemed to like the idea of staying at the cabin right on our property and…well, I think it's a good choice. You can take things at your own pace without getting overwhelmed." His father grinned and gave his head a prideful tilt. "Course, here I am talking about you getting overwhelmed when you're the owner of a big corporation and all."

Brooks grinned. That apple not falling far from the tree again. "And here you are with this very prosperous horse farm in Texas. You have a great reputation for honesty and quality. Look Away Ranch is top-notch." Aside from having Beau Preston investigated by Slater, Brooks had Googled him and found nothing lacking.

"It's good to hear you say that. Look Away has been a joy in my life. I lost my wife some years ago, and this place along with my sons helped me get through it. You'll meet your half brothers soon."

"I'll look forward to that. And I'm sorry to hear about you losing your wife."

"Yeah, it was a tough one. I think you would've liked her. I know Mary Jo would've approved. My Tanya was a good woman. She filled the hole inside me after losing your mama."

"I wish I could've known her, Beau."

His eyes snapped up. "Son, I'd appreciate it if you called me Dad."

Dad? A swell of warmth lodged deep in his heart. He'd never had the privilege of calling any man that. While growing up, he, Carson and Graham had always been the boys without a father. Grandma Gerty had made up for it in many ways, her brightness and light shining over them, but deep down Brooks had wanted better answers from his mother about his father's absence in their lives. "You're better off not knowing," she'd say, cutting off his further questions.

Brooks gave Beau a smile. "All right, *Dad*. I'm happy to call you that after all these years."

His father's eyes lit up. "And I'm happy to hear it, son. Would you like to get settled in? I can drive you to the cabin. It's barely more than a stone's throw from here, only a quarter mile into the property."

"Yeah, that's sounds good."

"Fine, and before we do, I'll give you the grand tour of the house. Tanya did all the decorating and she loved the holidays, so we've kept up the tradition of putting out all her favorite things. We start early in December, and it takes us a while to bring the trees in and get the house fully decorated in time for our annual Look Away Ranch Christmas shindig. C'mon, I'll show you around now."

"Thanks. I've got no doubt I'm going to like your place."

"I hope so, son."

After his father left him at the cabin, a rustic, wood-beamed, fully state-of-the-art three-bedroom dwelling that would sell for a million bucks in the suburbs of Chicago, Brooks walked his luggage into the master suite and began putting away his belongings in a dark oak dresser. Lifting out the shirt Ruby had worn just this morning, Brooks brought the collar to his nose and breathed in. The shirt smelled of her still, a wildly exotic scent that had lured him into his best fantasy to date.

He'd hold on to that memory for a long time, but now he was about to make new ones with his father and his family. Brooks walked the rooms, getting familiar with his new home—for the next few weeks, anyway—and found he was antsy to learn more, to see more.

He grabbed a bottle of water from the fridge, noting that Beau Preston didn't do things halfway. The fridge was filled with everything Brooks might possibly need during his stay here. If Beau wanted him to feel welcome, he'd succeeded.

Locking the cabin door with the key his dad had given him, he headed toward the stables to explore. What he knew about horses and ranching could fit in his right hand, and it was about time to change that. Brooks didn't want to admit to his father he'd seen the saddle side of a horse only once or twice. What did a city kid from Chicago know about riding?

Not much.

Huddled in a windbreaker jacket fit for a crisp December day in Texas, his boots kicking up dust, he came upon a set of corrals first. Beautiful animals frolicked, their groomed manes gently bouncing off their shoulders as they played a game of equine tag. They nipped at each other, teased and snorted and then stormed off, only to return to play again. They were beauties. *His father's horses.*

The land behind the corrals was rich with tall grazing

grass, strong oaks and mesquite trees dotting the squat hills. It was unfamiliar territory and remote, uniquely different from what Brooks had ever known.

He ducked into one of the stables. Shadows split the sunshine inside, and a long row of stalls on either side led to a tack room. The stable was empty but for a dozen or so horses. Beau had told him to check out Misty, an eight-year-old mare with a sweet nature. He spotted her quickly, a golden palomino with blond locks, not too different in color from his own.

"Hey, girl, are you and I going to get along?" The horse's ears perked up, and she sauntered over to hang her head over the split door. "That's a girl." He stroked the horse's nose and looked into her big brown eyes. "Hang on a sec," he said and walked over to the tack area. The place smelled of leather and dust, but it was about as clean and tidy as a five-star hotel.

That told him something about his father.

"Can I help you?" A man walked out of the tack room and eyed him cautiously. "I'm Sam Braddox, the foreman."

Brooks put out his hand. "I'm Brooks Newport. Nice to meet you."

The man's expression changed to a quick smile. "You're one of Beau's boys."

"Yes, I am. I just got here a little while ago."

"Well, welcome. I see the resemblance. You have your daddy's eyes. And Beau only just this morning filled the crew in on the news you'd be arriving."

"Thanks. I'm… I'm just trying to get acquainted with the place. Learn a little about horses." He scratched his head and then shrugged. "I'm no horseman, but Beau wants to take me out riding one day."

Sam studied him. "How about a quick lesson?"

"Sure."

"C'mon. I'll show you how to saddle up." He led Misty out of her stall and into an open area.

"Misty's a fine girl. She's sweet, but she can get testy if you don't show her who's boss from the get-go."

"Okay."

The foreman grabbed a worked-in saddle and horse blanket and walked over to Brooks. "Here we go."

Sam tossed the blanket over the horse just as one of the crew dashed in. "Hey, Boss. Looks like Candy is ready to foal. She's having a struggle. Brian sent me to get you."

"Okay." Sam sighed. "I'll be right there." He gave Brooks a glance and set the saddle on the ground. "Sorry about this. Candy has had a hard pregnancy. I'd better get right to it."

"No problem at all. I'll see you later, Sam."

"You okay here?"

"I'm gonna try my hand at it. I'll Google how to saddle a horse."

Sam gave him a queer look. "All right." Then he strode out like his pants were on fire.

"How hard can this be?" Brooks said to himself.

He fixed the blanket over the horse's shoulders, sheepskin side down, and then lifted the saddle. The darn thing weighed at least fifty pounds. He set it onto the horse and grabbed the cinch from underneath the horse's belly.

"You're doing it all wrong." The female voice stopped him short. What in hell? He whipped around, uneasy about where his thoughts were heading. Sure enough, there was Ruby of his fantasies coming forward. His mouth could've dropped open, but he kept his teeth clamped as he tried to make sense of it. He'd just left Ruby a few hours ago, and now here she was in the flesh, appearing unfazed at seeing him again. He, for sure, wasn't unaffected.

"Ruby?"

"Hello, Brooks."

She practically ignored him as she went about removing the saddle like a pro—a saddle that weighed probably half her body weight—and shoving it into his arms. "The blanket has to be even on both sides. You put it on closer to Misty's shoulders and then slide it into the natural channel of her body. Make sure it's not too far down on her hips, either. It's the best protection the horse has for—"

"Ruby?" He took hold of her arm gently.

She didn't budge, didn't face him. "I work here. I'm Look Away Ranch's head wrangler and horse trainer."

As if that explained it all. "Did you know who I was last night?"

Her eyes snapped up. "God, no." She shook her head, and the sheet of beautiful raven hair shimmered. "Beau told us about you only this morning. He wanted to make sure you were really coming before he shared his news. Welcome to the family, Brooks."

His heart just about stopped. "The family?"

She nodded. "Beau's like a father to me."

Brooks released the breath he'd been holding. She'd had him scared for a second that they could be related in some way. "Like a father? What does that mean?"

"My father worked for Beau all of his life, until he died ten years ago. I was sixteen at the time. It was hard on me. I, uh…it almost broke me. My dad was special to me. We both loved horses, the land and everything about Look Away, so when he passed, I couldn't imagine my life without him. But Beau and his boys were right by my side the entire time. Beau never let a day go by without letting me know I was welcome and wanted here. He took me in and I worked at Look Away, making my way up to head wrangler."

"You live here?"

"I have an apartment in town, but often I stay in the old groundskeeper's cottage, especially during the holidays. It's where my dad lived out the last years of his life. It's home to me, too, and Beau's family is now my family."

Brooks nodded at this new wrinkle in his life. "What about your mother?"

"Mom died when I was very young. I don't remember too much about her."

"I'm sorry." He put his hands on his hips. "So, what do we do now?"

"Now?" Her brows knit together. "What do you mean?"

"About us?"

Her olive skin turned bright pink, and her embarrassment surprised him. The Ruby he'd met yesterday had been fearless and uninhibited. "Oh, that. Well, it'd be best if we didn't discuss what happened between us last night. Beau wouldn't approve. It was really nice, Brooks. But not to be repeated."

"I see."

"Glad you do," she said, dismissing the subject with a flip of her hair. "You want to learn how to saddle this horse correctly?"

Dumbfounded, he began nodding, not so much because he gave a damn about saddling, but because Ruby living on his father's ranch blew his mind. "Uh, sure."

"Okay, so the blanket has to be even and protecting the horse from the saddle." Next this petite five-foot-something of a woman positioned the heavy saddle on her knee. "Put the stirrups and straps over the saddle seat so you don't hit the horse or yourself by accident when you're saddling up. Now use your leg for support and then knee it up in a whipping motion like this." With the grace of a ballerina, she heaved the weighty saddle onto the horse's back. "You want the saddle up a little high on the shoulders first, then slowly go with the grain of the horse's hair to slide it into place. This way you won't cause any ruffle to the hair that might irritate the horse later on. Proper saddling should cause your mount no harm at all. Doing it wrong can cause all kinds of sores and injuries."

"Got it."

Ruby gave Misty several loving pats on the shoulder. She spoke kindly to the animal, as one would to a friend, and the horse stood stock-still while she continued with a ritual she probably did every day.

Ruby adjusted the front cinch strap. "Make sure it's not too loose or too tight. Just keep tucking until you run out of latigo. Take a look at how I did this one and you do the back one."

"Okay, will do." He made a good attempt at fastening the cinch, Ruby standing next to him. His concentration scattered as she brushed up against him to fix the cinch and buckle it.

"Not bad, Brooks. For your first try."

Her praise flattered him. And her sweet scent filtering up to his nose blocked out the stable smells.

"Now that Misty is saddled, you want to make sure all buckles are locked in and all your gear is in good shape. Here's a trick. Slide your hand under the saddle up front." She placed her small hand under the blanket and saddle. "If your hand goes under with no forcing, you're good to go and you know your horse isn't being pinched tight. Isn't that right, Misty?"

As she stroked Misty's nose, the horse responded with a turn of her head. The two were old pals, it seemed. Ruby's big brown eyes lifted to him. "If you want some pointers on riding, I've got some time."

Mentally he winced. He had trouble focusing. He kept thinking about Ruby in his bed. Ruby naked. Ruby making love to him. Feisty, fierce Ruby. He should back away and make an excuse. Gain some perspective. But she was offering him something he needed.

Just like last night.

"Yeah, show me what you've got."

She stared at him for a beat of a second, her face coloring again. They were locked into the memory of last night, when she'd shown him what she had. And it was not to be equaled. "Stop saying stuff like that, Brooks. And we'll do just fine."

It was good to know that she wasn't as unaffected as she wanted him to believe.

"Right. All I can promise is I'll try."

Once Brooks was away from the stable and on horseback, Ruby could breathe again. She'd never expected her one-time, one-night fling to end up being Beau Preston's long-lost son. The irony in that was killing her.

"You're not a bad rider, Brooks," she said to him.

"I'll take that as a compliment." He tipped the hat she'd given him to wear. He didn't look half bad in a Stetson.

"Actually, you learn fast. You saddled up my horse pretty darn well."

"If you're trying to butter me up, it's working, honey."

"Just speaking the truth. And can you quit the endearments?"

He smiled. "You don't like me calling you honey?"

"I'm not your honey, Brooks. Ruby Lopez never has

been anyone's honey." Except for Trace's at one time, but the sweetness of the term had soured along with the relationship.

They rode side by side along a path that wound around the property. She wanted out of this conversation. Brooks didn't need to know about her lack of a love life. But for some reason, when he was around, she did and said things she normally wouldn't.

"Ruby?"

"Hmm."

"I find that hard to believe. There's been no one in your life?"

"No one I care to talk about."

"Ah, I thought so. You've been burned before. The guy must be a loser."

"He isn't." Why on earth was she defending Trace?

"Must be, if he hurt you."

"Remember what I told you? When you want the horse to stop, pull back on one rein. Not two. Two can toss you forward, and that's a fight you can't win."

"Yeah, I remember, but why—"

"See you later, Brooks!" Ruby gave Storm Cloud a nudge, and the horse fell into a gallop. The ground rumbled underneath her stallion's hooves, and she leaned back and enjoyed the ride, grinning.

She thought she'd left Misty and her rider in the dust, but one quick look back showed her she was wrong. Brooks wasn't far behind, encouraging Misty to catch up. Ruby had five lengths on them, at best. But it wasn't a race. She couldn't put Brooks in danger. For all his courage and eagerness to learn, he was still a novice. "Whoa, slow up, Cloud." A slight tug on the rein was all that was needed. Cloud was a gem at voice commands. Beau had given her Storm Cloud on her eighteenth birthday, and she'd trained him herself. They were simpatico.

Brooks caught up to her by a copse of trees and came to a halt. "Is that your way of changing the subject?" His mouth was in a twist.

She shrugged a shoulder. "I don't know what you mean."

"Cute, Ruby."

"Hey, I'm impressed you caught up."

"Because you let me."

"Okay, I let you. But I couldn't endanger Beau's long-lost son."

"*One* of his sons. I've got a twin brother."

"Oh, no. There are two of you?" She smiled at him. This morning Beau had briefed her on all the sad events of his early life. He'd lost the woman he loved and his twins when she ran away from her abusive father. It was something Ruby had heard rumored, but it was never really spoken about in the Preston household.

"Yeah, I'm afraid so."

She tilted her head. "Can the world handle it?"

"The world likes the Newport brothers for the most part. But the question is, can you handle it?"

"I already told you, I'm good with you being here."

"I might be staying quite a while."

It was time to set him straight, and she hoped to heaven she could heed her own warning. "You're a city guy who's out of place in the country. You run a big company, and I'm at home in a barn. You're also the son of my best friend and mentor. The man is almost a father to me. You'd better believe I can handle it. There's no other option, Brooks."

He gave her a nod, his mouth turning down. "You're right. But when I look at you and remember…"

"Don't look at me."

"You're hard to miss, honey."

Honey again? "It's time to head back." She didn't wait for his reply. She turned Storm Cloud around. "Let's go, Cloud." With a slight nudge of the stirrup, the horse took off in a canter.

"I didn't peg you for a runner," Brooks called out.

But that's exactly what she was.

This time.

With this man.

She wasn't lying. She had no other choice.

Four

"You're cooking?" Brooks asked Ruby as he walked into his father's kitchen later that day.

Ruby glanced at him from her spot at the stove. She wore a black dress that landed just above her knees, fitting every curve on her body like a glove. A pink polka-dotted apron tied at the neck and waist didn't detract from the look. Brooks was beginning to think Ruby looked sexy in everything she wore.

"I'm cooking. Beau wanted me to make you a special dinner for your first night here."

"Do you cook every night?"

"No, that's Lupe's job. She's the best cook in the county, but this recipe comes from my father's family, and it's something Beau likes me to cook on occasion."

Brooks walked over to the stove. "I'm the occasion?"

She smiled. "You're the occasion."

He lifted the top off the enamel pot. Steam drifted up, and the scents of Mexico filled the room.

"Be careful. It's hot," she said, shoving a pot holder into his hand.

"What is it?"

"It's called *receta de costillas de res en salsa verde*. It's braised short ribs in tomatillo sauce."

"Smells delicious."

"It's not too spicy for a gringo." Her mouth twisted.

"You're all the spice I can manage in his house."

Ruby whipped her head around to the kitchen door. "*Dios!* Don't say things like that," she whispered. "I don't like lying to Beau."

"How did you lie?"

"It was a lie of omission. I didn't tell him I've already met you."

She'd met him and slept with him. And Brooks was having a hard time forgetting it. "He won't hear it from me, Ruby." He wasn't a kiss-and-tell kind of man. "I'm starving. Can I have a taste?" he asked.

"I suppose."

She grabbed a fork and dipped it into the stew. The meat she pierced fell easily away, and she lifted the steamy forkful up to his mouth. "Here. Tell me if it needs anything."

Brooks looked into her dark brown eyes as she fed him a morsel. The heat on the stove didn't compare to how he was heating up just being close to Ruby again. And then he began to chew. The seasoned meat blasted his palate with savory goodness. "Mmm. The lady can toss a man over her shoulder, ride a horse like nobody's business *and* cook."

"So, you like it?"

He nodded and stepped inches closer to her. "Is there anything you don't do well?" She didn't back away, and he didn't bother pretending he wasn't talking about her prowess in the bedroom.

She nibbled on her lower lip. "Brooks."

He ignored her warning tone, sensing she was as caught up as he was. He leaned forward and focused on her tempting mouth.

"Well, I see you've met Ruby already, Brooks."

The booming voice startled him, and he quickly stepped away. Ruby turned back to the stove, and Brooks answered his father. "Yes, I've met Ruby. She was kind enough to give me a taste of her stew."

Beau nodded. "It's a favorite of mine. I figured you might like it, too."

He bypassed Brooks to give Ruby a gentle kiss on the cheek. "Ruby's like a daughter to me." He gazed warmly into her eyes, and Ruby gave him a sweet, affectionate smile. "She's been with us since she was a tot. Her daddy was foreman around here, and Ruby grew up at the Look Away for all intents and purposes. I don't think there's a better horse wrangler in all of Texas, and everybody knows it."

"Thank you," she said.

"Actually, Ruby and I went for a ride this afternoon," Brooks said, to add something to the conversation.

"Good, good." Beau beamed with pride. "I want you to feel comfortable on Look Away. Did Ruby teach you a few things?"

Brooks met her eyes. "More than a few things."

The feisty Latina with the killer body blushed and put her head down to stir the stew, avoiding eye contact with him altogether now. It was clear this meal was going to be awkward, to say the least.

"My boys—your half brothers—will join us another night," Beau commented. "They're giving us time to get better acquainted. I hope you don't mind it'll just be you and me. And Ruby, of course."

"I can give you two time alone, too, Beau," Ruby jumped in, obviously trying to remove herself from the situation.

"I won't hear of it," Beau said. "Not after you cooked all afternoon for us. You're gonna sit right down and enjoy the meal along with us, Ruby. You work too hard as it is. Tonight we're gonna relax and get to know Brooks."

Ruby's gaze dimmed, and Brooks hid his amusement, but somehow Ruby knew he was laughing at her. From behind Beau's back, she gave him the stink eye.

Now that she was at the ranch, he couldn't imagine keeping away from her. Not touching her again was messing with his mind. He had bigger problems, but the idea of delicate, petite Ruby Lopez sitting by his side at dinner had him tied up in knots.

She was about as off-limits as a woman could get.

Brooks had never run from a challenge in his life, as old man Sutton Winchester could testify.

But Brooks was used to getting what he wanted in life.

And he was beginning to think Ruby was all that and more.

Once they were seated at the table and diving into the food, Beau asked, "So, what do you think about the ranch so far? Seeing it on horseback is a good way to gain perspective on the property, son."

Son? Would there ever come a day when Brooks would tire of hearing his father call him that? For so many years, Brooks had wondered what it would be like to know his true father, to sit down with him and have a meal. Now he was living the reality, and it all seemed surreal. "It's... it's a great spread, pretty impressive."

"And I bet Ruby picked out a good horse for you to ride."

"He rode Misty," she said.

"Ah, good," Beau said, nodding. It was the horse Beau had suggested.

"You know, Brooks, Ruby learned from the best. Her daddy, Joaquin, was my foreman and head wrangler for many years." Beau's eyes once again touched on Ruby with affection. "It'd make me real proud and happy if you'd think of Ruby as family, son. I mean, once you two get better acquainted."

Ruby's olive skin flushed with color. She immediately scraped her chair back, rose from her seat and went over to open the refrigerator. "I forgot the iced tea," she mumbled.

Beau ran a hand down his face and gave his head a shake. "Uh, sorry, honey. I forget how independent you are. I didn't mean to make you uncomfortable."

"You didn't," she said, pouring tea into three glasses, her back to them. "I'm fine, Beau."

Brooks's gaze dipped to her rear end in that tight-fitting dress, her long hair falling down her back like a sheet of black silk. He wasn't about to touch upon this subject, so he stayed silent. His father's request only cemented his need to keep far away from Ruby, which wasn't going to be easy since they'd be living on the ranch together now. Every time he laid eyes on the woman, something clicked inside his head. And way farther south.

Shelve those thoughts, man.

She came back to the table, delivered the drinks and scooted back into her chair.

"Thanks," Brooks said.

"You're welcome," she said, giving him a quick smile.

"Yeah, thanks honey. Meal's real delicious."

"Yes," Brooks added. "You're a talented cook, Ruby."

Among other things.

Ruby escaped the dinner early, claiming a case of fatigue and a desire for Beau to get to know Brooks on a one-on-one basis. Beau was ecstatic to have his son finally home. She saw it in his eyes, heard it in his tone. And she was truly happy for him. He'd told her he'd been haunted for years, had searched for and lamented the loss of the children he knew were out there somewhere. Now he'd been given a second chance to father them and bring them into the family.

Twins, no less.

Dios, it was weird having Brooks here. He made her nervous, and she couldn't say that about too many things. She was a woman who usually didn't go in for one-night flings, yet the one time she'd indulged, fate pulled a fast one on her by bringing Brooks right to her doorstep. Weren't one-night stands supposed to be just that—secret liaisons that both parties could walk away from?

She needed to purge thoughts of Brooks Newport Preston. He'd taken up too much space in her mind today. She made a detour and walked the path to the stables. Checking in on her horses always made her feel better.

One peek inside the dimly lit stable told her all was right in the horse world at Look Away. Beau bred dozens of horses to sell, and it was her job to make sure they were healthy and happy and well-trained. She knew enough not to form an emotional attachment to most of them. She knew not to love them, because that bond was sure to be broken as soon as the sale became final. Her papa had warned her enough times when she was a young girl, and after a few pretty brutal heartbreaks, she'd learned that lesson the hard way. Now Ruby knew when to love and when not to love.

Unfortunately she hadn't been that astute when it came to men.

But the horses in this stable weren't in danger of being sold off. They all belonged to the Preston family, except for Storm Cloud. He was all hers.

"Hey, Cloud," she whispered, tiptoeing to his stall. "You still up?"

Cloud wandered over to her, his head coming over the split door to say hello with a gentle nudge. "Yes, you are." Ruby stroked the side of his face, pressing a kiss above his nose. The horse gave a little snort, and Ruby chuckled. "You want a treat, don't you?"

She grabbed her secret stash from a bag hooked on the wall and came up with a handful of sugar cubes. "Only a few," she said. "And let's be quiet about it. Or the others will wake up."

Cloud gobbled them within seconds, and Ruby spent a few more minutes with him before she said good-night. Feeling better, she walked toward the cottage she called home while she was staying on the Look Away. Carrie Underwood's "Before He Cheats" banged out of her phone, and she glanced at the screen.

Trace?

Her heart sped up. Why was he calling now, of all times? He hadn't had the balls to call her for six months. She'd invested almost two years in him, mainly during the off-season of the rodeo. They'd dated and had an amazing time together. But it wasn't all fun and games on her part. She'd fallen hard for the bull rider, giving him something she'd always protected and kept safe— her heart. Yet when the rodeo started up again this year, he'd left her high and dry. He hadn't called. He hadn't written. A few texts in the beginning, and that had been it, for heaven's sake. She'd spent the first months making excuses for him because the rodeo was an important part of his life. He was busy. He was focused on making a name for himself. But in the end, Ruby came to the conclusion that Trace had not only tried to make a name for himself but also made a damn fool out of her.

Carrie Underwood was about to carve her name in her guy's leather seats, and Ruby had a mind to do that very thing to Trace's truck if she ever saw him again. But her curiosity got the better of her. Before her cell went to voice mail, she answered the call.

"Hello."

"Ruby? Baby, is that you? It's Trace."

"I know who it is, Trace. Are you bleeding or on your last breath or something?"

Silence for a few seconds, and then, "No, baby. I'm not. What I *am* is missing you."

"You're not dying and trying to ease your conscience?"

"Ruby, listen to me. I know it's been a while."

"A while? Is that what you call six months of deafening silence? Why are you calling me now, Trace?"

"I told you, babe. I miss you like crazy. It's been hell on the circuit and I couldn't think straight, so I had to close off my mind to everything but what I was trying to accomplish. I needed the space to keep my head in the game. You can ask anybody around here. They all know about you, baby. They're sick of me pining for you. They all know I'm crazy about you."

Ruby's heart dipped a little. Trace was saying all the right things. He had charm and dark dastardly good looks. His voice, that deep Southern drawl, could melt an iceberg. But her wounds were deep, and she wasn't through being mad at him. "Not good enough, Trace. I'm sorry. I've got to go."

"Ruby, baby...wait."

"I have, Trace. For too long. Good night."

She pushed End and then squeezed her eyes shut. Pain burned through her belly, and those old feelings she'd managed to bury threatened to bust their way back up and slash her again and again.

He's like the horse I wasn't supposed to love.

Dios, why did he have to call her tonight?

She didn't want to think about him anymore.

Carrie's voice carried the same tune again, Ruby's cell phone drowning out the night sounds and coyote calls. No, damn it. She wasn't going to answer her phone again. No matter how many times Trace called. Her finger was ready to push the end button again. Until she saw the name flashing on the screen.

Serena.

Oh, thank goodness. She picked up quickly.

"Serena, hi," Ruby said anxiously. "I'm glad you called. You must've been reading my mind."

"Ruby, wow. Is everything all right? You sound stressed."

"I just got a call from Trace. And yeah, I'm a little stressed. I need to talk to you."

"Tell me. I'm listening."

"Oh boy, it's almost too much to explain over the phone. Can we meet for lunch tomorrow?"

"Of course, sure. That's the reason I was calling anyway. I wanted to catch up with you. It's been weeks since I've seen you. I miss my friend."

"I miss you, too. And there's a *whole lot* to catch up on. I'm buying. Root beer floats and sliders at the diner sound okay?"

"I won't pass up that offer. I'll see you there at noon."

Ruby sighed. Her bestie from high school was the only one she could confide in. "Thank you. I don't know what I'd do without you." Ruby didn't have a mom or an aunt or anyone female in her family she could talk to. Without Serena, she'd have been lost. Ever since they were kids, they'd shared their secrets with each other. Ruby ended the call, feeling a little better about things. Just knowing Serena would listen and not judge her made all the difference in the world. Though they didn't share bloodlines, they were sisters in all other respects. She'd relied on Serena's friendship to see her through some of the really tough times in her life.

"I'm eager to show you around Look Away, Brooks. Mind if we saddle up after breakfast and take us a ride?" Beau asked on Brooks's second morning on the ranch. "I'd love for you to see our operation."

"Uh, sure. I'd like that," he said, setting aside his coffee cup and patting his belly. "If I won't break poor Misty's back after the giant meal I just consumed. It was delicious, Lupe. I ate up everything in sight." Breakfast had included maple-smoked bacon, ham, eggs, chile-fried potatoes and homemade biscuits with gravy. "If I keep eating like this, I'll be as big as this house, but smiling all the way."

Lupe gave him a nod. "*Gracias*, Brooks. I'm happy to cook for Beau's son."

"Lupe is a triple threat to all of us. Breakfast, lunch and dinner. We have to work out hard around here to avoid putting the pounds on."

Beau's eyes were on him—the blue in them the exact same hue as his own—and he was beaming. Having his father look at him that way humbled him and made him feel as if he belonged. Even though ranch living was foreign to Brooks, it felt damn good knowing he was welcomed and—yes—loved by this obviously decent, successful and well-respected man.

A sudden case of guilt spilled into his good mood. Would Beau approve of the tactics he'd used to bring Sutton Winchester down? Brooks hadn't taken any prisoners on that score, too eager to exact his revenge on the man he believed had immeasurably hurt his mother and his family. Brooks had looked upon Sutton as his enemy and hadn't held back, using all the tools at his disposal to get back at the dying man.

But was Sutton the monster he'd made him out to be? Or had he simply protected his mother's secrets at her urging, thus refusing to reveal who Cynthia really was? Had Sutton truly loved his mother enough to withstand all the media and personal attacks Brooks had thrown his way? It was hard thinking of Sutton in softer terms, as a man who'd go the distance for a woman to protect her. Everything else about Winchester pointed to him being a ruthless bastard.

Brooks was still sorting this all out in his mind.

"Son?"

Beau was on his feet, waiting for him.

"Yep, I'm ready, Dad." His lips twitched, and suddenly he felt like a child being given an unexpected gift. He had a sense that Beau was feeling that way, too, as they walked out of the kitchen, ready to take a ride together as father and son.

Minutes later, Brooks had saddled up and mounted Misty. Beau was atop a stunning black gelding named Alamo. "I figured you'd be a fast learner. You saddled up that mare almost perfectly."

Brooks lowered the brim of his hat and nodded at his

father's praise. "Thanks. The truth is, I don't know much about horses. I don't get out of the city much. My friend Josh Calhoun owns a dairy farm in Iowa, and that's about the only time I've seen the backside of a horse. Let me tell you, it wasn't pretty."

Beau chuckled. "I think I learned to ride before I could walk, son. You'll get the hang of it, and if you need any help, just ask me or Ruby. She's actually the expert. She's got the touch, you know."

He knew.

"That girl can tame the most stubborn of animals."

Beau went on to explain that in the summer months, Ruby gave lessons to children three mornings a week, teaching them how to respect and care for the animals. "It's a sight to see. All those kids swarming around her, asking her questions. Anyone who knows Ruby knows she's not the most patient kind. She likes things to get done, the faster the better, as long as they're done right. But Ruby, with those kids...well, it's my favorite time of year, watching her school those young kids."

Ruby with kids? Now that was an image that entered Brooks's head and lingered.

They rode out a ways, Beau showing him all the stables and corrals and training areas. There were outbuildings and supply sheds and feed shacks on the property. They rode along the bank of a small lake and then over flatlands that bordered the property. Beau's voice filled with pride when he spoke of his land and the improvements he'd made on the horse farm through the years.

"Enough about me, son. I want to hear all about you and your brothers. And your life in Chicago."

"Where do I start?"

"From the beginning...as you remember it."

"Well, let's see. Going back to my earliest years, Mom

was always there for us. We lived with Mom's best friend, an older widow named Gerty, as you know. She was Grandma Gerty to us, and there wasn't a day that went by that my brothers and I didn't feel loved. As adults, we found out what a truly generous woman she was. She put a roof over our heads, raised us while Mom was working and helped all three of us get through college."

Brooks sighed, relieved. "That's good to hear, son."

"We had a good life, but all throughout growing up, Mom always told us we were better off that our father wasn't in our lives. I guess that was Mom's way of protecting us. And you, as well. I'm guessing she feared her fake identity would be discovered. Gosh, her father must've really done a number on her."

Beau's brows pushed together, and his scowl said it all. "You don't want to know."

Brooks nodded. Maybe he didn't.

He went on. "While she was pregnant, she worked for Sutton Winchester as his personal secretary. They fell in love, and she must've shared her secret with him about her life and the true father of her twins. I think he protected her secret all those years, and then things went bad between them. His ex was making all kinds of trouble, and Mom walked away, but by then, she was pregnant with Carson."

"It's quite a story."

"I know, but all through it, Mom was our constant. I miss her so much. But I will admit to being angry with her, with you, with Winchester. I became obsessed with learning the truth."

"Good thing, or we would've never found each other, son."

"That much is true. But I'm pretty relentless when I go after something."

"You saying you have regrets?"

He shrugged. "Maybe. But not about coming here and being with you, Dad."

Sitting tall in the saddle, riding the range with his father and learning about Look Away all seemed sort of right to him. Though he had a full life in Chicago, a successful business to run and family he could count on, being in Texas right now gave him a sense of belonging that he'd not had for a long time.

"I think we all have regrets," Beau said. "I shouldn't have stopped until I found Mary Jo. Gosh, son, you have to know how much losing her ate me up inside. After a time, I really thought she was dead. And I blamed her old man for it. He's a shell of what he once was, but I never knew a meaner man."

"He must've been for my mom to run from you and her hometown, the only place she'd ever lived. Only goes to show how strong my mother was."

"And brave, Brooks. I don't know too many women who would be able to assume a new identity, get a job, raise her boys and give them a life filled with love. Mary Jo was something."

"Yeah, Mom was that."

As they continued their ride, Brooks scanned the grounds, looking for signs of Ruby. She hadn't joined them for breakfast, which was a disappointment. He'd been looking forward to seeing those big brown eyes and the pretty smile this morning. He knew enough to stay away from her, but he had an uncanny, unholy need to see her again.

Now, as they headed back to the stables, he kept his eyes peeled.

"Ruby's got a date this afternoon," his dad said, practically reading his mind. Was Brooks that obvious about what he'd been searching for? He had no right to feel any emotion, yet the one barreling through his belly at hearing Ruby was on a date was undeniable jealousy. "Or she'd be on the ranch today. I've asked her to show you a little about her horse training program. Looks like it's gonna have to wait until tomorrow, if that's okay with you, son?"

"Of course. I'm on Ruby's schedule. She's not on mine. If she's seeing someone, that takes precedence." Damn, if those words weren't hard to force out.

His dad chuckled. "No, it's not like that. Gosh, I'm sure glad that ship has sailed."

"What do you mean?"

"Oh, the man she was seeing a while back didn't sit straight with me. I'm glad he's out of the picture now."

"Didn't like him much, huh?" Brooks shouldn't have been prying, but he couldn't help but want to know more. Ruby fascinated him in every way.

"No. Trace Evans wasn't the man for her. Hurt her real bad, too, and she's moved on. She's having lunch with a girlfriend, and you know how that goes. She could be gone for hours. I told her not to worry and to take all the time she needs. Man, it sure is different raising a girl, that's for sure."

Too much relief to be healthy settled in his gut. "I wouldn't know, having two brothers."

"Yeah, I hear ya. When Ruby came into the family, my boys had to clean up their act. Not a one of them ever disrespected her, and that's what I want for her. Whoever takes her heart better damn well treat it with tender care. I owe it to her and her daddy."

The more he was around Beau, the more respect Brooks had for him. He liked that Beau was watching out for Ruby, and again it underscored his need to keep their relationship platonic. If only he could think of Ruby as a half sister.

Instead of the sexy, hot woman who'd heated up his sheets two nights ago.

Five

Ruby bit into a pulled pork slider, and barbeque sauce dripped down her chin. She dabbed at it with her napkin. "Yum, I feel better already."

Serena Bartolomo chuckled as she lifted her slider to her mouth and took a big bite, too. When it came to settling nerves, there wasn't anything better than the Cool Springs Café's food, and the combination of being with Serena and downing pulled pork made Ruby's hysteria from yesterday seem like a thing of the past.

"So, let me get this straight, Rube. You've got two hot guys in your life right now, and that's what's making you crazy? I should be so lucky."

Serena had her own set of issues with the opposite sex; namely, she was looking for the perfect man. Someone kind, strong, honest and funny, *just like her daddy*, and all others need not apply. It was a tall order, and so far, Serena hadn't found the man of her dreams.

"Luck has everything to do with it," Ruby said. "Bad luck. I thought I had it clear in my mind what I wanted. If the right guy comes along, fine. That would make me happy, I guess. But if he doesn't, and I'm certainly not looking, then I'm good with my horses and family. I'm in no hurry to get hurt again."

"Yeah, Trace did a number on you. I can see you not wanting to jump back into that arena."

"But you should've heard him on the phone, Serena. He was really sweet, and he said everything I wanted to hear. How he missed me. How he's been thinking about me night and day."

"Are you buying it?"

"I shouldn't. But he sounded sincere."

"The rodeo season is over. What will you do if he comes knocking on your door?"

Ruby shrugged. It wasn't as if she hadn't asked herself that question a dozen times already. "I don't know. Wait and see. I'm not rushing into anything."

"That's good, hon."

She released a sigh that emptied her lungs. "And then there's Brooks."

"Yeah, tell me about him."

"Smart, confident, handsome. We had that one night together. A crazy impetuous fling, and afterward we parted ways amicably, only the next day he shows up at Look Away as Beau's long lost son. I never thought I'd see him again, and now he's a fixture at the ranch and I've got to pretend nothing's happened between us."

"Is that hard?"

She sipped from her float, the icy soda sliding down her throat as she contemplated her answer. "Well, it's not easy. Especially with the way he looks at me with those dreamy blue eyes. And he's funny, too. We laugh a lot."

"Uh-oh, that's dangerous. A man who can make you laugh—that's the kiss of death." Serena began shaking her head. "Do you think of Trace at all when you're with him?"

"*Dios*, no. I don't think of any other man when I'm with Brooks. He may not know it yet, but he's so much like his father."

"Being like Beau Preston is a good, good thing."

"So true. But Brooks has a sharper edge, I think. He's pulled himself up from humble beginnings, and this whole situation with not knowing who his real father was has hurt him and maybe made him bitter."

"Wow, that's heavy. Did he tell you that?"

Ruby dipped her head sheepishly, hating to admit the truth. "No, I Googled him. I wanted to find out more about him. He's entering the Preston family, and they've had enough heartache in their lives. Is that horrible? I feel like I'm spying on him."

"It's the way of the world, hon. Don't beat yourself up. You were concerned about Beau, right?"

"Yes, that's part of it. Anyway, now you know my dilemma. Brooks is off-limits to me. He's part of Beau's family now, which means he's my family, too. And then there's Trace. I have to admit, hearing from him last night really threw me off balance."

"Ruby, we've been friends a long time. I know how strong you are. You can handle this. You're Ruby Lopez. Anybody who messes with you lives to regret it."

Ruby laughed. "That's my persona, anyway."

"Hey, you're forgetting I've seen you in action. You've got self-defense skills any woman would love to have."

"Yeah, I can toss a man over my shoulder, no problem. But can I evict him from my heart? That's a totally different matter."

* * *

Texas breezes ruffled Brooks's shirt on this warmer than usual December day and brought freshness to the morning as he strode down the path toward the lake. He didn't mind the walk; it helped clear his head. Beau, so proud of his operation here, had recommended that Brooks check out Ruby in action. Hell, he'd already seen her in action. She'd downed a big oaf of a man in that saloon. And then he'd been private witness to her other skills in the bedroom. But of course, Beau had meant something entirely different.

"You want to get a better sense of what we do on Look Away, then go see Ruby down at the lake this morning," his father had said. "She's working with a one-year-old named Cider. Beautiful filly."

The truth was, Brooks hadn't laid eyes on Ruby yesterday, and he'd missed her like crazy. It baffled him just how much. Now, with his boots pounding the earth as he headed her way, his hands locked in his pockets Texas-style, a happy tune was playing in his head. He liked it here. He liked the sun and sky and vastness. He liked the howl of a coyote, the smell of hay and earth and, yes, horse dung. It all seemed so natural and beautiful. But mostly, it was Ruby in this setting that he liked the most.

And there she was, about twenty yards up ahead, near a nameless body of water his father simply called the lake, holding a lead rope in one hand and a long leather stick in the other. She wore a tan hat, her long raven locks gathered in a ponytail that spilled down the back of her red blouse. Skin-tight jeans curved around her ass in a way that made him gulp air.

He lodged himself up against a tree, his arms folded, to take in the scene for a few seconds before he made his presence known. How long had it been since he could simply enjoy watching a woman do her job? Probably never.

Ruby was sweet to the horse, though she wasn't a pushover. She spoke in a friendly voice, using the rope and the stick as tools to train the filly. She was patient, a trait he hadn't associated with Ruby, but then, he really didn't know her all that well. The time she took with the horse notched up his respect for her even more.

"Why don't you come away from the tree, Brooks," she called, catching him off guard. He hadn't seen her look his way; he thought her focus was mainly on the horse she was training. "Cider knows you're here, too."

Brooks marched over to her. "I didn't want to disturb you."

"Too late for that," she said quickly, with a blink of her eyes, maybe surprising herself. He got the feeling she wasn't speaking about the training session. "Actually, I'm glad you're here. Beau wants you to see how we train the horses. And I'm just beginning with Cider."

With gloved hands, she gathered the rope into a circle, her tone businesslike and stiff. It had to be this way, but Brooks didn't like it one bit. He knew she was untouchable, but of course the notion made him want her all the more.

"For the record, you disturb me too, Ruby." He didn't give her a wink or a smile. He wasn't flirting or teasing. He meant it.

"Brooks." She sighed, giving him an eyeful of her innermost thoughts by the sag of her shoulders and the look of hopelessness on her face. Then she turned her full attention to the horse, patting Cider's nose and stroking her long golden mane. "We need to be just friends."

She was stating the obvious.

"I can try," he said.

"For Beau."

"Yeah, for Beau."

Because they both knew if they got together and it didn't work out, Beau would be hurt, as well. Brooks didn't want friction in the Preston family. He was the newcomer. He was trying to fit in and become a part of this family. It would do no good to have a repeat of what happened at the C'mon Inn. His father and this family deserved more than that from him.

Brooks's brain was on board. Now if the rest of him would join in, it wouldn't be an issue at all.

That settled, he gave the horse's nose a stroke. Under his palm, the coarse hair tickled a bit, yet it was also smooth as he slid his hand down. "So, what are you doing with her today?"

"Today, we're working on gullies and water." Ruby jumped right in, eager to share her knowledge. "People sometimes think horses know what's expected of them from birth, but nothing is further from the truth. This girl is water-shy, and she doesn't know how to jump over a gully. Both frighten her. So I'm working with her today to make her more comfortable with both of those situations. Here, let me show you." She walked Cider over to a dip in the property, the gully no more than a yard across. "First I'll let her get familiar with the terrain."

Ruby released the lead rope and, using her stick, tapped the horse on the shoulder. "Don't worry, I'm not hurting her. The stick on the withers or neck lets her know she's crowding my space. When she gets scared, she closes in on me. I'm trying to get her into her own space."

Ruby worked the horse up and down the area. The horse avoided the gulley altogether. Ruby gave the horse room to investigate, leading her with the rope. "See that, Brooks? She's stopped to sniff and get her bearings. That's good. Now I'm going to bring her in a little closer. She won't like it much—she doesn't know what to do about the gully—but she'll figure it out. I keep sending her closer and closer to the gap and tapping, like this." She tapped Cider again and then gave the horse time to overcome her fear. Back and forth, back and forth. Then Cider stopped again, put her head down and sniffed around. The next time Ruby led her close to the gulley, she jumped. "There! Good girl. That's wonderful, Cider." She stroked the horse again, giving praise. "Good girl. Want to try it one more time?

"I'll keep this going," Ruby explained to him. "Leading her back and forth near the gully. And soon she'll be a pro at jumping over it. It's a start."

"It's amazing how she responds to you, Ruby. I saw a change in her in just a few minutes. Will she go in the water?"

"She'll go near it and take a drink. But she won't go into the water. That takes a bit more time. She's thirsty now, which will work in my favor. But I won't push her right now. She can have a peaceful drink."

Ruby let the rope hang very loose, taking off any pressure, and approached the water. Cider resisted for a few seconds. Then, without being prompted by the stick or the rope, she walked over to the bank and dipped her head to lap up water. "See how wary she is? She won't put her feet in. But she will, very soon."

"I never thought about horses not feeling inherently comfortable with their surroundings. I don't know a whole lot about horses, that's for damn sure. I guess I figured they were naturally at ease with jumping and going in the water."

"Yeah, I know that's the perception. But horses, like

children, need to be trained to do the things we know they are capable of doing. They certainly don't understand what it means when we put saddles on them or bits in their mouths. The truth is, when I train the horses, they tell me what they need help with. And I listen and watch. The reason this method works so well is that I give the horse a purpose. I kept sending Cider across that gully and let her figure out how to solve the problem. It's a matter of knowing what they need and providing it."

Brooks spent the remainder of the morning watching Ruby work miracles with this horse, completely impressed with her knowledge and the ease with which she worked. When his stomach grumbled, he grinned. "Are you going back to the house for lunch?"

"No. I'm not done with Cider yet. I brought my lunch out here."

"You're eating here?"

"Yep, under that tree you were holding up earlier."

He laughed. "Sounds peaceful."

She stared into his eyes. "It is."

"Okay, then, I should get going. Let you have your lunch."

He turned and began walking.

"There's enough for two," she said, a hitch in her throat, as if she couldn't believe she'd just said that. Hell, if she was inviting, he wouldn't be refusing.

He turned and smiled. "If it's Lupe's leftover fried chicken, I'm taking you up on it."

"And what if it isn't?" she asked.

"I'm still staying."

Ruby's mouth pulled into a frown as if she was having second thoughts.

"As your friend," he added.

Her tight expression relaxed, and a glint gleamed in

her pretty brown eyes. "I lied. It is chicken, and Lupe packed me way too much."

"So then, I'd be doing you a favor by staying and eating with you. Wouldn't want all that food to go to waste."

She rolled her eyes adorably, and Brooks was glad to see the Ruby of old come back.

She grabbed her backpack, and together they walked over to the tree where swaying branches provided shade on the packed-dirt ground. Ruby tossed her stuff down, but before she sat, he put up his hand. "Wait a sec."

She stood still, her eyes sharp as he pulled his shirt out of his jeans and began unbuttoning until his white T-shirt was exposed. "Never did like this shirt anyway." He took off his shirt and made a bit of a production laying it on the ground. Then he gestured to Ruby. "Now you can sit."

Her expression warmed considerably. "Galahad. You're too much."

"That's what they tell me."

She plopped herself comfortably down on his shirt so that her perfect behind wouldn't be ground into the dirt. "Thank you. You know, that's about the sweetest thing a man's done for me in a long while."

"Well then, you're meeting the wrong kind of men. Present company excluded. And boy, am I glad you're not into all that feminism stuff, or I'd be dead meat right now."

She smiled. "Who says I'm not? I believe in the power of women."

"So do I."

"But I can also recognize a gentleman when I see one, and I don't feel like it's diminishing my role in the world."

"And this is Texas, after all," he said.

"Right."

"And I have developed Southern charm."

"Don't press your luck, Preston."

Brooks blinked. And then he looked straight into Ruby's spirited chocolate eyes. "Thanks. It feels good to be called by my father's name."

"You're welcome. You've earned it."

He stared at her and nodded, holding back a brand-new emotion welling behind his eyes.

Brooks headed to the main house that evening, thoughts of Ruby never far from his mind. The more time he spent with her… Okay, forget it. He couldn't go down that road, especially when the main reason his thoughts had splintered was standing not ten feet away on the sweeping porch of the residence.

As soon as Beau spotted Brooks, he called him over with a wave of the hand. "Come here, son. Meet the rest of the family."

The three men—all wearing Stetsons in varying colors and appearing younger than Brooks by several years—stood at attention next to Beau. Brooks's half brothers.

He walked up, and Beau gave his shoulder a squeeze. "Brooks, I'm proud to introduce you to Toby, Clay and Malcolm. They're your brothers."

He shook each one of their hands and greeted them kindly. It was strange and awkward at first, but Beau's boys made him feel welcome.

"We're surely glad to meet you," Toby said. He was the oldest and tallest of the three. "I'm sorry we missed out on knowing you all those years."

"Yeah, I'm sorry, too. Life took me down a different path," he said.

Malcolm stood against the post, his boots crossed, his gaze narrowing in on Brooks's face. "But you're here now, and we're glad of it. You look more like Dad than any of us."

Beau chuckled. "Poor guy."

"Mom wouldn't agree," Clay said, chiming in. "She was always telling us how handsome you were."

"Yeah," Malcolm said. "Damn near gave us a complex."

Beau shook his head. "Your mama thought the sun rose and set on you boys, and you know it."

"Seems like your mom was a pretty great lady from what I'm told," Brooks said. He'd heard from Beau, but just about everyone else on the ranch had nice things to say about Tanya, too.

"That she was," Beau said, the pride in his voice unequalled.

"My brothers and I, well, we're sorry to hear news of your mother's passing, Brooks," Malcolm said. The others nodded in agreement.

"Thank you. Mom was also quite a woman. And she died unexpectedly. My brothers and I miss her terribly."

"It's not easy," Beau said, the brightness in his eyes dimming. "But we have each other now, and that's something to celebrate. Shall we go in to dinner? Lupe promised us a feast, and we're opening a few special bottles of wine to toast the occasion."

"I'm nearly starved," Toby said, patting his stomach.

"Yeah, me, too," Clay said. "Oh, and new brother?"

Brooks gave him a glance. "Yeah?"

"I'm apologizing in advance for the interrogation. We're all so dang curious about your life, I'm afraid we're gonna grill you. We want to hear about Graham, too. Dad says he's the spitting image of you."

"Yep, there are two of us. We're identical twins."

"You boys will meet him soon," Beau said as he ushered them all into the house. "I'm hoping Graham will be here by next week in time for our Christmas party."

"I don't mind your questions," Brooks added. "I've got quite a few for you. We all have some catching up to do."

In the formal dining room, on Beau's cue, Clay, Malcolm and Toby spent the next few minutes asking about Brooks's early life, his college days and how he came to build such a successful real estate development business. "Lots of hard work, long hours and a driving need to make my way in the world," he answered. "Mom was a survivor, and she raised her children to be independent thinkers."

Beau smiled, getting a faraway look in his eyes. Was he thinking about the young woman he'd loved and lost? Then, with a shake of the head, he shifted and turned his attention back to the conversation.

Lupe came in, carrying plates filled with twelve-ounce rib eye steaks, potatoes, creamed corn and Texas-sized biscuits. "Looks delicious, Lupe. Thank you," Beau said.

Toby and Malcolm immediately rose to help her bring the rest of the food in from the kitchen. And just as they were sitting down, ready to take their first bite, Ruby walked in.

She didn't immediately make eye contact with Brooks, so he looked his fill. Her jeans and blousy top were white, but her ankle boots were as black as the mass of long raven hair falling down her back. The contrast of black to white was striking, and he took a swallow of water to keep his mouth from going dry. "Hey, everyone," she said.

"Better late than never, Rube," Clay said, teasing. "Had another hot date with a horse?"

Toby and Malcolm chuckled.

"Wouldn't you like to know," she said, smiling and

scooting her fine little ass into her seat. "At least horses can take direction. Unlike most men I know."

Beau choked out a laugh.

Ruby arched a brow and shot daggers at Clay. Apparently she wasn't through with him yet. "And tell me again, who are you dating at the moment?"

"Oh, you've dug yourself a hole now, Clay," Malcolm said. "You know better than to get into it with Ruby. You're not gonna win."

"You see," she said, "Malcolm understands. At least he has a girlfriend."

"This is a picture of what it was like when the kids were growing up," Beau explained, grinning. "I gotta say, it's still amusing."

Ruby glanced at Brooks then, giving him a nod of acknowledgment. He smiled, acknowledging how Ruby held her own with Beau's boys. She was a handful, a woman with spunk who took no prisoners and didn't apologize for it. If only he could stop noticing all her admirable traits. As it was now, she was off the charts.

Wine was poured and Beau lifted his glass. Everyone at the table took his cue, and the deep red wine in the raised glasses glistened under chandelier light. "To my family," he said. "I couldn't be happier to have Brooks here. And soon Graham will join us. I love you all," he said, his voice tight, "and look forward to the day we can all be together."

Glasses clinked and Brooks was touched at the welcome he'd received by his new family at Look Away Ranch.

They settled into the meal. The steak was the most tender he'd ever had. Texans knew a thing or two about raising prime cattle and delivering a delicious meal. His brothers surely looked the picture of health—all three were sturdy men—and a sense of pride in his newfound family washed over him. He doubted he'd ever feel as close to these young men as he did Graham—he and Graham had shared too much together—but he hoped they'd all become the family Beau had longed for.

"Dad says our little sis taught you a thing or two about horse training," Toby remarked. "What'd you think?"

Brooks hesitated a second, finishing a sip of wine while contemplating how to answer the innocent question. He couldn't give too much away. He couldn't say that Ruby was the most amazing woman he'd ever met, or that her talent and skill and patience had inspired him. That would be too telling, wouldn't it? "What I know about horses, I'm afraid to say, can fit in this wineglass. But watching Ruby at work and hearing her thoughts on training gave me a whole new perspective. It's eye-opening. It seems Ruby has just the right touch."

Toby nodded. "She does. We've all had a hand in horse training growing up, and all of our techniques are different, but the honest truth is, when we'd come up against a stubborn one that gave us trouble, we turned to Ruby and she'd find a way. Now she pretty much runs the show."

Brooks looked at Ruby, giving her a smile. "I see that she pretty much runs the show around here, too."

Beau chuckled. "Didn't take you long to figure that out."

"There's an advantage to being the only female in the family," Malcolm said.

"I can speak for myself, Mal," she chimed in. "There's an advantage to being the only female in the family."

Everyone laughed.

Ruby's eyes twinkled, and in that moment, Brooks felt like one of them. A Preston, through and through.

* * *

The next morning, Beau suggested that they spend the day with Ruby. There was more she could teach Brooks, and if he really wanted to get a sense of how the operation was run, he needed to get his hands dirty.

"Ruby will put you in touch with your inner wrangler," Beau joked.

Well, she'd already put him in touch with *something*: namely, rock-solid lust. The woman turned him inside out, and there was no help for it.

Before Brooks had even met Ruby, he'd asked for this training, and Beau was more than happy to accommodate his request. But now it meant that Brooks and Ruby would get to spend more time together at the Look Away. Yet Brooks wanted to learn. He needed to catch up on the history of the ranch and the day-to-day operation of running it. It would give him a chance to meet Beau and his half brothers on equal ground. He'd have more in common with each one of them if he could grasp at least a basic knowledge of horses, training and all that went with them.

So they'd walked over to one of the corrals and stood by the fence, watching Ruby securing a saddle on an unruly stallion.

The air was brisk this morning, the sun shadowed by gray clouds. He huddled up in his own wool-lined jacket and noted that Ruby, too, was dressed in a dark quilted vest over a flannel shirt. Only Ruby Lopez could make regular cowgirl gear look sexy. "Morning," she said, greeting both of them.

"Morning," he replied. But she had already turned away, busy with the horse, restraining his jerky movements with a firm hand on his bridle.

"This is Spirit," Beau said. "He's got a lot to learn, doesn't he, Ruby?"

"He sure does. He's not taken kindly to wearing a saddle. He's going to hate it even more once I ride him. But that's not happening today."

The horse snorted and shuffled his feet, pulling back and away from her. "Hold steady, boy," Ruby said, her voice smooth as fine silk. "You're not gonna like any of this, are you now?"

The horse bucked, and Brooks made a move to lunge over the fence to help Ruby. Beau restrained him with a hand to the chest. "Hang on. Ruby's a pro. She won't put herself in danger."

Brooks wasn't too sure about that. The tall stallion dwarfed Ruby in size and weight. Watching her outmaneuver the animal made Brooks's heart stop for a moment. Hell, she could be crushed. She slid him a sideways glance, her beautiful eyes telling him she'd just seen what he'd done. What was it she called him? Galahad. Hell, he was no knight in shining armor. To most of the people who knew him in Chicago, that label would be laughable. But today, right in this moment, he didn't give a crap about what anyone called him. But he did care about Ruby, and it surprised him how much. He didn't want to see her get trampled. "Are you sure? That horse looks dangerous."

"He could be, but Ruby knows her limitations. She's got a way about her that outranks his stature. She's gaining his trust right now. Though it doesn't look like it, she's giving him some leeway to put up a fuss. This is his second day wearing a saddle. He's got to get used to it, is all."

"It takes a lot of patience, I see."

"Yep," Beau said. "For the trainer and the animal."

For the next hour, Brooks watched Ruby put the horse

through his paces. Every now and then, she'd inform him what she was doing and how the horse should respond. Nine times out of ten, the horse didn't make a liar out of her.

Beau had excused himself a short time ago. He had a meeting with his accountant, and though he invited Brooks to join in, he'd also warned that it would bore him out of his wits. Brooks had opted to stay and watch Ruby work with the stallion. He could watch that woman for hours without being bored, but he didn't tell his father that.

When Ruby was done, she unsaddled Spirit carefully, speaking to the horse lovingly and stroking him softly on the withers. Then she set him free, and he took off running along the perimeter of the large oval corral, his charcoal mane flying in the breeze.

Ruby closed the gate behind her and walked over to Brooks, removing her leather gloves and pocketing them.

"Impressive," he said.

"Thanks. Spirit will come around. He's a Thoroughbred, and they tend to be high-strung."

"Is that so?" Brooks met her gaze. "Sort of reminds me of someone I know."

Her index finger pressed into her chest. "Me?"

"Yeah, you." Her finger rested in the hollow between her breasts. If only he didn't remember how damn intoxicating it'd been when he'd touched her there. How soft she'd felt, how incredibly beautiful and full her breasts were. The thought of never touching Ruby like that again grated on him.

"Well, you're half-right," she said. "Both my parents were Mexican, so I'm a purebred."

"What about the other half?"

"I'm not high-strung or high-maintenance. I'm strong-willed, determined. Some have called me feisty."

"And they lived to tell about it?"

She snapped her head up and saw his grin. "You're teasing me, Galahad."

What he was doing was flirting. He couldn't help it. Ruby, being Ruby, was an aphrodisiac he couldn't combat. And he was beginning to like her nickname for him. "Yeah, I am."

She smiled back for a second, her eyes latching onto his. Then his gaze dropped to her perfectly sweet mouth. Suddenly all the things he'd done to that mouth came crashing into his mind. And all the things she'd done to him with that mouth...

"Spirit," she said, "uh, he'll bring in a good sum." She began walking. And now she was back to business and a much safer subject. It was necessary, but Brooks had to say he was disappointed. He walked beside her as they headed into the stable.

"He will?"

"Absolutely, once we find the right buyer."

He squinted to adjust to the darkness inside the furthest reaches of the barn. It was even colder in here than outside.

Ruby grabbed a bucket, a brush and a shoe pick. "Beau's been great about giving me input on who our horses end up with. Especially the stallions. They're in demand, but not everyone is cut out to own one."

"You mean you can tell when someone is all wrong for the horse?"

She handed him the brush and a bucket.

"Pretty much."

"That's a talent I never knew existed."

"It's no different than anything else. You wouldn't buy

a car you didn't feel was the right fit. A mom of three wouldn't do too well in a sports car. The same holds true for a single guy on the dating scene. He isn't going to buy a dependable sedan to impress a girl, now is he?"

Brooks smiled. "I never thought of it that way."

"The horses I train need to go to good homes. They need to fit. Spirit wouldn't do well with a young boy, for instance. He's not going to be someone's first horse. But a seasoned rider, someone who knows animals, will be able to handle him, no problem. Beau has built his business on putting his horses with the right owners. It's a partnership."

Ruby removed her hat and stuck it on a knob on the wall. With a flick of the wrist, she unleashed her mane of dark hair, and it tumbled down her back. It was the little uncensored, unknowing moves that made Ruby so damn appealing. She was pretty without trying and as free a spirit as the horse she'd just trained.

"What?" she asked, catching Brooks staring.

"Nothing." He stepped closer. "No, that's not true," he said. "I'm standing here, looking at you and wondering how the hell I'm going to keep from touching you again."

She got a look in her eyes, one he couldn't read, and bit down on her lip. "We, uh, w-we can't."

But it was what she said with her eyes, and her stutter when she denied him, that gave him hope. "It's hard for you, too. You like me."

"I like a lot of things. But I love Beau. And I don't want to—"

"Ruby." The bucket and brush fell from Brooks's hands and thumped to the ground. She gasped as he approached. He took hold of her arms gently, and her chin tipped up. He gazed into defiant eyes. Was she telling him to back off or daring him to kiss her? There was only one way to find out. "Ruby," he rasped and walked her backward against the wall. There was no way anyone could glimpse them from outside. They were alone but for dozens of horses. "You want this, too," he whispered, and then his mouth touched hers, and the sweetest purr escaped her throat. He deepened the kiss, tasting her again, her warmth, the softness of her lips burning through him.

She threaded her arms around his neck, tugging him forward, making him hot all over. She was a dynamo, a fiery woman who kissed him back with enough passion to set the darn barn on fire. Their bodies melded together, a perfect fit of small to large. They'd made it work one time before, and it had been heaven on earth. He wanted that again. He wanted to touch her and make her cry out. He wanted to strip her naked and watch her body move under his.

One kiss from Ruby had him forgetting all else. It was crazy. It was the middle of the day and they were in his father's stable. But none of that mattered right now. Brooks couldn't stop. He couldn't walk away from Ruby. He grabbed thick locks of her hair, the shiny mass silky in his hands. He gave a tug and gazed down at her, so beautiful, so full of passion. "Is there somewhere we can go?" His voice was rough, needy.

Her eyes closed for a second as she decided, the pause making his heart stop. But then she whispered, "My office behind the tack room. There's a lock."

Relieved, he gave a slight nod of his head and then gripping her bottom, lifted her. Her legs wrapped around his waist, and he carried her to the office. He maneuvered them inside, turned the lock and then lowered her down. As soon as her feet hit the ground, she moved to the window and twisted the lever to close the blinds.

It gave him a second to do a cursory survey of her office. Warm tones, a wood floor, a cluttered desk and a dark leather sofa were all he needed to know about the decor before he turned to Ruby again, taking her back into his arms and claiming her mouth.

It wasn't long before their desperate whimpers and growls filled the room. He stripped Ruby of her vest pretty quickly and then worked the buttons of her blouse. She helped, and then he pushed the layers off her shoulders and undid her lacy black bra. Her breasts spilled out, and he simply looked at her in awe for a few seconds before filling his hands. He flicked his thumbs over both nipples. She sucked in oxygen and squeezed her eyes closed, the pleasure on her face adding fuel to his fire.

As he bent his head and drew her nipple into his mouth, she moaned low and painfully deep. Her hands were in his hair, holding him there, as if he needed the extra encouragement.

"Galahad," she whispered softly.

"Hmm?"

"Get naked."

She was impatient, and maybe he was, too, because if he stopped to analyze this, to really think about what was happening and *where*, rational thoughts would intrude and possibly kill the moment. He couldn't have that. He was too far gone, and so was Ruby. He could tell by the sounds she was making and the desperate look in her eyes.

This was dangerous in so many ways, and yet neither of them could put a halt to what they were doing, so he quickly unfastened all the buttons on his shirt.

And then Ruby's hands were on him, pulling his shirt off and tossing it aside. Her fingertips began grazing his skin, probing his chest as she planted kisses here and there. She reached for the waistband of his jeans and pulled his zipper down. "You're right," he murmured. "You are feisty."

"Determined," she corrected him, and he actually chuckled through the flames burning him to the quick.

"Your turn," he said, dipping into the waistband of her jeans. Within seconds, he had her naked and trembling. He couldn't blame her; he was equally turned on. All the secrecy and danger might have added to it, but it could simply have been Ruby. She was a man's dream. Maybe she could've been *his* dream in a different life.

She was feathery light in his arms as he lifted her and carried her to the sofa. He laid her down and gazed at her for a moment. Her hair, her skin, her body, everything that was Ruby made him shiver and want to please her. He came down next to her, squeezing in beside her on the sofa. He kissed her hard then, crushing his mouth to hers while moving his hand to her sweet spot. She bucked as he began to caress her. "Enjoy this, Ruby. Don't hold back. You understand?"

She nodded eagerly.

And he worked up a sweat pleasing her, using his kisses to muffle her whimpers and moans. And when her final jolt released her ultimate pleasure, he was there with her to press his mouth to hers and swallow her soft cries.

It was a heady thing, satisfying Ruby, but they weren't through yet. He rose up immediately, and she helped him take off the rest of his clothes. He grabbed for the packet he carried in his pocket and sheathed himself before coming up over Ruby. She stretched her arms up, reaching around his neck to pull him down and kiss him again. He was ready, so ready, and when Ruby invited him into her warmth, he joined them together in one breathtaking plunge.

Aw, hell. It was better than he remembered. He stilled, absorbing the feel of her, loving the body that so readily welcomed him.

"Don't hold back, Galahad. You understand?"

Good God, Ruby was something. He kissed her again and again, and as he moved deeper, filling her body, she moved with him, keeping pace, rising and lifting and enjoying.

It happened swiftly, neither one wanting to wait, both desperate to find that place that would unite them on the highest ground. She called out his name, and quickly he muted her with a powerful kiss. Then her hips bowed up, and he propelled her even higher with one final all-consuming push. The rush made her convulse around him, and he couldn't hold back any longer. He came as close to heaven as any mortal man could.

Afterward he lay holding Ruby in his arms. "You all right?"

She nodded, unable to speak.

He kissed her forehead, stroking her arm and grazing his fingers over the peaks of her lush breasts. Then he slid his hand down to her legs. He caressed her there, taking in the smooth, soft skin under his palms, not knowing when he'd have the privilege of doing this again.

He heard the thud of footsteps coming toward the office. Voices filtered in.

Ruby's eyes rounded, and she gasped. "It's Sam and one of the boys," she whispered. "He may be looking for me. I left Spirit in the corral, and the grooming equipment is all over the ground. Damn it."

"Shh. Don't panic. I locked the door."

"But Sam knows I never lock the door when I'm working. If he knocks on the door, I won't be able to look him in the eye. Not with you in here. I've got to go."

She rose and donned her clothes hastily, then wove her fingers through her hair to tame the messy locks. "Get dressed, Brooks. And don't come out of the office until I get them out of here."

"Ruby, it wouldn't be the end of the world if they saw me in your office."

"Are you insane? I'd never be able to pull that off. Sam will know something's up and it's the last thing either of us need right now. Stay until it's safe for you to leave."

She opened the door and was gone.

Leaving him locked in the office, buck naked.

What the hell?

Six

Ruby sat down in front of her flat-screen TV and began eating cold chicken salad. She'd deliberately not gone to dinner at the main house tonight. How could she possibly have faced Brooks across the table, eaten a meal with her family and pretended there was nothing between her and Brooks? She was still at odds with herself for what had happened in her office this afternoon. They'd come very close to being discovered. Sneaking around wasn't in her DNA. She didn't like subterfuge.

But wow. And double wow. When it came to Brooks, she didn't seem to have much resistance. Just a look, a word from him, tied her into knots. She had trouble fending him off and found that most times, she didn't want to. She enjoyed his company a little too much.

A nighttime soap opera played on the screen, a story about oil and country music and cowboys who were too much trouble. She stared at the TV as she forked lettuce into her mouth, trying to concentrate on the story and not the city dude with the deep sky-blue eyes who had turned her simple ranch life upside down lately.

A familiar voice sounded and she blinked. Trace Evans walked into the picture and her spine straightened as she sat up and took notice. Trace was on television?

He had a bit part; he spoke a few words before he disappeared again.

Now, this was news. Trace hadn't told her anything about it. But then, she hadn't spoken with him in ages, except for that one phone call a few days ago. Funny that he didn't mention anything about being on *Homestead Hills*, even if it was only a small role. She continued to watch, finishing her salad and waiting for him to appear again.

He didn't.

A knock at her door made her jump. She clicked off the TV and rose from the sofa. Her mind still on Trace, she walked to the door and looked through the peephole. It was Brooks. Seeing him on her doorstep caused her belly to stir immediately. He always made her forget all about Trace and the heartache he'd put her through.

She opened the door and stared into smiling, deep blue eyes. He held a bunch of flowers in one hand and a lavender box from Cool Springs Confections in the other. "Hello, Ruby."

"Brooks, come inside." She ushered him in before someone spotted him with date night goodies in his arms. She scanned her yard before closing the door, thankful that no one was in sight. She had no business being alone with Brooks, but she wasn't about to throw him out, either.

He stood just inside her cottage and grinned. "You look uptight, Ruby."

If it wasn't for the light in his eyes, she might have

been offended. "Thanks to you. You really shouldn't be here."

"I do a lot of things I shouldn't do. These are for you." He handed her a dozen beautiful white roses and the box of chocolates. "Listen, I'm not courting you. Well, not in the usual sense."

"Not in any sense," she pointed out.

"Still, we've been thrown together and it's been... amazing." He pushed his hand through his blond hair as he struggled for words. "I don't know. I had to come. To give you something nice, something you deserve. The way you had to run out from the office after we made love didn't sit well with me."

"Thank you, Brooks. But you don't owe me anything. As you said, we're not dating. We never could be, and I did what was necessary."

"I've learned never to say never, Ruby." He glanced at her arms loaded with his gifts. "You want to put those flowers in water?"

"Uh, sure. Follow me," she said, leading him into the kitchen. She set the box of candy on the table and then opened a cupboard door. "They really are gorgeous."

"I'm glad you like them."

"I don't remember seeing such perfect white roses this time of year in Cool Springs."

"They're not from Cool Springs. I had them flown in from Chicago."

She craned her head around. "You didn't."

He shrugged and gave her a simple nod. Her heart beat a little bit harder.

"My florist is known for his perfect roses. Cool Springs didn't have anything that comes close."

She kept forgetting he was a zillionaire. He probably did this kind of thing all the time for the women in his life. Though that might be true, the sweet gesture and the trouble he'd gone through weren't lost on her. "It's nice of you, Brooks."

She found a crystal vase, an heirloom from her grandmother, and filled it with water. Arranging the flowers, she placed the vase in the center of her glass-top kitchen table. "Here we go."

"It's a nice place you have here," Brooks said.

"It was my father's house, and I've sort of made it my own."

Once Ruby was old enough to make changes, she had redecorated the place, adding modern furniture and window treatments that aligned more with who she was. The cottage wasn't rustic anymore but had a bit of style and flair. She enjoyed living here when she wasn't at her apartment in town.

"I can see your personality here," Brooks said.

Why did he always know the right thing to say?

"Then I've succeeded. It was a labor of love decorating the cottage."

Brooks looked down at the box of candy on the table. "I hear Cool Springs Confections makes a pretty good chocolate buttercream candy."

"That's what they're known for. Want to try one? I can make coffee, or—"

"Sure, I'll try one. And coffee would be great."

"Have a seat. I'll get the coffee going."

"Can I do anything?"

"Grab two mugs from the cupboard above the stove."

"Sure thing."

A few minutes later, she poured two cups of coffee and sat down with Brooks at her kitchen table, realizing this could be dangerous. Spending time with Brooks always seemed to be, yet he was easy company and someone she truly liked. She opened the box and glanced at a dozen luscious candies. "It's going to be hard to choose. Here's a buttercream for you." She pointed it out and he grabbed it.

"I think I'll try the raspberry chocolate," she said.

"Is that your favorite?" he asked.

"It is." She didn't wait for Brooks. She took a big bite and let the soft, creamy raspberry center ooze down her throat. "Oh, yum."

Brooks grinned and then downed his candy in one giant swallow. "Wow, that was good."

"Have another," she said. "I'm going to."

They sipped coffee between bites and managed to polish off half the box of chocolates. Brooks took a last swallow of coffee and then set down his mug. "We're not going to talk about what happened in the stable?"

She replaced the lid on the box, stalling for time, and then finally replied, "No. I don't think so."

"So we just pretend there isn't this *thing* between us."

"We don't have to pretend anything."

"All right," he said, rising and reaching for her hand. "No more pretending we're not hot for each other, Ruby. The truth is, I can't stop thinking about you." He gave her hand a tug, lifting her from her seat. He was deadly handsome, but more than that, he wasn't playing games with her the way Trace had. With Brooks she felt special and cared for, and maybe he was what she needed to get over Trace. She'd protected her heart and would continue to do so, but she had Brooks on the brain lately. She knew he would eventually go back to Chicago. He belonged in the city, and her place was here. Maybe they could keep things light. "I came here only to give you the flowers, Ruby," he said. "I had no ulterior motive."

"Really? I thought you needed a good reason to down half a box of candy."

"That, too." But the truth was in his eyes, and her heart did that thing it did when she was with him. It spun out of control.

She lifted herself on tiptoe and placed a soft kiss on his lips. "You're sweet."

He growled from deep in his throat, a desperate sound that resembled exactly how she was feeling right now, and then his gaze fell to her mouth. His eyes darkening, he backed up a step and put some distance between them. "It really was about the flowers, Ruby. I'd better go." He turned and headed toward the door.

Seeing him retreat put thoughts of the lonely night ahead in her mind. "You don't have to go," she blurted the second he reached for the doorknob. "I mean…you don't have to rush off. I was just going to pop a movie in and kick back. If you care to join me, I have popcorn."

"That was the deal breaker," he said, his lips twitching. "'Cause if you didn't have popcorn, I was out the door."

"Go sit in the living room, Galahad. I'll be right in."

"Thanks—and oh, I like lots of butter."

She rolled her eyes, and he laughed. "Anything else?"

"No, just you and the popcorn make it a perfect night."

Ruby hummed her way into the kitchen and grinned the whole time the kernels were popping.

Ruby sat cross-legged on the sofa next to Brooks, the fireplace giving heat and a warm glow to the room. They'd emptied the popcorn bowl a long while ago, and the movie was ending, but she wasn't ready for him to leave. She was nestled comfortably in the crook of his shoulder, and neither one of them made a move to separate when the credits rolled. There was a sense of right-ness when they were together, which should have scared her off. She wasn't looking to get her heart broken again. But it was harder to see him leave than it was to have him here. She didn't know what to make of that.

"That was good," she said of the classic Western they'd just watched. "I've seen it half a dozen times, and it never disappoints." What wasn't to like about horses and range wars and white hats against black hats? It was clear who to cheer for, who were the good guys. If only life was that easy to figure out.

Her body had been in a constant state of high alert since Brooks entered the house. She'd tried hard to tamp down her feelings, to treat him as a guest and not the man who'd turned her inside out. A part of her wanted him to go, so that they could end whatever they had be-fore he tore her life up in shreds. And another part of her wanted him to stay. To keep her company throughout the cold winter night.

She lifted away from Brooks and unfolded her pretzel position to stretch out her legs.

He planted his feet on the floor, bracing his elbows on his knees, and turned to her. "Thanks for the movie. I really liked it. But I think a lot of that had to do with the company."

She smiled. "Thank you."

"Welcome. Popcorn was good, too. I can't remember enjoying an evening like this back home."

"You don't go to movies in Chicago?"

He shook his head. "No, not really. I'm usually too busy. It's not high on my list of priorities."

"I guess Cool Springs is a totally different experience from what you're used to."

"It is, but not in a bad way. Back home, my phone is

ringing constantly. My life is full of dinner meetings and weekends of work. I don't get to play very often."

"Is that what you're doing here? Playing?"

"If you knew how hard I tried to find Beau, you wouldn't even have to ask. I went to great lengths and sometimes, now that I think back, didn't employ the most honorable means to locate my father. My coming to Look Away is very serious. But I am finding some peace here, and it's quite surprising."

"I meant with me, Brooks."

He reached out to grab her hand, then turned it over in his palm as he contemplated her question. "Not with you, either, Ruby. I don't make a habit of playing games, period."

"You probably don't have to."

"Meaning?"

"Meaning, you're handsome and wealthy and I bet—"

"You'd bet wrong. I'd be the first one to tell you I've been obsessed lately with finding the truth of my parentage. I haven't had a moment for anything else. I haven't dated in months, and I—"

She pressed her fingers against his lips. "Okay, I believe you."

He kissed her fingertips. "Good." He rose then and lifted her to her feet on his way up. "I really should go."

She waited a beat, debating over whether to have him in her bed tonight, to wake with him in the morning. Picturing it was like a dream, but she couldn't do it. She couldn't invite him to stay. The long list of reasons why not infiltrated her mind, making it all very clear.

"I'll walk you out." She tugged on his hand and headed to the door, ignoring the regret in his eyes and willing away her own doubts about letting him go. "Thanks for the candy and flowers, Brooks."

He bent his head and kissed her lightly on the lips. The kiss was over before she knew what was happening. "You're welcome. I had a nice time tonight," he said and walked out the door.

He had had no ulterior motive for showing up here tonight.

Her heart warmed at the thought.

Galahad had been true to his word.

The next morning, Ruby entered the shed attached to the main house. It was nearly as big as the Preston five-car garage. Back in the day, the Preston boys would play in here, pretending to camp out in the dark walled recesses and holding secret meetings. Ruby was never a part of that all-boy thing, but she had her own secrets in this place. The shed was where twelve-year-old Rusty Jenkins had given her her first kiss. It had been an amateur attempt, she realized years later, as the boy's lips were as soft as a baby's and he'd kinda slobbered. But it had thrilled her since Rusty was a boy she'd really liked. And every time she walked in here, those old, very sweet memories flooded her mind.

She lifted the first box she found marked Christmas in red lettering and loaded it into her arms. Ever since Tanya had passed on, Beau enlisted Ruby's help in decorating the entire house, claiming the place needed a woman's touch. And she was happy to do it. It was serious business getting the house ready for the holidays.

When the shed door opened, letting in cool Texas air, she called, "Beau, I'm back here."

"We're coming," Beau said in a nasal voice.

She turned to find not one but two Prestons approaching. She should've known Brooks would be with him. There was no help for it; Beau was anxious to spend as much time as he could with his son.

Immediately Beau took the box out of her arms. "Morning, Ruby."

"Good morning," she said to both of them. But her gaze lingered on Brooks, dressed in faded blue jeans and a white T-shirt that hugged his biceps. She looked away instantly—she couldn't let Beau catch her drooling over his son. Brooks had *hunk* written all over him, and how well she knew. Every time he entered a room, her blood pulsed wildly. It usually took a few moments to calm down. "Brooks is going to help us decorate the tree, if that's okay with you." Beau barely got the words out before he began coughing, and his face turned candy apple red.

"Are you sick, Beau?" she asked.

"Trying to catch a cold is all, Rube."

But he coughed again and again. Brooks grabbed the box out of his arms.

"Not trying," she said. "You sound terrible. You're congested, Beau."

"I think so, too, but he insisted on helping decorate the tree today," Brooks said.

Beau pursed his lips. It was the closest the man came to pouting. "Is it so wrong to want to put up a tree with my son for the first time?"

Ruby glanced at Brooks and then gave Beau a sweet smile. "Not at all, but if you're not feeling well, you should rest. The Look Away Christmas party is happening this weekend, and Graham and his fiancée will be here by then. You want to be healthy for that, Beau. A little rest will do you a world of good. I can manage the tree."

"I'll help, Ruby," Brooks added, nodding. "Why not take a rest and come down later for dinner?"

Beau turned his head away and coughed a blue streak. "Okay," he managed on a nod. He couldn't argue after that coughing spell. "I guess you two are right. I can't be sick when Graham and Eve get here. Not with her being pregnant and all. That's my first grandbaby." Pride filled his voice.

"Yeah, and I'm gonna be an uncle." Brooks's eyes gleamed, showing Ruby just how much Beau and Brooks looked alike.

"That you are." Then Beau drew out a sigh as if he wanted to do anything but rest on his laurels this morning. "I'll go now. See you both later on."

He walked away, and the sound of his coughing followed him out the door.

Now Ruby was alone in the shed with deadly handsome Brooks. He stared at her, a smile on his face.

"What?" she asked.

"You're a bossy mother hen."

She shook her head. "I already lost one father. Don't want to lose another."

Brooks flinched, and she wished she could take her words back. Brooks hadn't meant anything by his comment. He was teasing; it was what he did, and she shouldn't have lashed out. But the man made her a little jumpy and whole lot of crazy.

"I'm sorry. It's just that my father worked himself into the ground, and I was too young to know enough to stop him. Losing him as a teen was hard. I had no other family, and when Beau took me in and treated me as his own, well…it meant a lot to me. So I'm protective."

Brooks moved a stray hair from her cheek and tucked it back behind her ear. "I get that. I was only teasing."

"I know." She lifted her chin and cracked a small smile.

"Ruby," he said quietly. His eyes softened to a blue glow, his hand moving to the back of her neck to hold her head in place.

There was silent communication between them. She sensed that he understood, and in the silence of the shed, her heart pounded as she stared at him, wishing that he was someone else. Not Beau's son. Not a man who would eventually leave Cool Springs. And her.

"I'm not going to hurt you," he said as if reading her mind. As if he realized the pain she'd experienced losing her mother, her father and a lover who had abandoned her. Her heart was guarded. She'd built up an impenetrable wall of defense against further hurt and pain.

"I can't let you, Brooks."

"I won't. I promise," he said, his gaze dipping to her mouth. She parted her lips and he took her then, in a kiss that was simple and brief and sweet. Moments ticked by as she stared at him, sad regret pulling at her heart. And their fate was sealed. They had come to terms with their attraction and would put a halt to anything leading them astray.

It was quiet in the shed, and cool and dark. Ruby trembled, and that brought her out of her haze. "We should get these boxes into the house. We've got a full day of decorating ahead. Have you seen the tree yet?"

"No, not yet. We should get to it, then."

Brooks got right on it, pulling down two big boxes and loading up his arms while she grabbed one, too. "You know, I haven't decorated for Christmas since I was a kid," he said as they made their way toward the house. "My mom would get this small three-foot tree and put it up on Grandma Gerty's round coffee table. That made it look just as big and tall as the ones we'd see around town. Then Graham and I would put the ornaments on the taller branches, and my little brother, Carson, would decorate the bottom half."

"Did you use tinsel?" she asked, her mood lighter now as she pictured Brooks as a boy.

"My mom always made a popcorn garland. And my grandmother would give us candy canes to stick on the tree."

"My dad and I always used silver tinsel," Ruby said. "It wasn't Christmas until we had the tree covered in it."

"Sounds nice," Brooks said. "I'm sorry Beau isn't going to be decorating with us today. Seems silly now that I'm a grown man, doesn't it?"

"Not at all. You missed out on a lot with Beau. But you know what? I bet before we finish the tree, Beau will come down."

As they entered the massive living room, Brooks took one look at the tree and the ladder beside it and halted his steps, inclining his head. "Wow. Now, that's a tree. Must be a fifteen-footer."

"At least. Every year Beau has the biggest and best Douglas fir delivered to the house. Tanya loved filling up the entire corner of the room with the tree."

They set their boxes down. Brooks scanned the room again and sighed. "It's weird, you know. Having a family here I didn't know about. I'm not complaining. I had a good life. My mother made sure of it. But to think while I was decorating our Christmas tree at home, my father and his family were setting their own Christmas traditions."

"Just think, Brooks. Now you'll have both—a Chicago and a Cool Springs Christmas."

He chuckled. "You're right, Ruby. I guess that's not half-bad."

"No, it's not. Now, here," she said, digging into a box and coming up with a string of large, colorful lights. "Before we can hang any ornaments, we need to make this tree shine. Start at the top and work your way down, Mr. Six-Foot-Two. You've got a lot of catching up to do."

Hours later, Brooks put his arm around Ruby's shoulders as they stepped back from the tree to admire their handiwork. The tree was stunning, the lights in holiday hues casting a soft glimmer over the large formal living room. "It's beautiful," Ruby said quietly.

"It is. We went through six boxes on the tree alone."

"It looks almost perfect," Ruby said, noticing a flaw.

"Almost?"

"Yeah, I see a spot we missed."

"Where?"

She pointed to a bare space toward the top of the tree that had been neglected. "Right there. I'll get it," she said, breaking away from Brooks to grab a beautiful horse ornament, a palomino with a golden mane. "We'll just get this guy up on that branch."

She hugged the side rails of the ladder and began climbing. Making it to the highest rung, she thought was safe and reached out to a branch just as the ladder wobbled beneath her. "Oh!"

"I've got you," Brooks said, steadying the ladder first and then fitting her butt cheeks into his hands from his stance on the floor.

"Brooks." She swatted at his hands. "Stop that."

"What?" He put innocence in his voice. "I'm only keeping you from falling."

"Shh," she said, her entire body reacting to the grip he had on her. They'd worked together all day long in close quarters, and it was hard enough to keep from touching him, from brushing her body against his, from breathing in his intoxicating scent while trying to focus on the task. "Lupe might hear you. Or Beau might come down."

"Lupe went shopping for groceries, remember? And I heard Beau snoring just a second ago. Doesn't seem like he's going to come down anytime soon."

"Smart aleck. You're got it all figured out, don't you?"

"Hell, I wish I did, Ruby."

She ignored the earnest regret she heard in his voice. "I'm coming down. That means you can take your hands off my ass now."

He grinned and then released her. "I'll be right here, waiting."

"Why does that worry me?" she said as she lowered herself slowly down.

He stood at the base of the ladder, and when she turned around, he was there, crowding her with his body, his scent, his blue beautiful eyes. "I think I have a shelf life around you, Ruby," he said in explanation. "A few hours without touching you is all I can manage."

The compliment seared through her system and warmed all the cold spots. "I know what you mean," she said softly. She felt the same way, and it was useless to deny the attraction.

He gave her a bone-melting smile. "Now, that's honest."

"I'm always honest. Or at least, I try to be."

He held her trapped against the ladder, his arms roped around the sides, blocking her in. When he lowered his head, her eyes closed naturally, and she welcomed his kiss.

"Mmm," she hummed against lips that fit perfectly with hers. Lips that gave so much and demanded even more. The connection she had with Brooks was sharp and swift and powerful. They were like twin magnets that clicked together the minute they got close.

He took her head in his hands and dipped her back, deepening the kiss, probing her with his tongue. He swept inside so quickly she gasped, the pleasure startling her and making her pulse race out of control.

He whispered, "Come to my cabin tonight, Ruby."

"I, uh…" A dozen reasons she shouldn't swarmed into her mind. The same reasons she'd tried to heed before, the same reasons that had kept her up nights.

He kissed her again, meshing their bodies hip to hip, groin to groin. There was no mistaking his erection and the blatant desire pulsing between them. She had to come to terms with wanting Brooks. Not for the future, not because of the past, but for now. In the present. Could she live with that?

"Yes," she said, agreeing to another night with him. "I'll come to you," she promised. And once she said it, her shoulders relaxed and her entire body gave way to relief. She'd put up a good fight, but it was time to realize she couldn't fight what was happening between them. She could only go along for the ride and see where it would take her.

"Ruby, you sure you don't want to watch the end of the game with me and Brooks?" Beau asked from his seat at the head of the dinner table. "We can catch the last half. Looks like the Texans might make the playoffs if they win tonight."

His boys had invited them all to catch the game at the C'mon Inn as they usually did once a week, drinking beer and talking smack, but mother hen that she was, Ruby delicately squashed that idea. Beau needed his rest and some alone time with Brooks, since he'd missed out on being with him today.

"No thanks, Beau. I'll just help Lupe straighten up in the kitchen and then head home. You boys enjoy the game. And remember, don't stay up too late. You may be feeling better, but you still need to turn in early."

"Yes, ma'am, I promise," Beau said, giving her a wink.

He seemed much better than he had this morning. He'd coughed only once during dinner, and his voice had lost that nasal tone. She congratulated herself on getting him to rest today. It had done him a world of good.

"Thanks again to both of you for fixing up the house. Looks real pretty."

"You're welcome." Brooks looked as innocent as a schoolboy as he nodded at his father, but his innocence ended there. He'd been eyeballing Ruby all during dinner, making it hard for her to swallow her food. She was eager to be with him again, to have him nestle her close and make her body come apart.

"It was a lot of fun, Dad. Ruby taught me the finer points of decorating a tree."

Ruby wanted to roll her eyes. Everything Brooks said lately seemed to have a double meaning. Or was she just imagining it?

"She's had enough experience," Beau went on. "She took over from Tanya, you know. And I know my wife would approve of the way you both made the house look so festive. The party's on Saturday night, and son, I can't wait to introduce you to my friends."

"I'll look forward to that."

Beau smiled and then was hit by a sudden fit of coughing. Concerned, Ruby put a hand on his shoulder until he simmered down. "S-sorry," he said.

"Don't apologize, Dad. Maybe I should go so you can turn in early."

"Nah, don't go yet. It's just a tickle. I'm fine."

Beau seemed to recover quickly. He didn't want to miss out on watching football with his son. It was sweet of him, and Brooks seemed to understand.

"All right, then," Brooks said.

"I'm making you a cup of tea, Beau," Ruby said. "No arguments. Go have a seat in the great room and finish the game. I'll bring it in to you. Brooks, would you like some tea?"

"I'll just get myself another beer, if you don't mind. I'll meet you in the other room, Dad."

"Okay, sure," Beau said, heading out.

Brooks cocked his mouth in a smile and followed behind Ruby. When she was almost through the kitchen doorway, his hand snaked out and tugged on her forearm. He spun her around to face him squarely. "What?" she asked, her brows gathering.

"Look up."

She didn't have to. The scent of fresh mistletoe filled her nostrils from above, and before she could comment, Brooks was swooping down, giving her a kiss. It was short-lived, but filled with passion—a kiss that had staying power. "Shelf life," he whispered, searching her face with sea-blue eyes.

"You set me up." He'd put up mistletoe in half a dozen rooms in the house.

"Guilty as charged."

She shoved at his chest, but he didn't budge. "Go," she pleaded. "Watch football with your father." Lupe was clearing the dinner dishes from the dining room table and would be back in the kitchen any second.

"Bossy. I love that about you," he whispered over her lips.

Her skin heated at his seductive words. She pointed toward the great room. "Go. Pleeeze."

He saluted her. "Yes, ma'am. See you soon." Then he turned and walked away.

If he wanted to give her a preview of what was in store for her later that evening, he'd succeeded. The kiss had staying power; it had her nerves jumping and her body primed for his touch.

After delivering a steaming mug of chamomile tea to Beau, she bundled up in a warm wool jacket and exited the house. She was halfway home when her phone rang out—Carrie Underwood again, keying her ex-boyfriend's car.

The screen displayed the caller. "Trace," Ruby muttered.

She couldn't talk to him tonight. She let the call go to voice mail.

But curiosity had her putting the phone to her ear to listen to his message. "Hey, baby. It's Trace. I'm missing you like crazy. I'm coming home tomorrow. I need to see you, babe. We need to talk."

He sounded serious. Trace wanted to talk to her? The entire time they'd dated, he'd put her off about matters of the heart. He'd always said he would rather show her how he felt than ramble off meaningless words. And she'd bought that, hook, line and sinker. For a time, his actions had spoken louder than words. He'd been an attentive boyfriend, showing up with thoughtful gifts, taking her to country music concerts, letting her drive his most prized possession, his fully restored 1964 Ford truck. For a while Ruby had felt like the queen of the world. And she'd fallen hard for him, thinking him the perfect man for her—a man born and raised in Texas, a man who understood her love of horses, a man of the earth.

Together they could enjoy life here in Cool Springs.

But then something had happened. It had started out gradually. Trace had become restless. His attention had drifted. He seemed unsatisfied, as if he needed and wanted more out of life. He was systematically yet subtly pushing her away, and it had taken his being gone for months on the rodeo circuit without calling her for her to realize she'd been dumped. She'd spent many nights crying over him. Wondering what had gone wrong. She'd been in love with him. She'd banked her future on him, and she'd been sucker-punched in the gut when she realized they were truly over.

She'd asked herself if he'd been tired of *her*, or if it was his life that needed a big change. She didn't know, but what she did know was that he didn't want her anymore. Maybe he'd never really loved her. She'd wasted a great deal of time on a man who, in the end, didn't want a future with her.

She wouldn't be that gullible again.

So as she entered her cottage, she showered and changed her clothes and set her mind on keeping her feelings for Brooks neutral. He was a city guy, Beau's long-lost son and a man who'd be leaving town after the holidays. She couldn't give herself fully to Brooks, but she could enjoy spending time with him and look forward to the pleasures they could give each other. Once again she asked herself if her attraction to Brooks was real or simply a way to redeem her blistered and battered soul.

Brooks made her feel feminine and special and beautiful.

That was enough for now.

* * *

Shortly after, Ruby parked her car so it was completely hidden from sight behind a feed shed and walked up to Brooks's cabin. She knocked briskly. Her heart was pounding, her mind made up. When Brooks opened the door, she studied the handsome face, the beautiful blue eyes gazing back at her. "My shelf life for you has just expired."

Brooks's eyes flickered, and a growl emanated from his throat.

He took her hand and tugged her inside.

Then slammed the door shut behind them.

Brooks seemed to know. He really seemed to know she didn't need mindless words as he peeled her dress down her arms and over her hips until she was clad only in a pink bra and panties. His groan of approval gave way to him ripping at the buttons of his shirt and yanking it off. Then he lifted her silently, his strong arms under her legs and his mouth covering hers as he moved down the hall. He didn't let up on her lips until they reached the bedroom. His room was bathed in candlelight—a nice touch—and the soft beams delicately caressed the bedsheets.

Instead of lowering her onto the bed, Brooks guided her down his body until her feet met with cool wood floor planks. He reached around and unhooked her bra, then slipped his fingers under the straps, pulling them away and freeing her breasts. He gazed at them for several heartbeats before he hooked her panties with a finger and slid them all the way down her legs. With the slightest move of her feet, she stepped out of them.

It amazed her how much she trusted him. How she allowed him to bear witness to her naked body without worry or shyness. Maybe it was the glow of admiration in his eyes, the way they seemed to touch and warm her at the same time. Her nipples tightened under his scrutiny, and he noticed. "You're cold."

She shook her head no.

She wasn't cold. She was turned on. Ready for whatever Brooks wanted to do.

He walked around her and pressed his body to hers. The length of his manhood rubbed against her backside, and her eyelids lowered ever so slowly. He reached around and cupped her heavy breasts in his hands much like he had her rear end earlier in the day, and then nibbled lustily on the back of her neck. If he was trying to drive her crazy, he was doing a good job. Her body was throbbing now, hot and eager for more.

He wasn't through tormenting her. Next he used his palms to mold her skin from her shoulders down along the very edge of her breasts. He smoothed his hands to the hollow curves of her waist and lower still until his fingertips touched the apex of her thighs, teasing and tempting, bringing her immense pleasure. Instincts had her spreading her legs, welcoming the onslaught, and her breathing escalated. She couldn't think of anything but what he was doing to her. What she wanted him to do to her.

He rubbed against her as he brought her closer still, pressed so tight there was no doubt about his own thick arousal. And then his hand moved to her core, making her gasp and silently plead for more. His fingertips worked the folds of her skin and drew her out with tender but targeted strokes that jolted her body. "Easy now," Brooks whispered as he wrapped his free arm around her waist to steady her while he continued his torment. She was so ready, so primed that it took only a few more infinitely refined strokes to send her sailing over the edge.

She rocked back and shuddered long and hard, the

spasms ridiculously powerful. When they were over, Brooks braced her in his arms, bestowing kisses on her shoulders, her back, and then spun her around and looked deep into her eyes.

Ruby was in too much awe to say a word.

Brooks wasn't much in the mood for talking, either. He whipped off his belt and then removed the rest of his clothes. Her eyes dipped to his beautifully ripped and aroused body, and she fell to her knees before him and gave him the same pleasure he'd given her. He groaned from deep in his chest with utter approval, and it wasn't long before he was reaching for her, lifting her up.

"I need to be inside you," he rasped.

"Lie down, Galahad."

And once he was in position, taking up the length of the bed and wearing protection, she threw her leg over his hips and straddled him. "Ah man, Ruby," he said. "You have no idea how you look right now."

"Like I'm about to ride?"

Even through his heated expression, he chuckled. "You comparing me to a horse?"

"Take it as a compliment," she said as she pressed herself down onto him. A low, guttural sigh emerged from his throat as her body took all of him inside. Then she began a slow, steady climb. Brooks's hands were on her hips, holding on or guiding her—she couldn't tell—and then the pace changed, surging and building to a crescendo that had her crying out.

Brooks, too, was there, grunting and sighing in a mix of pain and pleasure.

The climax hit them hard together, and their cries echoed from the cabin walls.

Ruby fell atop him and he gathered her in, holding her tight, cradling her in his arms.

She was spent, her limbs like jelly.

It was a good thing she had Brooks on the brain tonight.

Tomorrow she would have to deal with Trace.

Seven

Ruby stood at the gates of the Cool Springs Christmas Carnival on the outskirts of town. She used to barrel race at these fairgrounds as a young girl. Ruby smiled at the memories. Oh, how she'd always loved it when the carnival came to town. With her father looking on, she'd put her horse through the paces, leaning and reining and guiding those sharp turns, feeling at one with the animal. She'd brought home a few trophies in her day, but once her papa had passed on, Ruby turned to something she loved even more: training horses. It was his legacy that she now carried on at Look Away.

Strings of twinkling lights crisscrossed the carnival grounds. There were giant holly wreaths as well as red-and-green banners announcing the holiday. The chatter of fun-seeking crowds, children's laughter and shouts from hawkers selling cotton candy and funnel cakes brought it all home. Ruby smiled.

It was here that Trace Evans first kissed her, back behind the shack that now sold hot chocolate and coffee. Her heart warmed despite the brisk December night as she stood there taking it all in.

And then she saw him.

Trace.

Approaching from inside the gates, his smile was as broad and sure as she remembered. His polished snakeskin boots leaving dust behind, the six-foot-tall hunk of man worked his way through the crowd as if all the others surrounding him didn't exist, his deep, dark eyes set only on her.

Just like it used to be.

All the worries she'd been plagued with in coming here vanished the instant she laid eyes on him. Seeing Trace, tall in his Stetson, broad in a black-and-white snap-down plaid shirt and giving her a megawatt smile, flooded her senses, and a shiver of warmth ran down her body. Crap. She was here only to put him off. To tell him they were officially over, so that they could both move on with their lives.

She needed to do this face-to-face.

But his *face* was filled with genuine joy. "Ruby," he said, his voice husky and laced with that down-home drawl. "It's good to see you."

She stood there immobilized as he paid for her ticket and tugged her through the gate. She realized he held her hand, and when she tried to pull away, he drew her up close, bent his head and gave her a quick kiss. "Sorry," he said, dipping his head in that charming way he had. "I've been dreamin' about doing that ever since you agreed to meet me here. Gawd, you look good, Ruby. I've missed you, honey."

"Trace." She put force in her words, ignoring the crazy, mixed-up stirrings in her heart. "I'm here only to—"

"I know, I know. You're not happy with me right now. I get that. How about we enjoy the evening a little before we get all serious? Look over there. Funnel cakes. I'm dying for one. I bet you are, too."

"I, uh..."

"Don't you remember how much we used to crave those things? With all the fixin's, too. Strawberries and whipped cream, the more powdered sugar the better. You game? Come on," he said, taking her hand again. "I'm about to die of starvation."

She rolled her eyes, but a big smile emerged regardless of the company she was in. She was craving a funnel cake, too. They were available only once a year, at this carnival. This was her chance to indulge in a gooey, deep-fried concoction with all the heart-stopping extras. "Okay, sounds good."

"*Delicious* is a better word, sweetheart."

She wasn't his sweetheart and she was ready to tell him, but a few young women and two school-age boys butted into the line, asking Trace for his autograph. He seemed genuinely delighted, giving them each individual attention as he took their names and signed their tickets, flyers, whatever paper article they could produce. Trace had made a name for himself in the field of bull riding. As far as rodeo champions went, he was equivalent to a soap opera star rather than an Academy Award winner, but to the folks around these parts, he was a local hero. Trace ate up all the attention.

"Sorry about that, Ruby," he said, guiding her toward a two-seater café table.

"Do you get that a lot?" she asked, curious now.

"Some," he said, trying for humble, though his grin gave him away. "More and more."

Then his grin faded as his gaze roamed her face, and he sighed from deep in his chest. "I'm sure glad to see you. I've been lonely for you, honey."

"Last I checked, you broke up with me, Trace."

"I never did. Not officially. I, uh, like I told you on the phone, I had to focus on my career, and that meant blocking out everything else."

"That's not exactly comforting, Trace."

She'd felt fully and totally dumped, and there was no way he could salvage what happened between them by using phony excuses.

"Only because being with you was so damn distracting. When we were together, you were all I could ever think about."

He was talking like a man still in love, and if Ruby was that same gullible girl he'd left behind, she might have swallowed that line again. "When you care for someone, you call. You want to know how they're doing. You—"

"I made mistakes. I'm not denying it." He played with his fork but didn't dig into the funnel cake he craved. "But I'm home now, for good."

"What does that mean, for good?"

"It means I'm gonna stay on in Cool Springs."

"You quit the rodeo?"

He smiled sadly. "I think it quit me, Rube. I'm not cut out for the life. I'm never gonna make it big. Not like I wanted. I gave eight years of my life to the rodeo."

"But you love bull riding." He'd been nineteen when he won his first local rodeo, and the entire town had gotten behind him. Some small businesses in the area sponsored him so he could pursue his dream. It seemed strange to her that he would give it up now. Yes, it was a young man's sport, but he still had years left in him.

"I did. I loved it, but it didn't love me back, Ruby. I gave it my all, and I hope I didn't lose you as a result of my pursuit. I just never got where I wanted to go, and I'm done with all of it. So I'll be home now, just like we'd planned. If I'm lucky enough to win you back, I'm staying put right here."

For her equilibrium's sake, she had to ignore the winning-you-back part. This was all too much to take in. She straightened in her seat to keep from showing her total surprise. "So, what will you do?"

He shrugged. "Dad's getting on in years. He wants me to take over the ranch full-time."

It didn't sound like Trace. He'd always had big plans, and none of them included becoming a local rancher. He was Texan through and through, but Ruby had begun to believe his true heart was elsewhere.

"I saw you on television the other night. *Homestead Hills*?"

"Oh, that. Yeah, I did that on a whim. Met some casting guy at the rodeo who said I'd be perfect in the role. I gave it a try, is all."

"A try?" From what she'd heard, people busted their butts and did all sorts of crazy things to win a role in a hit TV series.

"Nothing much came of it," he said dismissively.

"You haven't touched your funnel cake," she said, finally raising her fork and digging in. The airy pastry, all sugared up, got her taste buds going. When she finally swallowed, a burst of deliciousness slid down her throat. "Mmm, it's good. I shouldn't, but I think I'm going to eat every last bite."

Trace smiled, his gaze focused on her mouth for several beats, and suddenly her insides quaked and her belly quivered. Those familiar yearnings returned. She couldn't believe that one year ago, they'd been doing this very thing: eating funnel cakes and talking about their future.

"Soon as I start," he said, lifting his fork and gazing into her eyes, "this here dessert is gonna be history."

True to his word, Trace demolished his funnel cake.

Ruby wound up leaving half of hers behind. Her stomach was tied in knots once everything Trace had said to her finally sank in. She'd been raised to forgive with an open heart. But would she be a fool to do so?

As they rode the Ferris wheel, circling to the highest point, sitting hip to hip, their legs brushing, they took in the nighttime view of all of Cool Springs, the moon and stars appearing close enough to touch. Trace took her hand, entwining their fingers, and gave her a slight squeeze. In that moment, she saw a glimpse of what life with Trace could be like again.

And a few moments later, Trace set his money down at a gaming booth and wasn't satisfied until he hit the bull's-eye target with a dart gun to win her an adorable stuffed reindeer. "Here you go, miss," he said, bowing and presenting her with the toy.

He used to be her hero.

Could he be again?

She was as confused as ever, with the Trace she remembered returning to her and saying all the right things, making her feel like she mattered to him. She was a long way from forgiving him...and then there was Brooks.

A sigh blew from her lips, and Trace turned to her. "What?"

She shook her head. "Nothing. I should go."

"You sure? We haven't gone into Santa's Village yet."

"I'm sure."

Disappointment dimmed the gleam in his eyes. "Okay, I'll walk you to your car."

He took hold of her hand again. She didn't want to make a fuss by pulling free of him, so they walked hand in hand into the parking lot.

Now's your chance. Tell him you're not taking him back. Tell him he hurt you and...

The words didn't come. She couldn't yank them out of her throat. Not when he was being so dang sweet and trying so hard to impress her.

When they reached her car, she hoped to make a quick getaway. Launching into her handbag for her key fob, she moved away from him, breaking their connection. "Good night, Trace. Thanks for the funnel cake," she said, opening the car door.

He glanced at her hand on the door handle and knew enough not to press her tonight. "I'll call you tomorrow."

She should tell him no. There was no point. "Okay."

Before he could say anything more, she slid into the seat and pressed the ignition button.

The car didn't rev right up. In fact, nothing happened. She pressed the button again, giving the engine gas.

Again nothing.

Shoot. Trace walked over. He had a keen sense of cars, and judging by the expression on his face, this couldn't be good. After fiddling with the ignition button, he spent a few minutes under the hood and came up looking bleak. "You want the good news or the bad news?"

"Bad."

"The car's not going anywhere tonight. Not without a tow."

Ruby silently cursed under her breath.

"The good news is, I can give you a lift home."

* * *

Parked in front of her cottage now, Ruby slid across the pristine leather seat, angling for the truck's door handle. "Thanks for the ride, Trace." Her head was spinning from spending time with him tonight. It was almost too much to take in. What they had once was pretty darn remarkable. Being with him tonight at the carnival had brought back memories of the good times they'd shared when Trace had loved her.

Before he'd had second thoughts.

Before he'd turned into a jerk.

"Hold up a sec, Ruby." The urgency in his voice stilled her. He climbed out of his truck and spun around the hood to open the door for her. He offered his hand, and she fitted her palm inside his as she stepped out. Now that they were alone under beautiful moonlight, she waited for the butterflies to attack her stomach, but nothing seemed to happen. No flip-flops. No queasy feeling. No little bursts of excitement.

That was a good thing, right?

As soon as her boots landed on Preston soil, she pulled her hand free, grabbing for her purse, ready to end this night. Earlier, rather than have her wait for a tow, Trace had insisted on taking her home. His good buddy Randy over at Cool Springs Auto promised to tow her car to the shop and take a look at it first thing in the morning. Ruby couldn't argue with that logic. She would've had to do the same thing, and Trace had effortlessly taken care of everything for her.

Ruby had always thought of herself as an independent woman. She could fend for herself, but having Trace take over the reins tonight and deal with her car issues was nice for a change.

"I'll walk you to your door," he said.

She didn't like the prospect of Trace giving her a good-night kiss, one more potent than the one he'd given her at the festival. He'd been her first love, and the splinters of his betrayal were still stabbing her. The pain wasn't as strong as it had once been, but it left behind scars that had yet to heal. She couldn't be a fool twice. "There's no need, Trace." Her door was ten feet away, and having him walk her there implied much more than she was willing to concede right now.

"Okay. But before you go, Ruby, I, uh…"

Brisk night breezes put a chill in her bones as she faced him, her back against the bed of the truck. He stepped closer and removed his hat, hesitating as if searching for the right words. Whatever he had to say had to be important for him to stumble this way. Usually confident, he rubbed at the back of his neck and inhaled from deep in his chest. She'd never seen him quite like this, and she almost wanted to put a hand on his arm to steady him. Almost.

"I wanted to say I'm sorry…deeply sorry for the way I treated you. I should've realized what we had was special, and now that I'm home to stay, I want to make it up to you. I want to start fresh. You and me, we were good together. I want that—"

The sound of footsteps crunching gravel came from the road behind them. She swiveled her head as a figure came out of the shadows and into the ring of moonlight surrounding them.

Trace saw him, too. "Who in hell is that?" he asked none too quietly.

Ruby tried not to react. "Beau's son."

Now that Brooks was upon them, his brows arched as his inquisitive glance went from her to Trace and back again. "Evenin'," he said. He was picking up a Texas drawl, probably from spending time with Beau. She almost chuckled, except seeing her ex-boyfriend meet up with her current lover wasn't a laughing matter.

"Hi, Brooks." There was cheery lightness in her voice worthy of a big Hollywood award.

"Ruby."

"Oh, um, Brooks, I'd like you to meet Trace Evans. Trace, this is one of Beau's twin sons, Brooks. He's visiting here from Chicago, getting to know the family."

Trace sized Brooks up as he put out his hand. "Nice meetin' ya."

"Same here," Brooks said without much enthusiasm as the two pumped hands.

"So, you're one of the lost boys Beau's been searching for. I heard about you. Not from Ruby, though. She didn't say a word about you all night, but word spreads quickly when someone new shows up in Cool Springs."

"I met Trace at the Christmas carnival in town," she was quick to explain. "My car broke down and Trace offered me a lift home."

Trace took a place beside Ruby against the truck. "Yeah, just like old times. Ruby and I go back a ways. Don't know if she told you about us, but I'm back in town now." He gave Brooks a smile. Was he warning Brooks off or simply making conversation? Trace had no reason to suspect anything, not that it mattered anyway. He didn't have a claim on her anymore. "So, how are you liking Cool Springs so far?" he asked.

"I'm liking it just fine." Brooks said the words slowly, giving nothing away by his tone. Yet his gaze shifted to her every so often as if puzzling out what was happening. "I'm beginning to feel right at home here at Look Away."

Ruby edged away from Trace. If he put his arm around her to haul her closer, she'd cringe.

"Must be, if you're out taking a walk this time of night in the cool air."

"I'm used to cold weather. Chicago winters can be brutal. Actually, I wasn't out walking for the sake of walking. I came to ask Ruby a favor. Is all," he added.

Ruby kept her lips buttoned. Brooks playing the country bumpkin was enough to make her laugh. But she didn't dare.

"That so?" Trace asked.

"Yeah."

"Ruby and I were in the middle of a conversation," Trace announced, as if that wasn't obvious.

"Was I interrupting?" A choir boy couldn't have appeared more innocent.

"You were, actually," Trace replied, his chest expanding as he stood a bit taller.

This was not going well, and it was clear Brooks wasn't going to back down.

"Don't let me stop you," Trace said, gesturing with a royal sweep of his arm. "Go ahead and ask Ruby your favor."

"Actually Trace, I'm not up for this conversation tonight," Ruby said. "It's been a long day, and I'm tired. Brooks, can your question wait until tomorrow?"

He glanced at Trace, eyeing him for a second before nodding. "Sure thing. It can wait."

"Okay, then. We'll talk tomorrow. And Trace, thanks again for the lift."

"You're welcome. I enjoyed our date, honey."

It wouldn't do any good denying it was date. Trace had it in his head it was.

Both men stood like statues, refusing to move.

"Well, good night, then." She made her way past Trace and rolled her eyes at Brooks as she brushed by him. His lips twitched in amusement, and for that split second, devilish images of tossing him over her shoulder played out in her head.

She left them both standing there and walked to her door. Curiosity had her turning around briefly to see Trace waiting until Brooks was well on his way before getting into his truck and starting the engine.

Men.

"So what's with your ex showing up?" Brooks wasted no time with pleasantries, yet his tone coming through her cell phone was more curious than accusatory.

"Where are you?" It hadn't been but ten minutes since he'd left her. Cozy in her pajamas and tucked into bed already, she really was unusually tired tonight and…confused. She hadn't expected the man she'd banked all her dreams on once to show up with apologies and promises.

Promises that she'd waited so long to hear.

"I'm at my place. Sitting here wondering what's going on with you. Are you okay?"

"I'm okay. It wasn't really a date, Brooks. Trace wanted to talk to me and apologize, I guess. I agreed to meet him at the Christmas carnival."

"So, are you forgiving him?"

"I don't know what I am at the moment, Brooks."

The line went silent. A moment ticked by, and then a sigh came through. "Is it none of my business?"

Now, that also was unexpected. Brooks had a way of getting to the heart of the matter. "It may be your business, a little, since we've been seeing each other."

She hadn't had to deal with the reality of their relationship until now. But it was evident Brooks had made her no promises and he was bound to leave for Chicago after the holidays, while Trace was offering her something that she'd always wanted. "I want to continue seeing you, Ruby."

"I, uh, I just don't know, Brooks." Could she be blunt and tell him she couldn't afford to get her heart broken again if she gave in to her feelings for him and he left town? Could she tell him that he hadn't offered her the sun, the moon and the stars the way Trace once had? It was silly to think Brooks would. They'd known each other only a couple of weeks. Though things had been humming along very smoothly until Trace showed up. "I can't be pressured right now."

"I don't want to pressure you, Ruby. But this guy's hurt you once, and I wouldn't want to see that happen again. I care about you."

"I care about you, too, Brooks. But we both know…" She hesitated, biting her lip, searching for a way to put it that wouldn't seem callous or crude. The truth was, they were hot for each other. They'd had a chance meeting in a bar—the cliché hook-up—and it would've ended there if Brooks hadn't turned out to be a Preston. Now they couldn't seem to keep their hands off each other.

"What do we know?" he asked.

"We've been thrown together under strange circumstances, wouldn't you say?"

"I suppose. When I first met you, I never once thought you'd be a part of the Preston family. Shoot, it blew my mind when you walked into the barn that day. But I'm not sorry you did. Are you?"

The truth was, no. She wasn't sorry she'd met Brooks. She liked him, and maybe her feelings went much deeper than that, but she wouldn't face them. She couldn't. It wasn't just because he was Beau's son. Or because of all of the secrecy and guilt involved in seeing Brooks. No, she couldn't face deeper feelings because her heart wasn't healed enough to let another man inside. So even though she'd slept with Brooks, readily giving him her body, she'd held a small part of herself back. She couldn't give herself wholly to him, and at this point, he hadn't asked that of her, either. "No, I'm not sorry." Enough said for now on the subject. And because her curiosity was tapped, she asked, "Did you really come by to ask me a favor, or was that a little fib?"

"No fib. Although I'll admit, I wanted to see you tonight." His voice turned husky, and whenever it deepened like that, she melted a little inside.

"Did you want to go out for another ride tomorrow or something?"

"I'd love to. But that's not the favor. The truth is, I've been thinking about my grandfather. I need to make my peace about him, and I've been putting off a visit to his nursing home. I'm not sure I'm ready to go it alone and face him. That man caused my family a lot of grief, and I don't know how I'm going to react. But I need to put it behind me so I can move on."

"Would you like me to go with you, Brooks?"

His relief came in the way of a quick sigh. "Would you?"

"Yes, of course. I'll go with you whenever you want."

"Really? That's great. I'm... I'm thinking I'll arrange an appointment sometime before the holiday party this weekend. I want to—"

"I'll clear my calendar whenever you can arrange it."

"Okay," he said, his voice cracking a little. As if he was barely holding it together, as if this visit to his grandfather had been festering in his mind. "It means a lot." Breath whooshed out of his lungs. "Thank you, Ruby."

"Of course."

Sadness swept through her when she heard the pain

in Brooks's voice. It only served to prove how much she cared about him. If she could do anything to bring him some peace and sense of closure, she was right on it. But it was more than that. She wanted to be by Brooks's side, to give him the support and encouragement he might need to make that visit easier for him.

He was her friend, at the very least.

Eight

Brooks stood shoulder to shoulder with Beau on the steps of the ranch house as a black limo pulled up and parked. His father took a deep breath in anticipation of seeing his other son for the first time. "I'm the better-looking twin," Brooks said, smiling.

Beau's chuckle caught in his throat as Graham stepped out of the car. "My God."

"Yeah, I know." It was the typical reaction people had when they met the Newport twins for the first time. One face on two very different men. "Graham cut his hair a bit shorter than usual just so you could tell us apart."

"That's...smart," Beau said with a catch in his throat. Then he took off straight toward the limo, and Brooks followed.

Graham was reaching inside the limo to help his fiancée out of the car. It had been a while since Brooks had seen Eve Winchester. Because she was Sutton Winchester's daughter, she'd been an immediate adversary, and he hadn't liked her for a time, but Graham was head over heels in love with Eve, and Brooks had finally made his peace with her.

"Welcome, son," Beau said, trying his best to keep his composure. As Brooks sidled up next to him, he spotted tears glistening in his father's eyes. "I've waited a long time to meet you."

"So have I."

The two men embraced, and Brooks gave Eve a smile and a peck on the cheek.

Graham broke away first from the bear hug, taking Eve's hand and gently tugging her forward.

"Beau, I'd like you to meet Eve. My fiancée," Graham said.

Beau embraced Eve carefully. Despite the beige leather jacket and blouse underneath, Eve's baby bump couldn't be missed on her slender, athletic body. "Pleased you meet you, Eve. Welcome to my home, and congratulations on the little one. I couldn't be happier about all of this. My two sons, a new soon-to-be daughter and a grandbaby on the way."

"We're excited about it, too," Graham said, and there were smiles all around.

"I'd appreciate it if both of you called me Dad."

Graham shot Brooks a quick glance as if to say, *Finally. We have a dad.* "I think we'd both like to do that, right Eve?"

Her green eyes glittered. "Yes, of course."

Beau's lips curved up in a wide smile. Then he scratched his head, shifting his gaze from Graham to Brooks. "You two boys are certainly identical. That much can't be denied."

"No, but I've wanted to deny this guy was my brother

a time or two," Graham said, eyes twinkling. It was meant as a joke, but there was some truth there, too. They'd had their differences, especially lately. Graham hadn't exactly approved of the tactics Brooks had used to go after Sutton Winchester.

"Is that so?" Beau asked, puzzled.

"But it's all good now, right Graham?" Brooks was quick to point out.

"Right." His brother had the good grace to nod and agree. Brooks didn't want to dredge up the past, not now, when they'd finally found their family. It was all about the future now.

"Graham, I've gotten a chance to get to know Brooks, and he's told me some about the two of you growing up. I can't wait to get to know more about you and get acquainted with Eve. I have to admit…there was a time when I didn't t-think this day…would e-ever come." Beau choked up.

Graham's eyes watered a little, too. "Well, we're here now for a few days and we'll have lots of time to catch up."

"You'll stay for the holiday?"

"Of course."

"I'm happy to have you here for as long as you want. Let's get out of the weather. Come on inside. I'll show you to your room."

The chauffeur brought the bags in behind his family as they entered the house, but Brooks held back. There was something missing, or rather, *someone*.

He did a quick scan of the grounds, looking for signs of Ruby. Since their conversation two days ago, he hadn't stopped thinking about her or his reaction to seeing her with Trace Evans. Jealousy had surged as strong as he'd ever felt it, making him stop and assess exactly what was going on between him and Ruby. He'd never met a woman quite like her, and the thought of her going back to her ex put an ache in his gut.

His hands were tied right now. Ruby didn't want anyone to find out about their affair, and he couldn't openly date her. But he wanted to. And that surprised him. He'd never let a woman get close to him. He'd dated, but only halfheartedly and without any notion of commitment. He'd been married to his work and, more recently, too obsessed with finding his true parentage to pursue anyone seriously.

In the back of his mind, he'd always thought that if he met the right woman, all things would fall into place. That had never happened.

With Ruby, it wasn't just about sex. He'd figured that out straightaway. It wasn't even that she was forbidden in every sense of the word. Although that had been dangerously exciting. Everything about her seemed to turn him on. Her independence. Her spunk. The way she never gave in or gave up.

But love and romance had taken a backseat in his life lately, and he couldn't trust what he was feeling. He was out of his element here on Look Away and more vulnerable than he'd ever been before. Yet the more comfortable he was becoming on the ranch, the more he could begin to see himself with Ruby Lopez.

That's why he'd picked up the phone yesterday and placed a call to Roman Slater to find out more about Trace Evans. A secret little investigation from his friend, a top-notch PI, seemed in order. Brooks had a feeling Trace wasn't what he seemed. Beau didn't have a good opinion of the guy, either, and the last thing Brooks wanted was for Ruby to get hurt again.

Then his gaze hit upon the beautiful raven-haired Latina approaching the barn some distance away, and just seeing her again sent his pulse racing. Dressed in a black quilted vest, skin-tight jeans and tall riding boots, she was a vision in her work clothes. He couldn't believe how badly he wanted to be there when she met his brother. He wanted to be the one to introduce them.

"Ruby," he called out as he began to take long strides in her direction.

She'd finally spotted him and stopped in her tracks, staring at him from just outside the barn.

"Ruby," he said again, more softly this time, as he finally came face-to-face with her.

"Hi, Brooks." Her almond-shaped eyes widened in a curious stare, waiting for him to speak.

"Hi." He smiled like an idiot. He couldn't even pretend to be cool around her anymore. "Good seeing you."

She nodded but said nothing more. Yet the question in her eyes gave him pause.

"Are you working this afternoon?" he asked.

"Yeah, I was planning on taking Spirit out. Why?"

"My brother's here with his fiancée. They just arrived. I wanted to introduce you."

"Right now?"

He shrugged. He felt like an ass. And Ruby was trying not to look at him as if he'd lost his mind. Beau had invited everyone for dinner tonight to meet Eve and Graham, and as far as Brooks knew, all of the half brothers and Ruby were coming. "Well, yeah. I want you to meet Graham and Eve right now."

Ruby's brows drew together. "It's important to you?"

"It'll take only a minute or two, and yeah, it's important to me." Ruby was becoming *important* to him, more and more. It had taken seeing her with her ex to make him realize it. He was having some heavy-duty trepidation about his relationship with her and where it was going. Or not going. He'd grown up in a small family, without a father figure to look up to and sharing this part of himself with her meant a great deal to him.

Ruby eyed him for a short while, making up her mind, and then nodded. "I can do that."

"Okay, great." He wanted to wrap her up in his arms and kiss her senseless right there on the spot. He wanted to tell her she was more than a fling to him, more than a secret affair. She was beginning to fill up the voids inside him that he hadn't even known were there. But now was not the time to tell her.

"I'll just go to my place and change."

"Change? Good God, Ruby." He took in that shining sheet of black hair, those incredible cocoa eyes, the way her clothes hugged her body. "You don't need to change a thing. You're perfect just the way you are." He put out his hand. "Come with me?"

She flushed pink at his compliment. "Galahad. You do have a way about you."

And when Ruby put her hand in his, a sense of peace settled over him.

The introductions had gone well yesterday and Brooks was glad of it. Who knew Eve and Ruby would hit it off so well? The pretty green-eyed president of Elite Industries, soon to be his new sister-in-law, and Ruby, horse trainer extraordinaire, had talked fashion, country rock music, Cool Springs versus Chicago, and football, of all things. And because Graham and his fiancée were anxious to see some local Texas color, he and Ruby had brought them to the C'mon Inn for drinks tonight.

Now, as the Newport brothers nursed their whiskeys at the very place Brooks first set eyes on Ruby, the girls chatted and filled the corner booth with bright laughter. Both women were beyond pretty. Both were strong-willed and determined and accomplished.

Sitting beside his fiancée, Graham reached for Eve's hand, claiming the woman as his, while Brooks looked on, wishing he could do the same with Ruby. His brother kept his eyes on Ruby and him, and that twin thing happened. Graham had figured out something was up. Brooks would be hearing about it later. Graham wasn't one to keep his thoughts to himself.

The conversation turned to the feud between the Winchesters and the Newports, and Eve was trying to put things as delicately as she could. "So, you see, Brooks had this vendetta against my father and dug up some dirt—that proved not to be true, by the way—and went to the media to reveal the whole sordid scandal."

Ruby's gaze fell solidly on him. "That doesn't sound like Brooks."

"How well do you know my brother?" Graham was teasing, but the comment fell flat.

"I thought I knew him well enough," she answered.

"It's a long story and the bottom line is, we've resolved those differences," Brooks said in his own defense. "Haven't we, Eve?"

The uncertain look in Ruby's eyes was knifing through his gut. What she thought of him mattered, and he didn't want to lose his Galahad status with her. At the time, he'd had good reason to go after Winchester, but that was over and done with, and he'd made his peace with his brother's fiancée.

Eve was cordial enough to agree. "Yes. Thanks to Graham. He took back all the allegations and, well, stole my heart in the process. But I will confess that Brooks thought he was justified in going after my father. For a time, it was thought that my dad, Sutton, could've fathered the twins, since he and their mother had been in love. And Brooks thought Sutton was hiding something."

"As it turned out, Sutton is our younger brother's father," Graham said. "But our mom hid that pregnancy from Sutton and moved on with her life. He only recently found out Carson was his son."

Brooks sipped whiskey. The entire mess that was his life these past few years was coming to light. He wasn't ashamed of his actions—he'd thought he had good reason—but if he had to do it over again, he might've done some things differently.

His obsession with Sutton Winchester was coming to a close. The man was dying, and there'd been enough grief and heartache already over the mistakes and actions of the many people involved. It wasn't just Sutton. Brooks's mother wasn't entirely faultless. Nor was his Grandma Gerty. There was enough blame to go around.

"Well," Graham said. "It all turned out okay since I now have Eve and a baby on the way. So something wonderful came of all of it."

Brooks raised his glass. "I'll drink to that."

Graham brought his tumbler up, and the women raised their iced tea glasses.

"To family," Brooks said, staring into Ruby's eyes.

"To family," they all parroted, and then clinked glasses and sipped their drinks.

"Ruby, would you like something stronger?" Brooks asked.

"No thanks. I think I'll lay off tonight. I ate too much of Lupe's tamale pie at dinner."

"Gosh, me, too. It was delicious," Graham said, patting his stomach. "I hear you're a pretty good pool player, Ruby."

"She's a hustler," Brooks said, grinning.

"Is that right? Eve's pretty good, too."

The women exchanged glances.

"Want to?" Ruby asked.

"Sounds like fun," Eve replied.

"This I gotta see." Graham rose from his seat to let Eve scoot out.

Brooks did the same, and Ruby's exotic flowery scent wafted to his nose as she brushed by him. His lust had to give way to decorum. He and Ruby were in a standoff right now, and he doubted she'd be inviting him into her bed anytime soon.

The women headed to the pool table at the back of the room, secured pool sticks and cued up as Brooks and his brother leaned against the far wall. "Go easy on her, Ruby," Brooks called. "She's a guest in Cool Springs."

"Go easy, nothing," Eve countered, the fierceness in her eyes indicating she was ready for battle. "Don't hold back, Ruby. I can handle it."

Graham chuckled and said quietly, "She can. She's pretty amazing."

"It's good to see you happy, bro."

"Yeah, I am. I managed not to blow it with Eve. Thank God for that. And meeting Beau was pretty great, too. I wasn't sure about any of this, coming here to Texas and being brought into a whole new family. But Beau's made it real easy. He's a good man, and there was no awkwardness between us."

"Because I paved the way," Brooks said, giving his brother grief. "As usual."

"Smart-ass. So what's with you and Ruby? And don't tell me nothing's going on. I can practically see the steam rising between the two of you from across the booth. Have you fallen for her?"

Brooks drew oxygen into his lungs and kept his voice low. The women were preoccupied; Eve was about to make the first shot. "I'm in the process, I think." What the hell kind of answer was that? He was in the process of falling for her? While trying to keep things light with Ruby, it had gotten hot and heavy real fast. "It's complicated."

"I hear you. Couldn't be more complicated than me falling for Winchester's daughter, now, could it?"

"I don't know about that. Ruby's like a daughter to Beau, and if I hurt her, there'll be hell to pay. Not exactly the impression I want to make on our father."

"Hell, man. Make it a priority not to hurt her, then."

Brooks stared at his brother, letting his words sink in. Was it that easy? Did he want Ruby? He darted a glance at her. She was taking aim, her hot body stretched across the pool table, her eyes laser-focused, her kissable mouth pursed tight as she drew back the stick and *clack*, the cue ball sailed across the table and hit its mark. The striped ball dropped into the side pocket.

Hell yeah, he wanted Ruby. From the moment he'd first laid eyes on her right here at the C'mon Inn, he'd been drawn to her. She had substance and class and a sassy mouth that made him smile, even when that sass was aimed at him. He admired her passion and knowledge of horses and her open method of teaching that came straight from the heart. He couldn't imagine not seeing her day in and day out. Not speaking to her and not laughing with her. Up until this moment, he hadn't thought about the time when he'd have to go back to Chicago for good.

He'd never been really serious about a woman before. For one, he'd been preoccupied with work, striving for and finally attaining the financial independence he'd craved ever since the more humble days of his youth. He'd worked hard building the Newport Corporation and didn't have time to play much. As a result, women had come and gone in his life. Rightfully so. He hadn't been ready for a strong commitment. He had only so much to give, and getting serious with the opposite sex had taken a backseat to all else. More recently, he'd been too caught up in meeting his father after years of searching to let his mind go anywhere else. But now that he was faced with the possibility of losing Ruby to her ex-boyfriend, he had to make a stand.

Sooner rather than later.

But first, there was something he had to do.

And he wanted Ruby by his side.

Hutchinson's Nursing Home, twenty miles outside Cool Springs, sat nestled inside brick walls and a set of wrought iron gates. The grounds were groomed carefully. Right now, the cold Texas weather prevented any flowers from blooming in the beds next to the long, sweeping veranda, but Ruby could picture them thriving there in the spring, their color cheering up the dementia patients who would sit in patio chairs outside to get a little air.

Brooks rested his arms on the steering wheel, staring at the large mansion-like brick home with its pretty white shutters. He sighed. "This is it."

It wasn't going to be a loving homecoming, this much Ruby knew. But she understood his need to come here for closure, while his brother Graham had no desire to meet his grandfather. The twins may have looked exactly alike, but they were two very different men in the way they dealt with life.

Ruby reached for Brooks's hand and squeezed. "We

can make this quick," she said. "And I'll be with you every step of the way."

"Thanks." Brooks rubbed the back of his neck and gave her a solemn look. "I don't think I could do this without you." His blue eyes melted her heart. She felt honored and a little awed that Brooks had counted on her so much. That he needed her.

It was one thing to be wanted.

But to be needed by such a strong man was something else entirely.

"I'm here, Brooks. Let's go meet your grandfather."

Once they were inside a few minutes later, a nurse escorted them to the visitors' room, where they were told to stand just inside the doorway. The woman walked over to a man with a shock of pearl-gray hair seated by a window and spoke a few words to him. He barely acknowledged her, but he turned his head slightly to the door, his expression blank but for a sliver of light entering his eyes.

Ruby felt Brooks freeze up, his body stiffening. He closed his eyes, and she tightened her hold on his hand. "It's going to be okay," she whispered.

"Yeah," he said quietly, but he hesitated.

The nurse waved them over and placed two chairs by the window to face the old man, who was slumped over in his seat.

"Ready?" Ruby asked.

Brooks nodded. She was by his side as they walked over and sat down.

"Hello," Ruby said first. "I'm Ruby."

"You're a pretty thing," the old man said in a childlike voice. "I don't know you, do I?"

Ruby shook her head. "No."

He blinked and seemed to stare straight through her.

The nurse put her hand on Bill Turner's shoulder. "Mr. Turner, this is your grandson, Brooks."

"My grandson?" Bill stared blankly at Brooks. "I don't have a grandson."

"You have two grandsons," Brooks said. "Twins. I have a brother named Graham."

As the nurse walked off, the man began shaking his head.

"They are your daughter Mary Jo's children," Ruby offered.

At the mention of Mary Jo, Bill Turner's eyes switched on. "My daughter? She sits by the fireplace and reads. She likes to read. Quiet little girl. Where is Mary Jo? Is she coming?"

"No, she's not coming today," Brooks said, moisture pooling in his eyes.

Ruby ached inside as she watched Brooks swipe at his tears.

"Maybe she'll come another day," the old man said. "I would like to see her."

"Maybe she will," Ruby said. "How do you like it here, Mr. Turner?"

He shrugged. "I guess I like it fine."

"The people seem nice."

"Where's Mary Jo?" He looked toward the doorway. "She likes to read. Her nose is always in a book. She's a smart girl."

"She is a smart girl," Brooks managed to answer. "And s-she loves to read."

"Do I know you?" Bill Turner's brows gathered. The wrinkles and blankness on his face hid the handsome man he'd once been. "I don't think I know you."

"No," Brooks said, his gaze turning Ruby's way, hopelessness in his expression. He tried again. "You don't know me. But I'm your grandson. Mary Jo was my mother. You are my grandfather."

He shot Brooks another blank stare. "I'm your grandfather?"

Brooks nodded. "Yes."

Bill Turner looked out the window, focusing on a bird hopping on the ground beside a mesquite tree just a few yards away.

"Mr. Turner?" Ruby put her hand on his arm.

He swiveled his head slowly back to them. "I used to build things, you know. I built my own house. This is not my house. I didn't build this."

"No, but it's your home now, Mr. Turner," Ruby said quietly.

"Yes. It's my home now." The light in his eyes dimmed. Then he popped his head up, in search of the nurse. "I think it's time for lunch."

Brooks stared at him for several heartbeats, then sighed and rose from the chair. Ruby witnessed a depth of sadness and pain in his eyes she'd never seen before. "We have to go now, Mr. Turner," he said, taking Ruby's hand again. "Have a good lunch."

They exited without saying another word, and Brooks stopped as they reached his parked car. "It's so damn unfair."

"What?" Her stomach churned. She could guess what Brooks was about to say.

"He's like a child. He doesn't remember his abuse. He doesn't remember hurting his family. He's blacked out the bad times."

"You're angry," Ruby said.

"I'm...yeah, I guess I'm pretty pissed. I wanted to meet the son of a bitch and lay into him about my mother. Someone needed to defend her and look out for her.

Someone had to stand up to him. Even though I'm years late, I had it in my head I'd come here and tell the old guy off." He fisted his hands. "But he's in a world of his own. Nothing I'd say to him would sink in."

"Probably not, Brooks. That's the sad thing about dementia. He's trapped in his own head," Ruby said.

Brooks dropped his gaze to the ground, shaking his head.

Ruby stepped closer and stared into his handsome face, which was tightly lined in raw pain. He was fighting to keep the tears away. "It's okay to feel all the things you're feeling. Coming here will give you closure, trust me. It will. When you get back home and think about this, you'll feel better. You'll begin to feel whole again."

Brooks slowly wrapped his arms around her waist and drew her closer. She laid her head on his chest. His heart was beating so fast she placed her hand there to calm him, to give him the balm he needed right now. Nestled in his embrace, she waited for the beats to slow to a normal pace.

"How come you know me so well, Ruby?" He brushed the top of her head with a kiss.

"I just do, I guess."

He tightened his hold, locking her against his body as they swayed ever so slightly together to the music. Electricity sizzled. It always did when they were this close. "You feel so damn good in my arms."

"Humph."

"I didn't mean it that way."

"I know how you meant it, Brooks." He welcomed her comfort. He needed her here, and she wouldn't want it any other way. "I'm just giving you jazz."

"Because that's what you do."

"Yeah, that's what I do."

"Don't ever stop doing that," he whispered into her ear.

Something fierce and protective crackled and snapped inside her. And in that moment, Ruby knew she never wanted to stop giving him *anything*. She'd fallen in love with him. She loved him so much, she wanted to take away his pain, absorb it and tuck it away in some deep, dark place, never to return. She loved Brooks Newport.

But did she still love Trace, too?

Right now, in Brooks's arms, she was giving him all he needed. She wouldn't think about the future and the fact that Brooks would be leaving after the holidays.

He had a home in Chicago.

A thriving business there.

And none of it included her.

The next day, Ruby licked around her cone of dark chocolate fudge ice cream, enjoying every second of her indulgence. Sitting beside her at the Fudge You Ice Cream Factory, Eve was doing the same, digging into her chocolate cone, and Serena, who was happy to join them today, sat across the booth, devouring a dish of French vanilla scoops topped with caramel sauce.

"Yum," Eve said, crunching down on the sugar cone. "I can't remember the last time I had ice cream."

"You don't crave ice cream?" Serena asked. "Isn't that the go-to craving when you're pregnant?"

"That's what I hear. But for me it's more potato chips and dip. Give me salt and I'm happy. But I'd never turn down good ice cream. If I don't watch it, I'll be floating away like a balloon soon."

"Eve, you look fantastic. You don't have to watch anything," Ruby said, hiding the fact that it was her craving for ice cream and not Eve's that had brought them here today.

Eve chuckled. "Thanks for that. The ice cream is amazing. And so is the company." Eve smiled at both of them.

"It's your reward for beating me at pool," Ruby added. "I told you if you won, I'd have something fun in store for you." Fun and indulgent. Ruby needed that, too, now more than ever. Coming here with Eve and Serena was much better than suffering alone at her cottage and digging into a pint or two of decadent ice cream in front of the television set, pining over the state of her love life.

How could one man make her so happy and so sad at the same time?

Brooks had been hurting yesterday and it was only natural for her to comfort him, to allow him time to grieve over his grandfather...because that's exactly what he had done. He'd met Bill Turner for the first time and said farewell to the old man, probably never to see him again, all in one afternoon. The ordeal had shaken Brooks, and seeing him that way had sent her own wobbly emotions out of whack.

"Actually, it's really sweet of you to entertain me today while Graham and Brooks are out riding with Beau," Eve said. "Graham couldn't wait to ride on one of his dad's Thoroughbreds."

Ruby turned her attention back to the girls. "Are you kidding? My stomach is doing somersaults right now. It's been too long since I've had Fudge You ice cream. I'm happy to do it."

"This does beat eating lunch," Serena said. "I'm glad I'm on winter break right now so I could join you."

"Serena is the new principal of Cool Springs High School," Ruby explained to Eve. "The kids love her over there. She's made going to the principal's office a cool thing."

"Oh, really? How so?" Eve asked, her brows lifting as she turned to Serena.

"Well, there are still times it sucks getting summoned to the principal's office," Serena said, "but now, if students do something remarkable like helping a fellow student out of a jam or achieving higher grades than expected because of hard work, I reward them."

"She takes them to lunch," Ruby said, "or lets them skip gym for a week, or gives them a season pass to the football games."

"Among other things," Serena said. "It gives the kids an incentive to do well. They seem to like it."

"They sure do," Ruby said, praising her friend. "And they like Serena a whole helluva lot more than we cared for Mr. Hale, our principal back in the day. That man never cracked a smile."

"I like your creative approach," Eve said. "I can see why the kids adore you."

Ruby gobbled up her cone before the girls were halfway through theirs. She gazed longingly at the mounds of ice cream under the glass case, wishing she could have another cone or maybe a sundae with whipped cream and cherries on top. What was wrong with her? Even with the Trace-and-Brooks-induced stomachache she'd had lately, her appetite was voracious.

Too soon, all the cones were history, and Serena was rising from her seat. "Sorry to dash out, but I've got an errand list a mile long for this afternoon. It was nice meeting you, Eve. I hope to see you again."

"Same here, Serena," Eve said. "I'm glad you joined us."

"Serena's coming to Look Away for our Christmas party, so you'll see her again," Ruby said.

"That's great," Eve said. "Well then, I'll see you in a few days."

"I'm looking forward to it. Bye girls." Serena exited the shop.

"She's nice," Eve said. "You've been friends a long time?"

"We have. Serena's like a sister to me."

"And Beau's like a father."

"He is. He's a good man. I'm fortunate to have the Prestons. We're pretty tight."

Eve sipped water and smiled. "I can see that. It's really refreshing. My family…well, we've had our differences. But my sisters and I are close. You know, in a sense, you and I will be sisters, too. In-laws, but sisters."

"Yeah, I'm happy about that."

"So am I," Eve said. And then, suddenly she gripped her belly, and the blood drained from her face. "Oh."

"What's wrong?" Ruby rose halfway out of her seat.

Eve waved her off. "Nothing. Just a bout of queasiness. I get that sometimes. But I'm… I'm okay."

Ruby sat down, relieved.

Seconds ticked by before the color returned to Eve's face. "Pregnancy sometimes knocks you for a loop, you know."

Ruby didn't know. None of her friends had children yet, so she didn't have any firsthand knowledge of the subject. She knew how mares gave birth and had pulled foals on the ranch under the supervision of her father, but the whole human pregnancy thing was new to her. "How do you mean?"

"Well, first off, you get all these weird sensations. In the beginning, you're hungry all the time and feel like you can't get enough food in you. One day, and I'm ashamed to admit this, I consumed two omelets for breakfast and a thick foot-long sandwich for lunch, and I still had room for a barbeque chicken dinner with chocolate cake for dessert. I inhaled food in those early weeks. I couldn't believe it."

"Eating for two?"

"More like an army," Eve said, her eyes twinkling. "But that's passed. Now I'm sensitive all over." She pointed to her chest. "I'm full and tender here all the time."

Ruby froze up, holding her breath tight in her throat. The only thing moving were her eyes. And they were blinking rapidly. She'd been feeling those very sensations lately, too. If she put her bra on too hastily, her nipples would tingle and actually hurt. The pain was foreign to her, and it would take a while before it disappeared. She hadn't thought much of it, but now, as she took another glance at the mountain of ice cream sitting in the refrigerator case, her stomach grumbled. She was still hungry. She could do major damage to those big cartons. Chocolate. Strawberry. Vanilla. And every other flavor.

Good God. Had she missed her period this month?

"Ruby?"

She tried to calculate back in her mind.

"Ruby, you're turning green right before my eyes. Are you okay?"

Ruby stopped blinking and focused on what Eve was saying. She forced herself to recover from the shock and shoved her doubts to the back of her mind. "I'm fine. Um, are you ready to see the best Cool Springs has to offer by way of shopping? It's no Rodeo Drive, but there's a shopping district that has some pretty neat boutiques."

Eve's brows knit together as she subtly scrutinized her, making Ruby wonder if she'd actually fooled her. "Sure, I'd love to. We can walk off the ice cream calories." Eve reached across the table to touch her hand. "Thanks for making me feel welcome in Cool Springs. I think of us as friends already." There was a flicker in Eve's eyes that said she was willing to listen if Ruby needed to talk.

"I feel the same way," she replied genuinely.

Astute as Eve was, Ruby suspected she had already guessed about her involvement with Brooks. But admitting it would make it all too real, and there would be questions she couldn't answer. And feelings she'd have to face. About Trace. About Brooks. And the wrinkle that she might be carrying a child even though she'd been very careful, was all too much for her right now.

It was better to put her head in the sand and let the world keep on turning for a while.

Nine

Brooks gave the living area of his cabin a final once-over. Dozens of roses he'd had flown in from his home-town were arranged in vases and glass bowls all around the room. Their unequalled beauty and sweet scent reminded him of the woman who had stolen his heart. He had pillar candles ready to flicker at the strike of a match. Ideally tonight, after the Christmas party, he would finally show Ruby how much he cared about her.

It had been days since he'd touched her, days since he'd held her in his arms and kissed the daylights out of her. He totally understood that Ruby was torn in two by the return of her ex. She'd banked her future on Trace Evans and had envisioned a life with him. And Trace had failed her. The guy wasn't good enough to shine Ruby's boots, and tonight was Brooks's chance to win her over. To show her that they needed more time together, that what they'd started at the C'mon Inn was worth pursuing.

In just a few hours, he'd be face-to-face with her, and he wouldn't let up until Ruby was his.

A knock at his door shook him out of his own head. It was his brother Graham.

"Hey."

"Hey. Thanks for showing up on time."

"My brother calls and I come."

Graham stepped inside the cabin, immediately took in the romantic setting, lifted his nose in the air and grinned. "Smells like a funeral home in here."

Oh man, Graham was such a pain sometimes. "Don't make me sorry I let you in here."

"You're doing this for Ruby?" Graham walked farther into the room.

"Yep. You know I don't like to lose. And Ruby is worth winning."

Graham eyed him carefully. "Just don't blow it, Brooks. Seems weird saying this, but she's family now. And you'd have the entire Preston house come down on you if Ruby gets hurt."

"I don't intend to hurt her," Brooks said, hearing the commitment in his voice.

"Man, you're really hooked, aren't you? I mean, you two are polar opposites."

"Let me worry about that. And we're not that different when it comes right down to it."

"Hey, I have my hands full with wedding plans and the baby coming. I'm not going to say another word, except you deserve to be happy." He looked over the place again. "Nice touch with the candles. Ruby will love what you've done. I hope it works out."

The sincerity in Graham's voice made up for his crap from earlier. "I appreciate that."

"So, what's up?"

"I've been thinking."

"About Bill Turner? I do plan to see him one day, but after what you told me, apparently there's no rush. He won't know who I am, right?"

"Probably not, but if you need to see him, to meet with him, I wouldn't stop you. Ruby said..." Brooks paused. Everything Ruby had told him was true. She'd gotten him through a tough day, and that was only one of the reasons he was crazy about her.

"What did Ruby say?" Graham asked.

"A lot, and I'll tell you later, but first I want to run something by you. I think I'm ready."

"Ready?" His brother gestured to the decked-out room. "Obviously, if you've gone to so much trouble for Ruby—"

"I'm talking about my vendetta against Winchester. I think I'm through, Graham. Once and for all. I wanted to get your opinion. I want to make peace."

His brother's brows shot up. "Really?"

"Yeah. It's time. Being here at Look Away has cleared my head some. I'm not the same man I once was. Vengeance can be taken only so far before it destroys you. Coming here made me see that I want to look to the future and not bury myself in the past. What's done is done."

"I like what I'm hearing, Brooks. And Eve will be grateful if you could put the past behind you. She's come here to support me in meeting my father while her own father is very ill. Sutton isn't long for this earth. Eve, Nora and Grace are struggling with all of it. I mean, say what you might about the man, but he is their father, and he's dying."

Brooks drew breath in his lungs. He'd had a long-running feud with Sutton Winchester and had come to learn the man hadn't been guilty of many of the things Brooks had once believed. Winchester's biggest crime had been to love his mother, Cynthia, so much that he hadn't revealed her secrets. In a way, that had been honorable. Though it had caused the Newport sisters a lot of grief, Brooks's anger had softened recently. "Yeah, I know."

"I've already put the past behind me, for Eve's sake and for the sake of our baby. It's no good clinging to a grudge. I'm a happier man for it and I think you would be, too." Graham slapped him on the back. "You've got my full support."

"Wonderful. I'll make that happen soon. Now get out of here. I've got to get ready to sweep Ruby off her feet tonight."

Shortly after his conversation with his brother, Brooks got dressed in a Western tux, a bolo tie and a black Stetson. He took a final look at himself in the mirror. This was it. He would make his stand for Ruby's affection tonight and, he hoped, make this Christmas holiday one of the best ever for both of them.

Any doubts warring in his head were quickly replaced with positive thoughts as he exited his cabin and approached the Preston home. Surrounding oak, cottonwood and white birch trees glimmered with thousands of lights. The path leading up to the house sparkled from the ground up, and an array of colorful twinkling lights outlined the beautiful home's architecture.

Peace settled in his heart.

A part of him had always known there was something more for him than city life. A part of him had always known something was missing. Now, as he gazed at this home in all its magnificent yet simple splendor, a sense of true belonging nestled deep down in his bones.

Beau greeted him at the door with a big papa bear

hug. The man was not ashamed of wearing his emotions on his sleeve, and Brooks hugged him back with the same enthusiasm. "Welcome, son. The party's just getting started." Beau smiled wide, his eyes bright. "My dream of having my whole family under one roof is the best gift I could ever receive."

Brooks got that all too well. Except for Carson, everyone who mattered most to him now was right here at Look Away.

"Let me introduce you and Graham to some of my closest friends."

Brooks followed his father into the house. But as he began shaking many hands and making small talk with Beau's neighbors and friends, he kept one eye on the front door.

And then she walked in.

Ruby.

He swallowed a quick breath. And then excused himself from a conversation that couldn't compete with the stunning creature removing her coat at the front door. She wore her hair partly up in a sweep secured with rhinestones, the rest of her raven tresses flowing down her back. The dress she wore was ruby red, the color perfect for the holidays and perfect on her. The dress exposed her olive skin, dipping into a heart shape in the front that cradled her full breasts.

His heart beat wildly at the vision she made. And suddenly, his legs were moving and his focus was solely on her. He couldn't seem to get to her fast enough as he strode the distance to put him face-to-face with the Ruby of his fantasies.

"Ruby, you look incredible." He hadn't seen her since he'd visited his grandfather. "That dress on you...is a knockout."

"Thank you." She gave him a smile. "You do a pretty good version of a cowboy for a city dude."

"I tried."

"I love the tie on you." She gave it a sharp tug. "And the hat."

He removed it immediately. "Uh, sorry. I, uh…" Why was he tongue-tied?

"It's cool, Brooks." She took the hat from his hand and set it back on his head. "I like the look. Don't take it off on my account."

He ran his hands down his face. Tonight any guests with eyes in their heads would figure out that Brooks had it bad for Ruby, and he wasn't about to hold back. No more pretending. No more hiding out. He was ready to make his claim on her. "Come with me for a second?"

"Sure, but where are we going?"

"You'll see." He took her hand and tugged her through the festively decorated rooms until they reached the kitchen doorway, out of sight to all but a half-dozen caterers. Her knowing eyes glittered. "Look up."

Mistletoe again, and this time she understood exactly where she was and what he was about to do.

He brought his mouth to hers. From the moment their lips met he was a goner, lost in the taste and pleasure and sweetness of her. It was too hot, too amazing to let up. He'd waited for her, craved her and now she was in his arms and he didn't give a good goddamn who saw them or what they thought about it. He was consumed by Ruby. She was his anchor. He'd never had feelings this strong or powerful. The little throaty sounds she was making turned him inside out. She wasn't immune to him. They worked. And he had to make her see that.

"Ruby," he murmured near her ear, the desperation coming through clearly in his voice. "I miss you like hell."

She lifted up on tiptoe and whispered, "If you're talking about making love, I miss you, too."

"Oh, yeah, I am," he said, but he was talking about much more. And he had to bide his time until the end of the evening to show her just how he felt about her. "For starters."

"Starters? Sounds promising, Galahad." Her breath fanned over the side of his face, making his nerves go raw. This woman was a tease, but he didn't mind as long as her teasing was aimed his way. At least she wasn't refusing him. Had she made up her mind about Trace?

"Come back to the cabin with me. We can leave the party right now."

Ruby set a hand on his chest and tilted her head to look into his eyes. "No, we can't. Beau has waited too long to have you here with him."

She had a penchant for being rational and right, and if Brooks wasn't so damn head over heels for her, that would have annoyed the life out of him.

"Just enjoy the party, Brooks."

"As long as you're by my side, I can do that." God, the truth in that was powerful.

"That's where I want to be, too," she whispered.

Brooks breathed a sigh of relief. He had to be respectful of his father and his new family. Wisely, Ruby had put him in his place. He was glad of it, but it was torture just the same.

Christmas music with a country twang streamed into the house, and it seemed everyone was beginning to make their way to the backyard to listen.

"It's a local country band," Ruby offered. "They're pretty good. Beau's hired them for the night."

"Yeah, he told me about them. TLC or something?"

"It stands for Tender Loving Country," she said.

"There's a dance floor set up. Will you dance with me?" He offered her his hand.

"Of course."

And they walked outside hand in hand and danced under the electric warmth of strategically placed heaters. The night was cool, but thankfully devoid of Texas breezes that could make your hair stand on end. Brooks didn't need the artificial heat blasting from the heaters, though; he was already revved up enough inside just holding Ruby in his arms.

"They *are* pretty good," he whispered, nuzzling her hair. She smelled of something tropical and exotic. He brought her as close as he possibly dared. He didn't want to make her uncomfortable—he'd gotten her message loud and clear—so he'd bide his time until he could get her alone in his cabin.

Where he would lay his heart on the line.

They danced every dance until the band took a break, and then Brooks led her off the dance floor. She began fanning herself. "That was fun, but I'm afraid I've got to go...*powder my nose.*"

Brooks chuckled. Ruby was something. He was about to suggest escorting her, but she was snatched away immediately by Eve and Serena. What was it about women going to the john in groups? He'd never understand that.

Toby walked up and caught him red-handed staring at Ruby's shapely ass. "So, you've got the hots for Ruby, huh?"

Brooks gave his half brother a sideways glance, unsure how to answer that.

"It's okay. We get it."

"We?" Brooks turned to face him.

"My brothers and me. We've all had a crush on her at one point or another in our lives, but Dad put a halt to any of that. Let's just say he didn't nip it in the bud—he slashed it to the ground until it was crushed to a pulp. But that was years ago, when we were teens."

Brooks swallowed hard. "That so?"

"Yeah, she's just our little sis now."

"Beau's plenty protective," Brooks said, his voice trailing off as he stated the obvious. He felt an ache in the pit of his stomach.

Toby noticed his change in demeanor and must've taken pity on him. "Actually, when Dad was out here watching the two of you dancing, he was smiling. Maybe he doesn't think it's so bad, you and Ruby. I'd say go for it."

Clay walked up, looking distracted as his gaze scoured the guests milling about. "Have you guys seen Ruby?"

"Who wants to know?" Toby asked.

"Trace Evans is outside the house. He's pretty liquored up, and he's asking to see her."

Brooks blinked. "He's crashing the party?"

Clay shrugged. "I suppose. He wasn't invited."

Now the back of Brooks's hair really did stand on end. He didn't want the guy within fifty feet of Ruby, much less snatching her away from the Christmas party in a drunken state. "I'll take care of it."

Toby gave Clay a crooked smile. "He's a Preston, all right."

It was a compliment Brooks appreciated. "Tell Ruby I'll be back soon." And then he stalked off, ready to face his rival head-on.

Brooks found Trace leaning against his pickup truck, taking a chug from a bottle of whiskey. Wearing jeans and a chambray shirt, his hat tipped back off his forehead, he wasn't exactly dressed for the occasion.

"What do you want, Evans?"

Trace shot back a hard glare. "Ruby. I want Ruby."

Brooks ground his teeth at Trace's possessive tone. "She's not coming out here to see you."

"She'll see me. I have things to say to her."

Brooks held his temper in check. "Now's not the time. She's enjoying the party."

Trace's lips pulled into a twist, and he pointed his index finger straight at Brooks. "You don't speak for her, Newport."

"Why don't you get the hell out of here and sober up. Better yet, I'll get someone to take you home. You're in no shape to drive."

Trace threw his head back in a hearty laugh and gestured with the bottle. The amber liquid inside sloshed back and forth. "What? You mean this? You're obviously not a Texan. This is nothing. Trust me, greenhorn, I'm not blistered. And I need to see Ruby."

"Why, so you can lie to her and hurt her again?"

"You don't know squat about me and Ruby. We had something real special and I made a mistake, is all."

"You made *a lot* of mistakes. Like screwing a married woman. Yeah, I know about your mistakes, Evans. You owe thousands from gambling, and you got kicked off the rodeo circuit for banging the rodeo boss's wife. Now you need Ruby to bail you out."

Evans came toward Brooks with venom in his eyes. "What are you doing snooping into my private life?"

Brooks stood firm. He could take Trace if it came to a fistfight. "Ruby deserves much better. So yeah, I hired an investigator and found out all your dirty little secrets."

"You son of a bitch. I was going to tell her all about it. That's why I needed to see her."

"It's too late to confess your sins, Evans. Just give up."

"I have no plans of doing that. Ruby loves me."

"Yeah, well, she's been loving me lately."

Evans's free hand fisted, and his eyes hardened to stones. "I should knock you to hell and back."

"I'm shaking in my boots." Brooks shouldn't have let the guy get to him. He would've never betrayed Ruby's trust like that otherwise. He wasn't a kiss-and-tell kind of guy. But hearing Evans say Ruby loved him was like a knife twisting in his gut.

"How much cash would it take for you to leave Ruby alone?" Brooks asked. "I want you out of her life, *for good.* Twenty-five thousand? It's enough to cover your gambling debts. I'll write you a check right now."

"Asshole. You think everything can be settled with money."

"*Fifty* grand?"

Evans's brows rose in interest. "You bartering for Ruby?"

"I'm trying to protect her." The man's pride was keeping him from grabbing the brass ring. Brooks had to press him. "I'll make it a *hundred* grand. You want the deal or not?"

A loud gasp came from behind them, and his stomach clenched in dread as he pivoted around. Ruby stood just five feet away, her arms tight around her middle and her eyes spitting red-hot fire. The burn seared through him like a scorching poker. "Ruby, how long have you been out here?"

"Long enough to hear you both acting like jerks."

"Hey, he was the one trying to buy me off," Evans shouted.

"And you were about to accept my offer."

"Don't listen to him, Ruby." Evans took a step toward her.

She put up a halting hand that said, *Don't you dare come close*. Unfortunately, the gesture was meant for Brooks, too. "I. Am. Not. Going. To. Listen. To. This. I'm done with both of you. You can go straight to hell." With that, she spun on her heel and marched away, her shoulders ramrod stiff but the rest of her body trembling.

Brooks watched helplessly as she walked away. Her words cut deep, but nothing hurt as much as seeing the disappointment and accusation on her face.

"Looks like you blew it, Newport."

"Screw you, Evans."

Brooks took off after her, following her to the steps of the house. "Ruby, wait!"

She spun around instantly. The big, fat tears welling in her eyes stopped him in his tracks. "Leave me alone, Brooks."

Serena and Eve stepped out of the house just then and, noting Ruby's upset state, immediately ushered her into the house, flanking her like a human fortress. With a turn of their heads, the two women shot him glares that could have downed an F-16.

He ran his hands over his face, pulling the skin taut. Then he punched the air out of frustration. He should've known Ruby was enough of her own woman not to need his interference. Had he learned nothing from the past?

Now she was hurt and furious.

It was the last thing he wanted.

And yet somehow, he ended up being the bad guy in all of this.

In black spandex and her comfy Horses Are a Woman's Best Friend sweatshirt, Ruby sat on her sofa, going over the events from last night in her head. Her emotions had been on a high after spending the better part

of the evening with Brooks, but when she walked outside and found him in a bidding war *over her* with Trace,
she couldn't believe her ears. Brooks had been trying to
pay her ex off to stop pursuing her, as if Ruby couldn't
make that decision on her own. As if he had the right to
decide for her. The worst of it was facing the fact that
she really didn't know Brooks Newport at all. Was he
the ruthless manipulator that she'd read and heard about?
Was he trying to control her? Or had he really believed
he was protecting her?

Her phone buzzed and she glanced at the text. It was
Brooks again. He'd called and texted her last night until
after midnight, apologizing in every way imaginable.
She'd refused to answer any of his messages, but in each
he'd called himself an imbecile, a jerk or a fool for hurting her, and that had put a smile on her face. The lofty,
self-confident man was trying. She had to give him that.

But today's text was different. Today he wrote,

I'm going to Chicago today to make all things right in
my life. And then I'm coming back...for you.

A warm shiver ran up and down her body. "Oh, Galahad."

Her doorbell chimed and she rose, checking the peephole before opening the door. Eve had called earlier to
check up on her and invited herself over. Ruby was grateful she had. She needed a good friend today, and Eve was
quickly becoming that. "Good morning."

Eve's warm smile immediately faded. "Oh, Ruby. You
look exhausted. I bet you didn't get a wink of sleep."

"Maybe an hour or two. Come in."

"Are you sure? I can come back later if you want to
rest."

"Heavens, no. Moping around isn't my thing. I could use the company."

Eve entered and wrapped her arms around Ruby, pulling her in tight. The hug was exactly what she needed at the moment. "I'm sorry you're upset."

"I'm...yeah. I guess *upset* is the right word. My emotions are all over the place."

"I'm here if you want to talk," Eve said.

Spilling her heart out wasn't easy, but Eve was a thoughtful listener and someone Ruby knew she could trust. They entered the living room and took seats on the sofa next to each other.

Ruby faced Eve and didn't hold back. She told Eve everything about Trace, how she'd fallen for him and waited for him like a fool all those months. She explained how he'd returned to Cool Springs and laid his heart on the line, trying his best to make up with her, offering her everything she'd wanted from him, a life...a future. None of the things Brooks had ever hinted at. She explained about meeting Brooks for the first time at the C'mon Inn and how they'd hit it off from the start. How surprised she'd been the next day to find out that he was one of Beau's long lost sons.

Last night, after dancing with Brooks, she'd finally come to realize she wasn't in love with Trace anymore. And that was before she'd heard about his indiscretions. That was before she'd learned he was trying to use her to bail him out of a financial jam.

"As painful as it is, Ruby, at least you know the truth about Trace Evans," Eve said. "You can cross him off your list. I'm sorry he hurt you, but you dodged a bullet. And don't be mad at me for saying this—Brooks did you a service by exposing him."

Ruby lowered her head and rubbed at her temples.

"My brain knows you're right, Eve. But my heart…isn't so sure."

"According to Graham, Brooks is crazy about you. Believe me when I say this. He wouldn't have gone to this extreme with Trace unless he was all in with you. Brooks has his flaws when it comes to confronting adversaries, but he's passionate in what he believes and a really good guy."

"Do good guys take off at the first sign of trouble?" She searched Eve's earnest face, hoping to gain better perspective.

Eve took hold of her hand, and her warmth seeped into all of Ruby's cold places. "He went to Chicago for all the right reasons, Ruby. He's making his peace with the past. Graham and I believe it's so he can come to you with an open heart, as cliché as that sounds."

"No, that sounds…pretty good. If I can believe it. He hasn't stopped messaging me."

"Maybe you can cut the guy some slack?"

Ruby smiled. "Maybe."

Eve took both of her hands now, holding her gently at the wrists, and adjusted her position on the sofa to face her full-on. "I have something for you, Ruby. I hope I haven't overstepped a line here, but…" She released her wrists to dig into her handbag and came up holding a pink rectangular box. "Being in your shoes a few months ago, I kind of recognize the signs," she said, softening her voice.

Ruby's eyes widened. She wasn't ready for this. But maybe it was time to stop procrastinating. It wasn't like Ruby Lopez not to face life head-on. She took the box from Eve and, seeing the concern on her face, gave her a smile. "Do you always walk around with an extra pregnancy test in your purse?"

Eve chuckled. "Oh, Ruby, I was worried how you

would take it. You might think us city people are too pushy."

Ruby shook her head. "Yeah, well, city folk are more upfront, I will say that. Country folk tend to gossip behind your back. It all washes out the same."

"It's okay, then?"

"Of course. I should've done this myself. I think I needed the nudge."

"You think you might be?" Eve's voice escalated to a squeak, and a twinkle of hope sparkled in her eyes.

Ruby shrugged. "I don't know. I'm eating like the world is ending tomorrow, and lately I get supertired. Emotionally, I'm a wreck. But that just might be Brooks's doing. I guess... I'll find out soon. Thank you, Eve."

"You're welcome. I'll get going now and let you rest." Eve stood up and Ruby didn't try to stop her, although resting was the last thing on her mind. Her grip on the pregnancy test tightened. She had some major thinking to do, no matter what she found out.

She walked Eve to the front door, and they hugged. "Call me if you need to talk again," Eve whispered.

"I will. And thanks again." Ruby closed the door behind her and leaned against it. Sighing, she glanced at the pink box with light purple lettering in her hand. To think, peeing on a stick could change her life forever. Ruby placed her hand on her belly, and tears misted her eyes as she made a heartfelt wish.

Something she hadn't done since before her daddy passed away.

Ten

Brooks stood on the threshold of Sutton Winchester's master bedroom as one of his nurses laid a plaid wool blanket on his lap and turned his wheelchair around. Brooks came face-to-face with his adversary. With a man he'd hated so powerfully, he'd wanted to destroy him. Now, his emotions raw, he hoped to God that Winchester would hear him out, because he was also the man who had loved his mother dearly and had fathered his younger brother, Carson.

"He's having a good day today, Mr. Newport," the nurse said.

"I'm glad to hear it," Brooks responded as he and Winchester exchanged glances. "Good afternoon, Mr. Winchester."

Cancer seemed to have sucked Winchester's onetime bluster and hard-nosed demeanor right out of his frail body. Hunched over, he appeared a shell of the man Brooks had opposed so vehemently in the past. Warm-colored walls, floral bouquets and December sunshine streaming in the windows contrasted sharply with the sterile environment of medical equipment, drips and tubes, and the constant *blip*, *blip*, *blip* of a monitor over the soft music piping in from hidden speakers.

With a feeble wave of his hand at the nurse, Winchester stopped the music. "You know me well enough to call me Sutton, boy."

"Okay, thanks. I will."

"Did you come here to gloat?" He lifted his head to look into Brooks's eyes.

"No, sir, I would never do that."

"Have a seat," the older man ordered in a voice that had long lost its depth.

Brooks sat in a chair three feet from Sutton's wheelchair. "Thank you."

"How is my Eve?" he asked.

"She's doing well. Graham brought her down to Texas, as you know. She's looking wonderful, excited about the baby."

Sutton turned his head to gaze out the window. "That's good. I want my children to be happy."

"Sutton, I know how much you loved my mother."

Slowly Winchester turned his head back and raised his brows, looking him square in the eyes. "Cynthia was a special woman. I wished she would've told me about Carson, though. She left me without telling me she was pregnant. I missed out on my son's life."

"Mom had a lot of pride."

"She was a stubborn one." His eyes twinkled as if he admired that trait. As if he'd loved every single thing about Cynthia Newport. He and Brooks had that in common.

"I'm glad you loved her, Sutton. I'm glad because if

you didn't, she wouldn't have had Carson. So I guess I have you to thank for my brother. And I'm doing that now. Thank you."

Sutton stared at him and then acknowledged him with a nod. "I have no intention of cutting Carson out of my will, by the way. As you can see, I'm not long for this earth. Carson is my son and an heir. He will get what is rightfully his."

It had been a bone of contention these past months, something that had grated on Brooks. That his younger brother wouldn't be acknowledged by his father. That he would lose what was due him, being an heir to the Winchester fortune. Carson had already been robbed of a father growing up—they all had—but this was one thing that could make things right in principle. "Carson knows that now. It wasn't ever about the money."

"We have agreed that when the time comes," Sutton said, speaking slowly, "his inheritance will go to charity. That's fine by me. Whatever the boy wants. He deserves it." His voice crumbled a little. "I have many regrets when it comes to Cynthia. Things I should've done differently with her. I lived my life a little recklessly, but I never betrayed her trust. I never told her secret. Seeing how it hurt you and Graham, maybe that wasn't the smartest thing to do."

"We've all made mistakes. I'm here to make peace between our families. I'm here to tell you that I was wrong for pursuing vengeance against you. I was wrong to try to destroy Elite Industries. I understand why you kept my mother's secret all those years. I've only just recently come to understand the crazy things one will do out of love. I, uh, I get it now. So I'm throwing in the towel. I've ordered my attorneys to back off. There'll be no more legal battles. No more disparaging comments to the press.

No more trying to undermine you or your company. I've already spoken to Eve, Nora and Grace about this. I've made my peace with them. But I wanted to face you in person. To say it's over."

Sutton nodded, the movement slight, all he could manage. "It's over."

All those months of personal attacks and secrets and truths coming to the surface were finally coming to an end. There would be no more harsh statements, conniving or retribution. The Winchester-Newport feud was done. Finished.

Brooks had one more thing to accomplish to unite the families. "That being said, I'm also here to invite you and your family to Cool Springs for Christmas. On behalf of my father, Beau, and his family. We'd all like the Winchesters to share the holiday with us. Carson and Georgia will be coming. And your daughters are onboard if you think you can make the trip. I'll send a private jet, and you'll have expert nursing care while you are there. I promise you'll be as comfortable as possible. It'll be a time of healing for all of us."

Sutton inhaled slowly, closed his eyes and seemed to give it some good thought. "I'd like to be with my family for Christmas. One last time. Yes, I'll make the trip."

Brooks put out his hand, holding his breath. There'd been a lot of bad blood between them, but he hoped they could put it all behind them. Sutton glanced at Brooks, then slowly offered his frail hand. It was putty soft, devoid of any strength, but he shook with Brooks and then smiled. Something Sutton Winchester rarely did. "It's a deal."

"Deal," Brooks said. "I'll work with your staff to make the arrangements."

"Thank you."

Brooks sighed in relief. He was making strides, and it felt like a heavy weight had been lifted from his shoulders. He was free now to head back to Texas and make things right with one hot gorgeous woman. He only hoped Ruby would agree to see him. She was a stubborn one, too. She hadn't answered any of his messages. Which worried him. But once he returned to Look Away, he vowed not to take no for an answer.

Brooks stood on the veranda with Beau, looking out at the cloudless night. There were hundreds of stars decorating the Texas sky, twinkling brighter than he'd ever seen before. He hugged his wool coat around his middle against the chilly winds. The Douglas fir tree decorating the veranda released the fresh scent of evergreen. It was Christmas Eve, and to spend it with his father for the first time locked up his fate good and tight. Brooks knew what he wanted to do with his life.

"Well, Dad. Here I go. Wish me luck."

"You won't need luck, son. Just tell the truth. There's power in that, and you'd be surprised how much it's appreciated." Beau faced him. "I certainly appreciated hearing it from you tonight."

Beau wrapped his arms around him good and tight, drawing him close. Beau was a hugger, and Brooks loved that about him. When they broke apart, his father said, "I'm behind you one hundred percent."

He had his father's love and support and, like a young boy would, he beamed inside. "Thanks, Dad."

"All right now, go. I've got a houseful of guests I don't want to neglect."

The Winchesters had arrived this morning, and Beau had been a cordial host. Any awkwardness that might have occurred had been wiped clean straightaway by his father's warm hospitality.

"I'm going. I'm going."

Beau grinned and pivoted around to enter the house, leaving Brooks alone to make his move. He took a deep breath and sighed, a smile spreading across his face. What the hell was he waiting for?

Holding Ruby's image in his mind, he climbed down the steps and walked the distance to her cottage. A light was on in her living room, which was encouraging. He took a moment to gather himself and then knocked. When nothing happened, he knocked again, harder this time. "Ruby, it's Brooks."

Silence.

He reached for his cell phone and called her number. When no one answered, he sent her a text.

Still no reply.

He closed his eyes and sent up a prayer. He hoped he wasn't too late. He hoped Ruby hadn't gone back to Trace Evans. Though he couldn't imagine it, Brooks knew she had a soft spot for the guy. Who knew what lies Evans might have told her to claim his innocence? Had Brooks waited too long? Had his lack of commitment sent Ruby back into Trace's arms?

Brooks's shoulders sagged. He'd stand out here all night waiting for her, but catching pneumonia out in the cold would be a fool thing to do. He had no other option but to go home and try to speak with Ruby tomorrow. She'd be at the house bright and early for Christmas breakfast.

His hopes plummeting, he began the trek to his cabin, wishing now he'd thought to drive. The wind kicked up, lifting his hat from his head. He caught hold of it right before the darn thing sailed away and kept it flattened to his head as he walked on.

Oh man, his bones were chilled, and he had no doubt it was going to be a long, cold, sleepless night for him. Once he reached his cabin door, a wreath of pine and holly berries greeted him, something that hadn't been there when he'd left for Chicago three days ago. The staff or maybe Beau himself must've put it up as a way of welcoming him back. Or maybe it was simply a Preston tradition to decorate every door on the ranch. Christmas cheer seemed especially important on Look Away.

Brooks entered the cabin, and as soon as his boots hit the wood planks, warmth rose up and smacked him in the face. It went a long way in taking the chill off from his cold trek. The fireplace crackled, and his gaze traveled to the tangerine flames partially lighting the room. He stepped farther inside, removing his coat and hat, rubbing at the back of his neck and wondering about the fire.

"Brooks?" Ruby's soft voice had him turning toward the bedroom doorway.

As soon as he spotted her, his breath caught tight in his throat. She stood at the threshold clad in one of his white dress shirts, the sleeves pushed up and the tail reaching to midthigh on her gorgeous legs. Firelight christened her face and was reflected in her dark chocolate eyes. The lovely vision she made heated his blood, and hope sprang to life inside his body. Good God, she was beautiful.

And *here*.

"I hope it's okay. Beau gave me the key to the cabin."

Tongue-tied, Brooks barely got the words out. "No, uh, it's fine."

"I did some decorating."

He tore his gaze from her to scan the room. A tree sat on a corner table. This one would make Charlie Brown proud. The awkward branches were filled with tiny ornaments and multicolored lights. It was a clear winner and perhaps his favorite Christmas tree ever.

Centered in the middle of the dining room table, a big glass bowl of shiny red and green Christmas balls caught his attention. Atop the mantel, a family of snowmen and Santa trinkets along with cinnamon-scented pillar candles added to the holiday warmth.

"I like it." He was a little dumbfounded, standing there, drinking in the sight of Ruby in his cabin after days and days of no communication. "So, does this mean you're talking to me again?"

"If you want an answer to that, you'll have to come here."

"Baby, you don't have to ask twice." Her subtle, familiar scent, sheet of glossy hair raining down her back and mysteriously sexy voice lured him in. He took the steps necessary to come face-to-face with the woman of his fantasies, giving him the little boost he needed to lay his heart on the line. He'd been a fool not to claim her before this. Not to tell her what she meant to him.

"I like your shirt," he said, tracing a finger on her rosy lips, then skimming it along her sweet chin to her neckline and down to the hollow where the shirt dipped into her mind-numbing cleavage.

"Ask me why I'm here."

"With you dressed like that, I'm supposed to think straight?"

She chuckled, the deep sound coming up from her throat catching him off guard. "Try."

"You picked me?"

"Galahad, it was never really a contest. Trace isn't the man for me."

"You ditched him?"

"I told him I didn't love him anymore. That we weren't meant to be. I'm not happy about you bribing him, but afterward I had a heart-to-heart talk with him, and he was honest with me about everything. He's messed up his life and swore up and down that he never meant to hurt me."

"And you forgave him?" *The cheater, the creep*, Brooks wanted to add, but he was in too hopeful a mood to press his luck.

She nodded. "It's easier when you're no longer emotionally invested. He'll get on the right track again. He got an offer to do a reality show on a country cable television station, and he jumped at the chance. He'll be moving to Nashville soon."

"That's good to hear, because I wouldn't have let you go. I wouldn't have given up on you."

"Because that's what white knights do?"

"Because I'm crazy about you, Ruby. I'm out of my mind in love with you."

Ruby's face brightened, and she smiled. "I love you too, Brooks. This isn't a passing thing for me. This is the real deal."

Thank God.

He didn't need the mistletoe above their heads for permission to kiss her. He circled his arms around her waist and brought her up against him. Her chin tilted, and he gazed into the most stunning pair of dark eyes he'd ever seen. The glow in them promised more than he could ever hope for. Ruby was going to be his. And then his mouth came down on hers, meeting her flesh to flesh. Her soft lips slid over him exquisitely. Her petite body, all five-foot-two of her, crushed against him and put his brain in jeopardy of shutting completely down.

He broke the kiss to her defiant whimper and then dipped down to lift her. Her brows arched in question, but she didn't stir otherwise. Her arms automatically roped around his neck, and he carried her to a chair beside the sizzling fire. A log broke apart, and golden flames climbed the height of the fireplace, bringing intense heat. He sat down in the warmth, and Ruby wiggled in his lap. But Brooks had to contain his lust for just a few more seconds. "Ruby, I thought I'd blown it with you. Foolishly I left town without telling you how I felt about you. Maybe I shouldn't have had Trace investigated..."

"You think?"

"Okay, I get it. It wasn't my business to interfere, but I was trying my best to protect you from getting hurt again. Ever since the night we met at the C'mon Inn, when that guy was pestering you, I've had this need to protect you."

"Are you apologizing?"

"For not trusting in you? Yes. You're more than capable of making up your own mind about things."

She gently took his hand in hers and stroked his fingers, sending tingles up and down his arm. "I didn't mind the first time, Brooks. I thought it was really kinda sweet of you, coming to my rescue. You didn't know me, and still you were willing to help me. But with Trace, it was different. I really don't want to talk about him anymore tonight. It's over and done with. I know in my heart you had good intentions."

"I did and I still do, sweetheart. Actually, you call me Galahad, but in truth, you're the rescuer in this duo. You've saved me, Ruby. From the very moment I met you, my life changed. I've become a better person, a more tolerant man, because of you. I came here looking for my true father and found a new way of life, as well. I've discovered something within me that I wouldn't have realized if not for you. You taught me about the ranch and how things work in the country, but you also helped ease the pain of my past. Coming with me to meet my grandfather for the first time meant a lot. That was a hard reunion, but having you there comforting me and showing me how to let go worked miracles for me. You helped me turn away from the past and look forward. To the future. You gave me something special that day. You made me see what my life could be."

He lifted her fingertips and kissed each one. Just looking at her filled his heart with so much joy, he could hardly think straight. "I've always felt something was missing in my life. I thought it was because of my childhood. I thought it was because I never knew my father. In a sense, that's true. I missed knowing Beau as a boy, having his guidance and love, but I've come to realize I've also missed this place. Look Away and Texas. It feels right being here, with you. I've known only city life, but now that I'm here, I don't want to leave. I'm going to work it out so that I can stay closer to my family. The company is in good hands. I can run it long-distance."

"You're staying?" The hope in Ruby's voice swelled his heart.

"I want to, yes. I hear there are some pretty nice ranches for sale close by." Brooks rose with Ruby still in his arms. Her warmth mingled with his, and as soon as he lowered her down and her feet touched the floor, he felt the loss. "I went to your place looking for you. And nearly died when I couldn't find you."

"I had a surprise for you, Brooks."

"Having you here was the best surprise I could ever hope for," he said. And then he dropped to one knee and gazed into a pair of astonished eyes as firelight caressed her beautiful face. "Ruby Lopez, I promise to love and cherish and yeah, probably protect you for the rest of my life. I can't help it. I'll always be your Galahad." He fished inside his pocket for the wedding ring he'd brought with him from Chicago, a diamond ring that had once been his Grandma Gerty's. It was all he had left of the woman who'd taken his family in during a precarious time in their lives.

Brooks held up the ring, and it glistened under the firelight. Clearing his throat, he presented it to her and said, "Ruby, this ring was given to me by my grandmother. She told me one day I'd give it to a special woman. That day has come, sweetheart. I want to give you this ring and along with it, my heart and soul. I ask that you do me the honor of marrying me. Ruby, will you be my wife?"

Tears spilled from Ruby's eyes, raining down her face without warning. Brooks held his breath, hoping they were happy tears. "I went to Beau and asked for his blessing, Ruby. I asked him for your hand in marriage, and he was touched and happy for us."

"Oh, Brooks," she said, grasping his wrists as he rose. "That's the sweetest thing…"

Facing her now, he stared into her eyes, waiting patiently for her answer. "Ruby?"

She began nodding quickly, the tears still trekking down her cheeks. "Yes, Brooks. I'll marry you. I'll be your wife."

He laughed, and the sound of his relief and joy filled the room. "You had me worried there, sweetheart."

"No, no. It's just that I didn't expect this."

Using the pads of his thumbs, he wiped at her tears, carefully drying her eyes. Cupping her face, he said softly, "I didn't expect it, either. It happened so darn fast, but it's the right thing. For both of us. I promise you, Ruby, we'll have a great life."

"I know we will." And then she took his hand and walked him over to the scraggly Christmas tree. Turning to face him, she smiled sweetly. "You've given me this beautiful ring and a promise of your love. It's a wonderful gift, and now I have a gift for you, my sweet love." She handed him a small box decorated with snowmen and reindeer wrapping paper. "Merry Christmas."

He lifted the lightweight box in his hands and jiggled it. Nothing moved. He shot her a glance. She gave nothing away, and he had no idea what she was up to, but her expression was hopeful, and her eyes positively beamed. "Let's see," he said, ripping away the wrapping and opening the small box. After separating the tissue paper, he lifted out a small white garment.

"It's called a onesie," Ruby said softly.

Puzzled, Brooks read the printed saying on the front. "Future Look Away Ranch Wrangler."

He blinked. And blinked again. Normally he wasn't slow on the uptake, but this…this was like a lightning bolt striking his heart. Something else lay at the bottom of the box. Cute, small, adorable tan leather baby boots.

He stared at them for a second. "A *baby*? Ruby," he said, tears burning the backs of his eyes so hard he could barely get the words out, "are we having a baby?"

She began nodding her head. "Yes. We're going to have a baby, Brooks."

Joy burst inside him, and his face stretched wide as he grinned. Thankfully he didn't shed tears, but his emotions were off the charts. "A baby…" he said, awed, as he pulled Ruby back into his arms and kissed her cheek, her chin and finally her lips. "It's the best Christmas gift in the world."

"Yes," she whispered. "I think so, too. But I wasn't sure how you'd feel…"

"I love you, Ruby." He set his hand very gently on her belly. "And I love our baby already. I couldn't be happier. To have you and our child in my life, it's a dream come true."

"I love you, too. You'll be a great father, Brooks." Ruby covered his hand with hers and positioned it where new life was growing inside her. Then she leaned in to kiss him. The kiss bonded them together forever, and Brooks had never been happier in his life. He was complete. His life held new meaning and purpose.

Here on Look Away Ranch, he had finally found home.

Epilogue

Christmas morning on Look Away was usually a chaotic affair of eating, joking, opening gifts and spreading the love, and today was no different, except that the family had expanded to include the Winchesters. Ruby had coordinated with the household staff to make sure they were as comfortable as possible.

Sutton Winchester had his own set of nurses, and the older man who'd played a role in Brooks's, Graham's and particularly Carson's lives was holding his own this morning. His wheelchair was right next to the warm flames of the fireplace, and he seemed to be in good spirits. Occasionally Ruby would see him smile at his daughters, Nora, Grace and Eve. For a powerful man who wasn't long for this earth, his eyes still held a bit of mischief, and though he spoke seldom, what did come out of his mouth was witty and charming.

Ruby knew the history he had with Brooks's mother.

Last night, while in bed with her new fiancé and father of her unborn child, Brooks had recounted to her all he'd known of their relationship. Sutton was Carson's father, and it was sad that Carson had come to know him only in the last months of his life.

"Gather around the tree, everyone," Beau said after they'd eaten a Christmas morning meal that would probably stay with them throughout the entire day. Except for her. She was still ravenous. And now Brooks was watching her like a hawk, eyeing her with love in his eyes, but also concern over every little move she made. It was sweet, for now, as they were both getting used to the idea of her pregnancy and overjoyed at the little one who'd be making an appearance in eight months.

Married now, Nora and Reid Chamberlain took their places along with newly engaged Grace and Roman Slater. Carson stood with his fiancée, Georgia, next to Sutton's wheelchair, and his allegiance to his ailing father was inspiring. Toby, Malcolm and Clay were to Beau's right, and next to him on the other side were Graham and Eve.

Brooks grabbed Ruby's hand and angled them beside Graham.

"Want to sit down?" he asked her.

"No, I'm fine," she told him quietly. Ruby's heart was thumping wildly in her chest. No one knew their news yet, and she was enjoying this special secretive time with her new fiancé, but a part of her just wanted to scream it from the rooftops. The ring, which she'd hated taking off, was in Brooks's pocket.

Lupe came around with a tray of mimosas and sparkling cider. Brooks snapped up two ciders and handed Ruby one, giving her a quick, adorable smile.

"Thank you all for making the trip to Look Away for

the holiday," Beau began, holding up his glass. "I'm not one for making speeches, but it seems lately there's a need. So I'll make this toast short. The past has been hard on many of us. But looking around this room, I have renewed faith in the future. I see love here in many forms, and it's heartwarming."

Beau's gaze found hers, and his smile made Ruby blush down to her toes.

"I, for one, am grateful that Graham and Brooks are here with me this holiday. They have met their three half brothers and our Ruby, and it's been all that I had hoped. And I'm so happy having Carson here, along with all you wonderful Winchester girls and your father. It's all a blessing.

"I cannot hold a grudge about the past. It serves no purpose and so, with that in mind, I hope that this coming together of the Prestons, Newports and Winchesters brings with it peace to all families. Let's set aside our differences, put salve on our wounds and try to move forward. Especially at this time of year, when goodwill abounds, let's have ourselves a very Merry Christmas."

Glasses clinked and good-natured chatter began. The families were united and, at least for this holiday, all was well.

"Dad, if you don't mind, I'd like to say something." Brooks's tone was reverent, and everyone stopped talking to listen.

"Of course, son."

Brooks's arm came around Ruby's shoulder, tugging her in even closer, and many sets of eyes rounded in surprise. "I didn't know what to expect when I came to Look Away. I'd been hell-bent on finding my father, as everyone here knows. And when I finally met him…well, when I met you, Beau…" Brooks said, speaking directly to his father now and choking up a bit. Ruby put her arm around his waist, supporting him. She'd always be there for him when he needed her. "When I met you, Beau, saw you for the decent, kind man you are, I was floored, inspired and thrilled to know you. To be your son. But I also felt one with this land. It was like a part of me became suddenly alive again. And I knew I belonged here. I knew that Texas and Look Away was my real home. Ruby played a role in that."

He spoke to her now, and she lifted her chin to look into his eyes. "Ruby and I have fallen deeply in love. With Beau's blessing, I've asked her to marry me, and she said yes. We are officially engaged as of last night." Brooks dug into his pocket and formally put the ring on her finger.

Applause and congratulations broke out. Brooks bent his head and brought his lips to hers, giving her a taste of the passion that would always consume their lives. She had no doubt.

"There's one more thing," Ruby said, raising her voice above the din. Everyone grew silent again. "It seems that Graham and Eve aren't the only ones who will be making Beau a grandfather."

Gasps broke out, and Ruby thought she heard Eve chant, "All right!"

"Brooks and I are going to have a baby."

Tears poured down Ruby's cheeks again. Even though she tried her best to maintain decorum, she couldn't help it, and Brooks did his best to wipe them away.

Beau was the first to come over, wrapping his arms around both of them and hugging tight. "Congratulations, you two. I couldn't be happier." His voice broke, and Ruby knew he was crying, too. "You've got yourself a wonderful girl, son."

"I couldn't agree more," Brooks said, brushing a kiss across her cheek.

After everyone congratulated them and the Christmas festivities moved on, Brooks took her by the hand and led her outside to the front veranda. Wrapping his arms around her from behind, he bestowed kisses on the back of her neck as they swayed back and forth in full harmony, gazing out on the land, the pasture, the horses, all that was Look Away. "We're going shopping tomorrow," he announced quietly.

"For baby things?"

He chuckled. "First I need to put a roof over our heads, sweetheart. We're buying our own ranch, one we can call home. And even though I'm in real estate—"

"You're not *in* real estate. You're the king of real estate."

"But you're the expert in ranching. I value your opinion in all things, but I especially defer to you when it comes to Texas and ranches."

"You're letting me choose?"

"I want you to have your heart's desire, Ruby. The house, the ranch. I'll build it for you if you can't find something you absolutely love."

"I already have."

Brooks's brows arched. "You found a place?"

"I found something I absolutely love."

And then she roped her arms around his neck and kissed her handsome fiancé something fierce with all the love she had in her heart, thanking her lucky stars she'd met her very own knight in shining armor that night at the C'mon Inn.

"You, Galahad. I found you."

* * * * *

COMING SOON!

We really hope you enjoyed reading this book. If you're looking for more romance, be sure to head to the shops when new books are available on

Thursday 15th November

To see which titles are coming soon, please visit
millsandboon.co.uk

LET'S TALK
Romance

For exclusive extracts, competitions
and special offers, find us online:

- facebook.com/millsandboon
- @MillsandBoon
- @MillsandBoonUK

Get in touch on 01413 063232

For all the latest titles coming soon, visit
millsandboon.co.uk/nextmonth